EXIT PLAN

FORGE BOOKS BY LARRY BOND

Dangerous Ground
Cold Choices
Exit Plan

**FORGE BOOKS BY LARRY BOND
AND JIM DEFELICE**

Larry Bond's First Team
Larry Bond's First Team: Angels of Wrath
Larry Bond's First Team: Fires of War
Larry Bond's First Team: Soul of the Assassin
Larry Bond's Red Dragon Rising: Shadows of War
Larry Bond's Red Dragon Rising: Edge of War
Larry Bond's Red Dragon Rising: Shock of War

LARRY BOND

EXIT PLAN

 A TOM DOHERTY ASSOCIATES BOOK

NEW YORK

This is a work of fiction. All of the characters, organizations, and events portrayed in this novel are either products of the author's imagination or are used fictitiously.

EXIT PLAN

A Forge Book
Published by Tom Doherty Associates, LLC
175 Fifth Avenue
New York, NY 10010

www.tor-forge.com

Forge® is a registered trademark of Tom Doherty Associates, LLC.

ISBN 978-0-7653-3146-5 (hardcover)
ISBN 978-1-4299-5705-2 (e-book)

First Edition: April 2012

Printed in the United States of America

0 9 8 7 6 5 4 3 2 1

This book is dedicated to U.S. Navy SEALs, past and present. You have done so much for our nation, with many of your accomplishments shrouded in secrecy, that mere words cannot describe the debt we collectively owe you. All we can offer is our heartfelt thanks, and prayers for your safety and future success.

In particular, we wish to recognize the loss of 66 SEAL warriors who have fallen since September 11, 2001. These brave men paid the supreme sacrifice to defend our freedom and way of life. Rest, warriors. You have diligently stood your watch, and are relieved.

ACKNOWLEDGMENTS

Our deepest thanks go to Captain Ryan McCombie (SEAL) USN (Ret.), BUD/S class 50E, for patiently guiding us along the path toward understanding an inscrutable group of elite warriors—U.S. Navy SEALs. Ryan kept us on the straight and narrow as we struggled to maintain an accurate reflection of the SEAL mind-set and culture. He also backstopped us on weapons, communications systems, and other pieces of cool gear that Special Operations Forces get to play with. A true gentleman and a scholar, his wise counsel was greatly appreciated.

Thanks also to Dave Hood and Angela and Michael Pelke, for their friendship as well as their sharp eyes.

AUTHOR'S NOTE

I've known Chris Carlson for more than thirty years, and we've worked on dozens of projects together. Still, this is only our third novel, and we are still working out the best ways of collaborating. We don't disagree often, and those are quickly resolved. It's more often about which scene has to happen first, or one of us wandering too far from the story.

Writing is fun: Creating realistic, interesting characters, putting them in exciting situations, and then figuring how to get them out of the trouble they're in is a blast. But it's also work—sustaining momentum over a long project is hard. Working with someone else, especially someone with a lot to contribute, makes the work easier. Chris's knowledge of submarines and, in this story, SEALs, makes this story possible, but he's also a good story-teller.

Jerry Mitchell owes as much to Chris as he does to me for his existence. Telling his story without Chris would not only be impossible, it wouldn't be as much fun, either.

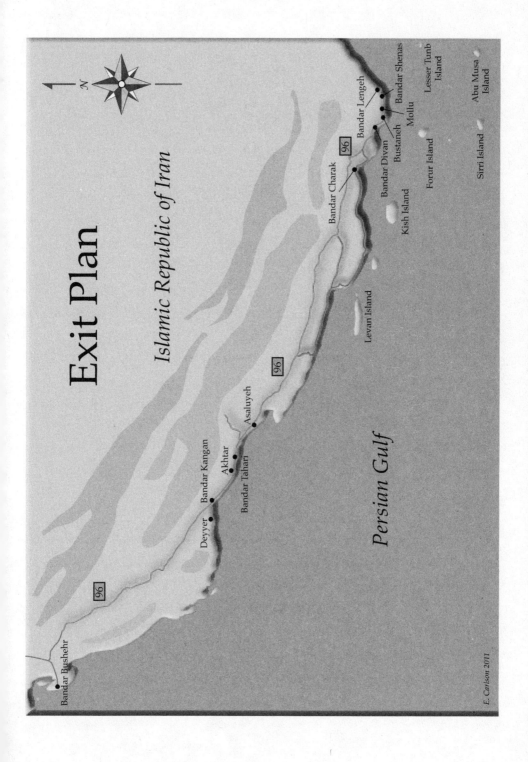

Exit Plan

Islamic Republic of Iran

Persian Gulf

Bandar Bushehr

Deyyer

Bandar Kangan

Akhtar

Bandar Tahari

Asaluyeh

Bandar Charak

Bandar Divan

Bandar Lengeh

Bustaneh

Mollu

Bandar Shenas

Levan Island

Kish Island

Forur Island

Lesser Tunb Island

Sirri Island

Abu Musa Island

96

E. Carlson 2011

PROLOGUE

6 February 2013
Uranium Pilot Enrichment Plant, Natanz, Iran

"I smell smoke!" Shirin Naseri, assistant engineer in the centrifuge-testing department, had opened the blast door into the test cell. Her superior, Dr. Davood Moham, quickly looked up, first with confusion, then irritation, and motioned for her to shut the door.

"What is the problem now?" snapped Moham. "And why did you open the door?"

"I said, I smell smoke," replied Naseri patiently. She had to be careful of her tone; her boss was in one of his less collegial moods. "A good engineer doesn't just look at the gauges, and my nose tells me something is overheating. We should shut down the test and find out what's wrong."

Moham slammed his clipboard on the console, making test technician Faraz Yazdi almost jump out of his seat. He stalked over to the blast door, muttering about "fussy women," and yanked it open. The whirring din from sixty-four centrifuges engulfed them. Taking a deep sniff, his face soured even more. "I smell nothing."

"It's been six days, *Doctor* Naseri." Moham had used her title with contempt, as if it was a mistake. "You thought we weren't ready for this, that the design was still flawed. It's been six days, with no problems whatsoever, and now that it's almost over, you're still looking for bad news."

Naseri shook her head. "No, sir. I want this design to succeed, but I'm very sensitive to smells right now, and . . ."

"And pregnancy makes you smarter?" Moham looked up, as if speaking to the heavens. "Why did I ever think a woman would be useful?"

Naseri, twenty-eight, was one of Moham's assistants. She'd done well enough in school to impress even the opinionated Moham. A petite and beautiful young woman, she was as outspoken as Yazdi was timid. The technician was still working on his doctoral thesis, and looked like a graduate student—skinny, with a spare beard and pale complexion from spending too much time indoors. He was the nervous type, intimidated by Moham's reputation and Naseri's competence, and had been especially wound up for days, ever since the final test had started. Naseri certainly was.

Moham, director of the centrifuge program, was their boss, but more than that, their beacon. Brilliant, arrogant, and charismatic, he'd brought them and others as new blood into a program that Moham would redeem and save. Now, three years later, he'd lost weight, and gray had appeared in the thirty-eight-year-old's jet-black hair and beard. His expression was just as intense as it was at the beginning, but now it wasn't all power and knowledge. He was also afraid.

This was the final test of their latest centrifuge design—his latest design, and his last chance. None of the others had come this far, and if it passed, it meant success, vindication, reward. And failure meant more than just professional loss. Others in the nuclear program had been accused of sabotage or spying, never to be seen again.

All three stared through thick safety glass at the two rows of cylinders and piping, as if they could pull more information from the machines by gazing intently at them. The computer displays that filled the test console told them anything they wanted to know: revolutions per minute, gas flow, bearing temperatures—any physical metric that they could imagine. After all, Moham and the others had designed the console. But did it tell them what they needed to know?

The brightly lit test cell appeared almost empty. Only a small fraction of the available floor space, designed to hold several hundred machines, was being used. The ceiling was heavily patterned with electrical cables, piping, and flexible tubing that supplied power, cooling water, and the uranium hexafluoride gas to the centrifuges.

Sixty-four hand-built examples of their latest centrifuge design stood neatly aligned in two rows of thirty-two, connected in a long chain called a cascade. A full cascade usually had 164 machines, but given the "encouragement" from their seniors for faster progress, smaller test cascades were now the norm.

Everything was contained within walls of thick reinforced concrete. The panels, doors, and windows around the control room were also of reinforced construction. Some of the previous tests had ended violently, and while uranium hexafluoride gas was not highly radioactive, it was dangerously toxic.

For something so important and complex, the centrifuges themselves were rather plain. Each smooth silver cylinder stood about three-and-a-half-feet tall and six inches in diameter. Spaced about ten inches apart, they looked like rows of stacked juice cans without their labels. Their importance lay beneath their shiny silver exterior. Inside each canister, a carbon-wound rotor spun in vacuum at ninety thousand revolutions per minute—six times faster than a high-performance race car engine.

"Faraz!" yelled Moham. "Are any of the centrifuges overheating?"

"Ahh, no, Dr. Moham," responded Yazdi. "But several have lower bearing temperatures that are higher than I'd like," he added carefully.

"Are they within acceptable limits, Technician Yazdi?" demanded Moham impatiently.

"Yes, Doctor; just barely."

Turning back to Naseri, Moham sneered and said, "See! There is no basis for your concern. We will continue the test."

"Doctor, we both know there can be a time lag between when a component begins overheating and when the heat actually reaches the thermocouple. I'm convinced that at least one of the centrifuges is in serious trouble." Naseri's tone was urgent, almost pleading.

Moham breathed in deeply, his face crimson with anger. "Engineer Naseri, I have no intention of ending this test until it reaches its successful conclusion! We will continue the test, and that is *final*!"

Naseri surrendered and took her post again, sitting next to Yazdi, and monitored the computer displays and gauges, while Moham, supervising, paced back and forth in the narrow space. Moham kept glancing at his watch, and unconsciously reached for the pack of cigarettes in his shirt pocket. Then he would put them back. There was no smoking in the control room.

They'd barely started checking the displays again when the computer confirmed Naseri's fears. Centrifuge forty-two's lower bearing temperature was rising rapidly. Cross-checking the rotor vibration display showed it was getting disturbingly large as well. A quick glance toward Yazdi showed that he saw it, too, but he remained silent. Dashing to the blast door, Naseri threw it open. A foul odor washed over the three of them. "Can you smell it now?" she demanded.

Her supervisor reacted with anger, but that quickly transformed into shock as the unmistakable odor of burning electrical insulation took hold. Moham froze.

Before Naseri could say anything else, a loud alarm buzzer sounded.

"High temperature in number forty-two!" shouted Yazdi. "Lower bearing!"

Moham stared, disbelieving, at the display; all the color disappeared from his face.

"Doctor Moham? What do you want me to do?" asked the technician.

He didn't reply, and instead stared at the displays, finally saying, "It has to be an error in the sensors. Maybe if we reset the system . . ."

Naseri slammed and bolted the blast door, yelling commands. "Execute test shutdown sequence. Start coasting down the centrifuges. Close the uranium hexafluoride gas feed."

Yazdi hesitated for a moment, looking to see if Moham would countermand Naseri's orders. When the director just sat there, muttering to himself, the technician started the shutdown protocol. He kept up a running commentary on the centrifuge as he punched the commands.

"The temperature is spiking. Vibration readings are very high as well. Wait, now it's gone to zero . . .

"Now it's high again." The technician checked the control settings. "It's like the sensor can't handle the data."

"Never mind, Faraz, we don't have time," exclaimed Naseri. "That rotor will tear itself apart any second now. We have to leave." She hit the red button on the console. The emergency alarm for the building started shrieking. Reaching down under her seat, she grabbed her gas mask from its storage bag and started putting it on.

The technician was busily putting on his mask, but Moham was fumbling with his, still confused as to what was going on. Naseri grabbed him and started pushing him to the exit.

The two of them managed to drag their supervisor out of the control room just as the centrifuge blew, a loud pop mixed with the screech of tearing metal. The blast-resistant windows shuddered, but held. The test cell was immediately filled with a brownish-yellow smoke. The swirling clouds near the ceiling also showed the fire suppression system had been activated, flooding the cell with carbon dioxide gas. Uranium hexafluoride could burn when mixed with the air.

A staccato of explosions punctuated by the sound of thuds and crashes continued, as if two giants were fighting in a junkyard. They felt each explosion through the floor, and they were hard enough to knock dust and debris down from the ceiling.

As Naseri and Yazdi made sure the control room door was latched shut, several men in firefighting gear came running down the hallway with hoses and portable extinguishers. Their leader pointed to the test team, motioning for them to move to a safer location. Escorted by two of the firefighters, Moham, Yazdi, and Naseri quickly found themselves outside; a crowd was gathering, with people streaming toward them from other buildings. The sound of sirens mixed with the diesel engines of fire equipment.

Colonel Zamanian, the base commander, leapt out of a jeep as it slowed.

"Davood! What happened? What went wrong?"

"Disaster!" wailed Moham. "May Allah be merciful!" The director began to weep, and would have collapsed if not for the firefighters supporting him on each side.

Zamanian turned to Naseri and Yazdi. "Engineer, Technician, tell me what happened."

"A bearing failed on one of the centrifuges. It tore itself apart," replied Naseri frankly. The engineer shuddered, reliving the experience. "There were many explosions, Colonel."

Zamanian became pale. "Why? What caused the bearing to fail? I thought we solved that problem months ago."

"I don't know, sir. Nothing obvious. There was a temperature alarm in centrifuge forty-two and it blew up soon thereafter. We'll have to analyze the test data." She looked over to her partner. "But I believe Technician Yazdi was able to save the data. We should be able to identify the cause."

"How much of the cascade did we lose?"

"I do not know," answered Naseri, annoyed that the man seemed more interested in centrifuges than people. "But as I said, there were many explosions. It may be a total loss."

Stunned, Zamanian nodded, then gathered himself. "I must report this unfortunate incident. The medical staff will tend to you and the others." With a weary smile he added belatedly, "I'm glad that no one was hurt. We at least have that to be thankful for. Allah be praised."

1

EPIPHANY

8 February 2013
Uranium Enrichment Facility, Natanz, Iran

Natanz lay only 150 kilometers to the north of his headquarters in Isfahan, so General Moradi had flown up early in the morning with his aide, Captain Hejazi. Moradi's staff had urged him to wait, to not rush up there the same day, that afternoon. "They won't know anything," Colonel Nadali had warned. "They'll bury you in raw data and argue with each other."

The general had learned to listen to Farzad Nadali, his chief of staff. The colonel's patience and good humor complemented Moradi's own fiery temperament. Nadali had counseled Moradi to wait until the scientists had something to tell him.

So finally, two days later, they were flying north in an Islamic Revolutionary Guards Corps Mi-17. Instead of jump seats for troops, the Russian-made transport helicopter was fitted for VIP travel, with increased soundproofing, comfortable seating, and fold-down work surfaces. A few hundred meters below them, the landscape was empty and broken, painted in shades of brown and gray, with stony hills rising from the left. It was still winter, and the morning cold did nothing to soften the desert landscape.

Moradi had made the trip often, and hardly noticed the harsh beauty of the ground below. Instead, he studied a briefing prepared by the scientists and e-mailed to his headquarters that morning. The general was sure they'd

been up all night working on it, but he was not sympathetic. A few more
sleepless nights might have prevented this disaster.

Captain Hejazi's voice interrupted his review. "Sir, Natanz is in sight."
Moradi understood that his aide was referring to the uranium enrichment
facility. They'd spotted the town of Natanz proper five minutes ago. The
facility was thirty kilometers farther to the north, surrounded by desert and
rocky hills, but not isolated. Its front gate was just south of the Isfahan-
Kashan road, a six-lane highway that actually passed through the outer ring
of air defenses. A moment later the aide added, "Major Sadi is monitoring
our approach."

Moradi nodded, acknowledging the report. Sadi was in charge of the
facility's air defenses, and simply because they were a scheduled flight didn't
mean they couldn't be shot out of the sky.

The enrichment site itself was a rough square, a kilometer and a half on
each side. A perimeter fence enclosed the pilot enrichment plant, the gigan-
tic buried centrifuge halls, and the support buildings for those two vital
facilities.

A few hundred meters out, a road paralleled the perimeter, connecting
dozens of antiaircraft gun emplacements and watchtowers. Each gun position, a pair of manually aimed 23mm or 35mm autocannons, was ringed
with sandbags and sited on an earthen mound to give it a better field of fire.

Farther out, a second ring bristled with even more guns: larger four-
gun batteries of 100mm weapons, radar-directed 35mm batteries, scores of
the manually aimed guns, and half a dozen batteries of surface-to-air missiles. Three early warning radars covered Natanz and the surrounding area.
It was possible that Natanz was the most heavily defended place in Iran,
except, of course, for Tehran itself.

And a lot of that was Moradi's doing. Since he'd been placed in charge
of the nuclear weapons program five years ago, he'd tripled the number of
SAM batteries and ordered a second ring of antiaircraft guns placed around
Natanz. He'd also handpicked Sadi for his post. The major was inexperienced, but competent, hardworking—and loyal.

Moradi felt the helicopter descend, and he saved his notes and closed
the laptop. As Hejazi packed up the general's computer, the helicopter hovered and then set down smoothly. The crew chief moved aft to open the side
door, and Moradi remembered to remove his uniform cap before the rotor
wash snatched it away.

The blades slowed, and figures outside ran toward the open door. A few were ground crew, but most were officers, with a few civilians scattered through the group. Moradi recognized the Natanz facility's commander, Colonel Zamanian, with his staff, including Sadi, and Nadali, who'd arrived yesterday to manage the recovery and the investigation. Colonel Nadali was a great organizer, and he'd been right to go ahead and manage things. Moradi knew he'd probably have fired the lot on the spot.

The officers immediately fell into two ranks, and the civilians wandered about for a few moments, deciding where to stand. There was more than a little tension between the scientists, engineers, and the military. The civilians seemed reluctant to fall in line, but finally formed a knot at one end, not quite in line, but not sticking out either.

Nadali, who'd placed himself at the near end of the front rank, saw Moradi appear in the open door and called "Attention!" The officers saluted as one, and even the civilians managed to stand a little straighter.

Brigadier General Adel Moradi of the Islamic Revolutionary Guards Corps, the *Pasdaran*, stepped from the helicopter. The Revolutionary government's propaganda machine had dubbed him "The Lion of Karbala," for his bravery in the war with Iraq, but he knew his real nickname, the one his staff thought he didn't know about: "The Rhino."

Smoothly slipping on his uniform cap, Moradi returned the salute. His hat was a dark olive green ball cap, matching his fatigues and emblazoned with the emblem of the Pasdaran in gold thread. The symbol was repeated on his breast pocket.

In his late fifties, Moradi was trim, almost athletic. His aide, Hejazi, was taller, but Moradi was still six foot one. Solidly built, his physical presence had always been an asset, both on the battlefield and in politics. Trimmed close, his beard was only lightly threaded with gray. It outlined a broad, weathered face that seemed to settle naturally into an impatient scowl.

Nadali didn't wait for Moradi to speak. Shouting over the helicopter's slowing turbines, the colonel reported, "We're ready for you, sir." He pointed to a line of jeeps, and Moradi got into the lead vehicle without saying a word.

As Colonel Nadali climbed in the backseat, Moradi asked him, "Is there anything worth seeing at the pilot plant?"

Nadali shook his head sharply. "No, sir, and as a matter of fact, they're encouraging us to keep clear of the area while they make another sweep for radiation and toxicity." He saw Moradi's expression and continued. "When they spot-checked the first survey results, there were several errors—all underreporting."

Moradi's scowl deepened. "When will they be done?"

"They couldn't start until it was daylight this morning. It will be late this afternoon."

"Wonderful," Moradi rumbled. "I wonder how many other mistakes they've made." His tone made it clear that he was sure there were more. The other jeeps were pulling away, and Nadali ordered their driver to head for the administration building.

Nadali took the general to a conference room. Pasdaran sentries, armed with automatic weapons, flanked the door, and Nadali led the staff inside. When one of the civilians tried to go in the room, Nadali waved him back. "The scientists will brief the general in half an hour. We just have some housekeeping and organizational issues to go over." The civilian nodded nervously and hurried away.

As soon as the general was seated, a middle-aged major looked over at Nadali, who nodded. "The room has been swept, and is clear," the officer reported. "The spaces on all sides of us, and above and below, are occupied by my people." Major Hassan Rahim was Moradi's intelligence and counter-intelligence officer. He also belonged to VEVAK, the Ministry of Intelligence, but although everyone knew it, nobody ever mentioned it.

"It was a careful sweep, Rahim? There are some clever people here," Nadali observed.

"Not from what I've seen," Moradi countered. "What have you found, Hassan?"

Rahim was a small officer—short, and older than would be expected for a major. There were rumors that his real rank was much higher, but changed to match the assignment. His glasses gave him a professorial look, but his gaze was hard, and his tone cold. "The centrifuges failed on their own, sir. I can find no sign of sabotage, either from foreign agents or someone inside."

"It's hard to prove the absence of something," Moradi offered.

Rahim pulled out a notepad and flipped through the pages. "This is already one of the most secure installations in Iran. My people have enhanced those measures. We've been able to correlate the movements of everyone on base that day with the entrance and exit logs for each building. Dr. Sabet has helped us with scenarios for sabotage, and who would have the knowledge to perform it. Everyone on the list is being watched. Most have been questioned."

Moradi nodded as he took in the information. He'd expected this result. If Rahim had found anything amiss, the perpetrators would have been arrested instantly. VEVAK might have different masters than the Shah's SAVAK, but they used the same methods.

"Could it have been that damned computer worm again?"

"Unlikely, sir. I had every computer on the installation checked, as well as all personal computers in the dormitories. Every CD and flash drive was also examined. There was no sign of the Stuxnet worm. As you recall, we found this worm on dozens of computers when the cyber attack was first discovered three years ago," remarked Rahim.

Stuxnet was a devilishly effective piece of malware that sought out and attacked the motor controllers on the centrifuges, causing them to undergo wild variations in speed. This greatly reduced an infected centrifuge's performance, and even caused damage to the main support bearing. But even though the worm destroyed itself after having completing its dirty work, numerous computers were infected as the malware worked its way from its original source to the centrifuges.

"Have any of the staff suffered a family tragedy, or had some other personal crisis?" Moradi knew he was reaching, but he had to ask.

Rahim shook his head. "No, sir. I've reviewed the local security officer's records, and confirmed their accuracy with my own sources, as well as the reliability of the officers themselves."

"Thank you, Major. You've removed the possibility of malign influence. Unfortunately, that would have been the simpler answer."

The next meeting was the important one, with the physicists and engineers who had failed in their fourth attempt to create an improved centrifuge design. Iran had built a working centrifuge, but it was primitive, "first-generation" technology, and it was based on a design provided by a Pakistani nuclear scientist, A. Q. Khan. Centrifuges separated two uranium isotopes from each another by spinning uranium hexafluoride gas at tens of thousands of revolutions per minute. One isotope, U-238, was marginally heavier than the other, more desirable U-235. The difference of three neutrons pushed the heavier, unwanted U-238 toward the outside. The gas near the center, slightly richer in U-235, was removed.

But the increase was infinitesimal. Natural uranium contained less than

1% U-235 by weight. This had to be increased to about 4% to be used as reactor fuel, and to 90% for a weapon. And each centrifuge only enriched the gas by a few hundreds of a percent.

So the centrifuges were ganged together, each one taking the product of the one before and increasing the concentration of U-235 by some tiny amount. The sixty-four-centrifuge test cascade that had torn itself apart produced a trivial increase. The buried halls at Natanz had thousands of centrifuges installed in series, but even then the product had only just exceeded 4% thus far.

And that was the problem. It was taking too long to produce even small amounts of reactor-grade material. Iran needed to move quickly from reactor-grade to weapons-grade levels, and in large quantities. They could not build just one bomb. They needed several, at least a half dozen, to have a viable nuclear weapons capability.

Unfortunately, the Pakistani first-generation centrifuge design was inherently inefficient, and the Iranian versions didn't even reach that low mark. That meant an improved centrifuge design was absolutely essential. But it had to work before they could begin production, and they needed to produce them in the thousands.

Although they didn't fill the auditorium, it was a sizable group. Moradi saw Colonel Zamanian and his staff seated together on one side, then in a separate group, the scientists and engineers, with Dr. Moham, the head of the centrifuge program, fidgeting in the front row.

Davood Moham was young, brilliant, and outspoken. He'd been picked for the job three years ago, after the "second-generation" centrifuge design had failed. The physicist had been critical of the attempt, correctly predicting how it would fail. Now, after two major failures of his own, he was looking over his own shoulder. Only in his thirties, he looked much older, his hair thinning, and his face drawn. It looked like he hadn't gotten a lot of fresh air.

Dr. Rashid Sabet, the civilian who managed the entire nuclear weapons program, had flown in last night from Arak, looking for his own answers. If Moham represented youth and energy, Sabet was experience and wisdom. Even hardened war veterans knew Sabet's reputation. The Iranian government and people treated him almost like a national treasure. In his seventies, thin and almost frail, he projected a presence almost as strong as Moradi's, and while Sabet technically reported to the general, Moradi sometimes felt like a university student, and found himself deferring to Sabet almost automatically.

Moradi heard the chatter die as he approached the stage. They would be scared, defensive. They knew his reputation, and some were nervously glancing toward "Major" Rahim. Frightened people were not helpful.

Instead of heading for his own seat, the general turned and walked over to the pair, greeting Moham and Sabet warmly. Smiling and offering his hand to Moham, the general said, "Dr. Moham, I'm glad nobody was injured in the accident." Surprise flashed across the civilian's face, but he quickly hid it and rose to shake the general's hand. "I'm sure we'll be able to recover from the setback quickly," Moradi continued. "I'm looking forward to your recommendations."

"Yes." Moham paused, unsure of how to answer. Moradi could tell that his positive tone had unsettled the physicist. That was good. Nodding to Dr. Sabet, Moradi took his place with his staff. Conversation immediately stopped, and Moham stood and announced, "Mr. Yazdi will start with a summary of the accident and what we have learned."

Yazdi looked like a university student, with glasses and longer-than-fashionable hair. Nervously, he walked to the podium and opened a laptop computer. He pressed a key and the auditorium's screen came to life with a simple title, "Natanz Centrifuge Cascade Failure Reconstruction." The corners of the screen labeled the presentation as "Top Secret."

"General, Dr. Sabet, this briefing will describe our investigation and findings of the accident." The engineer pressed a key on his laptop and the next slide appeared—a time line.

Moradi waited for the third slide before speaking up. "Is this the same material I was sent?"

Yazdi, a little flustered, quickly nodded. "Yes, sir. We didn't know if you'd had a chance to review it."

"Well, ask before you waste my time. Is there anything new in this? Any changes since you sent it to me?"

"Ah, no, sir."

"Then go to the last slide," Moradi ordered impatiently.

Yazdi fiddled with the laptop for a moment, and a page labeled "Conclusions" appeared on the screen.

Moradi spoke after a moment's quiet. "Why did you stop the investigation at this point?"

Yazdi, who was supposed to be briefing the general, seemed surprised by the question. After a moment, he answered, "Sir, we are confident that we've found the cause." He pointed to the screen, quoting the text. "Voids created by improper curing allowed microfractures to form, causing carbon fiber delamination at high rotational speeds."

"That's all fine," Moradi answered. "But what steps are you taking to correct the error? Who was supervising the curing process? Why didn't they follow proper procedure?"

Yazdi looked hopefully at his director, and Dr. Moham rose. "General, we reviewed all the steps in production as a part of the investigation. Every procedure was followed and double-checked. An error might cause an anomaly in one or two centrifuges, but not the whole cascade. Once we knew what to look for, we found voids and microfractures in every centrifuge, even the ones that were only damaged—hence our conclusion of improper curing."

Moradi appeared confused, but also irritated and impatient. "And you are saying all the centrifuges were manufactured improperly? Why was such a serious error allowed to occur? Who was responsible?"

Dr. Sabet now stood to join Moham. "General, please. There was nothing that suggested there was an error during the manufacturing process. We developed the procedure ourselves; we had to due to the sanctions. It was incorrect. But now we know better and we'll devise a better curing process."

Moradi now understood, but clarity didn't bring enlightenment. "How long?"

Sabet looked to Moham, who didn't answer immediately. Several expressions passed across his face, all of them thoughtful. "We only confirmed the cause late last night. It will take a few days just to develop a systematic plan." He paused again, then estimated, "It will take at least several months."

Moham warmed to the plan as it took shape in his mind. "We'll investigate every part of the process. It's most likely the epoxy resin chemistry, but it could be the temperature, or even something mechanical like vibration or rotation during the curing process." Moham's tone was earnest, full of dedication. "We can't tell right now. I wouldn't even hazard a guess. But we'll find it, General. I'm sure we can make this process work."

"But you can't predict how long it will take to find a solution," Moradi answered.

"I won't even guess until we've narrowed down the possibilities. As I said, at least several months—and first we have to rebuild the lab, or set up a new one." He paused, realizing what kind of news he was delivering. When he continued, the physicist's tone was less animated, but more earnest.

"We're in unexplored territory, sir." Dr. Moham gave a small smile. "The technical challenge is what attracted me to this position. This is new technology. It can't be rushed. If we had access to high-quality steels, this would be much less expensive, in both time and money."

"Don't wish for what we can't have," Moradi growled. Improved centrifuge designs required maraging steel, a high-strength, high-temperature alloy that could be used in guided missiles, jet engines, and enrichment centrifuges, as well as dozens of peaceful applications. But Iran couldn't make it. Iranian metallurgy wasn't up to the task, and would not be for the foreseeable future. And they couldn't buy it abroad. The sanctions did have some effect.

So they tried end-arounds and substitutes. Moradi often thought of the Germans, late in World War II. Denied strategic metals and petroleum, they developed processes to turn coal into gasoline, and built fighters out of wood. But it was always harder and took longer. Engines didn't work as well using substitute gasoline. And some of the fighters crashed.

And sometimes, the centrifuges failed. And failed again. And again.

Moradi let Colonel Nadali run the rest of the meeting. The test facility had to be rebuilt and materials for the new test program obtained. As they hammered out plans, the general studied them, half-listening, wondering if it was all wasted motion.

He had handpicked these men for the most important task in Iran, just as the Supreme Leader, Grand Ayatollah Ali Khamenei, had chosen him. Had he made a mistake? The Supreme Leader had given his personal assurance that Moradi could call on any resource the country had. Surely with the entire nation behind them, they could construct a nuclear device.

Or could they? Fifty-five years after the first atomic bomb was built, knowing the design and bringing it into existence were two different things. And while Iran was a large country, it was not very wealthy—despite its petroleum resources—and the world was arrayed against them.

Moradi expected that. It was part of, almost required by, the Revolution and what it represented. Iran stood alone, and wanted to stand alone. She had been invaded, occupied, and manipulated by other nations since Darius had been beaten by Alexander the Great. She was surrounded by ethnic enemies like Iraq and Saudi Arabia, or historic ones like Russia, and was now ringed by American bases in Turkey, Iraq, Afghanistan, and Pakistan.

He could feel the pressure as a physical thing, a wall trapping them, or a net being drawn tighter. America talked openly of "containing" Iran, using the Cold War tactic of encircling an enemy nation and strangling it. Sanctions, spies, alliances, wars, all were part of an American plan to destroy the Revolution and replace it with another one of their puppets. He sometimes imagined what it would be like if Iran could trade freely, healing the wounds they still carried from the war with Iraq. What would Iran look like then? What would the Islamic Republic be able to do?

Nuclear weapons would elevate Iran among the world's nations, demanding respect, commanding leadership in the region and the Islamic world. Pakistan had the bomb, but the fractured and crippled government could not use it except as a counter to India's weapons. Iran could use it to break the sanctions, a demonstration of national will in the face of any opposition. . . . If they could ever get it built.

Moradi watched the meeting break up. Nadali had them motivated and almost rushing out the door, eager to get back to work. Moham led the charge, and Moradi and his staff found themselves alone in the auditorium. The colonel started organizing the trip back to their headquarters in Isfahan. There was nothing more to do here, but Moradi interrupted him. "Colonel, I'd like to speak to Dr. Sabet privately. Have Major Rahim set up security again." Rahim had been listening, and with a nod from Nadali, rushed off.

Moradi and the elderly scientist took their time, and when they finally returned to Nadali's temporary office, the sentries were posted, and Rahim reported the area was secure. Nadali ushered the two men in, Moradi following the older man. The general had said a "private meeting," so Nadali stepped out, closing the door behind him.

Someone had left two cups of tea on the desk, and Sabet picked one up, sitting across from the empty desk. It was a subtle acknowledgment of his position. Moradi had been given charge of the nuclear program, but Sabet was the guiding intellect. The general respected the scientist's experience and achievements, his piety, and his dedication to the Revolution, but he lacked Moradi's sense of urgency, and to Moradi's mind, pushing was how the big jobs got done.

The general sat down behind the desk, and sipped his tea quietly, almost afraid to ask the next question. "What is the news from up north?"

Sabet said, "No more bad news; a little good news. They have almost finished debugging the simulation. It can model the thermal and hydraulic performance of a malfunctioning reactor."

Moradi almost laughed. "We have one of those, Doctor." Near Khondab, about ninety kilometers southwest of Arak, Iran had built a nuclear reactor, following the plans provided by the Pakistani nuclear scientist. It used natural uranium fuel with no enrichment, which Iran could produce. Transformed by the nuclear reaction, the spent fuel contained about 1% plutonium by weight, most of which was Pu-239, which could be extracted and used to make a nuclear bomb. It was the second doorway into the nuclear clubhouse, bypassing the complex, time-consuming, and so far unattainable uranium enrichment process. All one had to do was build a specialized nuclear reactor.

Unlike the civilian and very public pressurized light-water reactor at Bushehr, built to a Russian design, the "IR-40" at Arak used heavy water to moderate the nuclear reaction. Heavy water paired two deuterium atoms, an isotope of hydrogen with an extra neutron, with an oxygen atom. It looked like regular water, and while it wasn't as efficient as regular water at slowing down neutrons, heavy water didn't absorb neutrons as readily as light water and this enabled a reactor to use natural, unenriched uranium as fuel.

The IR-40 reactor was entirely an Iranian enterprise. The Iranian scientists had a good theoretical understanding of nuclear reactor design, and they had been running small research reactors for decades. Using the plans provided by Pakistan, it should have been a straightforward task. However, the transition from theory to practice is rarely a smooth road. And in the case of the IR-40, the road was more of a goat path.

For some reason that they didn't understand, the IR-40's main cooling system wasn't working properly. In several of the narrow coolant channels, the water was starting to boil, reducing the flow of water over the adjacent fuel rods, which then started to warp and crack. Moradi knew it had to do with the design of the core, but he depended on Sabet and his people at the facility to understand and fix it. That was not only frustrating, but was thus far unproductive.

The core of the IR-40 had to be redesigned, but how? Their basic understanding of reactor core design had to be improved, and quickly. For Moradi, everything had to be done quickly.

Sabet saw his expression. "General, I truly believe computer simulation is our best option. You can't use trial and error with nuclear reactors. Mistakes could be deadly, even worse than what happened here, and their effects last for decades. Modeling the core's behavior in a computer will improve our understanding, as well as enable us to explore different core designs. Such techniques are used in Europe and America all the time."

But Iran had not been able to acquire the software, again because of sanctions. Theft, espionage, and black-market purchases had provided the software, but then it had to be documented, adapted, and finally completely understood. Otherwise they would have no idea whether the computer's output was a bug or a correct result. That process had taken almost a year.

Intellectually, Moradi could accept Sabet's explanation. Simulation was the logical course, but it reduced the struggle to develop a plutonium bomb to a roomful of computer geeks arguing over a printout. Moving ones and zeroes around on an invisible battlefield made it impossible for the general to see any progress, or any way to improve the situation.

Moradi's frustration was clear in his tone. "We are pouring resources into both the enrichment process and the heavy-water reactor because it gives us two paths to a nuclear capability." He sighed heavily. "Both are effectively stalled."

"Moving forward slowly," Sabet corrected quietly. "Sometimes it's difficult to see, General, but even a failure can be viewed as progress. I've been involved in projects that had even worse setbacks. You have to take the long view."

Moradi's answer had an edge to it. "We don't have an infinite amount of time, Doctor. The West, and now even Russia are aligned against us. They work to undermine not only this program, but also our government and our economy. They are hurting us, and I'm not sure how much more damage we can stand."

Sabet nodded, agreeing with Moradi, but the general pressed his point.

"Doctor, you don't understand. The government can issue all the press releases it wants, but the sanctions do have an effect. And it's getting worse. The situation is not static, nor is it in our favor."

The doctor answered, "Of course, you may have access to information I don't. Is there anything specific we need to worry about? Is there a deadline?"

Moradi shook his head. "Nothing specific. But eventually, we won't be able to find a key material or technology, even on the black market. What do we do then?

"This is a battle, Dr. Sabet. Even without guns and trenches, the rules are the same. A short battle is better than a long one. Move slowly and your opponent has time to react. He may block your advance or even find a way to defeat you." He gestured toward the crippled pilot plant. "And it gives your own people more time to make mistakes."

"You approved the test schedule. . . ."

"Based on their recommendations. I'm not a fool, Doctor, or a scientist. I will let the specialists practice their craft, as long as they get results. And I don't see any."

"Are you saying it's fruitless to . . ." Sabet started to ask.

"No, Doctor, your scientists and engineers should redouble their efforts. Tell them time is limited, and precious. But if we're blocked on two paths, it's time to look for a third."

"A short cut? General, we are already cutting corners."

"A bypass, an end-around," Moradi replied. "We've gotten quite good at those."

General Moradi bid Dr. Sabet farewell by the Mi-17, then followed his staff onto the helicopter for the trip back to Isfahan. Their mood was upbeat, chatting happily as they belted in, pleased to be returning home after a few days away. Moradi's own feelings were harder to define. He wasn't as angry or frustrated as he'd expected to be, or depressed about the program's setback. Certainly his conversation with the Supreme Leader would be unpleasant. As the helicopter took flight, he realized he'd reached a conclusion.

This wasn't going to work.

2

SEQUENCE

Ed Randolph walked into the conference room to find it jammed, buzzing with conversation. Thankfully, government buildings were nonsmoking, but it was still stuffy. With even the janitors cleared for Top Secret, classification hadn't been much of a barrier to attendance. And there had been rumors. He quickly walked to the front of the room, past the two briefers setting up.

He held up his arms, and the murmur quickly faded. "There are too many people in this room. If you're not a principal or designated representative, leave. If you're not from the WMD, Near East, Military Issues, or Science and Technology Offices, leave." One analyst rose to protest, but Randolph forestalled him. "Yes, Clark, you're entitled, but not yet. This is only a preliminary meeting. The Office of Transnational Threats will get their chance to review and comment on the draft product." He raised his voice. "And the fewer discussions I hear in the halls, the better." There were no more arguments, and people began to file out of the room. As the National Intelligence Officer for Weapons of Mass Destruction and Proliferation, Randolph had the authority to limit the meeting's attendance.

The Chairman of the National Intelligence Council, General Duvall, appeared in the door and the stragglers made a path for him, then hurried out. Randolph checked his watch: 1500 exactly. He checked the two briefers. One was now standing at the podium while the other tended the computer. They had dealt with the general before. Randolph knew what he expected.

As Duvall sat, the analyst behind the podium smoothly launched into his brief. "Good afternoon, General. My name is Todd Allison. I'm the senior imagery analyst assigned to the Weapons Intelligence, Nonproliferation and Arms Control Center, Central Intelligence Agency. This briefing is classified Top Secret, NOFORN, and contains information from a sensitive HUMINT compartment." To emphasize that fact, the second slide listed not only the security classification, but all the categories of intelligence involved, and the classifying authorities.

"Next slide," Allison directed. The bold lettering, "Key Judgments," at the top of the slide was somewhat misleading, as there was only one short bullet.

"Sir, based on all source analysis, we believe with a high degree of confidence that the Iranians are preparing to test a nuclear device—no earlier than two weeks, but possibly in no more than a month."

Randolph watched the reactions from those in the room. Gene Cooper, Allison's boss and the head of WINPAC, sat to one side. He was nodding of course, as was Duvall, who'd been told the reason for the sudden change in his afternoon appointments. Everyone else, the other analysts and the department heads, sat up straighter. Some pulled out notepads. A few turned to speak to their neighbors, but were quickly shushed.

"We understand this runs counter to the last three NIEs, and we've taken care to verify both our analysis and sources." The NIEs, or National Intelligence Estimates, are the official positions of the U.S. intelligence community on a wide variety of issues that affect the security of the United States. It was the National Intelligence Council's job to draft, coordinate, publish, and update them as needed, combining the data and analytic talent from the entire intelligence community. It took a lot of hard work to get the intelligence community to make up its mind about anything. Changing it was even harder.

"The first indicator was found by Ken Akamatsu at the NSA." He motioned to the analyst minding the computer. "Ken tracks Iranian construction companies, watching for activity that doesn't correlate with known projects, or projects that are larger than they should be."

"Khatam al-Anbia is one of the biggest construction companies in

Iran," Akamatsu broke in and explained. "One of their divisions, 'Hara,' recently opened a small office in Qermezin, 250 kilometers to the west-southwest of Tehran." A map flashed on the screen.

"Information on this came from intercepts of commercial phone traffic we obtained. The Hara division specializes in tunnel construction."

"The second piece was a sensitive HUMINT report," said Allison, continuing the presentation. "CIA's National Clandestine Service provided it to us six days ago after receiving it from a friendly nation." Randolph knew which nation, and most of the audience might guess it was Israel, but Allison didn't need to tell them that. "This source reported that Basij units in Markazi Province were ordered to provide troops to patrol an area in the northwest part of the province until regular IRGC units could arrive and set up proper security."

The Basij was a militia force, first formed during the Iran-Iraq war in the 1980s. Consisting of young men armed with infantry weapons, it was a paramilitary arm that could serve as irregular troops, civic event organizers, or political enforcers as the occasion required. They were locally recruited and often commanded by an imam in the community they came from.

Akamatsu pressed a button and the map zoomed out. "Qermezin is in the northwest part of the province.

"Based on these two reports, and with Mr. Cooper's approval, we asked NGA to survey the imagery of all Basij barracks in the area." He clicked again, and a circle appeared surrounding Qermezin, then small crosses appeared inside the circle.

"These are the locations we've checked over the past week. We saw increased activity at these five—" Some of the crosses changed color from white to red. "This led to a wide-area search for new construction. Our initial suspicion was a new underground facility was being started—purpose, unknown. What we found was this."

The map was replaced by a satellite image. "This is a low-resolution shot taken yesterday evening." It showed a collection of jumbled shapes scattered across a rocky surface.

Picking up a laser pointer, Allison systematically worked his way across the image. "This framework looks like a tower with a rectangular cross section. Measuring the components assembled nearby, its final height could be as much as twenty meters." He moved the light. "This is probably where they're going to be erecting the tower, over what looks like drilling equipment." Pointing to different places on the slide, Allison said, "These trailers appear to be typical construction offices, brought in to manage the work, but there are other trailers over here, almost a kilometer from the rest of the site. They aren't big enough to house the number of workers who would be working at a job like this, nor do they provide any services like meals or a dispensary. And they're bulldozing a berm between the trailers and the drilling site."

Duvall spoke for the first time. "And you think they'll hold instrumentation for monitoring an underground nuclear test." His tone was flat, neither agreeing nor disagreeing.

Allison answered, "The layout closely matches test sites we've seen in India, Pakistan, and North Korea. Khatam al-Anbia is owned and operated by the IRGC, the Pasdaran, who also control the Basij, and the nuclear program. There's nothing out there to drill for that we know of, neither water nor oil, and they're not close to any settled location. In addition to being sparsely populated, it's also very mountainous." He pointed to a wavy line that began at the work site and extended off the edge of the photo. "We traced this 'road,' if you want to call it that, back to the nearest paved highway. They just bulldozed any obstacles out of the way, and have made no effort to improve it. This implies that whatever they're doing, it's not a permanent installation.

"This area was last photographed several years ago, so there's no way to say when work started, but based on my experience, it all looks recent, and it also looks like they're in a hurry."

"And the time line?" Duvall asked.

Akamatsu pressed a key and a diagram appeared on the screen. Allison answered, "Typical underground test bores are drilled down to a depth of three-hundred-plus meters. Allowing for time to set up the drilling equipment and drill to that depth, then place a device and instrumentation in the hole, they could be ready in as little as two weeks. Four is more likely. I'm making two assumptions: First, they will make the shaft deep enough to fully contain the blast; they don't want anything going into the atmosphere that we could collect. The second assumption, and biggest variable, is the size of the device."

Allison shrugged. "The bigger the boom, the deeper the hole they have to drill. They can't make it too small. They don't have the technology, yet. And they won't make it too big, because they don't have that much material.

My estimate is in the twenty- to thirty-kiloton range." He nodded to his partner, who turned off the projector, and Allison sat down.

The chairman looked to the side. "Gene, your people have done good work."

Cooper smiled. "Thank you, sir. Todd really pulled it all together. But we had a lot of help from the nuke folks and NSA and NGA as well."

"And that's why I've asked Dr. Mizrahi to join us," Duvall answered. He turned to the NIO for Science and Technology. "Maurice. Do you or your people have any additional dots we could connect to this?"

"Not that I'm aware of, but we'll begin a complete review immediately."

"Do it quickly, but quietly, Maurice," Duvall instructed. "Too many people with clearances have reporters on their speed-dialers." His tone mixed frustration with contempt.

Duvall stood and walked to the front of the room and addressed the entire group. "We may have the 'whether' and 'when' to one of the biggest intelligence questions of this decade. The only problem is, it goes against everything we've been saying. Everybody here understands how thoroughly we have to nail this down. I've asked Dr. Mizrahi here because his office has the in-depth technical expertise, but I will be asking other NIOs, like Military Issues or South Asia to follow the thread that Todd Allison has described.

"Look for information that confirms or refutes this analysis, and ways for us to improve our knowledge. My intention is to have an intelligence community brief on this for the president within forty-eight hours. Our next meeting on this topic will be at eleven hundred tomorrow. Do your best work, everyone."

The meeting broke up quietly. Randolph was pleased, but wondered how long their restraint would last. He walked with the general back to his office, just a short distance. Once Randolph's door was closed, Duvall sat and took the china coffee cup Randolph offered.

"Here are my recommendations for retasking satellites and aircraft." Randolph didn't wait to be told what to do.

Duvall said, "Thanks," studied the document, and smiled. "This will keep everyone busy. I'll send it up the chain."

Randolph asked, "I wonder what the Israelis will do with this." The same agreement that allowed the U.S. to receive Israeli intelligence data required that the fruits of that data be shared with the Israelis.

"Shoot, Ed, I don't know what we're going to do with it." Duvall replied. "This is counter to everything we know about the Iranian program. That's why everybody was so shocked in there."

Randolph nodded. The U.S. had devoted considerable effort to tracking the Iranians' nuclear progress, and he'd seen plenty of both "technical intelligence," meaning satellite photos and communication intercepts, and "human intelligence," meaning agents on the ground. It all said that an Iranian bomb was years away. Now everything they knew was suspect.

"I'll review what we've got and look for holes or hidden assumptions," Randolph promised the general.

"See you at eleven tomorrow."

Officer's Quarters, Natanz Nuclear Enrichment Facility

They tried to eat together at least a few times a week. Between Shirin's long hours in the lab and Yousef's air defense duties, it was often hurried, with a return to work for one or both of them, or a solitary meal while the other worked through the evening hours. And sometimes, rarely, they both had the evening free.

Married only a few years, separations made evenings together all the sweeter. Shirin was out of her first trimester, and her appetite had partially returned. The meal was simple—kebabs, vegetables, and Lavash bread—and the maid had used a southern recipe, reminding Shirin of home. They avoided shoptalk, sticking to office gossip and plans for the baby's arrival. They discussed plans to visit Shirin's mother in a few weeks.

After dinner, over Shirin's protests, Yousef insisted on an evening walk. "It's mild enough with a coat, and the baby needs the exercise."

"Then let the baby do the walking. I'm tired."

"You sit in a laboratory all day." Strong-willed in so many things, she let her husband usher her out the door of their dormitory apartment. It was nice enough, suitable for a middle-grade Pasdaran officer, but not large.

They walked quietly for a while. In spite of what Yousef had said, the air was chilly, but there was no wind to speak of, and both were warmly dressed. They were alone on the street.

There were few places to go. The Natanz facility had been built for one purpose, and had few amenities. There was a mosque, of course, and a canteen and dispensary, and housing for the workers. So they strolled along the sidewalks, not going anywhere.

"Major Sadi says they're bringing in more guns, several batteries of fifty-seven millimeters."

"Those are smaller than the ones you command, aren't they?" Yousef was in charge of the heavy antiaircraft weapons, ten batteries of 100mm guns, four guns to a battery. They were updated copies of an older Russian design.

"The major says they'll close the gap between all the light stuff and my weapons." Her husband sounded unconvinced.

"You don't think it's a good idea." Shirin sounded a little worried.

"If the Israelis or Americans attack, they will probably use GPS-guided weapons. They can loft them from twenty or thirty kilometers away, well beyond the range of my guns, much less the smaller ones." The captain sounded disgusted. Ten batteries of radar-guided heavy guns sounded deadly enough—if you were dropping dumb iron bombs. His guns didn't even reach out to ten kilometers. "My only hope of shooting down anything is if our attackers display gross stupidity."

"What do you know about the work they're doing to the south wing?" Shirin asked. The pilot plant where she worked was shaped like a plus sign with one building in the center and four others laid out from it in the cardinal directions. "We have some offices in there, and Moham says we have to be out in two days. He also said they're setting up a new department, just like the centrifuge program, with its own director."

Yousef didn't answer for a moment, then said, "I think it's for bomb assembly."

"What?" She stopped suddenly, and he took a few steps past her before turning back to face her. He looked around, but there was nobody in sight.

"I'm sorry," she apologized, and continued in a softer voice. "I was just surprised. That goes against every plan I've seen since I joined the program. Fabrication was supposed to take place at Isfahan. They already have a shop that works with exotic metals, and it's close to Moradi's headquarters." Shirin paused, and Yousef could imagine her working through the information, trying to fit the pieces together.

Finally, she started walking again. "What makes you think they will assemble the weapon here?"

"It's why they're improving the defenses. Sadi says there may be other 'secret weapons,' brought in as well. I think he's talking about some GPS jammers. He said 'the final stages of our jihad will happen here.'"

"And Moham said the new department head was coming from Isfahan, along with specialized equipment. This explains why I saw Dr. Sabet so upset yesterday. He was complaining about 'arbitrary decisions.' First the test site, and now an assembly facility. Those were supposed to be built at the last minute, after we had enough material for several bombs. In fact, we weren't going to test the first bomb we assembled. We're confident enough of the design that we were going to make three, then test one."

Yousef nodded. "You can hide a bomb-making lab from satellites, but not a test site—or the test itself. That's why it was going be done last, and quickly. The period of greatest danger is when the Israelis think we are close, but haven't actually detonated a device. The Jews have already said that is when they will attack. Once we actually have a bomb, they won't dare strike."

They'd discussed all this before, of course, but academically. "My friend Assef went up to Qermezin to help set up the equipment at the test site. Are we really that close?" Shirin asked incredulously. Hope flared for a moment, but reality pushed back. If their lack of progress with the centrifuges and the Arak reactor was to be believed, completion was still a long way off.

"Could we have acquired a weapon from somewhere else? Or fissionable material perhaps?" she wondered aloud.

"Maybe . . . that would be consistent with why he needs the assembly facility," Yousef replied. "But what country would give us a kit for an atomic bomb? And if it's a complete bomb, why do we need to test it?"

"And that still doesn't explain why they will assemble it here instead of Isfahan," she persisted.

"Better security, maybe? That bloodhound Rahim's been all over this place. Perhaps he doesn't trust someone at Isfahan."

Shirin laughed sarcastically. "I don't think so. You know what happens if you lose Rahim's trust."

He smiled grimly in agreement, but demanded, "Do you have an answer, then?"

"No, but I have friends and contacts throughout the program. I will find out," she declared.

"Regardless of the explanation, we are now in real danger." Yousef's tone was intense. "We can't hide that test site. The Israelis will see it. We all know it's a provocation, and we're not ready to use it. What is the general thinking? I know there's a bomb shelter in the basement of the pilot plant, but we need to find a safe place for you near our quarters."

"I'm more worried about you, Yousef. If there's a raid, won't the command post be a target?"

"Not likely. They won't waste bombs on a military target. The centrifuge halls, the labs, and"—he patted her shoulder—"engineers are their targets. Besides, if there actually is a raid, I'll probably be out untangling the ammunition supply for one of the batteries."

"In the open?" She stopped walking again and struck a pose of mock anger. "And that's supposed to make me feel better!" She punched his shoulder, maybe a little harder than she needed to.

"Ouch," he said softly. Deliberately changing the subject, Yousef asked, "So will you chat with your uncle tonight?"

"Yes," she replied. "Should I mention the new guns?"

"No," he replied sternly. "Definitely not! I am a loyal Iranian military officer, and I will not compromise our defenses."

"But you will send information about our nuclear program out of the country."

"You're the one doing the talking," he pointed out. "You believe it is a waste of resources, and a path leading to disaster. I do it because our leaders, however pious they may be, should not possess nuclear weapons. They are too eager to use them." A moment passed, and he added, "They are unfit."

"Your brother made you believe that," she commented softly. Yousef's younger brother, Ali, had still been in graduate school when the protests broke out after the June 2009 elections. Both brothers, like many Iranians, had believed the election was stolen by Ahmadinejad, but Ali had taken to the streets, part of the "Green Revolution."

He'd been arrested, taken to Evin Prison, and had disappeared. Inquiries about Ali's welfare had brought questions about the family's loyalties, and threats about their fate if they pressed the matter too strongly. Later, after word of the deaths at Evin Prison leaked out, Ali's name appeared on a list of those who "died resisting arrest" released by the Ministry of Justice. The family was never officially notified, and his body was never returned.

"Yes, at first, that was my reason, but it isn't just about Ali anymore, or the others that died." They came to a corner and Yousef paused for a moment, looking as if he was choosing which direction to walk. There were a few people on the street now. They were all at least a block away, but he turned nervously, taking her down an empty street. "We've said enough." He kept his voice so low, that Shirin could barely hear him.

A chill found her, and she said, "It's time to go back." She kept her arm tight around Yousef, pulling him close as they walked quickly back. Venturing one last comment, she said softly, "I miss Ali, too. And I think you are being very brave." She patted his shoulder, and they didn't speak until they returned to the apartment.

General Moradi's Headquarters, Isfahan

Moradi may have been a general, and handpicked by the Supreme Leader to command Iran's nuclear program, but when he wanted to speak with Rahim, he went to the "major's" office.

Rahim's part of the building had been purpose-built, with the entire intelligence section enclosed in a "screen room." Electrically grounded metal sheeting built into the walls shielded the area from electronic eavesdropping, and prevented unwanted transmissions from computers or other electronic devices from going out. If one had private matters to discuss, this was the perfect venue.

Moradi was sure his conversations there were being recorded by Rahim, simply because Rahim taped everybody, including himself. The general wasn't worried about Rahim possessing a record of their conversation. He was VEVAK. If they wanted to accuse him of a crime, they could easily make up any charge they chose, with evidence to match.

Even Moradi didn't know Hassan Rahim's actual rank, if such things mattered in VEVAK, but he'd been assured by Khamenei himself that Rahim was their best man—efficient, thorough, and utterly ruthless. Thankfully, Moradi found Rahim shared his views on many things. That had been important before, but it was utterly vital now. His plan could not work without the intelligence chief's cooperation. And with it, he was almost assured success.

Moradi returned the guard's salute, turned in his cell phone, and signed in. Instead of a conventional door, the entrance to the intelligence section was bare metal, with security warnings in bright colors. Moradi pulled on a lever to open the door, as if he was stepping into a refrigerator. It even made the same kind of noise.

Inside, another guard greeted him and logged his entry. The hallway inside was unremarkable, lined with filing cabinets, with gaps for doors to the offices on either side. Space was at a premium. Above the cabinets, portraits of Supreme Leader Khamenei and President Ahmadinejad in different poses were mixed with other religious leaders.

The door to Rahim's office was flanked by an oversized image of Grand Ayatollah Khomeini. The door was open, and as Moradi entered, Rahim's aide sprang to his feet and greeted the general. Moradi noticed the assistant's right hand moving down, away from his sidearm. "The major's waiting for you," the young soldier reported. Knocking once lightly on the door, he quickly opened it for the general, then stepped aside.

Rahim was standing, almost at attention. Gesturing, he invited the general to sit. A fresh pot of tea was already waiting, and as Moradi sat down and accepted a cup from the major, he heard the door close and lock behind them. He knew Rahim's aide would make sure they were not interrupted.

As Moradi sipped his tea, Rahim reported, "The information was sent, but there has been no reaction from the Americans or Israelis. It may still be in transit."

Moradi was silent for a moment, considering. "Will we be able to tell when the information has been received?"

"Only by their reaction. We know it was sent." Rahim smiled grimly. "Our 'friend' is watched very carefully. He's been well trained by his handlers, but tradecraft is designed to help someone avoid notice. If you're already watching, and expecting him to act, then it's trivial to watch him send a message."

"So when will the enemy react?"

"You really mean, will they believe and act on it?" Rahim asked. "I understand your eagerness, but we could paint a sign on the roof that said 'nuclear weapon being built here!' and they still might not respond."

Moradi nodded. "They won't believe it's worthwhile unless they steal it from us."

"Exactly!" Rahim almost exploded. "And they won't move quickly.

Even the Israelis will argue for a while, and we both know how long it takes the Americans to make up their minds."

"It will be the Israelis," Moradi insisted. "They are our true enemy. They want to strike us."

"It is as God wills," Rahim replied. "But imagine it: Their intelligence agencies collecting, analyzing bits of information, just as we do. Some will become convinced that we are in the final stages. Others will not. We must supply the enemy with enough evidence, from different sources, to convert even the most cautious doubters. We will give them more than one 'smoking gun.'"

"Like the IAEA inspectors," Moradi said.

Rahim nodded. "A week from tomorrow, on their regular monthly inspection, they will find traces of uranium enriched to much higher levels than is needed for any reactor. The amounts will be minute, but within their analytical capabilities.

"They are looking very hard for evidence of our progress, so we will give them exactly what they are looking for. And they will decide they have to stop us. As if they have the right to decide our actions." There was anger and defiance in Rahim's words.

"And they will strike Natanz, brutally and thoroughly," Moradi continued. "The pilot plant, the buried centrifuge halls, anything connected with the nuclear program will be completely destroyed." Both of them had seen the accuracy and destructive power of modern ordnance delivered by a first-line air force. And they had no illusions about the effectiveness of Natanz's air defenses—or the national air defense organization. The raid might suffer casualties, but it could not be stopped.

"The world, and especially our enemies, will believe they have stopped our nuclear program, but they will start a war," Rahim declared with finality. But after a pause, he asked, "Is this really the only way?" His question had a reluctant tone.

Moradi reassured him. "Our leaders want a war. They always planned to strike Israel, to deal it a mortal blow. I am convinced that under the current conditions, we will never be able to produce a nuclear device. And if we can't, then we have to find some other way. A cold-blooded attack by Israel or America will rally all the nations in the region to our side. Even the Saudis would have to acknowledge that we were the aggrieved party. We will lose Natanz—which will finally justify its existence—and some lives, which is regrettable but necessary.

"And what if Israel attacks unilaterally, without informing America? They've done it before." Moradi smiled at the idea. "The damage to their relations would be catastrophic—for them. Dissention among our enemies."

"At the very least, Israel would be crippled, too weak to ever recover," Rahim agreed. Then he asked, wondering, "But what if it isn't enough? What if the Twelfth Imam is waiting for the actual destruction of Israel before he returns?"

"*Insh'Allah*," Moradi replied. "As God wills. And nobody knows. You know the *hadiths* better than I do. They say 'a time of chaos and civil war.' Some people say we live in a time like that right now. But if we are, why hasn't Muhammud Al-Mahdi returned?"

Moradi raised his hands. "I do not question Allah or his will, but we all await the Imam's return, and are commanded to do all we can to hasten it. The Israelis or Americans could attack tonight, and I would be a happy man."

"They won't," Rahim replied. "It will be as least a week, maybe two. The information I fed to our tame traitor and the IAEA report will take at least that long to percolate through the spy agencies. And then our enemies will have to gather their courage."

"What about Dr. Sabet?" Moradi asked. The program's scientific leader had not been brought into Moradi's plan and had recently found out about construction of the site near Qermezin and the changes at Natanz.

"He was definitely not pleased when he discovered you had changed the plan and given orders behind his back," Rahim answered. "He is being watched. His questions are being deflected to your office. And you've been 'difficult to reach.'"

"It would be best if we could share our plans with him," Moradi suggested.

"We can't, and we've discussed this." Rahim's tone was firm. "His piety is beyond reproach, but I do not believe he would be willing to make the sacrifices required by your plan. And he would not agree with your assessment that the program is doomed to failure. He is too emotionally committed to its completion."

"I agree," Moradi replied, "but he has access to a great many people outside the program. If he reaches out to them—"

"Which is why he is being watched." Rahim assured him. "If he does reach out, he will be detained." Forestalling Moradi's protests, he quickly added, "He will not be harmed. I would never permit such a thing. If our plans are successful, he would only be held incommunicado for a short while, until the attack."

"They will attack," Moradi answered. "And soon."

3

APRIL FOOLS

1 April 2013
2030 Local Time/1630 Zulu
USS *Michigan*

"Please tell me this is just another bad joke," pleaded Jerry Mitchell, as he looked up from the report in his hand.

"Sorry, sir," replied Lieutenant Jaime Manning, USS *Michigan*'s medical officer, "but this isn't part of today's festivities. Alex has really fractured his left arm, and I have to ground him from any further ASDS operations."

Jerry winced at the word "ground." Even after a decade that word still had some bite to it. He rubbed his right forearm, just above the wrist, almost by reflex, feeling the scars from the rough landing after ejecting from his Hornet so many years ago.

Not bothering to hide his frustration, he threw the report onto an already impressive mound in his in-box. As the executive officer of the blue crew on USS *Michigan*, his world revolved around paperwork. And while overseeing the ship's administration was only one of his duties, it seemed to take up most of his time. Despite his best efforts, he scrambled just to keep up. Everything was getting done, but the process wasn't pretty, nor was his stateroom. This little incident would add another report or two to Jerry's growing to-do list. Turning back toward the doctor, he asked a one-word question. "How?"

"Well, XO, as you recall, last night's movie was *300*."

"Tell me about it," replied Jerry sarcastically. "I've been listening to the SEALs chanting *HAROO!* all day long!"

Manning nodded sympathetically. "Yeess, it has been getting a bit tiresome. But anyway, Alex and Holt got into a lively debate over the scene where King Leonidas kicks the Persian messenger into the well. Alex claimed the segment had to be computer animation because there was no way a real human being could kick like that, with any force. Holt, of course, disagreed, claiming he had used a similar kick before and that it was very effective. The discussion got a little animated, and ended up with Alex challenging Holt to prove it. So they went off to missile compartment lower level to conduct a *Mythbusters*-like experiment and settle the issue."

Jerry sighed deeply as he rubbed his face; he had no trouble seeing why this story had a bad ending. Lieutenant (jg) Holt Barrineau was the assistant officer-in-charge of the SEAL platoon assigned to *Michigan* for the exercise with the Pakistani Special Forces. Holt was built like a truck—a very large truck—that made squeezing his powerful six-foot-four frame through the submarine's constricted passageways and hatches a challenge. The crew called him "Gutzilla," partly because of his huge size and aggressive demeanor, and partly because of his nearly insatiable appetite. Jerry had personally seen the young officer consume unbelievable quantities of food. Holt didn't just eat; he refueled.

Lieutenant Alex Carlson was physically a polar opposite. Skinny as a reed, he barely made it to five-foot-ten inches in height and weighed in at 160 pounds when soaking wet. Barrineau easily had 100 pounds on him. But despite the significant differences in size, shape, and Navy training, Carlson and Barrineau were close friends. Carlson, as the Advanced SEAL Delivery System, or ASDS, pilot, worked far more closely with the SEALs than anyone else on *Michigan*. SEALs also hold a special respect for non-SEALs that take the same risks to bring them in and out of harm's way. The mutual respect quickly turned into friendship. Jerry was confident that none of the individuals involved thought anyone would get badly hurt. He doubted thought entered into the discussion at all, but the basic physics of the situation were entirely in Barrineau's favor, and by a wide margin.

"After a few slow trials to get the positioning right," continued Manning, "Holt attempted the real kick. Unfortunately, as he raised his right leg, his left foot slipped and he rotated the kick instead of making it head on. The kick caught Alex between the fifth and sixth ribs on his left side, spun him about, and threw him into a missile tube where his left ulna took the brunt of the impact. It was a clean fracture, just above the wrist, and was easily set, but Alex will be in a whole arm cast for a couple of months, maybe three."

Jerry shook his head and looked upward. "Lord, save me from the synergistic stupidity of knuckleheaded young men."

"I believe the underlying medical condition is called testosterone poisoning, sir," added Manning wryly.

Jerry didn't immediately respond to the doctor's quip. He simply frowned while he groped around on his desk for the clipboard with the exercise master events list. Quietly, he looked it over, then tossed the clipboard back onto his desk.

"I'm assuming that Alex can still stand watches."

"Yes, sir. Between his arm and a couple of bruised ribs, he'll be a bit sore, but he is able to stand regular watches on board *Michigan*. He just can't pilot the ASDS."

"That's fine, Doctor. We only have one more event in this exercise, and it doesn't include the ASDS, so this injury goes into the annoying vice inconvenient category." Jerry paused momentarily, thinking. "Still, I'm going to have to give it some thought on how to describe this incredibly stupid stunt officially."

"If it's of any help, XO, some of the SEALs are calling it the 'Spartan kick gone wrong.'"

"Spartan kick gone wrong, eh?" Jerry mulled over the doctor's suggestion. "It certainly is catchy. It would make a great title for a YouTube vid . . ."

He froze in midsentence as that dreadful thought finally worked its way into the conscious part of his brain. Leaning forward, a guarded expression on his face, and speaking softly, he asked, "*Please* tell me no one recorded this foolishness?"

Startled by her XO's sudden change, Manning stammered, "I . . . I don't think so, sir. Why would they do something so dumb as . . ."

Her response slowly drifted to a stop as Jerry adopted the classic "XO look," a foundation of stern impatience with a dash of irritation.

". . . and I'll find out and get back to you ASAP," concluded Manning quickly.

"Correct answer," replied Jerry with a slight grin. "The last thing I need is for a video of this incident to go viral on the Internet the moment we get back to port. It would complicate my life and I don't need any help with that. Capiche?"

"Yes, sir. I understand, completely."

"Good. Now concerning your qual board . . ."

The sudden antiquated ring of the Dialex internal phone system rudely interrupted their conversation. Holding up his right index finger, signifying "Wait one," Jerry reached over and unclipped the handset. "Executive officer," he answered.

"XO, Officer of the deck, sir. The skipper asked me to pass on that we are receiving flash traffic. He is already in the radio room and requests that you get your, quote, carcass up there immediately, unquote, sir."

"Understand we are receiving flash traffic. Is it related to the exercise?" Confused, Jerry reached again for the events list.

"Negative, sir. This is a real-world message."

A flash precedence message for *Michigan* meant something very big was happening in her part of the world, and the powers that be wanted her to do something about it.

"Thank you, Erik. I'll be right up."

Jerry rose quickly as he secured the handset in its cradle. Manning had already stepped out of the stateroom, clearing his path.

"Doc, we'll have to work on your board later," said Jerry, as he bolted for the ladder well. She made a reply, but Jerry didn't hear it. His attention was elsewhere.

"Gangway. Make a hole!" he shouted, as his foot hit the first step. The sailors at the top of the ladder well rapidly dispersed. Grabbing the bridge access hatch ladder railing, Jerry propelled himself around the corner and found Lieutenant Erik Nelson, *Michigan*'s communications officer, already holding the radio room door open. "The skipper's forward reading the message," volunteered Nelson.

Jerry only nodded as he entered the room. The solid thump from behind told him Nelson had closed the heavy door. Hunched over a table, motionless, studying the message stood Captain Kyle Guthrie. A seasoned submariner, Guthrie had an outstanding record full of highly successful assignments. *Michigan*'s blue crew was his second command tour, a rare occurrence in the U.S. submarine force, and everyone on board knew he enjoyed every minute of it.

Jerry considered himself lucky to work for a man like Guthrie, who seemed to know everything about subs and submarine warfare. The guy had been there and done it all: patrols on a ballistic missile submarine, tours at NAVSEA and the Pentagon supporting submarine design and procurement, as well as XO and CO tours on attack submarines. He'd been on boats that had fired virtually every weapon a U.S. submarine could possibly carry including Trident II D-5 ballistic missiles, Tomahawk cruise missiles, and various flavors of Mark 48 torpedoes. Operationally, Guthrie had a lot of experience in land-attack strikes, intelligence-gathering missions, and had even worked with embarked SEALs before. In short, he was the perfect commanding officer for a converted *Ohio*-class submarine. His reputation as a demanding captain was well founded, but at the same time he was courteous, fair, and totally dedicated to his crew. While he worked them hard, he also made damn sure they had all the tools they needed to get the job done.

"Ahh, XO," said Guthrie, while waving for Jerry to come beside him. "Glad to see you made it. What took you so long?" The smirk on his face made it clear he was jerking Jerry's chain, particularly since it hadn't even been thirty seconds since Jerry had received the phone call.

"Sorry, Skipper, there was a little congestion on Highway 3," said Jerry without blinking. He had Guthrie's dry, and sometimes sarcastic, sense of humor down pat and knew the gibe wasn't personal. Indeed, his reference to the main road outside of the Bangor Submarine Base earned an appreciative nod from his commanding officer.

Before he could even ask about the message's contents, Guthrie calmly handed it to him. "These orders come straight from the top, Jerry. We're through with the exercise and are to proceed at best speed to the central Persian Gulf. We've been ordered to extract two individuals with critical information on Iran's nuclear program. Apparently we are a last-minute backup plan and have to get to the rendezvous location in less than forty-five hours." He emphasized that last point by repeatedly poking at the message paragraph containing that little tidbit.

Guthrie's rapid-fire summarization made it difficult for Jerry to read the message and listen at the same time. He saw the "Z" prosign in the message header signifying a "FLASH" precedence message. This meant the sender had to process and get this message out as fast as possible, preferably in less than ten minutes. The list of information addresses was impressive, starting with Special Operations Command, Naval Special Warfare Command, Commander, Submarine Forces Pacific, and on down to *Michigan*'s submarine squadron and SEAL Team Three, the parent unit of Charlie Platoon. He also noticed the message was classified at the Top Secret level with limited distribution. As he hit the meat of the message, Jerry found it contained little more than what Guthrie had already said, along with "more information to follow."

Guthrie gave his exec twenty seconds before shooting out a string of commands.

"We'll have to put the spurs to her if we're to make it, but even so it's gonna be dang close. Get the OOD to change course to due west, bring the reactor coolant pumps online, and get us up to seventeen knots. Then have all department heads, the COB, and SEAL platoon members muster in the BMC in five minutes."

"Change course to cardinal west, bring reactor coolant pumps online, and make seventeen knots. Muster all department heads, the COB, and SEAL platoon members in the BMC in five minutes, aye, sir," Jerry replied; a complete verbatim repeat back of an order was standard Navy operating procedure to ensure that it was properly heard and understood.

"Good, now git to it."

"If I may, Captain. There is a medical issue that I need to report. Lieutenant—"

"Is it life-threatening?" interrupted Guthrie.

"No, sir."

"Then it can wait, Jerry. It's more important right now to get us heading toward the rendezvous point."

"Begging your pardon, sir, I believe this is relevant . . ."

"I said later, XO." Guthrie's firm response signaled the end of the discussion.

"Aye, aye, sir," responded Jerry, chastened.

Turning to leave, he placed the message on the table and then walked swiftly toward the door. He heard the radio room watch stander say, "Skipper, another message is coming in on the new mission," as he shut the door.

The control room was barely ten paces aft of the radio room and Jerry marched directly to the periscope stand where Lieutenant Nelson stood with eager anticipation.

"OOD, change course to two seven zero. Have maneuvering bring the reactor coolant pumps online and get us to seventeen knots ASAP. Then announce over the 1MC for all department heads, the COB, and SEAL platoon members to muster in the battle management center."

Nelson accurately recited the orders. While he began to carry them out, Jerry moved over by the fire control consoles to get out of the way. The XO's presence could be something of a distraction, since most of the time his presence was the harbinger of yet another drill. But this time it was the real thing, and being out of the direct line of sight of the watch standers helped to reinforce that this wasn't another training evolution.

USS *Michigan* was the second of eighteen *Ohio*-class nuclear-powered ballistic missile submarines, also called SSBNs, built in the 1980s and 1990s. After completing thirty-three strategic deterrent patrols, the Navy decided to convert her and three of her sisters into cruise missile–carrying submarines, or SSGNs, as they came due for their major overhaul. *Michigan* began the conversion process in January 2005. The systems for the Trident II D-5 ballistic missiles were removed and replaced with equipment that supported large numbers of Tomahawk cruise missiles and berthing for Special Operations troops; in most cases Navy SEALs.

The missile tubes were refitted to hold insertable modules that allowed them to store equipment for the SEALs, carry Tomahawk land-attack cruise missiles, or house unmanned vehicles. Tubes one and two were converted to diver lockout chambers, letting up to five SEALs per chamber leave a submerged submarine. They were also fitted with docking ports that allowed an ASDS minisubmarine, and/or dry deck shelters to ride on *Michigan*'s back.

Tubes three through ten were switch-hitters and could hold either stowage canisters for SEAL gear or seven-celled canisters for the Tomahawk cruise missiles. Tubes eleven through twenty-four normally only had missile canisters in them. But on this patrol, tubes twenty-three and twenty-four held two experimental Cormorant unmanned air vehicles. Theoretically, a single SSGN could carry up to 154 Tomahawk cruise missiles, but between the UAVs and a SEAL platoon's worth of gear, *Michigan* had only 84 Tomahawks on board.

As substantial as the missile tube modifications were, virtually all of *Michigan*'s electronics had been ripped out and replaced with more advanced gear. She had an upgraded sonar suite and fire control system that gave her many of the same capabilities as the new *Virginia* class attack submarines, something Jerry very much appreciated. The Trident missile control center had been gutted and replaced with six new consoles to program and launch the Tomahawk cruise missiles.

When the Tomahawk missile had first been introduced in 1983, each weapon had to be programmed at a shore facility and the disk packs with the programming transported to the launching vessel. It took a lot of time. Now, the Tomahawk Weapons Control Center not only gave *Michigan* the ability to program the missiles herself, but also gave her access to the reconnaissance photos and the intelligence information needed to pick the targets.

The old navigation center was converted into the Battle Management Center or BMC, a space dedicated for SOF mission planning and ASDS or dry deck shelter operations. The navigation equipment that once took up the entire room was now condensed into two cabinets tucked away in the back. The BMC used the same type of information that the Tomahawk missiles used, but in this case, it was used to plan SEAL operations.

Finally, the radio room had undergone a thorough overhaul, giving *Michigan* unusually large communication "pipes." The greater bandwidth effectively made an SSGN a covert command ship, able to receive large amounts of targeting and intelligence information and quickly convert that information into Tomahawk strike missions or SEAL operations. Following the usual sea trials and tests, *Michigan* returned to service in June 2007.

But the physical alterations to the submarine weren't the only changes. In 2010, the U.S. Navy lifted its ban of women serving on submarines, and by early 2012 female officers started reporting to the crews of *Ohio*-class SSBNs and SSGNs. This was a controversial decision that sparked a lot of grumbling within the small and tightly knit submarine community. Women had, on rare occasions, deployed on SSBNs in the past. But these were engineering duty officers or medical doctors, like Lieutenant Manning, going out on a patrol as part of their qualification process; they were riders, not part of the official crew. *Michigan*'s blue crew had their first female ensigns show up just before the beginning of the current patrol. And as expected, it caused a bit of a stir, particularly among the older crew-members and their wives, who felt their way of life was being turned upside down by "social engineering politicians."

Jerry was neutral about assigning women to submarines. He'd seen the integration of the sexes before in the surface and aviation communities, and while there were a lot of problems at first, eventually things worked themselves out. He knew the fraternization problem hadn't gone away, but the dire predictions of whole-scale collapse of ship cohesiveness and readiness didn't occur either. His views were also tempered by his first deployment on USS *Memphis*. They had embarked two women for a special intelligence-gathering mission off the coast of Russia.

Captain Guthrie, on the other hand, was strongly against the policy change. He'd said it was inappropriate to have mixed crews on submarines due to the extremely close quarters and limited habitability space. In his opinion, "to expect young men and women to not act like young men and women was the height of hypocrisy." To his credit, he treated his two female officers no differently than any other member of his crew. He was just as civil, and pushed them just as hard as his other junior officers, and so far Ensigns Laura Tillman and Sandy Wagner were making satisfactory progress toward completing the lengthy qualifications for their dolphins—the symbol of an accomplished submariner. Of course, Guthrie made it clear to the entire crew that "any transgressions would be dealt with to the maximum extent the Uniform Code of Military Justice allowed. He would not tolerate fraternization on board his boat, and the individuals involved *would* live to regret it." So far, no one had tested the waters to see if the "Old Man" was bluffing.

The momentary dimming of the lights told Jerry that the reactor coolant pumps were being started and he could feel the vibration in the deck plates as *Michigan* accelerated. One aspect of the *Ohio*-class design that made them so quiet was the S8G reactor plant. The reactor was built to take advantage of the basic principle that hot water rises and cold water sinks. By using these thermal currents, cooling water would naturally circulate without the need for pumps; but only up to a certain point. For greater power, coolant pumps had to be engaged to increase the flow and keep the core at a safe operating temperature. This forced circulation mode was needed whenever *Michigan* had to move at high speeds.

The noise and traffic in the control room soon increased as the SEALs, Master Chief Eichmann, *Michigan*'s chief of the boat, and the ship's department heads began filing into the BMC. While taking a mental muster, Lieutenant Isaac Simmons, the navigation and operations officer, looked at Jerry and gestured "what the hell is going on?" Silently, Jerry pointed toward the door of the BMC. Simmons responded with a sloppy half-salute. Immediately after him came Barrineau and Carlson. *Dumb and dumber*, thought Jerry as he saw the cast on Carlson's left arm from just below the shoulder all the way to the wrist. "The skipper isn't going to be happy when he sees that," he muttered to himself.

A quick glance at his watch showed that the five minutes were nearly up. Moving forward to the front of the periscope stand, Jerry took up a vantage point from where he could see the radio room door. He was never very good at waiting, but with a high priority mission before them, Jerry was more impatient than usual. He just couldn't let it show.

"XO, we are on course two seven zero, and our speed is thirteen knots coming to seventeen." Nelson's report yanked him back from his temporary vigil.

"Very well, OOD," Jerry replied flatly.

"So what's going on, XO? This can't be part of the exercise. We're going in the wrong direction. The last event is closer to the Pakistani coast," prodded Nelson.

"You're right. It's not. But I don't know a whole lot more than we're to make for the Persian Gulf toot-de-sweetie," answered Jerry. "The captain is getting the specifics on our new mission as we speak and should be out any second now to brief us."

As if waiting for his cue, Guthrie abruptly emerged from the radio room, clipboard in hand. By his general body language one would be hardpressed to say that anything unusual was happening, but Jerry had spotted the glimmer of excitement in his captain's eyes.

"Mr. Nelson, report," demanded Guthrie, as he hopped up onto the stand.

"Sir, we are on course two seven zero. Our speed is currently fourteen knots, accelerating to seventeen."

"Very well." Then turning toward Jerry he asked, "XO, is the congregation assembled?"

"Yes, sir. All interested parties are in the BMC awaiting your presence. Bursting with curiosity, I might add."

Feigning sincerity Guthrie exclaimed, "Well, we can't have that now, can we!?" Then with a subtle sweep of his hand, he motioned toward the BMC and added, "After you, XO."

"Yes, sir," responded Jerry, as he turned and headed for the door. He had just cracked it open when a loud voice shouted, "Feet!"

Inside, Jerry saw Lieutenant Travis Frederickson, SEAL Team Three's targeting and operations officer, and the detachment officer-in-charge, standing by the access to the planning cell spaces. Stepping aside, Jerry let Guthrie enter first. Frederickson brought up the rear.

"As you were," Guthrie said, as he positioned himself in front of the two-dozen people crowded in to the planning cell.

"Moments ago we received a flash-precedence message giving *Michigan* and the embarked SEAL platoon a new mission. I'm going to read the message and then I'll give you your instructions. Save any questions till the end," instructed Guthrie.

The captain took his reading glasses out of his poopie suit pocket, put them on, and opened the clipboard.

FROM: Commander, United States Central Command
TO: Commanding Officer, USS Michigan SSGN 727.
SUBJECT: Fragmentary Order 05-13.

Terminate participation in Exercise Display Unity and proceed at best possible speed to coordinates latitude 27° 35' 49" N, longitude 051° 55' 29" E in the central Persian Gulf. Once in position, elements of Charlie Platoon, SEAL Team Three will rendezvous with and extract two Iranian nationals who have detailed information on the Iranian government's WMD program. The rendezvous has been scheduled for 1630Z hours on 03 April. This time cannot be altered due to a lack of communications with the Iranian individuals. Presidential approval to violate Iranian territorial waters is in process.

Commanding Officer, USS Michigan, has operational control of the mission, while SEAL Team Three Detachment OIC has tactical control. More information to follow.

A low murmur arose as soon as Guthrie finished reading. Jerry snapped his fingers twice, calling for silence.

"Alright, gentlemen, and lady," added Guthrie, nodding in Manning's direction. "We have a no-shit hi-pri mission on our hands, and not a lot of time to get in position or prepare. We are already on course for the Persian Gulf, moving as fast as we can, given the stress limits imposed by the ASDS and the dry deck shelter docked on the turtleback. If you factor in the time for ASDS launch and transit, we have a tad over forty-three hours to get where we are supposed to be. So everyone will have to be at the top of their game."

Flipping through the paper on the clipboard, Guthrie quickly read from a list of orders.

"Mr. Hogan and COB. Please coordinate with the XO on additional damage control drills." Lieutenant Daniel Hogan, the damage control assistant, acknowledged the orders, as did Master Chief Eichmann with a terse "Aye, aye, sir."

"Mr. Zelinski," Guthrie continued, "I want an updated status report on all ship's weapons and the UAVs. I don't expect a fight, but the Iranians don't always act rationally and I want to be ready just in case they make it necessary for us to defend ourselves."

"Yes, sir," replied the weapons officer. "I'll have it to the XO in a couple of hours."

"Good. Also work with the XO to schedule some additional battle stations torpedo and strike drills." Checking off two more items, Guthrie turned toward his navigator.

"Mr. Simmons, I need you to figure out our best avenue of approach once we enter the gulf. I want an optimized plan that gets us to the desired coordinates as fast as possible, while keeping us in the deepest water possible."

The young African American frowned. He was not happy with this assignment. "Skipper, we are talking two hundred feet of water at the very best, probably a lot less. It's going to be frickin' hard to maintain a decent speed without generating a visible wake on the surface. It's hard to hide a hippo in a swimming pool!"

Jerry had to grin at Simmons's metaphor, for while it was a little crass to compare *Michigan* to a hippopotamus with her skipper present, it was an apt analogy. Submarine skippers, especially nuclear submarine skippers, weren't comfortable in less than three hundred or four hundred feet of water, and preferred six hundred feet—a hundred fathoms.

"You don't see me smiling about this either, Isaac," Guthrie replied sympathetically. "Just do the best you can, and while you're at it please avoid shipping lanes if at all possible. I really don't want to be in a sequel of *Hartford*'s collision."

The frown on Simmons's face quickly mutated into a grimace at the mention of the collision between the *Los Angeles*-class attack submarine USS *Hartford*, and USS *New Orleans*, a *San Antonio*-class amphibious assault ship in March 2009. *Hartford* was submerged, crossing the main shipping lanes just inside the Strait of Hormuz, when her sail was struck by the amphib, causing significant damage to the submarine.

Still uneasy, Simmons nodded and said, "We'll get right on it, Captain."

"Mr. Frederickson"—Guthrie shifted his attention to the SEAL detachment OIC—"begin your formal mission-planning process. I want the brief back on the platoon leader order in thirty hours."

"Understood, sir. Mr. Ramey has that for action." Frederickson pointed toward Lieutenant Matthew Ramey, Charlie platoon's leader, as he spoke.

"Very well," said Guthrie as he checked his list. "One more thing for you and your SEALs to keep in mind when you start putting together your intelligence requirements for reachback support. Every time you want to transmit requirements or receive data, we have to slow down. The masts can't handle speeds in excess of ten knots. We are operating under a very tight time line for this mission, and we can't afford losing time for repeated periscope depth evolutions so you can phone home. So as you put together your essential elements of information needs for NAVSPECWARCOM or ONI to fill, please do so efficiently."

"Understood," responded Frederickson and Ramey simultaneously.

"Mr. Carlson, I want a complete check of the ASDS systems, particularly the batteries . . ." Guthrie's speech came to an abrupt stop as he looked up from his clipboard and saw his ASDS pilot clearly for the first time.

Jerry saw his captain do a double take. He then removed his reading glasses and took yet another look, followed by, "Alex! What the hell happened to you!?"

Carlson just stood there silent, embarrassed.

"Uhh, I did, sir," replied Barrineau sheepishly.

Guthrie turned toward Jerry, a look of total confusion written all over his face.

"The, uh, medical issue I mentioned earlier, Skipper," remarked Jerry as gracefully as possible. It's almost always a bad thing for an XO to let his boss be surprised in public, as this violates one of the primary duties of an executive officer to not let his captain look bad.

A deep calming sigh came from Guthrie. "My bad, XO, not yours. Now what do we do about this unexpected complication?" Facing Manning he asked, "I don't suppose Alex is medically cleared to pilot the ASDS?"

"No, sir," the doctor answered. "The fracture is in a very bad spot, just about the wrist, and I had to severely restrict that arm's range of motion if it's to heal properly."

"I can do it, sir," implored Carlson. "Just give me a shorter cast for this run so I can still handle the controls."

"Absolutely not!" Manning stated firmly. "Your strength in that arm is compromised. Trying to manhandle watertight hatches and other equipment will result in more damage."

"Alex," injected Jerry. "You're not going to win this one. Been there, done that, bought the wardrobe." He bared the scars on his right wrist to emphasize the point.

"I can pilot the ASDS," said Lieutenant Vernon Higgs. "I'm qualified and can still perform my other duties once the minisub is in position."

"That's too risky, Vern," Carlson countered. "You can't work the lockout chamber controls and support the diver egress and just let the boat sit there, even anchored, that close to the shore. And we have very little information on the bottom topography and the currents along the Central Iranian coast. Operating that boat with one of your squads going in and out is definitely a two-man job."

"What other option do we have, Alex?" Higgs argued. "I don't think we can get another qualified pilot out here in time."

"Even if the Navy could find one and get him out here quickly, you're still talking twenty-four hours at a minimum. By that time we'll be in the Persian Gulf, probably close to the Iranian coast; how do we get him on board without drawing attention to our position? If we divert to a safer location, we'll lose a lot of time," Simmons added with growing frustration.

Guthrie listened intently to the brainstorming, remaining silent to allow his junior officers room to freely voice their ideas and concerns. By their expressions and comments, the SEALs all believed that the risk was acceptable for Lieutenant Higgs to perform both jobs. The submariners strongly disagreed.

Guthrie did as well. "I can't allow Higgs to do the job alone. Too many bad things could happen. But to be honest, I'm not keen on telling my boss that I can't do my job without help, and I don't want to do this unless there is absolutely no other choice available to us."

The assembly grew quiet as two-dozen brains chewed on the problem. After about fifteen seconds of awkward silence, Jerry finally spoke up. "I can pilot the ASDS, Captain."

Every head in the room snapped in his direction. Guthrie looked quizzical, and intrigued. "Okay, XO, explain yourself."

"Yes, sir. You know I attended some of the training sessions before this patrol, to get a better appreciation of ASDS operations, and I've spent some time on the simulator. I went out with Alex during both the workups and on one of the exercise events. I even managed to get some stick time. I believe I have a good feel for how the ASDS handles, and Vernon can assist with the launching and landing evolutions. I'm also a qualified Navy diver, all of which makes me the closest thing to a spare pilot."

Guthrie took stock of his peoples' reactions as Jerry explained his plan; both Higgs and Carlson were nodding their agreement, a good sign.

"Alex can provide some additional training while we're en route, and Vernon and the others can make sure I understand the SEAL aspect of this mission. This should reduce the risk to an acceptable level," concluded Jerry.

"Comments on the XO's idea. Alex?" Guthrie asked.

"The XO's legit, sir," responded Carlson favorably. "He has an intuitive feel for the minisub; he can do it."

"Vern?"

"Concur with Alex, sir."

"Travis?"

"Concur, Captain."

A visibly relieved Guthrie turned to Jerry and said, "Okay, XO, you got the job."

Facing the assembly, Guthrie offered a final opportunity for comment. "Anything else?"

"Yes, sir," answered Frederickson. "Captain, I'd like to request restricted access to the BMC and missile compartment lower level to enable my guys to properly prepare for this mission."

Guthrie had seen SEALs go into a similar isolation mode in the past. It helped the SEALs mentally prepare for a mission. He thought it was a little strange, but it was their way and it did seem to bear fruit. "Granted, Travis. Only the navigator, Mr. Carlson, the XO, and myself will have access. Everyone else has to get your permission. Jerry, make sure you pass the word."

"Aye, aye, sir,"

"Thank you, Captain," responded Frederickson.

"Alright, people, we have a job to do, so get hot," ordered Guthrie.

Everyone in control clearly heard the SEALs. "HOOYAH, Skipper!"

4

SORTIE

Joanna Patterson concentrated on staying two steps behind the national security advisor. Ray Kirkpatrick was shorter than her by a good six inches, but he walked fast, and she worked to keep up. They were a little late, and that only added to her adrenaline level.

She knew the West Wing very well, and had been in the Oval Office dozens of times, but this was a new job, with a new administration, and of course, a new boss—two new bosses if you counted Dr. Kirkpatrick. A close friend of President Myles, he'd been a deputy undersecretary of defense in the Huber administration. It was a big jump from deputy of whatever to national security advisor, but Kirkpatrick had made a name for himself. Energetic, almost to a fault, with good communications skills and ambition, he'd transformed his little acre in the Pentagon from a disaster to "a model of efficiency," according to the cover of *Pentagon Weekly*. Kirkpatrick also understood the value of good press.

Getting the briefing perfect had taken a few minutes too long. They arrived almost breathless, five minutes late, but the president's secretary waved them inside. "You're not the last. We're still waiting for Admiral Hughes."

"Thank you, Mrs. McDowell." Kirkpatrick headed inside and Patterson followed. A memory, of going to the dean's office with a professor to ask for a grant, flashed in her mind.

She'd only met President Kenneth Myles a few times, and then only briefly, without getting a real chance to talk with him. She'd enjoyed a long relationship with President Huber, based on their common advocacy of environmental issues. Her relationship with the new president was based on a glowing recommendation from Huber and a vetting by the Myles transition team.

The room was crowded, in her opinion much more than necessary. The secretaries of state and defense waited near the president. It seemed like half the U.S. Intelligence apparatus was in the room: General Duvall, Chairman of the National Intelligence Council was here, as well as his boss, Gregory Alexander, the Director of National Intelligence, and Dr. Randall Foster, Director of the CIA. The military side included the secretary of defense, chairman of the joint chiefs, and General Ramsdale, head of Special Operations Command. Too many people drew too much attention and too much talk.

The president was speaking to the Secretary of State, Andrew Lloyd. Lloyd was an old-school diplomat, with over thirty years of experience in the state department. Myles's vice president had been picked to balance the ticket, but Lloyd was Myles's closest political ally. He'd helped shape the president's foreign policy platform before the election, as well as taking state after the inauguration. They'd been friends for decades, sharing interests in Asian history and Italian cooking.

President Myles had taught in Asian studies and written extensively before becoming involved in foreign policy, and then politics. He had the gravitas of a scholar, with a shock of snow-white hair that the political cartoonists loved, over an angular face with a strong jaw. Politically, he was more pro-business than many Democrats would like, but Patterson approved of his environmental record, and he'd said all the right things about national security. This would be his first real test.

Admiral Hughes, the Chief of Naval Operations, hurried in and took a seat next to the General Dewhurst, Chairman of the Joint Chiefs of Staff.

"We have a quorum, gentleman, and we're ten minutes late," Myles's chief of staff announced. "Dr. Foster, please begin."

The CIA director's tone was grim. "Good morning Mr. President, ladies, and gentlemen. Nothing has changed since the initial briefing last week.

ever, a couple out for a stroll on the beach during the evening glow is not an unusual event, even in Iran."

"How long will the SEALs be exposed?" asked Secretary of Defense Springfield.

"If Opal is at the right place, at the right time, ten, maybe fifteen minutes. Even with civilians, the use of GPS significantly increases the chances of a quick rendezvous. Opal has a GPS device and he knows how to use it."

"And if they're discovered?" asked Myles.

"They run back to the water, hopefully with Opal, and leave," Patterson answered. "They only risk exposure when they actually leave the water to make contact, and if bad guys are in sight, they just won't go ashore."

She added, "CENTCOM will have an RC-135 SIGINT aircraft on standing patrol in the gulf. It will monitor radio and phone transmissions in the area. They're also tasking a medium-endurance UAV to monitor the rendezvous point. If either one sees anything amiss, we can warn the SEALs off."

Myles looked at his notepad. "What's the thirty-fathom curve?"

She answered, "The line on the chart where the water depth becomes less than thirty fathoms, a hundred and eighty feet. Nuclear subs can't maneuver well in shallow water, especially ones as big as *Michigan*."

"How far is that line out from shore?" the president asked.

"At that part of the coast, a little over eight nautical miles, sir." Opening her folio, she took out a map and handed it to the president. "This shows the route of *Michigan* and the proposed pick-up point. This is Bandar Kangan, the nearest major city—really no more than a small town." Myles nodded and returned the sheet. She quickly put it away, and did not show the map to anyone else in the room.

"There is a risk," Lloyd insisted. "If the Iranians discover us in their waters, they'd consider it an act of war."

"They won't find *Michigan* or the ASDS," the SECDEF replied confidently. "The Iranian Navy operates to the east of the Strait of Hormuz, in the Gulf of Oman. The IRGC Navy has responsibility for operations inside the gulf, and they have no antisubmarine warfare capability whatsoever."

Hughes and Ramsdale both nodded in agreement, but Lloyd didn't look satisfied.

"Why does *Michigan* have to go into Iranian territorial waters?" Myles asked.

Patterson answered, "To shorten the run for the ASDS."

"Could the ASDS travel the distance if *Michigan* stayed outside the twelve-mile limit?" he asked.

Joanna paused, considering a moment before answering. "Yes, sir. It has a range of a hundred and twenty-five nautical miles at five knots."

"So a total run of what?—twenty-five or thirty miles, is well within its abilities, and at least *Michigan* is in the clear. Will it affect the timing of the operation?"

Patterson studied her notes. "Not significantly, sir. *Michigan* will be on station well before the ASDS is launched. It will double their time inside the ASDS, but it's 'dry,' so fatigue isn't the problem it was with earlier vehicles."

"Then is there any other reason to put a nuclear submarine inside Iranian waters?"

Patterson looked at Kirkpatrick, Hughes, and Ramsdale. They'd built the plan together but had never considered keeping *Michigan* back. They all looked unhappy, but nobody spoke.

"Then change the plan so that *Michigan* remains outside Iranian territorial waters. Also, add in a slight buffer to guard against any navigation errors," Myles ordered.

"We're still violating their territory," Kirkpatrick reminded him.

"I understand that, Ray, but perceptions are important. And in this instance, there is a very big difference between the ASDS and a very large cruise missile–armed nuclear submarine."

Patterson nodded, making notes. "We'll make the change immediately."

"It would be better if we didn't have to send anyone into their territory," Lloyd insisted. "If we're discovered, the Iranians will turn it into a major incident."

"Like they need an excuse," the SECDEF muttered.

"Let's not hand them one," Lloyd countered, annoyed. "Imagine the propaganda campaign if they capture U.S. commandos lured ashore by someone pretending to be an American agent."

The SECDEF shook his head. "They don't show themselves until it's clear, and they'll only be on the beach for ten or fifteen minutes. Mr. President, I agree with Ray and his people. Either we do this, and accept the low risk, or lose Opal and the information he carries. And what about the propaganda coup if VEVAK arrests Opal?"

Lloyd persisted. "I'm assuming there's nobody else in Iran—anywhere—that we can use to get Opal out of the country."

Patterson started to answer, but Foster broke in. "That was our first choice, Mr. Secretary, but again, without giving too much detail, Opal's movements are being watched. We are using this *secondary* plan," Foster said, emphasizing the word, "because my people don't have any safe way to get him and his wife out quickly." He motioned toward Hughes and Ramsdale. "When we couldn't do it, we asked the Navy and SOCOM to help."

The CIA director turned back to Patterson. "*Michigan* will be on station by 1600 hours local time tomorrow. With your approval to proceed, the operation will start about an hour later. By this time on Thursday, Opal should be safe and the information should be in our hands."

Myles and Patterson both scanned the room. Lloyd looked unhappy, and Duvall grim, but there we no dissenters. "All right, Dr. Patterson, gentlemen, proceed with the operation."

South of Shiraz
Bushehr Province, Iran

They headed south on Highway 65, another couple on an excursion to Bandar Kangan. They'd made reservations for three nights at a modest hotel near the ocean. After a drive to the coast and lunch in Bandar Tahari, Shirin and Yousef would explore some of the ancient Persian ruins before arriving in Bandar Kangan by midafternoon. The next day, they'd visit a national park farther down the coast before beginning the return trip home.

Shirin's mother, Mehry, had completely approved. "You spend too much time indoors, Shirin. Maybe underground, if the stories I've heard are true."

"Mother, please don't repeat rumors."

"Go. Take walks by the ocean. Get some fresh air. We'll have plenty of time to visit later."

So they'd made their plans and left Mehry's home, a little later than planned, because their car had developed some sort of mechanical fault that Yousef couldn't fix. They'd intended to get on the road early, and none of the garages were open, so Mehry traded cars with them. Shirin had protested. "Mother, what will you use?"

"I'll ring Yashar once his garage is open. I'm sure he can come round today and fix it." Yousef and Shirin had a Chinese-made Cowin, their first purchase as a married couple. It was a little extravagant, and much nicer than her mother's twelve-year-old Peykan.

It had taken only moments to shift their luggage, and they drove off, only half an hour behind schedule.

Shirin kept it inside until they were outside of town. They'd driven silently for a while, each with their own thoughts. Finally, Yousef said, "It's good we can leave her with the Cowin. It's a much better car. . . ."

And she'd started to cry. Clutching Yousef's arm as he drove, she sobbed into his shoulder, breathing in gasps. All her worries, the fear, and the grief of parting poured out of her. She tried to speak, and Yousef did his best to listen, but he could understand only a word here and there. One question barely squeaked out, "Will she be safe?"

"I don't know, probably," Yousef half lied. The Pasdaran weren't usually kind to family members of traitors. He had no concerns for his own mother; the woman who had lovingly raised him had been gone for over a year. Her body still functioned, but Alzheimer's had destroyed her mind. She no longer remembered him, and could barely talk. Yousef relived the pain he felt when he told her she was going to be a grandmother and all she did was stare vacantly and drool. Death would be more merciful.

An eternity later, when Shirin had finally stopped crying, she drew a slow breath and said quietly, "Yousef, I'm very afraid. For mother, the baby, for you, and me."

Her admission shocked him. She'd always been as determined as him, as passionate about their cause as he was, although for her own reasons. Both were scared, of course, but they'd never spoken of it. He thought of her as the strong one.

He had to say something. "It's a simple plan," he finally said. "We drive along the beach. We stop for a walk to admire the sunset, and happen to meet some strangers. Who happen to be wearing wet suits. And have a submarine."

She laughed in spite of her tears. "Oh, well, that's fine, then. I love walks on the beach." There was nervousness in her voice, but she was smiling. "I am glad we left our car with mother. This thing smells."

"It may smell, but the Peykan doesn't have any tracking devices on it,"

Yousef replied. "Remember yesterday, after we arrived and I went out to check the engine? There were marks on the lower body—streaks where the dirt had been rubbed off. I couldn't see anything underneath, but you never really know how small those devices can be. They could listen to what we say, track our location, and perhaps even disable the engine if they wanted to. I suspected as much.

"That's when I put the dirt in the Cowin's fuel filter. Our car will tell Rahim and his jackals that we are staying at your mother's for the next three days. And if we miss the meeting tomorrow, we will stay at the hotel for the next two nights and have a nice excursion by the shore. We can return to your mother's house, and then go back to Natanz with nobody the wiser."

She shook her head. "No. If they aren't 'wiser' now, they will be soon. I can't describe how nervous I was when I arranged my leave. The security people lectured me for half an hour, and Major Rahim himself kept 'passing by,' asking questions about my mother and our plans, especially when we'd be back. The whole time, my stomach was in knots." She hugged herself. "We can't go back. I couldn't say good-bye to mother like that again."

"If this doesn't work—" She lowered her voice. "If the Americans don't meet us tomorrow tonight, we have to escape on our own. We get a boat—rent, buy, or steal one and just leave. You know what's waiting for us. We can't go back!"

Yousef wanted to agree. With freedom a possibility, the thought of returning to Natanz repelled him. But crossing the gulf in a small boat? Two hundred kilometers of open water with a pregnant wife? And there were Pasdaran patrol boats, on the lookout for spies and smugglers. Spies like the two of them, he admitted to himself.

But arrest and Evin Prison held a special terror for every Iranian. Risking death in an open boat might be preferable. "We can talk about that later," he finally answered. "Let's see what happens tomorrow tonight."

"Where will we live?" she asked. Shirin wanted to imagine the future, to think about things she'd kept locked in a corner of her mind for years. She was beginning to consider the possibility that they might actually leave Iran. "Do you want to live in America? We don't have to, you know. We could live anywhere—France, or Brazil."

"We'd both have to learn French or Portuguese," Yousef answered. "At least you speak excellent English. Much better than me." He shrugged. "I should have studied harder."

"Then what about England or Australia?"

"It's pleasant to think about," he agreed. "We haven't had a lot of choices for the last few years."

"The Americans will help us," Shirin asserted. "They owe us, and even if they didn't, the flash drive has enough to pay for our passage."

They drove though the uneven landscape. Highway 65 wove and twisted across crestlines and valleys, always seeking the smoothest way south. Scrubby short plants stood out in different shades of green against dull brown, but it wasn't all desert. They also passed by fields and orchards that surrounded small farming communities.

Shirin took out the GPS navigator and checked their progress. It showed their planned route. "We should be in Bandar Kangan by three o'clock."

They would drive south to the coast and then northwest on Highway 96. Their route to Kangan took them right past the place where they would meet the Americans. The spot was nine kilometers southeast of the town, at a place where the highway passed very close to the water. It would be natural for a couple to pause by a narrow, rocky beach and watch the sun go down. Lingering long enough to see the sky erupt into bright colors during twilight— exactly at twilight. The Americans would arrive shortly after that.

Yousef had arranged their trip so they could see it first in the early afternoon, in full daylight. They could also check for any activity. It didn't have to be VEVAK or a Basij patrol. Fishermen, roadwork, anyone nearby would prevent their escape.

They had a latitude and longitude for the rendezvous point, but they had not entered that into the device. Both had memorized the numbers, and would simply drive, then walk until the readout matched their recollection. Shirin didn't think she'd ever forget them.

3 April 2013
1100 Local Time/0800 Zulu
USS *Michigan*, Battle Management Center

The final authorization for the mission had come in late last night, but it came with a twist. *Michigan* now had to stay in international waters, some fifteen nautical miles from the coast, while the ASDS made the longer trip in. This eliminated more than half of their time reserve, which wasn't a whole lot to begin with. Now they only had thirty minutes from the moment they arrived on station to the ASDS undocking and heading toward the shore.

Aside from Jerry, now the substitute ASDS pilot, the skipper, Lieutenant Commander Mike Harper, the boat's engineer, and Lieutenants Simmons and Carlson were the only members of *Michigan's* crew present. As navigator, Simmons had to make sure *Michigan* was in the right place both for departure and rendezvous—especially for the rendezvous. Harper, as the next senior officer, would be the acting XO while Jerry was off the boat. Lieutenant Carlson, cast and all, had been allowed to attend because of his expertise with the ASDS.

Jerry distractedly scratched the three-day growth on his chin. The rest of the SEALs had "gone native" as soon as they'd gotten underway. The Pakistanis were more comfortable working with bearded Americans, and the SEALs all had well-developed facial hair. Jerry had only started his after being tapped as Carlson's replacement. It seemed pointless to him, but it might make the two Iranians more comfortable when they came aboard the ASDS. He was looking forward to shaving it off the moment they returned to *Michigan*.

The BMC included enough table and chair space so everyone could sit and see the screen. Lieutenant Ramey, the platoon leader, ran the brief. The other three members of the team, Lapointe, Fazel, and Phillips sat together on one side, with their wheel books open and pencils ready. Jerry and Lieutenant Higgs, the two ASDS pilots, sat across the table. Lieutenant Frederickson, the ops officer, and Chief Special Warfare Operator Yates, the SEAL platoon chief, watched.

The rest of the SEAL platoon had already had their say during the planning stages. Now, with *Michigan* less than six hours from the launch point, they prepped the team's personal gear, and along with *Michigan's* crew, checked out and loaded the ASDS.

Although the extraction mission was a straightforward "template" operation, the SEALs had taken the plan apart, doing their best to break it. Worst-case scenarios had included everything from uncharted underwater obstacles to an ambush on the beach to *Michigan* being forced to abandon the rendezvous.

Lieutenant Ramey, thirty-one, and the platoon's officer in charge, was on his third deployment. He'd given his platoon instructions to look for every possible contingency and develop a plan to deal with it. "I've seen plans go south in a heartbeat. The worst case isn't watching the wheels come off. It's having a mission go bad and you don't even know it. That's when people die."

So they'd added problems like surface radar surveillance, or mines on the approach, or the beach itself, as well as obvious ones like the asset being used as bait, knowingly or unknowingly. They'd constructed a dozen different ambush scenarios, using satellite photos of the rendezvous area. How far ashore could the SEALs get before they couldn't escape? What were the best weapons to break an ambush? Something big and noisy, or small and less noisy? What if one of the SEALs goes down? Or two? What if it's one of the Iranians? The "what if's" had gone on endlessly.

Jerry attended many of the planning sessions. Theoretically, his role was simple: Pilot the ASDS to a point two hundred yards from the beach, keep the minisub on station while the SEALs made the pickup, recover the swimmers with the "precious cargo," and then head back to *Michigan*.

But Jerry had to know what to do if the SEALs had to move while they were on the beach. What if the team was ambushed? What if the Iranians were at the wrong location? Should the ASDS break down and couldn't recover the SEALs, where would they go? Each rally point and alternative rendezvous location was marked and noted. Each one had its own code word and specific instructions. Jerry's actions not only had to be automatic, but intimately understood by everyone, so they all could react instantly to a changing situation. Even if the group was separated, they could work seamlessly with minimal communications.

As the team lead, Ramey kicked off the briefing on the platoon leader's order by going over the situation, mission objective, and a general overview of the action to be conducted and the means of execution. He then went into the current and projected weather, including tides and moon rising, setting, and phase. Next, a detailed map came up on the large display that illustrated the beach landing site, the initial rallying points, and the individual SEAL positions along with fields of observation and fire. Ramey pointed out the lack of any significant obstacles: the beach was essentially clear with a slight grade to a small berm thirty meters from the waterline, as well as the few areas with appreciable cover.

The enemy's order of battle near the beach landing site was largely made up of small detachments of Basij militia and IRGC ground forces, although the former would be the most likely enemy forces should there be an encounter. The nearest Iranian Army units were located in Shiraz, approximately 125 miles to the north. The nearest naval facility was the IRGC naval base at Asaluyeh, thirty-six nautical miles to the southeast. The assets there were almost entirely lightly armed fast patrol boats.

The platoon leader then went over the rules of engagement, dealing with each scenario in detail. Since the mission was clandestine, denying the enemy any knowledge of the team's presence was paramount. Therefore, weapons fire was restricted to self-defense only. If the enemy was firing at you, he already knew you were there. To minimize the chance of an ambush, CENTCOM was allocating an RC-135 SIGINT bird, to monitor the electronic environment, and a medium endurance UAV with the best infrared sensor package available in theater would have "eyes" on the beach landing site.

Ramey then began walking through the mission-phase diagram box by box. He recapped the original mission order, along with an overview of the equipment loaded onto the ASDS. He then described the weaponry and equipment to be carried by the extraction team, followed by a discussion of the communications plan. To prevent the Iranians from detecting their presence, any communications with *Michigan* would be with the directional PRC-117 SATCOM radio. Comms between team members and the ASDS would use the PRC-148 MBITR personal radios on the lowest power setting.

His laser pointer then moved over to the fifth box that said "Mobility," followed by the bullet "ASDS Launch."

"We will launch at 1630, two hours and forty minutes before last light. XO, please brief your part of the mission."

Jerry stood and moved so he could point to their track on the screen. "After launch, initial course is zero zero zero true for forty minutes, then a turn at Point X-Ray to zero three zero for an hour and a half, all at eight knots and a depth of one hundred feet. The transit time accounts for the tide, which is ebbing at that location and will throughout this op. The dogleg adds a few miles to the run in, but we avoid a large shoal area to the east. Total length of the run is 18.3 miles, and the total time is two hours twenty-five minutes. We arrive at 1855, with fifteen minutes of margin for the 1910 diver lockout.

"There are no known large underwater obstructions within several miles of our route and the bottom slopes gently toward the shore, with the average water depth starting at one hundred eighty feet and gradually reducing to forty. When we reach Point Yankee, we slow to four knots and make a quick periscope observation of the landing area. We should be one mile from the shore at that point and we should be able to see our passengers on the beach. The last mile we creep in at four knots at an initial depth of thirty feet, coming shallower as we get closer. We stop at Point Zulu, three hundred meters from the shore, rise to a keel depth of fifteen feet and hover there at neutral buoyancy."

Ramey nodded, following Jerry's narration in his notes. "Petty Officer Lapointe."

Petty Warfare Operator First Class Nathan Lapointe was from Baton Rouge. Short and compact, he was an excellent swimmer, even among the SEALs. He was also the communications expert, and the senior petty officer on the team. "The four-man element locks out by 1910 and approaches submerged to within a hundred meters of shore. I surface to do a quick look, and if it's clear, the swim pairs split and complete the approach on the surface, blacked out in a combat swimmer mode. Fazel is with me and Petty Officer Phillips is with Mr. Ramey.

"Both swim pairs reach the beach by 1930. We come ashore about fifty meters apart, flanking the precious cargo that should still be on the beach. If that's the case, I'll go and take up an overwatch position here." He pointed to a spot on a satellite photo of the beach. "I can watch the road, the beach landing site, and the dead space behind this rise.

"Once I'm ensconced, I'll signal you that I'm in place and that the coast is clear. If at any time I see problems, I'll alert the other element members and extract by the secondary route. I don't make contact with the precious cargo, but provide cover for the rendezvous, and the withdrawal. Once the precious cargo is safely in the water, I'll abandon the overwatch position, link up with my swim buddy, and we withdraw from the objective area together."

"And once you send the 'All clear,' the rest of us will move toward the rendezvous point," Ramey continued. "Fazel on the left, Phillips and I are on the right. Fazel and Phillips establish a security perimeter while I make contact and establish the assets' bona fides. The pass phrases are typical CIA, cutesy, but simple, and they should be sufficient. The phrases are the two stanzas from the nursery rhyme, 'Star Light, Star Bright.' I give the first stanza in Farsi. They respond with the second stanza in English. Harry's been getting my Farsi up to speed, but since he's a native speaker I'll want his ears close to me just in case there's an issue. Once we are sure of whom we have, I'll fit them with swim bladders and Petty Officer Phillips and I get them into the water. We'll conduct a surface swim back out to the ASDS, which hopefully will be able to get closer. The main concern is the water temperature. The latest data shows the surface water running about sixty-seven degrees Fahrenheit, a bit chilly for civilians."

Special Warfare Operator Second Class Heydar "Harry" Fazel was the team's medic, a hospital corpsman second class and the next senior after Lapointe. Every SEAL mission included a medical specialist, and Fazel's skills would have made him a physician's assistant in the civilian world. Although a medic, he would be armed to the teeth like the other members of the extraction team. "I cover left and stand by in case you need translation, but stay close enough to Pointy to lend assistance as needed." Fazel was a first-generation American, born in the U.S. after his parents had fled the Iranian Revolution in 1979.

"After the Boss, Philly and the precious cargo are back in the water, I wait for Pointy at the water's edge, and we egress together. I also signal Commander Mitch—I mean the XO—that we are feet wet. After we are back on board the ASDS, I'll check our guests for hypothermia, just to be safe."

Jerry finished. "Higgs and I will keep the ASDS at periscope depth with both masts exposed, about a foot of mast out of the water. Once we receive your signal we'll move in to meet you as water depth allows. Once the swimmers are close by, I'll broach the ASDS to allow access to the upper hatch. After everyone is back aboard, we get as deep as we can and retrace our route back to *Michigan*."

Lieutenant Ramey nodded approvingly. "That's the plan. Now, last chance. Any more thoughts on the last-minute change?"

Jerry replied first. "Doubling the distance is still well within the margin for the batteries. The usage curves on the exercises we ran were close to the manufacturer's specs. The only issue was the power surge during the last run. Alex, have you been able to run that issue to ground?"

"We think so, sir," replied Carlson. "We replaced a motor controller on one of the aft thrusters that had an intermittent ground. We've checked both the new motor controller and the batteries with three diagnostic runs and they've come up green each time."

Fazel chimed in and said, "I've already raised my concern. If there are casualties, it doubles the time until they're treated."

Captain Guthrie answered, "If you need to get back aboard quickly, I'll bring *Michigan* in to meet you. Of course, I'll have to get permission, but we'll have a mast up, and line of sight to the RC-135 if the SATCOM doesn't work."

Ramey nodded politely, but didn't' look reassured. "If we've been shot at, sir, there may be pursuit."

"Not a problem, Lieutenant. We've got to rendezvous submerged, and the IRGC Navy has no ASW capability at all, either with planes or their surface craft. As long as we can avoid visual detection, we'll be able to rendezvous safely."

"And since the rendezvous will be after dark," Jerry added, "they'd have to be right on top of us even to see *Michigan* while at periscope depth."

"And if all goes according to plan, sir, we won't have to ask." Ramey looked around the space. "Anyone else? No? Then we muster here at 1515 hours for final checks." He grinned. "And remember to pee! There are no rest stops along the way."

5

"ABANDON SHIP!"

3 April 2013
1615 Local Time/1315 Zulu
USS *Michigan*

Jerry and Guthrie emerged from the captain's stateroom and walked casually to the ladder well that led up to the control room. Jerry had traded in his dark blue coveralls for a set of desert cammies. Other than the pixelated combination of tan, brown, gray, and olive drab colors of the Type II Navy Working Uniform, there were no rank insignia, nametag, warfare patch, or anything else that could identify the wearer as belonging either to *Michigan* or the U.S. Navy. He was also armed. The SIG Sauer P226 pistol rested in a paddle holster on his right side; while four fifteen-round magazines were on his left. At first, Jerry had protested that this was a bit over the top. After all, he was just piloting the ASDS, nothing more. Ramey and Higgs were adamant that Jerry be armed. But it was Alex Carlson who broke through when he pulled his XO aside and said, "Just wear the damn thing, sir. I would if I were going."

"Status, Mr. Simmons," barked Guthrie as he entered control.

"We are on station, hovering, Captain. Depth is one three zero feet with forty-eight feet beneath the keel. We've had twelve sonar contacts. Four are classified as tankers and are well to the west and south of us in established shipping lanes. Six are classified as fishing trawlers, heading toward either Bandar Kangan or Dreyyer. They are all past CPA and opening. The last two were probably patrol boats, as they were moving quite fast. One was headed in the direction of Lavan Island. We just lost the other as it headed north into shallow water. No contacts are estimated to be within eight thousand yards, and ASDS launch stations are manned and ready."

"Well done, Isaac," Guthrie complimented his navigator. Then, with a touch of sarcasm he added, "See, it wasn't that hard."

Simmons laughed wearily. Jerry knew the junior officer had been doing port and starboard watches to ensure that they made the deadline, without being detected or running into something. And with the exception of one rude surprise, the transit to the launch site went off without a hitch.

"Thank you, sir. But I don't think I need that many gray hairs just yet," replied Simmons, visibly relieved.

"Nonsense! It suits you. Besides, you need those occasional surprises to add spice to your life." The captain was clearly in a good mood, although he was just as surprised as everyone else when the loud *THUMP, THUMP, THUMP* of a ship's propeller had been heard through the hull.

Two hours ago, a large ship, probably a supertanker, had passed very close to *Michigan*, and none of the submarine's sensitive sonar arrays had heard a thing until it was right on top of them. Looking at the ship's course as it passed by, it became clear that the bow of the tanker had been pointing directly at *Michigan*. Even a large noisy ship, normally easy to detect, can become a ghost if a sonar array is looking straight at the bow. The phenomenon, called a bow null, occurs when the ship's structure and cargo absorb the noise from the propulsion plant at the very back. Simmons had turned pale when he estimated that there might have been as little as fifty feet between the tanker and *Michigan*.

"Sir, surprises like that lead to heart attacks," Simmons countered heartily.

Guthrie shrugged his shoulders as he reached over to the intercom. "Sonar, Conn. Report all sonar contacts."

"Conn, Sonar," responded Lieutenant Junior Grade Andy Buckley, *Michigan*'s sonar officer. "We currently hold eleven sonar contacts. Sierra seven eight is classified as a tanker. He bears zero nine eight and has just dropped anchor. Sierra eight zero bears one two two and is heading southeast at high speed. Classified as a patrol boat. Sierra seven nine and eight two are tankers, bearing two one zero and two five six. Both are heading northwest. Sierra eight three, also classified as a tanker, is currently in our baffles. Contact is tracking to the southeast. The remaining six contacts are all fishing trawlers off our port bow, heading home to either Deyyar or Kangan. No close contacts."

Guthrie took in the report as he quickly glanced at the fire control display's tracks for the eleven contacts. Satisfied that his people had good situational awareness, he hit the intercom button again. "Sonar, Conn. Woody, we're coming up for an observation. With us at a dead stop, keep a sharp ear."

"Conn, Sonar, aye."

"Mr. Simmons, bring her up to eight zero feet," Guthrie ordered.

"Bring her to eight zero feet, aye, sir."

While Simmons had the ship's diving officer and chief of the watch bring *Michigan* to periscope depth, Guthrie turned to Jerry and said, "We'll take a quick look around and if all's clear, we settle back down to a hundred and thirty feet and get you and the SEALs on your way."

"Sounds good to me, sir. I'd like to get this excursion started," replied Jerry with a smirk. "The SEALs are beginning to get that trapped animal look, and I was afraid they might start chewing off limbs to escape."

"Long stays on a boat are agonizing for SEALs," stated Guthrie. "They tolerate it just as long as there is a meaningful reason for being here. For them, it's all about being down range and in the thick of it. They think we're absolutely crazy for staying in a steel sewer pipe for seventy-five days at a crack."

"Yeah, well, anyone who intentionally leaves a perfectly good submarine isn't all there in my book, Skipper. And yes, I'm including myself in that category."

Guthrie chuckled at Jerry's comment. "Well, just get in and out as fast as you can. I'd like to let the SEALs off before one of them pops a gasket. I think Holt has managed to imprint his forehead on just about every piece of kit above the six-foot mark."

It was Jerry's turn to laugh. On more than one occasion he had heard a dull thud, immediately followed by some very salty language, only to see Barrineau roughly massaging his head. The young man needed to learn to duck.

"Passing one hundred feet, sir," Simmons reported.

"Very well, Nav. Raise the photonics mast."

"Raise the photonics mast, aye. Chief of the Watch, raise the photonics mast."

Guthrie stepped down to the BVS-1 control workstation. Jerry followed. Unlike a standard periscope, the BVS-1 photonics mast didn't have the ocular box and large barrel that penetrated the pressure hull. So instead of dancing with the "gray lady," one just watched a flat panel display. While Jerry appreciated the multiple camera capability and excellent definition display of the high-tech mast, it was all very sterile. It lacked the dash and romance of a periscope observation characterized so well in the movies.

At first, the display showed a hazy greenish-blue background with shadows streaking across the screen. The operator spun the sensor head around, looking for any large shadows or evidence of a nearby ship. Then suddenly a brighter picture appeared as the camera cleared the water. The speaker for the electronic surveillance system started beeping and chirping as the antenna on the photonics mast detected the emissions of several radars. All were surface search sets and the signal strengths were weak. None were close. A couple of quick circular sweeps showed there were no close contacts. Guthrie grunted his approval and ordered *Michigan* back down.

"OOD, get us back down to one hundred and thirty feet. I'm going with the XO to missile compartment second level. I'll be back before we launch the ASDS."

Simmons acknowledged the order as Guthrie and Jerry headed down the ladder. Both walked quickly along the narrow passageway; several sailors had to flatten themselves against the wall to let the two by. Once through the watertight door, they crossed the compartment to SOF tube one. The large hatch in the tube was open and several SEALs were just coming out. Carlson was also waiting.

"She's all loaded and ready to go, XO," he reported as he handed Jerry a clipboard. "Here's the prelaunch checklist and the compensation calculations."

"Thanks, Alex. But shouldn't you be in the BMC right now?" asked Jerry. There was a stern edge to his voice.

"Ah . . . yes, sir," the lieutenant replied uncomfortably. "I just wanted to make sure everything was squared away for the mission, sir. That's all." Then after a slight pause, "She is my baby."

"Yeah, I know." Jerry understood exactly where the winged ASDS pilot was coming from. And while he was sympathetic, it was still his job as the executive officer to train the junior officers assigned to him to think things through and do the right thing. "Vernon will make sure I don't screw up too much, and I promise I won't scratch the paint . . . Dad." Jerry grinned with the last word. "Now report to your station."

"Aye, aye, sir. Good luck, XO. Captain." Carlson's spirits were clearly buoyed, for as he approached the watertight door he spun about and said, "Remember, XO, mind the big rocks!"

Jerry snapped his fingers and pointed at the watertight door, encouraging the young man to get going.

"Nicely handled, XO," commented Guthrie. "But shouldn't you be getting your carcass up into the ASDS? You wouldn't want to be late for your first mission."

"No, that wouldn't look very good. I'll see you in a few hours, Skipper."

"Good luck, XO. And do watch out for big rocks." Guthrie smiled as he slapped Jerry on the shoulder and then stepped back to allow his exec access to the hatch. Once inside the tube, a SEAL closed and dogged the hatch. Jerry quickly climbed up the ladder into the lockout chamber. Barrineau and Higgs were waiting, and as soon as Jerry had pulled himself into the ASDS they secured the two hatches. Hunched over slightly, he worked his way up through the operator's compartment to the pilot's seat, sat down, and strapped himself in.

The displays were all up and running, showing the status of the trim system, propulsion, battery charge, navigation, as well as the minisub's attitude, course, and speed. A quick look at the status board showed mostly green, with only the docking skirt and the docking pylon latches being red. Jerry reached over and grabbed the logbook for ASDS-1 and started to make the proper entry; the paperwork gods must be appeased.

Higgs climbed into his chair and buckled up. As the copilot, he was responsible for life support, sensors, communications, and operating the lockout systems. He also helped to monitor propulsion plant and battery status.

"Pilot, ASDS is ready for launch. Docking skirt and the pylon latches indicate red," Higgs reported.

"Very well, Copilot." Jerry flipped on the underwater communications system switch. "Starbase, Gray Fox. Comms check, over."

"Gray Fox, Starbase. Read you loud and clear, over."

"Starbase, Gray Fox. Flood docking skirt, over."

"Gray Fox, Starbase. Flooding docking skirt."

There was a brief bubbling noise as the air in the space between the docking skirt and *Michigan* was vented to sea. The indicator on the status panel turned green.

"Pilot, docking skirt indicates flooded," said Higgs.

"Very well," replied Jerry, then hitting the transmit button again, he said, "Starbase, Gray Fox. Release docking pylon latches, over."

"Gray Fox, Starbase. Releasing docking latches."

A loud *KA-CHUNK* resonated through the hull as the four docking latches in the pylons bolted to *Michigan*'s outer hull swung to the unlocked position. The ASDS was now held to the mother submarine by only a few hundred pounds of extra water in her trim tanks.

"Pilot, docking latches indicate unlocked. The ASDS is ready for launch in all respects."

"Very well, Mr. Higgs. Pumping from trim tanks to sea." Jerry punched up the ballast control screen and told the computer how much water he wanted pushed overboard.

"XO, remember to apply a little upward thrust once two hundred pounds have been pumped out," cautioned Higgs. He wanted a clean launch. Bouncing around on the mating ring was the sign of a sloppy takeoff, a sign that would be heard by those in the tube and the BMC, and gleefully noted on their return.

"Understood, Mr. Higgs." Jerry knew what he needed to do next, but his copilot was just doing his job by reminding him. As the readout passed 190 pounds, Jerry gently pulled back on the joystick. Slowly, the ASDS lifted off of *Michigan*'s turtleback; a subtle scrapping noise being the only external evidence the two submarines had separated.

"Nice," murmured Higgs with approval.

"Starbase, Gray Fox. We have separation, over," declared Jerry.

"Gray Fox, Starbase. We hold you clear of the deck, over."

"Starbase, Gray Fox. Roger that."

Jerry waited a few more seconds, then turned toward Higgs. "Copilot, activate the forward looking soar."

"Activate the forward looking sonar, aye. Pilot, the sonar is on line."

Normally, a transmitting sonar would be a significant vulnerability. But the collision avoidance sonar on the ASDS operated at very high frequencies and low power, which made it difficult to detect unless you were really close. Still, Jerry would only keep it on as long as it took to ensure they had completely cleared *Michigan*.

"Pilot, the ASDS is clear and free to maneuver."

"Very well, Copilot. Secure the forward looking sonar."

As Higgs turned off the sonar, Jerry brought up the autopilot menu and selected the pre-stored course, speed, and depth for the first leg of the trip. The display looked similar to that on a Garmin or Tom Tom, just without roads. Once the route was confirmed, he pushed the transmit button.

"Starbase, Gray Fox. We are clear of your position and are proceeding to Point X-ray, over."

"Gray Fox, Starbase. Roger that. Godspeed. Starbase out."

Jerry reached over to the main propulsion motor panel and selected "all ahead two-thirds." Once the ASDS had some forward way on, he lightly pulled the joystick to the left. "Coming left to course zero zero zero," he announced. Higgs acknowledged the report as he monitored the propulsion system display. Within ten minutes, Jerry had the ASDS up to her flank speed, a blazing eight knots. Satisfied that everything was in order, he activated the autopilot and leaned back into his chair.

Taking it all in, Jerry had to admit that the Advanced SEAL Delivery System was a serious improvement over the old Mark 8 Swimmer Delivery Vehicle or SDV. The Mark 8 was considerably smaller, less than a ton in displacement compared to the sixty-ton ASDS, and could only carry four combat swimmers in addition to the pilot and navigator. The ASDS could carry eight fully equipped swimmers along with a pilot and copilot. The SDV also had shorter legs, only about half the range of the ASDS, and was slower when fully loaded. But by far and away the biggest difference was that the Mark 8 was a "wet" platform, meaning the passengers and crew had to use scuba systems to breathe, and they were exposed to the elements. While riding was much better than swimming long distances, cold water saps a swimmer's strength over time. The ASDS provided the SEALs with a dry environment, which meant they reached the beach at peak performance.

All in all, the ASDS was clearly a superior platform—at least in theory. In reality, it had been dogged by numerous technical problems. Initial testing showed significant design flaws with many of the onboard systems, the original propeller was too noisy, and the rechargeable silver-zinc battery wasn't providing the required power. The attempts to fix the problems took time and, more importantly, money—lots of money. In the end the program was canceled after huge cost overruns and seemingly unending reliability problems. While the Navy hierarchy reevaluated its plans, they took the lone remaining minisub and continued to work on improving its performance. The well-proven and safer silver-zinc batteries were traded for cutting edge lithium-ion batteries to solve the power issue.

Even after all of these fixes, the ASDS continued to experience equipment failures that made the minisub a maintenance nightmare. *Michigan*'s techs and the SEALs had to spend several hours maintaining and tweaking the ASDS's systems for every hour it spent underway.

After twenty minutes, Jerry stifled an urge to yawn. Absolutely nothing was happening. The autopilot was faithfully executing its orders and all systems were operating within spec. This was the part of the mission where one person could handle both jobs, largely because there wasn't all that much to handle.

"Any sonar contacts, Mr. Higgs?" Jerry asked. He knew his copilot would have said something if there were, but he needed some interaction to help stay alert.

"Negative, XO, but then we don't have the same 'Dumbo' ears that *Michigan* has." Higgs grinned as he dissed *Michigan*'s high-tech sonar suite.

"Oh, ho, ho, you might want to consider your words a little more carefully, Mr. Higgs. Woody wouldn't take it kindly you talking trash about his gear."

"I can handle Buckley, XO," Higgs replied confidently.

"True. Of that I have no doubt, but it's not Woody I'd be worried about. All he has to do is mention that you're doing an under-hull survey and somehow one of his guys will not only forget to red tag the fathometer out, but they'll forget to turn it off! Not that I would condone such negligence, mind you." Jerry fought hard to maintain a dispassionate expression.

Higgs winced at the thought of being underneath a fathometer when it transmitted. He'd suffered that unpleasant experience once in his career. A diver has little warning that a fathometer is actively pinging since the beam points directly downward. If you can hear it, you're too close. Unfortunately, the acoustic pressure wave has an impact similar to that of a fast moving baseball bat, and it hurts, a lot. There were procedures in place to prevent this, but it depended on people doing what they were supposed to.

Undaunted, Higgs returned fire. "Well, I guess I'll just have to be busy when it comes time to do the next under-hull security sweep. Besides, you wouldn't rat on me now would you, sir?"

"Absolutely not!" said Jerry with feigned sincerity, but then after a slight pause, he added, "Well, maybe. But my silence can be bought, and at a reasonable price."

"How magnanimous of you," grunted Higgs. Both men laughed.

It grew quiet again as Jerry and Higgs went through their monitoring routine, looking at the status of all the systems on board. Nothing was amiss.

After several minutes, Higgs broke the silence with a loud yawn, stretching. "Yea-uh-ahh. This is the part I hate, XO. The destination promises to be exciting and sexy, but the trip there is boring and a pain in the ass. I feel like one of my kids, 'Are we there yet?'"

"Please don't go there," Jerry groaned, as unpleasant memories of his childhood flashed into his head.

"Hey, XO, we've still got a long way to go. Do you want me to take the conn, while you get up and stretch a bit? Not that you can do a whole lot of that in this overgrown sardine can."

Jerry immediately took Higgs up on his suggestion. "Yeah, I think I will take a little break. Thanks, Vernon." He unbuckled himself and vacated the pilot's position. Higgs was seated before he had a chance to turn around. Arching his back, Jerry stretched while at the same time carefully avoided hitting one of the internal frames with his head. Looking aft, he caught a glimpse of the other SEALs through the windows in the watertight doors. He hadn't seen them when he'd climbed aboard, and dropping by to say "hi" seemed like a good idea. Besides, he was curious to see how they were going to lug all the equipment that had been talked about during the mission planning.

"Mr. Higgs, I'm going aft to the transport compartment. I'll be back in a few minutes."

"Understood, sir."

Jerry stepped into the lockout compartment and closed the watertight door behind him. The compartment was a great big ball in the middle of the ASDS and had a hatch in both the overhead and the deck. Separated from the operator and transport compartments by hull-strength watertight doors, it could be flooded to permit the SEALs to leave or return while the ASDS remained fully submerged. Entering into the transport compartment, Jerry saw Ramey, Lapointe, Fazel, and Phillips going over the operation plan yet again.

All were in the same Type II desert camouflage uniform that Jerry was wearing, but there the similarities ended. Each SEAL was completely covered in gear from head to toe. There were literally encased in wires, tubing, electronics, scuba tanks, respirators, ammo magazines, weapons, and numerous bulging pockets on their uniforms and chest harnesses. With their black wet-suit hoods and gloves they looked a lot like Borg drones from *Star Trek*. Jerry could easily see the SEAL community adopting the Collective's favorite expression, "Resistance is futile."

Each member of the team had a variant of the Special Operations Forces Combat Assault Rifle as his primary weapon. Known by its quaint acronym, SCAR, it had replaced the older M16A2 and M4A1 as the weapon of choice for U.S. Navy SEALs and other Special Forces personnel. During the mission-planning stage, Ramey had taken Jerry to the armory in missile tube five and gave him a quick introduction on how a SEAL unit selects its weapons for a particular mission. Ramey also made sure Jerry was familiar enough with the SCAR to use it if he needed to.

Right up front, the platoon leader stated that they were looking to go "light" on this mission. Since they weren't looking for a fight, the emphasis was on self-protection and not a pitched battle; so heavier weapons with a longer reach weren't as necessary. And because they had to swim in, weight was a key consideration. Grabbing a SCAR from one of the racks, he handed it to Jerry and explained that he and Phillips would carry a stock standard Mark 16 SCAR-Light, while Lapointe would have the same weapon fitted with a 40mm grenade launcher. Fazel, on the other hand, would be armed with the heavier, but longer ranged, Mark 20 SCAR-Heavy sniper rifle. By the end of their conversation, Jerry was convinced that a properly outfitted four-man SEAL element had the firepower of a small army. He also had to admit that their definition of "light" differed drastically from what he had in mind. In looking again at the four men, and seeing all the equipment they were carrying, he wasn't certain that they wouldn't just sink to the bottom after they left the ASDS.

"Hey, XO," greeted Fazel. "What brings you to the economy section?"

"Just seeing how you guys are doing. We're near Point X-ray, but you still have an hour and half before we get close to the beach."

"Understood, sir," Ramey responded. "We'll be ready to go when you give the word." His tone and mannerisms were all business.

You look more than ready to me right now, Jerry thought. He also got the feeling from Ramey's body language that he was intruding. Paying attention to one's gut intuition was something Jerry firmly believed in, and his gut told him to get out of the lieutenant's hair. "I'll have Vernon give you a thirty-minute warning. If you need anything else, you know where to find me."

"Yes, sir." Ramey spoke in an almost mechanical manner, with little or no facial expression. The hair on the back of Jerry's neck stood straight up as he returned to the operator compartment. There was a stark difference between the man in the transport compartment and the platoon leader he had gotten to know on *Michigan*. This Ramey, the one he had just left, was far more intense, focused, and eerily menacing. The image of Doctor Jekyll and Mister Hyde popped into his mind. He was still mentally chewing on this when he relieved Higgs at the pilot's station. Seeing the perplexed look on Jerry's face, the copilot asked, "Anything wrong, XO?"

"Huh? Ah, no, Vernon. It's just that Mr. Ramey is acting rather . . . well . . ."

"Strange?"

"I was going to say different," Jerry replied defensively.

Higgs chuckled. "Matt's got his game head on now. From the moment he boarded the ASDS until after the debrief, it's nothing but the mission for him."

As far as explanations go, this one wasn't very helpful and Jerry's confused expression showed it. "I don't get it, Vernon. We've been working on mission preps for almost two days and he's never been like this."

"Planning a mission is one thing, XO, executing a mission is another. Matt is one of those guys who mentally has to throw a switch between going downrange and normal living. Others, like Lapointe or Fazel, can go back and forth without thinking about it. It's not a deficiency on Matt's part; we all have personality quirks of one kind or another. His methods are just different and more discernable than some of the other guys, that's all. But in the end, he gets results. He has an excellent reputation among the SEAL teams for his tours in Afghanistan. I'm surprised you didn't see this during the exercise?"

"I never went out with Ramey during the exercise. If you recall, I only went out with you and Alex once, and that was when Barrineau and the chief led the squad. I had to back out from the other event, remember?"

"Oh, yeah. That's right, I'd forgotten that you ditched us for some paperwork," said Higgs with a grin. "So, XO, now you know what Matt is like in his über SEAL mode."

"I don't think I'd like to meet him in a dark ally when he's like that," commented Jerry, more as a joke than a factual statement.

"No, sir, you would not," responded Higgs soberly. Jerry felt a chill when Higgs spoke those words. And for the first time, he wondered how many men the mild-mannered Ramey had killed in his career.

"Well, if Matt's reputation is that good, then this mission should be relatively easy in comparison with Afghanistan," Jerry concluded.

Higgs's demeanor didn't change, and his voice remained stern. "The only easy day was yesterday, sir."

Jerry had heard the SEAL motto several times during the last couple of weeks, and every time it was spoken as if it were holy writ. The reason why yesterday was easy, he had been told, was because it was over and you couldn't do anything about it. By definition the present was always harder. From his admittedly limited perspective, this philosophy sounded overly negative to Jerry and he said as much. "You SEALs really are a pessimistic bunch, aren't you?"

A brief look of surprise flashed across Higgs's face, or perhaps it was annoyance, but whatever it was, he recovered quickly and respectfully countered Jerry's accusation.

"Absolutely not, XO. We are not a herd of Eeyores; nor are we blind optimists. We are realists. We do hope for the best, we truly hope everything goes according to plan, but we always train for the worst. Because usually something does go wrong, and we have to quickly adapt to the new situation if we are to win. And a SEAL has it ingrained in him from the very beginning that it pays to be a winner."

As Higgs turned back toward his console, Jerry looked on in silence. The short, but cogent rebuttal shined new light on a number of misconceptions that Jerry had about this unique community within the U.S. Navy. He considered asking some more questions, when his concentration was broken by an annoying beeping sound.

"One thousand yards to the turn, Pilot," reported Higgs.

"Very well, stand by to come right to zero three zero in three minutes forty-five seconds." The navigation computer could have told him the time remaining, but Jerry preferred doing a little mental gym himself; it helped him to refocus on the job at hand. The discussion had definitely piqued his curiosity and he wanted to understand the SEAL mentality better, but he also had a feeling that now probably wasn't the best time. There would be ample opportunities on the way back to hit Higgs and the others up with his questions. But one thing was certain, he had learned more about SEALs in the last ten minutes than he had during the last two weeks.

The next hour went by faster than Jerry expected: Partly because they were well inside Iranian territorial waters, and getting closer to the coast with each minute, and partly because Higgs had picked up two high-speed contacts on the ASDS's passive sonar. One was heading northwest, the other southeast at thirty plus knots. Both had passed close by. "My guess is that they are IRGC Navy patrol boats on the prowl," said Higgs.

"A safe bet," Jerry observed. "It's very unlikely they are fishing dhows." The ubiquitous, boxy, wooden fishing vessels common to the Persian Gulf would be hard pressed to make ten knots.

"They could be smugglers," Higgs suggested. Jerry detected a note of playful cynicism in the copilot's voice. The earlier transgression, if there had been one, was forgotten.

With a look of feigned astonishment, and dripping with sarcasm Jerry replied, "Seriously!?! Smugglers? At sunset, silhouetted by the sun, whizzing by within range of numerous coastal radar sites? What are you thinking?"

"Okay. Maybe they're dumb smugglers."

"Mr. Higgs, let's just stick with your initial call and move on." Then motioning aft he said, "Please inform Mr. Ramey that we are thirty minutes out. I told him we'd give him a warning."

"Aye, sir."

While Higgs notified Ramey of their current position, Jerry noticed that the water depth was starting to decrease. At a depth of one hundred feet, they only had fifty feet beneath them now, and that was slowly being nibbled away. He'd have to start coming up to a shallower depth soon, as the navigation chart showed the water depth at Point Zulu was only about forty feet. They were getting very close to the Iranian coast; they were deep inside Indian country.

Exactly twenty minutes later, a heavily laden Ramey opened the watertight door and strode up to Jerry and Higgs. "Status, Pilot," he demanded.

Normally, Jerry would have been a little irritated by the lieutenant's lack of military etiquette, but thanks to Higgs's counsel, he had a better understanding of the platoon leader's mind-set.

"We are fifteen hundred yards from Point Yankee, Mr. Ramey. Current depth is thirty feet, with thirty-four feet beneath the keel. We'll be coming to periscope depth soon to take the initial observation," he answered.

"Understood, XO."

"If you wish, you can look over Mr. Higgs's shoulder during the observation and see the lay of the land for yourself," offered Jerry.

"Thank you, sir. I intend to," was Ramey's response.

For the next ten minutes, Ramey stood rigidly over by the copilot's console. Jerry snuck an occasional look at the determined young man; the only time he could recall experiencing such intensity was during air combat maneuvering training at Fallon. Ramey was mentally pulling nine Gs.

Jerry had just started maneuvering the ASDS to periscope depth when an alarm suddenly sounded. Looking down, he saw a flashing red light on the aft battery status display.

"High temperature alarm," shouted Higgs. "Battery pack number two, aft battery."

"Reducing speed to three knots. Report temperature," Jerry yelled back.

"Two hundred seventy degrees and rising."

Without hesitation, Jerry turned to Ramey. "Lieutenant, get your men and all your gear out of the transport compartment ASAP."

"Aye, aye, sir," replied the SEAL as he bolted for the watertight door.

Jerry worked to stay calm. "Mr. Higgs, report temperature."

"Two hundred eighty-five degrees, and rising. Battery packs one and three also show elevated temperatures."

Not good, Jerry thought. He needed to get this under control quickly; if the temperature exceeded three hundred degrees the affected cells would become unstable and almost certainly start a fire. Worse yet, nearby battery packs could also be driven into thermal runaway. The resulting chain reaction would likely end in an explosion.

"Mr. Higgs, isolate the after battery," he ordered. Isolating batteries would reduce their power reserve by half, but this battery wasn't going to give them any more power today.

"Isolating the after battery." The copilot reached over to the electrical control panel and rotated the selector switch on the after battery breaker to open. Nothing happened. He tried again. No response.

"XO, remote breaker control failed. Battery temperature at two hundred ninety-eight degrees."

"Open the breaker manually," Jerry commanded.

Higgs launched himself from his chair and reached the breaker panel within a couple of seconds. He threw open the panel door, grabbed the breaker, and shoved it upward.

Jerry caught a bright flash out of the corner of his eye, followed immediately by a thundering noise. Momentarily stunned by the sound, Jerry tried to focus his eyes. The compartment was filled with gray smoke. The acrid smell assaulted his nose and lungs, forcing him to instinctively reach for his emergency breathing mask.

A flashlight beam pierced the smoky atmosphere as Ramey and the other SEALs crowded into the compartment. Ramey went over to Jerry. Fazel went to Higgs, who lay prone on the deck. He'd been thrown across the compartment by the blast.

The corpsman checked Higgs for a pulse, but it was a mere formality. The copilot was obviously dead. His face and hands were badly burned, his neck was canted at an odd angle, and there were ragged holes torn in his uniform. The larger ones had bloodstains growing around the periphery.

"XO, XO, can you hear me! Are you all right?" shouted Ramey.

Jerry looked at Ramey. The SEAL's image came into focus and Jerry could see that they were using their scuba gear to breathe. Ramey pulled the demand valve from his mouth and repeated himself, "XO, are you okay?"

"Temp . . . Temperature?" Jerry struggled to speak as he stood, shaking his head.

Ramey quickly looked over at the copilot console, it was dark.

"The displays are down, sir."

Jerry turned and saw that two of his displays were still working. He called up the battery-monitoring menu. The temperature was at three hundred fourteen degrees. They had very little time left. He reached over and pulled the emergency surface chicken switches, and turned toward Ramey. From such a shallow depth, the ASDS rose quickly to the surface.

"Matt, the after battery is probably going to explode. We are abandoning ship. Get your men out, *now!*"

Ramey hesitated for just a moment, then pushed his guys toward the escape hatch, instructing them to grab whatever they could on the way out. Fazel grabbed an additional first aid kit. Phillips nabbed a small inflatable raft. Ramey went to the lockout compartment and started opening the hatch.

While the SEALs prepared to abandon ship, Jerry programmed the ASDS to head back out to sea as fast as it could. He set the delay for one minute. Jerry briefly considered sending a "Mayday" but the Iranians would almost certainly pick it up and know they were there. Bad idea. In the end it didn't matter, as the communication system had been fried when the breaker shorted out. Jerry mentally ran down the the emergency destruct bill; there was one last thing to do.

Outboard of the pilot's seat was a cabinet that held two demolition charges. Jerry couldn't be one hundred percent sure the after battery would explode, although it was very likely, so he grabbed the charges, removed the backing, and plastered one on the hull above his chair. He set the timer for seven minutes. Popping his connection for the emergency breathing system he headed toward the escape hatch. Along the way he saw the after-battery breaker panel, or what was left of it. A one-foot-diameter circle was just plain missing, vaporized by the sheer amount of electrical power. He paused for just a moment to say "good-bye" to Higgs, then popped his connection again and went into the lockout chamber. He secured the watertight door and set the second charge, this time for six minutes.

Just as he had placed the second demolition charge, Ramey climbed down the short ladder and started opening the watertight door to the operator compartment. Jerry immediately grabbed him and shook his head "no." Ramey spit out his demand valve and shouted, "I have to get Vern."

Dumbfounded, Jerry pushed him back and said, "He's dead. There is nothing you can do."

The platoon leader acted like he didn't even hear Jerry. "I can't leave him behind!"

Ramey was a powerful man and Jerry physically couldn't hold him back, so he grabbed Ramey's harness and swung the SEAL around to face him. "I said abandon ship, Mister! The demo charges are set and that battery could go any second."

Ramey stood there confused; he looked at Jerry and then the watertight door. Jerry could see his mind racing, but had no idea what dilemma was causing his wheels to spin. Jerry in turn was getting frustrated and angry, he'd given this junior officer a direct order and he seemed unwilling to follow it. But before he could say anything else, the ASDS shook violently and Jerry saw flames in the transport compartment. Ramey saw it, too. They were running out of time.

With every ounce of strength, Jerry pushed Ramey against the ladder, grabbed his face, and yelled, "We are done here. Get your ass off my boat *NOW!*"

Reluctantly, Ramey climbed out and dove into the water. Jerry followed and closed the upper hatch just as water started pouring down into the lockout compartment. Another explosion threw Jerry off of the ASDS and into the cool waters of the Persian Gulf. Treading water, he watched as the minisub dove beneath the surface for the last time.

3 April 2013
1844 Local Time/1544 Zulu
USS *Michigan*

"Conn, Sonar," Buckley's voice boomed from the intercom, "Loud explosions bearing zero two two."

"Sonar, Conn. Repeat your last," Simmons replied anxiously.

"Conn, Sonar. Multiple explosions bearing zero two two."

"Sonar, Conn, aye." Simmons didn't even have to look at the chart. He knew exactly what was supposed to be on that bearing. He picked up the mike for the 1MC, the ship's general announcing circuit, keyed the mike, and said, "Captain to control!"

6

UNFRIENDLY SHORES

3 April 2013
1700 Local Time/1400 Zulu
Bandar Kangan

She'd forced herself to eat, in spite of her fluttering insides. She had the baby to think about, and had dutifully worked her way though rice and vegetables at dinner, although it was a mechanical exercise. She felt a little light-headed, detached from herself.

It seemed like a fantasy. Normal people didn't pass nuclear information to a foreign country. They didn't meet American commandos on a beach. Maybe they'd stopped being normal when the two of them had decided to act on their consciences. She wanted a place to work and live as a family. She wanted them all to be safe and unafraid. Was this the price?

After an early dinner in Bandar Kangan, they'd wandered the town, having explored it thoroughly that afternoon. It had let her walk off some of her nervousness before one final visit to their hotel room.

It was supposed to be a stop to visit the bathroom and pick up a jacket, but they'd never come back here again. She'd packed lightly, with clothes for three nights, but now she would abandon it all. The instructions had said no luggage or belongings, but she took photos of her parents and tucked them into her jacket pocket. She changed her scarf, putting on her favorite, and stuffed another piece of material, a gift from her father, in the other pocket.

Yousef came out of the bathroom. "Are you ready?" She nodded, hesitating at first, then firmly. He'd changed into his uniform, and was wearing
his sidearm. They'd discussed it, and had decided it might help if a Basij
patrol or the police stopped them. He wore the sidearm because it was part
of the uniform, not because he expected to use it. The idea of shooting one's
way out of Iran was ludicrous, not to mention he'd be shooting at other Iranians. The last thing he wanted to do was hurt someone just trying to do
their duty.

They had half an hour to go nine kilometers, so they took their time
driving around town, which let Yousef take one last look for unusual activity. Nothing had changed since their tour that afternoon, and they headed
southeast on Highway 96.

They parked about half a kilometer past the pickup point, and pulled off
the road onto a wide, smooth shoulder. The ocean lay a few dozen meters
away from the road here, across a gently sloping sandy beach. Low dunes dotted with dark green scrub lay landward. To the southeast, a few low houses
and buildings clustered along the highway, but behind them, in the direction
of the pickup point, the coast was empty.

Yousef made sure Shirin had her jacket, although the air was still
warm. "It will cool off quickly after the sun goes down." He locked the car,
partly out of reflex, but also to discourage casual investigation. He carried a
blanket, so she could sit while they waited, and a water bottle.

The sun was still a few minutes above the horizon, which suited them
both. "Watch your step," he admonished needlessly. "There are a lot of uneven spots." Gravel and sand crunched underfoot as they walked toward the
water. Gradually, the area between the water and the highway became
wider, until the road was hidden by dunes and scrub.

Half to himself, Yousef muttered, "This beach is so flat, so open. I wish
there was more cover." Then he added, "Is that why they chose it?"

Shirin nodded agreement, but stiffly. "I feel so exposed here." She
sounded tense. "What time is it?"

"Eighteen-fifteen. Almost sunset."

Shirin pulled the GPS device from her pocket and checked it. "We're
close, less than a hundred meters from the rendezvous."

"Watch for a big *X* on the ground."

She laughed.

They waited. Although they never saw it move, the sun crept toward the horizon, swelled, reddened, and eventually disappeared, taking the day-light with it.

When it was no longer possible to tell a black thread from a white one, she asked, "How much longer?"

"It could be any time," Yousef remarked.

They kept their vigil, alert for any sound, any movement. She tried counting the seconds in each minute, but lost count in the low two hundreds. After what seemed an eternity, Shirin finally looked at the clock on her GPS. It read 1940 hours. The Americans were late.

She watched toward the south, but the sound of waves and reflected starlight were the only signs of the gulf's existence. The dark landscape at least held irregular shadows. With no moon, the sea was simply blackness. The Americans could be a few meters away, or more likely, not there at all.

To pass the time, Shirin made a game out of trying to get as close to the latitude and longitude as she could: 27 degrees, 47 minutes, 18 seconds north latitude, 52 degrees 7 minutes, 30 seconds east longitude. At the equator a mile of latitude is 1,854 kilometers, which made one second of arc 31 meters. How many steps would that be?

Yousef complained about the GPS display being too bright, but there was no dimmer control for the screen. She shielded it with her hand, zoomed it in to its tightest scale, and walked back and forth. The seconds display flickered as she moved from east to west, but it didn't always de-crease. After watching it drop from 32 to 31 seconds east, a few more steps brought it back to 32.

"Remember the satellites," Yousef reminded her. You don't know what your error circle is. Maybe one went below the horizon."

Irritated, Shirin spun around to face him. Whatever she was about to say died on her lips as a voice called out from the dunes to the left. Yousef heard a few words, just a phrase, but he couldn't make it out.

Without thinking, he shouted, "Down!" and dropped to one knee, turn-ing toward the sound. His pistol was in his hand, and he searched for a target, expecting VEVAK agents or Basij troops. The landscape was empty.

The phrase was repeated, and Yousef realized it was in Farsi. But it was just a nonsense phrase about starlight.

Shirin was still standing, far too large a target, even in the dark. She stood a few paces away, and turned to face the voice. He started to tell her again to get down, but she looked back at him for a second, then responded, but in English.

Her reply was answered with another phrase in Farsi, telling them to stand. By this time, Yousef realized that they were being watched, and that the watchers were certainly armed, and well hidden. He carefully lowered his pistol and holstered it.

Whether it was her latest reply or him putting away the pistol, a new shadow appeared in the dunes. It might be holding a rifle, but he couldn't be sure. The stranger definitely held the advantage, but didn't seem hostile. If he'd wanted to shoot, he and Shirin would already be dead.

Yousef slowly stood, keeping his hands open and visible. The shadow stood as well.

"It's all right, Yousef, it's them," Shirin called, and he felt the tension drain out of him, almost taking his strength with it. Then a thrill of fear replaced it as another shadow appeared to his right. He also had a weapon, and had remained perfectly concealed, covering his comrade. Yousef offered a short prayer of thanks for his restraint.

USS *Michigan*, Battle Management Center

Captain Guthrie watched as a petty officer typed in commands, calling up a sequence of images. Lieutenant Frederickson explained each image as it appeared.

"These are all from the CENTCOM UAV. Its coverage includes the rendezvous point. Here's the first image. At 1815, two people appear on the beach. They're almost certainly the two Iranians we're supposed to pick up. They stay in the same spot for over an hour, hardly moving at all. Okay, Lawrence, second image."

The petty officer hit a key. "This image is just five minutes old, infrared only because it's dark. This is why we called you back. Five new people appear at the water's edge, while the original two stay put, as if unaware of their presence."

"Five people?" Guthrie asked, clearly worried, trying to understand. There were supposed to be only four swimmers.

"Okay, now in real time. The five new arrivals are joining the other two at the rendezvous point. Nobody's running, nobody's showing any violent motion, so we can assume the meeting is peaceful."

Guthrie looked up from the display to Frederickson. "This confirms what we suspected. The ASDS is down, and it looks like one man is missing."

"Probably dead," Frederickson observed frankly. "If he was wounded, he'd be with the others. They wouldn't leave him behind. If he's dead, his body heat won't show up on the infrared."

Guthrie frowned at the grim estimate. "That's harsh, but I can't disagree. Could he have been separated from them during whatever happened to the minisub?

Frederickson shrugged, but then shook his head. "He'd have to be incapacitated, and why didn't they stay to look for him? Anything's possible, but it's damn unlikely."

Guthrie turned to go. "I have to report this."

"Sir, I recommend we wait a few minutes more. Right now, there's no decision to make. Unless they've lost the comm gear, they'll report in. Then we'll know more."

He turned to the operator. "I need to see the UAV's coverage of everything between the coast and our position."

On the Coast near Bandar Kangan

Ramey called to Jerry, hidden farther back. "It's them, XO." Sighing with relief, Jerry stood and picked his way across the dark ground. After reaching the shore, Ramey had told Jerry to stay well back, and Jerry had readily agreed. The hour-long swim had exhausted him, far more than the SEALs, who were more heavily loaded as well. Jerry tried to control his shivering. The swim had drained the heat from every part of him; he couldn't remember ever being this cold.

As Jerry came over the dune, he got his first look at their "precious cargo." Ramey stood next to a uniformed figure and a woman. He couldn't see much in the darkness, except that both appeared to be about his age, and the woman was much shorter than her husband. Fazel stood to one side, weapon lowered but ready to cover the entire group. Lapointe and Phillips were not in sight, presumably still hidden.

As he approached the group, they turned toward him. Ramey said, "This is Jerry, my executive officer."

"You are in charge?" The woman spoke quickly and clearly. Her English had only a trace of an accent. Her companion remained silent, and his posture spoke of caution. One hand rested on his pistol holster, and Jerry hoped that was just habit.

"I'm the senior officer, ma'am. Matt, here is the team leader."

"I am Shirin, and this is my husband, Yousef. We are ready to go with you now. What must we do?"

Jerry looked at Ramey, who simply returned his gaze. No wonder he'd called Jerry over. He was the senior officer. Ramey was going to let him deliver the bad news.

"Our plans have changed," Jerry started. "There was an accident, a fire aboard our submarine—"

"A fire?" she interrupted him. Your submarine is sunk?"

Jerry tried to explain. "We had a small submarine that brought us to the beach, or was supposed to bring us here and take us back to another, larger, sub. On the way here, we had a battery fire and it sank—"

"Do fires happen often on American submarines?"

Jerry bristled, but simply replied, "Rarely."

"So you have no way to take us to the other submarine," she continued. "How far away is it? Can we swim?"

"About fifteen miles—nautical miles," he corrected himself. Jerry added, "Over twenty-five kilometers."

The husband, Yousef, broke into the conversation. Jerry could hear the impatience and questions in his tone. Shirin answered, but whatever she said didn't satisfy him. He looked unbelievingly at Jerry and Ramey, then fired another question at Shirin. As she started to answer he interrupted her, and she angrily countered.

Although they'd only been talking for a few moments, their rising voices reminded Jerry of their exposed position. "Matt, we've got to get off this beach."

Ramey motioned toward the two Iranians. "Concur, sir, but we need these folks to work with us, and they seem to have their own issues. Maybe Harry can help." He spoke into his chin mike. "Doc, to me. Pointy, maintain your position."

Seconds later, the second shadow silently trotted up to Ramey, Jerry, and the two Iranians.

Yousef listened to the American commando, if he really was American. He called himself "Harry," but spoke Farsi with a Tehrani accent. He was dressed in camouflage and armed like the others. He said he was a sailor, and a medic.

"Your wife is correct, sir," he said in Farsi. "Our minisub was lost, and we are stranded here. One of our team was killed in the accident."

Shirin asked, "How do you propose we get to your sub, then?"

Ramey replied, "Our backup plan is to launch a Zodiac—a rubber boat with an outboard motor—from the big submarine. It will come in to the beach and pick us up." As Ramey explained, Fazel translated for Shirin's husband.

"But we need to get under cover while I communicate with our submarine." Ramey pointed toward one dune. It was taller than the rest and ran parallel with the beach. "There. Let's go."

With the entire team sheltering along the dune, Jerry watched as Lapointe set up the PRC-117. Although they all had headset radios, Pointy carried the long-range gear. The husband, Yousef, saw the petty officer setting up an antenna and spoke quickly, urgently. Fazel translated. "He is warning you that the Pasdaran have radio listening posts all along the coast. If we transmit, he says we will be detected."

Ramey answered, "Explain to him this is a highly directional satellite communications antenna that uses frequency hopping. It is very hard to detect the transmissions."

He then turned to Shirin. "What rank is your husband?" Jerry could see the wheels in the lieutenant's mind turning. *The man's in uniform. Exactly whom am I dealing with?*

Shirin answered proudly, "He is a *Sarvan Pasdar*—a Pasdaran captain."

The SEALs looked at each other quickly, and Ramey shined a red light on Akbari's shoulder. The epaulet showed the four open rosettes of a Pasdaran officer.

"He is—" She paused. "He was responsible for part of the air defenses at the uranium facility at Natanz."

Jerry could feel the tension rise. There was a noticeable change in Ramey's tone.

"Tell the captain that our sub will launch a rubber boat with an outboard motor, a Zodiac. It's fast, twenty-plus knots—over forty kilometers an hour, and it's armed. It will take about forty-five minutes to get here once it's launched. It can hold us all, but it will be a little slower on the way back, about an hour. We can be off the beach and aboard the sub well before daylight."

Lapointe had finished setting up the antenna. Ramey took the handset. Comms were good, and Jerry listened as the lieutenant reported their situation.

Finally, he asked, "The beach is secure. We're ready for the boat as soon as you can send it."

Jerry already knew what the answer would be. He heard Ramey say, "Understood." He gave the phone back to Lapointe.

"They'll get back to us in ten," Ramey explained.

USS Michigan, Battle Management Center

Lieutenant Frederickson turned to Captain Guthrie as he hung up the handset. "Sir, I've alerted the CRRC crew and they're gearing up. I'll lead the mission. We can launch in five minutes." Michigan didn't even have to surface to launch the Zodiac or combat rubber raiding craft. The boat crew would launch from the dry deck shelter aft of Michigan's sail. The package containing the boat was buoyant, and would inflate by itself in moments once they pulled a lanyard.

"Have you looked at the surface plot?" Guthrie asked. "There are patrol craft between us and the beach. We've been tracking them with the UAV and by their radar emissions."

"They'll never see a Z-bird."

"They have good nav radars, Lieutenant. They're designed to spot small stuff in the water, and a wet rubber raiding craft has a decent radar cross section—you're not invisible. My guys have been laying out detection circles against a Zodiac-sized target. We're pretty good at figuring out how to stay hidden, too, but the patrol boats are just too close, and they appear to be showing up every hour or two. And every single last one of them is faster than a Zodiac, some are more than twice as fast. If they see you, there is no way you can outrun them."

"You can't call off the mission, sir." Frederickson almost pleaded.

"I don't want to, but the odds are against us. We are just too damn far away. It's very likely that the CRRC will get spotted on the way in, much less the way out. And that would draw attention to our people on the beach. If it was only on the outbound leg you might be able to fight your way clear. But if you get caught on the way in, there is no way you'll even reach the shore, and it will only make things worse.

"I'll tell them it's off for tonight while you work up a new plan," Guthrie ordered. "Then I've got another call to make."

On the Coast near Bandar Kangan

Jerry didn't believe it, even after Ramey passed the handset to him and he heard it straight from Guthrie. "Sir, we can do this," he protested.

"You can't make it without being spotted. Find cover and sit tight until sundown tomorrow. I'm going to try and get closer and then we'll send the Zodiac in for you tomorrow night."

"Aye, aye, sir."

Ramey took the phone, listened for a minute, and handed it back to Lapointe. "Our contingency hiding spot is several kilometers to the east of here." He turned to Shirin. "We'll hole up out of sight, away from the road."

"What about our car?" she asked.

"Where is it?" Ramey demanded. Jerry hadn't thought to ask how they'd gotten to the rendezvous.

She pointed east. "Back that way, about fifteen minutes' walk."

Shirin spoke quickly to Yousef, who nodded, frowning. "If it is found, it will lead them to my mother, and then to us," she explained. "If we had simply disappeared, it would not matter so much."

Ramey agreed. "We'll hide your car as well, then."

She replied, "Good. This way."

Ramey held up his hand. "Wait one." He spoke into his headset microphone. "We're moving east to find their car. Philly, tell me when you're ready."

Jerry heard their answers on his headset, and saw the other SEALs moving. There was only the slightest sound. Ramey explained to the civilians. "My men are taking screening positions. We can move in a moment—

with your permission, XO," he said, nodding toward him. Jerry thought he heard a hard edge on the remark.

A moment later, Ramey said softly, "Please, stay close," and motioned with his right hand. He raised his rifle and scanned ahead with his night-vision sight, then set off at a walk, his weapon at the ready.

Jerry followed, trying to be as quiet as possible, feeling clumsy. The two Iranians were behind him, walking close together. The young Pasdaran captain was holding his wife's hand. Each step on the gravelly surface sounded like a thunderclap. He wished for night-vision gear. Each of the SEALs had a set, but as the ASDS pilot . . .

Phillips's hushed voice came over the headset. "Two soldiers just got out of a jeep. Flashlights. They've got AKs, but they're slung. They're looking at a car parked along the road. Light-colored sedan."

"Hold." Ramey held up a hand and dropped to one knee. Jerry and the two civilians followed, more slowly.

"Philly says two soldiers are looking at a light sedan."

Shirin had whispered a translation to Yousef. "Yes, that is mother's car."

"Well, it looks like a Basij patrol has found it."

Even in the dim light, Jerry could see the confusion and fear in her expression. "What do we do?"

"We wait, and get ready in case we have to fight." Jerry heard Ramey give orders to Fazel and Lapointe, guiding them to positions flanking Phillips.

"Please don't shoot them," she begged.

"As long as they don't spot us, or call for reinforcements, we won't have to." Ramey's tone was matter-of-fact. Jerry knew the SEALs could kill the two soldiers in seconds, but that would not help their cause.

"They're both back in the jeep now and moving, heading west on the highway." Philly's voice was as flat giving the "all clear" as it was with the first warning.

After Shirin translated, Yousef spoke and she explained, "They'll report the car. The next patrol will check to see if it is still here."

Ramey ordered, "Okay, everyone, let's move. Philly, we're joining you."

A few minutes walk brought them to a dune where Phillips lay prone near the crest, facing the car. Spotting them, he eased back down the slope and knelt near the base. "Two guys in fatigues, in their early twenties. They had radios, but I didn't see either one use them. They wrote down the license plate."

3 April 2013
1150 Local Time/1650 Zulu
White House Situation Room

Joanna Patterson had come in early, and had heard *Michigan*'s signal that the ASDS launch had taken place as planned, at 0830 Washington time. The next call would not be until Opal and the team was safely aboard the ASDS, expected a little after eight in the evening local time, shortly after noon for her.

She'd brought along work and managed to get some of it done between glancing at the clock and checking radio intercepts. An RC-135 with the call sign "Pinto" was patrolling over the Saudi coast at high altitude. At that height it could pick up transmissions hundreds of miles away, including not just military and commercial radios, but cell phone and microwave communications as well.

The U.S. routinely kept a plane on station over Saudi Arabia, so Pinto wasn't directly connected with the operation. In fact, they knew nothing about it, but the operators on the plane had been told that signals coming from the vicinity of Bandar Kangan, on the south coast of Iran, were to have top priority for both detection and analysis.

So far, Pinto's reports had been routine. There had been some traffic: Basij units on routine patrols, Pasdaran boats off the coast, but it had been clear-language transmissions, and no reports of contact.

Images from the UAV signal had also been piped in to the Situation Room. Being shown on a supersized wall monitor didn't improve their clarity, but she'd seen two people on the beach waiting.

She'd fidgeted, sent out for some coffee, and thought about all the people who had waited while others risked their lives.

The SEALs were late coming ashore, and that was enough to start her worrying. What had slowed them down? Then the UAV's image showed figures arriving on the beach, and joining the other two, but they didn't leave. What had happened?

The ASDS was supposed to transmit one of a series of code words once Opal was aboard and they were headed back to *Michigan*. One meant a successful extraction; another meant they hadn't been able to find Opal at the rendezvous point; another would warn that they had been discovered, and so on. Instead, the call came from *Michigan*, and late. The communications specialist had passed her the handset.

Captain Guthrie's report was grim. After reporting the loss of the ASDS, Higgs's death, and the team's rendezvous with Opal, *Michigan*'s skipper said, "They're going to a safe layup position and we'll send a CRRC in for them tomorrow night." Guthrie made another request to bring *Michigan* inside Iranian territorial waters. The closer he got to the coast, the better the odds of recovery with a combat rubber raiding craft.

After giving her Higgs's name and rank, Guthrie listed the others on the beach. When she heard Jerry's name, she was surprised. What was *Michigan*'s executive officer doing on the beach? Guthrie explained, and she realized Jerry was the fifth man. Only four men were supposed to come ashore, and she cursed herself for missing that vital detail when she'd seen the UAV's image.

She'd known Jerry for years, and had once sailed with him on a mission. He was a dear friend. Jerry had also served under her husband, Lowell, before he'd left the Navy to run for congress.

Distracted by the news, Patterson automatically thanked him for the report and said she'd pass on his request. Her mind filled with activity. Someone had died, and there were things to be done. When a mission starts going bad, it often gets worse, quickly. Kirkpatrick would have to be briefed, and after that, the president.

And she would call Lowell, and see what he knew about Guthrie. She wanted to tell him about Jerry, as well, but that would mean telling him about the mission.

And the waiting was not over yet.

7

HUNKERING DOWN

3 April 2013
2000 Local Time/1700 Zulu
On the Iranian Coast near Bandar Kangan

Ramey ordered Lapointe to keep watch along the highway to the west. The petty officer split off from the group to take up a flanking position. The lieutenant sent Fazel to the east.

Jerry hurried with the others down to the car. It might have started out as a pale blue, but the sun had faded the upper surfaces to mottled white. There were dents in the grille and rear fenders. But it was transport, and his immediate thought was to get as far away from this place as possible.

The two Iranians, Yousef and his wife, were speaking softly in Farsi and looking at the car, then the SEALs, and back to the car. Finally, Shirin said, "You cannot all fit inside."

Ramey didn't hesitate. "Three guys go in the backseat, and two ride outside. We keep our weapons, but anything bulky goes in the trunk." After a pause, he added, "With your concurrence, XO."

Again the edge, but Jerry just said "Fine." This was not the time or place. "Is that all right with you?" Jerry asked the Iranian couple.

"What else can we do?" Shirin replied. "If we split up, the Basij or VE-VAK can still find us. And I do not wish them to find us."

The team leader explained, "There's an access road five and a half klicks west of here. It leads north to a high-voltage transmission tower. We should be able to go to ground there."

Yousef asked a question in Farsi, and Shirin translated. "How far off the highway is the tower?"

"A little over two kilometers," Ramey answered.

Yousef opened the trunk, then headed for the driver's seat, calling to Shirin. Ramey spoke into his headset, recalling the flankers. "XO, you're in the middle." That made sense. Not only was Jerry one of the shortest, but he wasn't a shooter. "Fazel and Lapointe are inside, Phillips and I will ride outside. There could be traffic down the highway at any time. Move."

Moving quickly, Jerry put his canteen and knapsack in the trunk, but kept his pistol. He climbed into the backseat of the small sedan. The space was claustrophobic enough, but the car had rear-wheel drive. The hump in the floor for the drive shaft pushed his knees up almost to his chin.

Clunks and thuds behind him meant the other team members were stowing their gear. Fazel piled in first on the left, behind Yousef, and Jerry didn't realize how far he'd moved to the right until Lapointe tried to get in from the other side. Jerry had to scrunch even closer to the medic, both pulling their elbows and shoulders in until it hurt. Ramey helped Lapointe position himself, then pushed the door shut. It jammed them together even more, but showed it was possible to fit three full-grown adults into the back of a Peykan.

They'd rolled down the windows on both rear doors before closing them. That was good, because there was no way Fazel or Lapointe could work them now. The two SEALs' weapons lay across their laps, barrels pointed out, but Jerry wondered how well they'd be able to shoot from such a cramped position.

Ramey and Phillips hopped up, putting their feet in through the open window and holding onto the edge of the door along the roof. Jerry found the space in front of him filled with boots and legs. Serving as "leg space coordinator," he pulled Ramey's feet in slightly and Philly's away so they didn't collide.

Once they'd settled, the two men slung their rifles over their shoulders. "We're ready," Ramey announced. The loading had taken less than a minute.

Yousef put the car in gear and started forward at a creep. Inside, Jerry felt the car lurch and tilt. He wondered if the shock absorbers had any play left in them at all. They were certainly overloaded, but hopefully not dangerously so.

The car rocked and wobbled across the uneven ground onto the shoulder, then up onto the smoother pavement. Yousef accelerated quickly and smoothly.

"The dirt road will be on the left," Ramey called to Fazel, who translated for Yousef. The Iranian nodded, his eyes ahead, accelerating. Shirin fiddled with her GPS device, but quickly announced, "The road is not on the map." Jerry thought that was a good thing.

How long would it take to drive five-plus kilometers? They all watched the road and the black landscape, except for Jerry, who could see little but the car's upholstery and combat boots. The enforced inactivity gave him time to think—and to remember: Higgs's disfigured body on the deck, his own sense of failure as the ASDS went down, and the long, cold swim to an unfriendly beach.

All he had to do was pilot the SEALs to a point off the beach, wait, and then take them back to *Michigan*. There had been no way to predict the battery fire, or any way to save Higgs. But it was his boat and Higgs had been his responsibility.

Jerry was still trying to shake off the thought when Ramey called, "There!" and pointed ahead and to the left.

Yousef held his speed as long as possible, then braked smoothly and turned onto the gravel access road. Thankfully, the car quickly slowed to a fast walk, making the ride bumpy but not bone-shattering. Jerry heard Ramey say, "Lights," with Fazel repeating it in Farsi, but Yousef was already turning off the headlights as he spoke. What little light they'd had was replaced with a single narrow beam from Ramey's flashlight. Although the SEALs had night-vision gear, Yousef did not, and Ramey kept the beam centered on the road in front of them. Yousef slowed the car even more.

Still pinned in the backseat, seeing only blackness out the windows, Jerry could only wait as the car crept forward on the access road. He could tell when the gravel stopped after a short while, giving way to a rougher dirt track, either poorly maintained or never more than crudely graded.

"There's the tower. Let's stop here." Ramey hopped down from the car as it rolled to a stop, his rifle already sweeping half the horizon. Phillips repeated the lieutenant's actions on his side. They were both using their night-vision scopes.

They opened the rear doors, and Jerry and the two SEALs almost tumbled out of the backseat, gratefully stretching. The SEALs quickly found their gear in the trunk and reequipped themselves. Jerry, still unfamiliar with the equipment, fumbled in the darkness for a moment before getting it right.

Phillips reported, "There's a cut in the hill off the right. It looks like a good spot to hide the car."

With his scope, Ramey completed a quick sweep of the terrain. He couldn't make out a lot of detail, but what he could see told him the ground was rough, hilly, and rocky. There were numerous dunes and shadowy gullies interspersed with more solid-looking rock outcrops and tufts of vegetation. *Good ground*, he thought to himself. Turning, he looked where Phillips was pointing. "Good, and there's level ground leading up to it. Keep a watch to the south, Philly."

Phillips trotted off in the direction they'd come from, while Ramey and Fazel walked over to speak with the two Iranians. Jerry hurried over to join them, but Ramey didn't wait for him. "Doc, tell him we can hide the car here and look for cover. This is a good location. We won't have to break cover until the CRRC's halfway to the beach."

While Fazel translated for Yousef, the lieutenant turned to Jerry. "I'm going to take Doc and Pointy and scout for a good hiding place for us, away from the car. Phillips will keep watch to the south, and I'd like you to stay here with the two civilians. Just back the car as far as you can into that notch in the hillside. Then sit tight."

"Of course," Jerry acknowledged. "Should we cover up the car?"

"No," Ramey answered sharply. "You'd just make a bigger mess. My guys will take care of it when we get back from scouting." Jerry bristled at the rebuke. Of course the SEALs could do a better job, but the lieutenant's hostility was unnecessary.

Three of the SEALs disappeared into the darkness, and with Phillips on watch to the south, Jerry was alone with the two Iranians. The woman, Shirin, looked at him expectantly, and after a moment, he turned on his own flashlight.

With Shirin translating Jerry's directions, Yousef backed the battered sedan slowly into the crevice. While relatively level, the ground was uneven enough to require care, or the Peykan might have gotten stuck, or worse.

At its opening, the cut was almost twenty feet wide, made by water in the steep slopes of a barren hillside. Jerry tugged and rolled a few large rocks out of the way to clear a path for the car, but the gap was deep enough so that the car was completely inside, with almost a full car length separating it from the front.

Once he'd made sure they could still open the doors and that there was a clear path out, Jerry stood near the opening, staring into the dark and hoping that he wouldn't see anything. Behind him, Yousef folded a blanket to make a place for his wife, and helped her sit. She drank some water from a bottle he carried, then leaned back against the wall of the crevice.

Still watching, Jerry picked his way over to where the two sat. He asked Shirin, "Are you hungry? I have some MREs." Seeing her expression, he explained, "Some field rations—food." Taking off his backpack, he found a plastic package and offered it to her.

She looked over to her husband and spoke. He answered by nodding, and she said, tentatively, "I am a little hungry."

Jerry had to open the outer package with his knife. Working by feel, he found something that felt like an energy bar and tore open the wrapper. She accepted it, and tasting it, nodded her appreciation. Jerry handed the rest of the package to Yousef, who sorted through the contents, asking Shirin and Jerry about the labels and ingredients.

A few minutes later, Jerry thought he heard something, but before he could react the three SEALs were back. Instead of a scouting report, Ramey asked, "What are they eating? Is that one of your MREs?" His tone was harsh, like a parent catching a child in some offense.

"Yes, Lieutenant," Jerry emphasized the second word slightly, "I thought it might be good for them to eat something."

"No ranks, sir," Jerry heard Ramey's emphasis on the last word. "We can't leave any trace of our presence. A piece of an MRE package would be a dead giveaway we were here. Please police the area carefully. The only thing I'm willing to leave behind is our footprints, and I wish I could avoid that."

"Right," Jerry replied, being careful to keep his voice neutral. "Did you find a place?"

"It's about a kilometer from here, but it's ideal. It's a small cave, but it's big enough for all of us. It's got overhead cover and has a good view of the approaches."

The SEALs went to work hiding the car. Each carried a section of camouflage netting. They combined these into a single piece large enough to cover the car, then added brush and rocks to break up its outline.

Yousef and Shirin stood to one side. She was leaning on him, and although their expressions were hard to see, his arms encircled her protectively. Jerry could also sense defensiveness in his posture, his watchfulness of not only the activity with the car, but the other SEALs as well. He didn't trust them, not yet anyway.

Ramey took his time to step back and check their work from several directions, but they were still done in a few minutes. "Let's get away from here," he ordered over the headset. "Diamond formation."

Jerry and the two Iranians were quickly corralled in the center of the formation, following Ramey. The other SEALs screened to the back, and both sides. They set off at a brisk pace, but had to slow when first Jerry, then Shirin, stumbled on the uneven surface. Grudgingly, Ramey promised to follow a smoother path.

There was enough starlight to see the ground, but not enough to reveal every obstacle. Yousef was especially solicitous toward his wife after her near fall, but she waved him off.

It was impossible to gauge distance in the dark. Jerry thought of counting footsteps, but his stride across the landscape was too irregular. He decided it would be best to just concentrate on watching Ramey ahead of him and picking his footing based on how he moved.

How far was a kilometer? Better than half a mile. In the dark? On an unfamiliar landscape? After a bone-chilling hour-long swim? He definitely hadn't planned on this when he'd gotten up this morning. He was breathing hard, and felt like he'd already run miles.

He wasn't the only one showing signs of fatigue. Shirin was moving more slowly, now leaning heavily on Yousef. The SEALs seemed unaffected by the evening's intense physical activity.

Jerry marveled a little when he thought about the husband. A captain in the Pasdaran. They were supposed to be Iran's shock troops, politically reliable and completely devout. What had turned him against his own service?

He tried to focus on the plan. They'd hole up tonight and tomorrow, then *Michigan* would launch a CRRC. They'd break cover once it was en route, meet on the beach, and an hour later they'd be back aboard. They were in a bad spot, but they hadn't been detected, and they had a plan.

Ramey motioned for Lapointe to go ahead; he ran to the cave and did a quick inspection. Jerry heard his report in his headset. "It's still clear, Boss."

A low line of hills loomed ahead, and they retraced the SEALs' earlier path. Turning right toward a high bank, then following it back, they came to a place where Lapointe stood next to a large shadow on the side of the bank.

"Pointy, take the first watch, everyone else inside." After giving the order, Ramey led the way. Once he was inside, he turned on his flashlight.

Shirin was surprised by the intensity of the beam. It seemed like a big red floodlight to her night-adjusted eyes, and she turned to see if it revealed their position. But the beam was directed into the cave, and little of the light was reflected back out.

When her eyes adjusted, she saw a space a little smaller than their bedroom. It was larger than she expected, but she hadn't spent a lot of time in caves. Water had eaten away the earth under a layer of rock, so the cave had a relatively flat, but rough ceiling. The floor was hard-packed sand with a band of pebbles running down the center, almost a gravel path.

Farther inside, Yousef was arranging a blanket for her to sit on. Suddenly she felt very tired, almost dizzy. With a small moan, she gratefully sank onto the spot, leaning back against the wall.

The Americans all turned at the sound, and Fazel asked in Farsi, "Are you all right?" When she didn't reply, he turned to Yousef. "Is your wife ill?"

Yousef, still helping Shirin sit comfortably, answered, "Not sick. She's pregnant."

The medic quickly knelt down beside her. One hand was on her wrist, taking her pulse. The other found her forehead. "How many weeks?"

"Nineteen," she answered almost automatically. She could see Yousef starting to protest. Normally such things were not discussed with strangers, but the American had medical training, and at least he spoke Farsi. Calming her husband with a hand on his arm, she said, "I'm just tired." *And under a great deal of stress*, she added to herself, but that was understood.

"I'm glad the walk wasn't any longer," the medic remarked. "You probably need something to eat, and please drink as much of that water as you can." He indicated the bottle Yousef was holding. "We'll make sure you have plenty of water."

Unslinging his pack, he pulled out a small square, which unfolded to a drab green thermal blanket. "Here. It will cool off tonight." Shirin noticed Yousef scowling, and so did the American. He offered the blanket to her husband, who took it with a polite "Thank you."

Yousef covered her and tucked the edges in around her. Although it felt light and flimsy, she felt warmer almost immediately, and drowsy. She closed her eyes as the warmth embraced her.

Yousef watched Shirin for a few minutes, peacefully asleep, then noticed the American medic doing the same thing on the other side. "I can take care of my wife," he said sharply.

"Of course," the American replied coldly. "But her welfare affects all of us, and we don't want to do anything that would endanger her and the baby."

"Isn't it a little late for that?" Yousef asked angrily. "We're hiding in a cave waiting for a boat to pick us up because you couldn't keep your submarine from catching fire."

"Our comrade died in that fire—coming here because you asked us to."

Yousef shook his head. "It's not my fault he died, and I'm not the person you're here to rescue. You can't get anything right." He smiled at the American's confusion, then pointed to his peacefully sleeping wife. "She's the one who has given you so much information. Shirin is an engineer at the Natanz Uranium Enrichment Facility." There was passion in his voice, and the words fell from him.

"She's risked her life for years collecting information on my country's nuclear weapons program and sending it to your government. It's not because we love America. I don't believe America is our enemy, but you haven't been our friend either. She was disgusted at how Iran has lied about making a bomb, and the waste of money and talent that have been spent on the program."

"What about you? You are Pasdaran. Surely—"

"My reasons are personal, and just as strong as hers. I won't betray my country, but we should not have nuclear weapons. They are un-Islamic."

"We won't ask you to do anything you don't want to. You don't even have to stay with us, if you think your chances are better on your own."

"No. We want to leave Iran any way we can." Yousef was firm. He tilted his head toward Shirin. "She doesn't want to go back to Natanz, no matter what. And neither of us want to go to Evin Prison."

The American nodded. "My parents told me stories about that place, both before and after the Revolution. And about the Pasdaran. The Basij beat my uncle until he was a cripple. The Revolutionary Guards seized my father's business and drove my parents from their home."

Yousef wanted to say it was all lies, American propaganda, but he knew the stories were true—about Evin, and the Pasdaran's zealous cruelty. He'd been a good soldier, but the Pasdaran was corrupt. They had their fingers in civilian businesses all over Iran, and he'd heard how the generals lived, more like rich executives than soldiers of the Revolution. He was unwilling to agree with the American, but could not argue. In the end, Yousef said nothing.

"I have to tell the others," Harry explained, and stood.

While Fazel had been taking care of Shirin, the others, with a few words from Ramey, had worked to improve their position. Jerry and Phillips camouflaged the cave mouth, while Ramey and Lapointe prepared firing positions, piling rocks and digging shallow ditches in the floor.

"XO, Boss, you need to hear this," Fazel called, then briefed Ramey and Jerry in a soft voice. Jerry was surprised to learn Shirin's identity, and dismayed at her condition. It was a complication they could have done without. The lieutenant's reaction was more extreme, almost hostile.

"And the fun just keeps coming." Ramey had been digging out a fighting position near the cave mouth. "Maybe I should just make this a little deeper and crawl in. Save us a lot of trouble."

Jerry said, "Matt, you can't blame yourself—"

"Shut up!" The SEAL's vehemence shocked Jerry. Ramey had put one hand on his weapon, and Jerry wasn't sure if it was just habit or deliberate intent. "It's your fault Higgs is dead, and then you made us leave him behind. I should have left you and taken him instead. We don't even know if he was really dead."

"He was dead, Lieutenant."

"So you say."

"I feel as bad about it as you do. I was responsible for him."

"Bullshit. You didn't work and train with him for a year and a half. How many deployments had he been on? How well could he shoot? Do you even know if he was married?"

The outburst had drawn everyone's attention, although to Phillips's credit, he continued to keep watch from just outside the cave mouth. Shirin was awake now, too, watching Ramey's angry rant with a confused expression. Yousef sat next to her, looking concerned. He knew Jerry was the senior officer. He also knew the Americans had lost a man.

Lapointe was the senior petty officer. Slowly easing himself over to Jerry, he said quietly, "Sir, let's go outside. Doc, can you help the Boss with his position?"

Gratefully, Jerry followed the petty officer outside. They found a spot a short distance from the cave, Lapointe sat down with his rifle across his knees.

Jerry stood, leaning against the hillside. Thoughts flew though his mind. Ramey was clearly upset, grieving, under great stress. But that was no excuse for his outburst; naval discipline had just been shattered. Admittedly this wasn't the usual senior-junior relationship. And weren't they all under stress?

Lapointe kept his eyes on the landscape. "Sir, I'm sorry about the lieutenant. We all feel like he does, but he's the guy in charge, so Higgs's loss hit him harder."

Jerry wasn't buying it. "I've lost people, too. It always sucks, but you don't fall apart. And you're SEALs. This may be a little harsh, but aren't you prepared to lose a man when you go on a mission?"

"Not like that, sir. From a freak accident? And when I said *lose*, I didn't mean *die*. SEALs never leave anyone behind, alive or dead. In Afghanistan, we've lost more people recovering a brother SEAL's remains than we have from our direct action missions, and nobody thinks it's a waste."

He saw Jerry start to speak, but interrupted. "I'm not kidding, sir. We've never left anyone behind before. At all. Ever. This would be the first time."

Jerry shrugged helplessly. "I've thought about almost nothing else since we came ashore. I sent him back to open the breaker. I'm not as familiar with the ASDS as Higgs and Carlson. Was there something else I could have done? Was there some sign that Higgs and I both missed? You can damn well believe an investigating board will be asking those same questions when we get back.

"But Higgs wasn't severely wounded, he was gone. Doc checked him before we left; he was dead. I've been trying to imagine how we could have gotten him out and ashore if he'd only been injured."

"We would have found a way," Lapointe answered flatly.

Mitchell nodded as Lapointe continued. "We would have tried our damnedest. Higgs might have died anyway, but the point is we would have tried.

"Maybe it's the lack of trying that the boss is mad about," the petty officer reasoned. "You didn't even try."

"We couldn't help him. He was dead, and trying to recover his remains would have risked more lives, and the mission. The batteries had already started exploding. I made the call to preserve as many lives as possible." Jerry was thinking like an XO now, his thoughts clearing.

"My brain agrees with you, sir, but other parts still need convincing. We just haven't had a chance to think about it much. There's something else, too."

"What? There's more?" Jerry tried not to sound too dismayed.

"The lieutenant is mission-oriented. Shoot, we all are. But he really takes a job on board, and we're on 'Plan C' at this point. It doesn't matter what the reason is. A mission failure is a personal failure for him. And he's never failed."

"He's worried about us making it back." It was a question, but Jerry made it a flat statement.

"He won't say so, but hell, yes, XO. We planned the bejesus out of this job, but if the pickup tomorrow doesn't go down, we start winging it. There is no 'Plan D. '"

Lapointe paused, and Jerry sensed that he was waiting for something from him. "So what do you want me to do?"

"We need Matt's, I mean, Mr. Ramey's head in the game until it's over. He's been shaken, and badly, and right now he isn't firing on all cylinders. He's starting to make mistakes."

Jerry's perplexed expression amused Lapointe. "You haven't been trained as a SEAL, so you don't know what to look for. The mistakes are little ones, but they're mistakes all the same. That has got to change. And the only way I can see that happening is you've got to stop being nice. You can't be oozing with sympathy, no matter how much he may be hurting inside."

"Are you serious?" Jerry exclaimed.

"Deadly serious, XO. Sympathy is between shit and syphilis in the dictionary, and it's about as useful. A SEAL doesn't respond to sympathy. When one of us is down the rest of us don't tell him everything will be all right, or that he did his best; we kick 'em in the balls and yell at him to get his ass in gear. Right now Mr. Ramey feels like a loser, and that kind of mentality is fatal. It's beaten into us from the very first day at BUDS that it pays to be a winner."

"Yeah, Vernon mentioned that," admitted Jerry.

"Well, he wasn't lying. I need—no, correction—we need Mr. Ramey to recalibrate his attitude and start wanting to win again. If the only way that happens is for you to be a flaming asshole, then, oh well. You're a big boy, you'll get over it."

Jerry stepped away from Lapointe as he considered the SEAL's assessment of the platoon leader's damaged psyche. It seemed to make sense, when viewed through the contorted lens of a SEAL mind-set. But Jerry knew he wasn't a "screamer," he just wasn't wired that way, and on those rare occasions when he did try, the results were pretty pathetic.

"I hear you, Petty Officer Lapointe," Jerry said as he turned to face him. "But I have to warn you, I make a lousy flaming asshole. However, I can be a demanding SOB if the situation warrants it."

Lapointe grinned. "If all you do, sir, is nag his ass, and don't cut him any slack, I think I can live with that."

When the two returned to the cave, they found Lieutenant Ramey waiting outside. Ostensibly, he was on lookout, but he motioned to Lapointe and the petty officer went inside.

"XO, sir. I was way out of line." Ramey's voice held little emotion, but Jerry could tell by the tightness in his jaw that he was fighting to keep it in check. "There was no excuse for what I said. Please accept my apology." He was almost at attention, maybe unnecessary for the circumstance but necessary for control.

"It's accepted, Lieutenant." Jerry could have said more, but his recent crash course on SEAL psychology told him to keep it short. "Are you able to lead the team?"

"Absolutely," Ramey answered, but the lieutenant's voice was strained.

Jerry wasn't convinced, but really had no alternative but to accept Ramey's answer. He searched for something else to say or ask, but again decided that less was more. "Let's get inside, then."

"Yes, sir."

Phillips came out to take lookout duty. Inside, the cave seemed bright, and warm, and then Jerry saw that the SEALs had set up a small stove. They were heating water and MREs, and Fazel was cooking. Phillips had finished first, but the others were still eating.

Doc gave a small smile. "It's only lukewarm, but it's tasty. It's my own creation—SEAL stew."

"Do I want to know what's in it?" Jerry asked, as he tried to peer into the MRE pouch.

"I can tell you, but it will be different next time. Depends on what's handy. There's no recipe, just a set of guiding principles." Nodding toward the two Iranians, Fazel added, "It is *halal*. No pork."

Yousef and Shirin were both eating steadily, if not enthusiastically. "Why is it called seal stew?" she asked. "I don't think this is what seal tastes like."

"No, ma'am," he said, pointing to the others in the team. "We are called 'SEALs.' It stands for 'Sea, Air, Land,' the different places we can move and fight."

"But you are commandos, aren't you?"

"Yes, but that's like saying your husband is a soldier. There's more than one kind. We're U.S. Navy. The best kind." He grinned.

Fazel handed Jerry a small bowl of the stuff. It smelled okay, but he was glad the light was dim. He'd heard stories of surviving on snakes and tree moss, but the SEALs hadn't had time to forage, and besides, he could see other open MREs next to the corpsman.

Lapointe nodded at the medic's explanation. "We specialize," he said, smiling.

"Is one of your specialties taking people off beaches?" she asked.

"Well, actually, yes," Lapointe answered. "We practice for this, among many other things. We've trained in snow, jungle, urban environments . . ."

"I have a flash drive," Shirin said abruptly. "It has over twenty-two gigabytes of files relating to our nuclear weapons program."

Jerry and the SEALs, surprised, all looked at Shirin, then at Ramey. The lieutenant was looking at Jerry.

"What kind of files?" Jerry asked.

"Schedules, purchase orders, test results, progress reports, e-mails, photographs, biographies—enough information to give a complete description of the entire program, and its potential. Because of security restrictions, I've only been able to send out a few files at a time. But this time I copied as much as I could find. Eventually the security checks will notice all the activity on the log at my computer, but I didn't plan to go back."

"Why are you telling us this?"

"In case things . . . go badly. You should know about it. But the data is encrypted. Yousef and I know how to open the files."

Lapointe said, "Sir, I recommend making copies of that data, encrypted or not." He pulled a laptop from his backpack. "The boss has one as well. We'll make two sets."

Jerry held out his hand. "May we copy the files?"

Shirin nodded, and her head disappeared under the blanket. After a few moments of rustling, her head reappeared, and then her hand, holding the device. She handed it to Lapointe, who plugged it into a USB port on his machine and began typing.

As Lapointe worked, Ramey asked him, "Can we uplink this stuff back to the sub, or somewhere else?"

"This is a lot of ones and zeroes, Boss. With the FPS-117's bandwidth, it would take tens of hours. Our batteries wouldn't come even close to lasting that long."

"There is a summary file," Shirin volunteered. "It lists the types of information on the drive, and I could decrypt one small file. It will help prove who we are and what we have."

"You don't have to do that," Jerry said. "We're not leaving you behind."

"Your government may have its doubts. I am not a professional spy, but they must rule out the possibility that we are lying. This does not offend me. It is prudent for them to make sure we are not double agents."

"I don't think I'd be that calm about it," Ramey commented.

"Done," Lapointe announced. "Everything has been copied onto my laptop."

"Then let me see the list of files, please." Shirin got up, still wrapped in the blanket, and walked over to where Lapointe was working. He turned the computer so she could see the screen as she knelt on the cave floor.

She studied the list for a moment, asked him to scroll down, then pointed out one. "Open this, please." When Lapointe double-clicked on it, a dialog box appeared, asking for a password. Shielding the keyboard, she carefully typed in a long sequence, and the file opened.

"It's a standard PDF file," Lapointe reported. Shirin repeated the process with a second file. "This is a presentation about centrifuge problems at Natanz. I was there when this happened," she explained.

Fazel leaned over and read the Farsi script aloud. "Natanz Centrifuge Cascade Failure Reconstruction. It's dated February of this year."

"Hoooly shit." Lapointe's exclamation matched Jerry's feelings. This was the real thing.

"The file sizes are good," Lapointe reported. "It will take about fifteen minutes to upload both, plus a few minutes to tell them what we're sending."

"Okay," said Ramey, "we will transmit this tomorrow night, just before we go to the pickup point. That minimizes the time for them to react if they detect the signal."

"I thought you said the signal was undetectable," Shirin asked.

"We're sending electrons into the ether. The chance may be very small, but I don't take chances if I don't have to."

She didn't look pleased. "That is tomorrow night. There is some . . . urgency in this data reaching your government."

Jerry asked, "Is some of this material time sensitive?"

"No, but Yousef and I have other information, very important information. And we need your government to believe in who we are and what we know."

Jerry considered for a moment, but realized he was hesitating. He knew which path he had to take. "Send it now," he ordered Ramey. "We shouldn't sit on this for a day."

"XO, I don't think this is a good idea," Ramey was visibly unhappy with Jerry pulling rank and making a decision that he wasn't trained to make.

"I understand your objection, Matt. But if I read this right, the information has strategic implications that go beyond our own situation." Turning to Lapointe, he asked, "Petty Officer Lapointe, what are the risks of sending such a long transmission?"

Lapointe looked first at his platoon leader, and then back at Jerry. "Technically, the risk is low. The Iranians likely don't know we're here and the radio is very secure—particularly for short transmissions. If the information is as important as you think, XO, the risk is acceptable."

"Very well," replied Jerry, as he stared straight into Ramey's eyes. "I do believe it is that important, and we need to send it up the chain . . . now."

Ramey was hard to read. His jaw was clenched tight again, but he didn't argue further. "Aye, aye, XO," he answered. "Pointy, do it when you're ready, and don't spend any time downloading the scores from the Red Sox's game."

"Aye, aye, Boss, and after that I'll copy the whole thing onto your laptop as well."

After Lapointe transmitted the files and finished transferring them to Ramey's laptop, the SEALs checked and cleaned their gear. Ramey set up a watch schedule for the night with two SEALs on watch at any one time. Ramey and Fazel took the first watch while everyone else tried to get some sleep. Each of the SEALs had a thermal blanket like Fazel's, they handed Yousef one and he snuggled up to Shirin; throwing part of his blanket over her as well. Lapointe and Phillips shared a blanket and bedded down near the cave entrance, just in case. By circumstance or design, Jerry found himself alone on the far side of the cave.

Feeling slightly left out, Jerry spent several minutes smoothing his place on the cave floor, removed some pebbles, and tried to remember the last time he'd camped out. He was still wondering if he'd ever get to sleep when fatigue claimed him.

8

A FINE MESS

"I thought this was supposed to be a low risk, routine operation, Mr. Secretary," exclaimed Myles angrily as he stormed into the situation room; a cloud of civilian and military advisors filed in behind him.

"Mr. President, our risk assessment was based on Iranian military capability, not on the possibility of a freak accident," replied Secretary of Defense Springfield. "Who could have possibly foreseen this extraordinary piece of bad luck?"

Joanna quickly took a seat behind Kirkpatrick, checked her notes, and scanned the synopsis she had prepared, along with Guthrie's proposed plan of action. Satisfied that she was as ready as she could be given the circumstances, she turned her attention to the president.

President Myles took a deep breath and let out an audible sigh. "I know, James. There was no way we could have anticipated this unbelievable complication. But as unfortunate as it is, it is now part of a much larger crisis after the IAEA report this morning and the Iranian general's press conference."

Earlier that morning, the International Atomic Energy Agency had released its long-awaited report on the latest inspection of Iranian nuclear facilities. The report was late, and it was a bombshell.

It stated that samples taken from discarded centrifuges at the Pilot Fuel

Enrichment Plant showed uranium hexafluoride residue with Uranium-235 enrichment levels of 85%, well beyond that needed for any civilian purpose. In its final paragraph, the Board of Governors had concluded that this was not a case of cross contamination from another source. The uranium was of Iranian origin, and there was only one purpose for U-235 concentrations of such magnitude—the development of nuclear weapons.

Less than an hour after the IAEA's report was released, IRGC Brigadier General Adel Moradi, head of security for the Iranian nuclear program, held a press conference broadcast by Iran's FARS News, Al Jazeera, and other news affiliates throughout the Persian Gulf, Europe, and Asia. Moradi first read from a prepared statement, denouncing the IAEA's findings as sheer propaganda; claiming the report constituted nothing less than slander against the Islamic Republic by its most hated enemies—the Zionists and the Great Satan.

He went on to say that this deception was purposely designed to create a more toxic environment, one that would make it impossible for Iran to have a fair hearing at the court of world opinion, and would embolden those on the UN Security Council to demand additional punishments—punishments that were as unjustified as they were evil. He then added that the IAEA report was undoubtedly a fabrication, that the samples, if indeed they were taken from Iran, were planted on the used centrifuges. It was widely known that their peaceful nuclear program had suffered numerous technical setbacks over the years—from malicious causes as well as inexperience.

Moradi had paused momentarily; he was shown grabbing the podium more forcefully, as if he was drawing strength from it, and then launched into the climax of his prepared statement. "Since the IAEA has shown that it is nothing more than a puppet institution for the enemies of the Islamic Republic to attack it, Iran is withdrawing immediately from all safeguard agreements of the Nuclear Non-Proliferation Treaty, including the additional protocols. The IAEA has forty-eight hours to withdraw all its inspectors from the country. All cameras and other monitoring devices will be removed from Iranian nuclear facilities immediately. Iran will weather this storm as it has the ones before, alone, resolute, and with faith that God will not abandon us."

With a final cry of, "*Allahu Akbar—God Is Great!*" the general had departed the podium. He did not respond to any of the questions shouted at him.

The two events had left everyone in Washington, D.C., in a state of shock. Unexpected, and almost unbelievable, the policy apparatus of the Myles adminstration was still struggling to regain its bearings.

"Agreed, Mr. President," injected Kirkpatrick. "I believe we should make the most of this respite to formulate a plan to deal with this crisis."

There were confused looks from all those seated at the table, including the president, whose response was snippy. "Respite? What respite? What are you talking about, Ray?"

"It is a statistically proven fact, sir, that bad things happen in threes. Well," he continued with a wide grin, "we've had our three. Certainly we are due a break now."

Even Myles had to crack a smile at Kirkpatrick's witticism, and the tension in the room dropped noticeably. His subtle message to the group had been received; stop complaining about what has happened, and start dealing with it.

"Sound wisdom as always, Ray," conceded Myles. "Since Secretary of State Lloyd is otherwise engaged with the Israeli ambassador, I believe we can begin."

"Yes, sir," said Kirkpatrick. "We'll start with a recap of the accident, followed by our current status and options." Looking around the room, he found the president's chief of staff over in the corner taking notes. "Milt, when is our video teleconference with Captain Guthrie?"

"It's scheduled for 1315, sir. In ten minutes."

"Then we'd better get started." Kirkpatrick signaled Joanna. She rose and began her briefing.

"Mr. President, at approximately ten thirty-five A.M., our time, the Advanced Seal Delivery System minisub suffered a catastrophic battery failure that resulted in the death of one crew member and the loss of the vessel. While there isn't any hard data for us to look at, the pilot reported a high temperature alarm in the after battery followed by a rapid and uncontrollable rise in temperature. We suspect that one or more of the lithium-ion battery cells experienced thermal runaway, became unstable, and exploded."

General Dewhurst, the Chairman of the Joint Chiefs of Staff, indicated he had a question. "Dr. Patterson, what do you mean by thermal runaway?"

"General, during thermal runaway an overheating battery undergoes an increase in its chemical reaction rate due to the excessive heat. This generates even more heat and the cycle feeds on itself until the battery cell ruptures or explodes. This can, and has led to fires. If you remember the laptop battery recall of six or seven years ago, there was a problem with some lithium-ion batteries manufactured in China that caused several laptops to burst into flames. Impurities in the composition of the battery plates likely caused those batteries to short-circuit and produce enormous quantities of heat."

"And this is what happened to the ASDS?" Springfield asked.

"It's our best theory, sir," replied Joanna.

"If lithium-ion batteries are prone to catching on fire, why would the Navy outfit a minisub with them?" asked a dumbfounded Dewhurst.

Before Joanna could answer the question, Kirkpatrick thumped the desk loudly with his fingers. "Gentlemen, we are not here to determine how and why the ASDS sank. We need to focus on the problem at hand: How do we get our people out of Iran? If you have additional technical questions, Dr. Patterson will be happy to address them *after* we are done here. Please continue, Joanna."

"Yes, sir," she replied, flipping to the next page in her notes. "The four-man SEAL extraction team abandoned ship approximately one nautical mile from the Iranian coast. The pilot abandoned ship right after he set two scuttling charges. The explosion of these charges was detected by USS *Michigan* at ten forty-four A.M. our time. At eleven forty-eight A.M., the SEALs successfully made contact with Opal and his spouse, and by eleven fifty-five A.M. they established satellite radio communications with *Michigan* and reported in.

"The contingency plan called for a Zodiac combat rubber raiding craft to be deployed from *Michigan* to recover the extraction team and the Iranians. Captain Guthrie, as the operational commander, scrubbed the mission at the last moment. He based his decision on the close proximity of IRGC patrol boats and that *Michigan* was too far away from the coast for the raiding craft to have a reasonable chance of slipping in undetected. Since the patrol boats are better armed and considerably faster than a Zodiac, he felt it was unwise to risk additional lives given that the probability of success was, in his words, 'less than slim to none.' He ordered the SEAL element ashore and the pilot to assume their preplanned layup position located in some hills approximately nine kilometers to the northeast from the rendezvous point. And that concludes my summary, Mr. President."

"Dr. Patterson, you mentioned that Captain Guthrie felt he was too far away to deploy the rubber raiding craft," noted Myles carefully, his tone stern. "Can I presume that he has requested permission to take *Michigan* into Iranian territorial waters?"

"Yes, sir. He specifically asked me to pass on that request."

"I see," responded Myles, as he threw his pen down on the table. His face grimaced with frustration.

"Sir, it's a logical and responsible request," argued the chief of naval operations. "I'd expect nothing less from one of my skippers."

"I'm sure you would, Admiral," Myles exclaimed with irritation. "I can even appreciate Captain Guthrie's viewpoint. But it doesn't change the fact that it is a myopic viewpoint. He's looking at the problem from a purely tactical perspective, the strategic aspect of this situation makes it far more complex."

Admiral Hughes was clearly unhappy with the president's response, but he remained silent.

"What are our options then?" asked Dewhurst.

"Very few, I'm afraid," Joanna answered. "Extraction by combat rubber raiding craft is still an option, although the risk of detection increases the farther *Michigan* is away. Stealing a fishing vessel from one of the local harbors is another option, but most fishing dhows are quite slow, about ten knots maximum speed, and the Iranians have beefed up their antismuggling patrols in the last two years making detection likely. We've also considered obtaining a fast boat from a neighboring country and having a SEAL team attempt to sneak in. If they are discovered, they'll at least have the speed to get away. We've ruled out an extraction by air, as there's an early warning radar at Tahari, less than twenty miles to the southeast. The Chinese radar upgrade at that location makes detection almost a certainty. With the tactical air base at Bushehr being only one hundred miles away, the probability of interception by fighters is high."

"Which option has the best chance of success?" Myles demanded.

Patterson hesitated, and looked down at Kirkpatrick who nodded.

"Sir, I can't give you a numerical probability of success for each of the options. We haven't had time to run simulations or even game it out. However, from a qualitative perspective, the consensus of the intelligence and special warfare people is that stealth is the primary factor. If stealth fails, then speed becomes the driver. The combat rubber raiding craft option has high stealth, but low speed. The fishing boat option has low stealth and low speed. The fast boat has moderate stealth and high speed. Since the raiding craft option maximizes stealth, it's the one that is recommended."

"And the closer *Michigan* can get to the coast, the better our chances become," emphasized Hughes.

"I'm not hard of hearing, Admiral Hughes," countered Myles. "I am fully aware of what you would like me to do. But I remain convinced that sending *Michigan* into Iranian territorial waters is pure, unadulterated foolishness. To be honest, I wasn't all that comfortable with sending in a minisub. But collectively you all made a good argument for the operation because it was believed the payoff was potentially substantial and the risk was low. Well, for whatever reason, the low-risk operation failed. And now I'm sensing considerable pressure to go against my better judgment and send *Michigan* in. All the Iranians have to do is see it and it's a *casus belli*. With the current unstable situation, this would be disastrous."

Hughes's face was taut, his speech measured. "Mr. President, I am merely doing my duty as one of your military advisors to ensure you have all the information you need to—"

"This is nonsense!" interrupted Myles angrily. "Can't you people see that we're at a tipping point? Can any of you give me a good reason why I should risk escalating this crisis further by allowing *Michigan* to enter Iranian territorial waters?"

General Duvall, the NIC chairman, raised his hand. "I can give you one reason, sir. Although, at the moment it may appear trivial."

"Go on, Gordon," Myles responded testily as he waved off his chief of staff. Alvarez had been pointing maddeningly at his watch; they were late for the VTC with *Michigan*.

"General Moradi's press conference was unusually timely and well orchestrated. Less than an hour after the report's release, he delivered a well-polished statement with excellent media coverage. He was also unusually forthcoming about their technical difficulties. Normally, the Iranians make up successes rather than admit failures. I could have bought this if it had been the usual extemporaneous ranting on just Iranian TV. But what we saw smacks of deliberate planning, as if he knew exactly what the IAEA's report would say. While I can't rule out the possibility of a leak, the IAEA has been excessively paranoid about their reports as of late and has success-fully kept them confidential until they are released. This latest report was several days late, with no explanation as to why from the Board of Gover-nors. The precise timing of all these events is a little too coincidental for my liking." Duvall paused as he gave time for this key point to sink in.

"Since March we've been getting wildly conflicting information on Iran's intentions and progress. We've seen two themes from multiple cred-ible sources that are at polar extremes. Logic demands that both cannot be right. Moradi's press release has only sharpened the contrast; one of these themes is false. I agree that we are at a tipping point, Mr. President, but with-out better insight into what is true and what is false, any action we take will be at a considerable gamble. I am convinced that the information that Opal possesses is absolutely critical to our understanding the true nature of this game."

Total silence descended on the conference room. Myles stared coldly at the NIC chairman, and slowly, a faint smile appeared on the president's face. "Well put, General. Well put. So we go with the rubber raiding craft option then?"

Before anyone could answer, Kirkpatrick chimed in. "I agree that the combat rubber raiding craft is the option we should go with, but I would also like to propose a compromise, sir."

President Myles leaned forward, intrigued. "What do you have in mind, Ray?"

"Sir, I recommend that you let Captain Guthrie walk right up to the line before he deploys the raiding craft. He can then back off while the SEALs make their run, returning again only to affect the recovery. By temporarily relaxing your restrictions a little, you can cut the distance the SEALs are exposed by twenty percent while minimizing the risk."

Joanna strained to maintain a calm expression; wanting to hide the ex-citement she felt as she watched her boss work. She had seen Ray Kirkpat-rick "pull rabbits out of a hat" before during the transition period when the president-elect had backed himself into a corner, and every time, Kirkpat-rick's solution had paid off big-time. This simple compromise would only reinforce the widely held belief among the White House staff that he was Solomon incarnate.

"Done!" shouted Myles with approval. "Milt, get Captain Guthrie on the · line."

3 April 2013
2125 Local Time/1825 Zulu
USS *Michigan*, Battle Management Center

Kyle Guthrie looked first at his watch, and then the clock on the bulkhead as he paced around the BMC. Shaking his head and grumbling, he continued doing laps around the planning table. Harper, Simmons, and Frederickson sat in absolute silence, doing their best impression of church mice; the skipper was pissed. The VTC was supposed to have begun ten minutes ago, and the screen was still blank. Agitated and impatient, Guthrie fumed as the seconds ticked by.

"What the hell is taking them so long," he growled. Guthrie always knew the beefed-up communications capability of a SSGN was a double-edged sword. It provided great benefits for planning and executing Tomahawk strikes or SEAL ops, and its impact on crew morale was without question, but it had its drawbacks as well—anybody in his chain of command could get a hold of him at a moment's notice. And to communicate, he had to stick a mast in the air, a mast that made *Michigan* more vulnerable to detection. High-level VTCs were a particular pain. They always went longer than he liked. On more than one occasion after an excruciatingly long-winded exchange, he was heard to mumble, "Silent service, my ass!"

"If that contact gets much closer, I'll have to dunk the masts and move," the captain snarled, as he pointed to an auxiliary display with fire control data showing an Iranian patrol boat nearby.

"Sir, it *is* the President," remarked Frederickson warily.

Guthrie's scowl made even the combat veteran a little uncomfortable. "I'm well aware of that, Mr. Frederickson. I'm also positive that we aren't the only problem on his plate right now given the news feed we downloaded. But to expect a covert platform that's a stone's throw away from a hostile shore to remain exposed for the sake of convenience is beyond stupid! I don't care who it is! Either they stick to their damn schedule or they call us when it's time to come up. Having my boat sitting here with two masts dangling in the air is just begging to be detected!"

Harper looked at Frederickson and made a cutting motion with his hand to "knock it off." The engineer knew his captain was not in the mood to debate the merits of his perception about the shortsightedness of his superiors. The young SEAL nodded his understanding.

"Do you think the president will approve your request, Skipper?" asked Harper, as he pulled out a chair for Guthrie. He'd often seen Jerry Mitchell use a mission-related question to pull the captain back on track whenever he found him caught on a specific detail.

"I doubt it, Eng," Guthrie replied, as he plopped down in the seat. "The man has only been in office for four months, and he's still trying to get his feet under him. I don't think he feels comfortable enough to make that kind of decision yet. You also have to remember he came from academia, and people of that ilk are loath to make quick decisions without first thoroughly researching the issue. Particularly if it's a risky decision."

"My guys and I can still make the run, sir," asserted Frederickson confidently. "Especially now that we know what the indications are for a patrol boat that is leaving port."

"Thank God that the Iranians like to talk. Otherwise we would have searched and searched for a deployment pattern that wasn't there," said Simmons.

"The CTs did a great job figuring that mess out, Isaac. We need to make sure that they get a commendation for their outstanding work. Please write up a draft when this op is finished," Guthrie ordered.

"Yes, sir. I already have a rough draft in the works, and Travis here has graciously provided a few good words from the SEALs," Simmons responded.

The cryptologic technicians had stumbled across the radio traffic of an IRGC patrol boat as it departed the nearby base at Asaluych. After analyzing the sequence of events, they managed to isolate the signal that indicated when the patrol boat had changed course to the northwest and started its patrol run. A little elementary chart work showed they had about forty minutes before the BQQ-10 sonar would pick up the patrol boat, and another five before the patrol boat would pass within radar range of the proposed route the Zodiac would take to the beach and back. Testing this theory against the last two patrol boats, they found that they had between forty-two and forty-nine minutes after the key signal had been transmitted. Unfortunately, there was no set pattern to the departures.

The length of a patrol appeared to consist of an hour-and-a-half trip up the coast, followed by a quick turnaround, and a backtracking along a reciprocal course back to port. A well-disciplined schedule would have had a patrol boat departing every two hours, but in reality it varied by as much as half an hour, which made part of the mission planning a bit more complex. And the problem wasn't the run in.

A lightly loaded F470 Zodiac combat rubber raiding craft with a fifty-five-horsepower outboard motor can do about twenty-five knots, which meant the fifteen-nautical-mile trip to the beach could be done in about thirty-five minutes. No, the issue that had the planners chewing on their pencils was the return trip. Fully loaded with ten people, the Zodiac could only make twenty knots, which meant a forty-five-minute trip back to the sub. If a patrol boat were noted leaving port just as the Zodiac reached the shore, timing would be very tight on the way back. But even with this near worst-case scenario, the SEALs felt the odds were still substantially in their favor.

At first, Guthrie was uneasy during the brief back, but Frederickson made a compelling argument that this was their best shot. They still had the element of surprise working for them, and the irregularity of the Iranian patrol schedule meant they would probably have more time, rather than less. He then addressed the low-probability, but high-impact scenarios that would require the SEALs to either fight their way out or abandon the Zo-diac, which included the possibility that an Iranian patrol boat skipper might get lazy on them and not bother reporting in as he started his route, thus denying *Michigan* of their indicator. When the captain pressed Freder-ickson on just what was the worst-case scenario, the young SEAL responded immediately that an unexplained increase in the number of deployed patrol boats would be "highly detrimental to mission success."

Guthrie had then looked directly at Frederickson and asked, "And what is your recommended course of action for this situation, Lieutenant?"

"I'd recommend scrubbing the mission, sir," Frederickson replied with-out hesitation. Without another word, Guthrie had approved the plan.

Guthrie looked over at the auxiliary display, and the Iranian boat was moving away from them. "That's better," he mumbled to himself. He then checked the clock on the bulkhead; it now read 2130. Just as he was about to let loose with a sigh of frustration, the screen flickered to life.

"*Michigan*, this is the White House Situation Room. Are you still with us?"

Guthrie reached over and tapped the mute button, turning on the micro-phone. "This is *Michigan*. Yes, we are still here. For a while there I thought

I'd have to pull the plug and reposition, but the offending contact has moved on."

"My sincere apologies for the delay. The president has been in some rather intense discussion with the CNO and the national security advisor on your proposed plan. Please standby while I get the rest of the VTC participants up on the channel."

"Roger, standing by." Guthrie tapped the mute button again and turned toward his junior officers. "Okay, gentlemen, you are about to enter the stratosphere. The president, several cabinet-level officials, and more stars than a planetarium will be on this teleconference in a moment. Just stay calm, and keep your lips buttoned. If I need anything from you, I'll ask. Got it?"

The three men nodded as they watched more and more windows opening up on the screen. The main screen showed the president talking to the SECDEF and the CJCS. The smaller windows around the periphery held the conference rooms of two combatant commanders and their subordinate commanders. Just about everyone had a flag officer at the center of the window.

"Oh. My. God," whispered Harper, his eyes wide with awe.

"*Sssh*," Guthrie snapped.

The unseen speaker in Washington announced, "Mr. President, all commands are present and we are ready to begin."

"Good afternoon, everyone. I first want to thank you all for dropping everything and making this VTC. I didn't give you a lot of time, but the situation in Iran demanded we get together and discuss the proposed plan of action for the ASDS incident," opened Myles. "I also owe you an apology, Captain Guthrie, for keeping you waiting so long. Admiral Hughes here commented that submariners have an inherent loathing of remaining exposed for so long, and that you had probably removed all your fingernails by now." The admiral's grin clearly showed he was joking.

Guthrie tapped the mike button. "Well, I hate to disappoint the CNO, sir, but my fingernails are *mostly* intact. But I must also admit that I'm still trying to get used to the enhanced communications capability of my boat. I'm not accustomed to speaking directly to my commander in chief while submerged on station."

"You're being gracious, Captain, and I appreciate that. Now before we get started, would you please introduce the three young men with you?"

"Certainly, sir. To my immediate right is Lieutenant Commander Mike Harper, my engineer and acting executive officer." Guthrie watched as every senior naval officer suddenly looked confused. "To his right is Lieutenant Isaac Simmons, my navigation and operations officer. And to my left is Lieutenant Travis Frederickson, the SEAL detachment officer in charge."

"Thank you, Captain. Now to the business at . . . What?" Myles looked annoyed as Hughes leaned over and whispered a question. Guthrie only heard a few words, but he was pretty sure the CNO wanted to ask him the one question he didn't want to answer. When President Myles gave his consent, Hughes leaned toward the mike and said, "Captain, did I hear you correctly that your engineer is the acting executive officer?"

"That is correct, sir."

"Captain, where is your XO?"

Guthrie took a depth breath before replying. "He is currently not on board *Michigan*, Admiral. He was piloting the ASDS during the mission."

"What!?! Explain yourself, Captain," demanded Hughes. It was a good thing the mikes were muted in the conference rooms at SUBPAC, Sub Group Nine, and the Naval Special Warfare Command as each commanding rear admiral had the exact same reaction.

"My ASDS pilot was injured during a physical fitness exercise with the SEALs less than an hour before we got the message to head to the Persian Gulf. My orders had a very challenging, nonnegotiable schedule I had to meet, and I did not believe it was feasible for me to request a replacement while adhering to the stealth and speed requirements explicit in my orders.

"Lieutenant Commander Mitchell was well versed in ASDS operations, had some experience in piloting the minisub, and is also a qualified Navy diver. I felt he met the spirit behind the ASDS pilot qualifications, if not the exact letter. My only other alternative was to let the SEAL copilot take the ASDS in by himself—an option I deemed unsafe."

"This is most unusual, Captain," commented Rear Admiral Fabian, Commander, Submarine Forces U.S. Pacific Fleet. "Don't you think you overstepped your authority to make that decision?"

Joanna leaned over to Kirkpatrick, who was growing tense as the discussion dragged on. "Sir, I personally know Lieutenant Commander Mitchell. He's a very capable and skilled officer. He served on my husband's boat during the special operations mission directed by President Huber to investigate spent nuclear fuel dumping sites in Russia. I participated in that mission and . . ."

Kirkpatrick motioned for Patterson to stop. "Thank you, Joanna. You've already told me this." Chastened, Patterson sat back in her seat, while Kirkpatrick reined in the VTC.

"Admirals, please, there will be a time for you to get answers to your questions," injected Kirkpatrick patiently. "But it is not now. As I've already explained to your *superiors*, I am not the least interested in how or why the ASDS was lost, or in why *Michigan's* executive officer went on the mission. Our primary concern is how we get our people out of Iran, along with the defectors who have information that is critical to the president's response to this crisis.

"Besides, I have it on excellent authority that Lieutenant Commander Mitchell is a highly resourceful naval officer who has served this nation very well in the past. I think we should consider allowing him a modicum of trust that he will do likewise during this situation."

Guthrie watched and listened as the national security advisor immediately silenced the cadre of unhappy admirals. *I owe that man a beer*, he thought.

"Now then, Captain," Kirkpatrick went on. "Please tell us your plan to extract said individuals."

"Yes, sir," Guthrie replied. He then went into a simplified mission-planning sequence, highlighting what they had learned about Iranian small boat patrols and how they intended to use that information to maximize the probability of mission success. He pointed out the timing issue, and while tight in some scenarios, the SEALs were confident that this was the best opportunity they would have as the element of stealth had been preserved. Carefully, Guthrie then brought up the issue of distance and its impact should the situation not evolve as anticipated. He wrapped up his presentation with a description on how the SEALs and the others would be recovered by *Michigan*.

"As the Zodiac approaches our location, the rest of the SEAL detachment will egress through the dry deck shelter and swim up with scuba gear fitted with a second demand valve. Once over *Michigan*, the Zodiac will be abandoned and the occupants will swim down into the DDS and through the lockout chamber into the boat. Under normal circumstances, I would broach the boat and recover the personnel without having to resort to a shallow dive with untrained individuals. But the circumstances are far from normal, and the risk of detection by a patrol boat close to Iranian territorial waters is extremely high.

"As the Iranians, my XO, and the others are swimming down, Lieutenant Frederickson and one other SEAL will scuttle the Zodiac by puncturing several of the air chambers. Once everyone is in the DDS and the hatch is closed, we make best tactical speed for Bahrain. That concludes our proposed plan, Mr. President."

"Thank you, Captain. Your proposal is sound and I appreciate the detailed planning that went into it. Your plan is approved. I did note, however, your concern about the distance."

Guthrie had intentionally pushed the topic; he'd tried to be diplomatic, but he just didn't know if he had pushed too hard. He wasn't sure whether he would be given permission or a presidential ass chewing.

"Yes, sir. It is the key factor in our evaluation of mission success."

"Yes, I know, Captain. Both the CNO and my national security advisor have already beaten me about the head on this," said Myles, smiling slightly. The smile quickly evaporated as the president leaned forward, his expression becoming sterner.

"I realize that my restrictions are not popular, Captain Guthrie. I have also been forced to realize that they are overly conservative. I will allow you to approach the twelve-mile limit to deploy and then recover the occupants of the combat rubber raiding craft. Between these events you are to back away to fifteen miles. Under no circumstances are you to violate Iranian territorial waters. Will this compromise ease your concern a little, Captain?"

Guthrie quietly let his breath go. He'd gotten part of what he wanted, and it was a meaningful compromise.

"Absolutely, Mr. President. This will make a big difference, particularly with those potential scenarios where timing is a very critical issue. Thank you, sir." He looked toward Frederickson who was obviously pleased and gave him a thumbs-up under the table.

"Just get your people and the Iranians out of there, Captain. The information your passengers are carrying is quite likely the key we need to understand just what the hell is going on over there."

"We'll do our best not to disappoint you, sir," replied Guthrie, as he signed off. The chances of pulling this off just got a whole lot better.

4 April 2013
8:00 AM Local Time/0500 Zulu
Shiraz, Iran

Mehry Naseri was washing up in the kitchen when the phone rang. Irritated at the interruption, she quickly dried her hands and snatched it on the fourth ring.

"I am trying to reach Captain Akbari. This is Major Sadi, his supervisor."

"Oh, Major, I'm sorry, he's not here right now. He and Shirin left for the coast yesterday morning. I expect them back tomorrow tonight, but it will be late."

"Do you know where I can reach him, then?"

"They are staying at a hotel in Bandar Kangan. I have the number." She read it off the slip of paper Shirin had given her. "They may be hard to reach. Shirin said they were going to take several excursions in the area."

"I'll try to call him there, then. Thank you, Mrs. Naseri."

Administration Building, Natanz

Sadi hung up the phone carefully. Major Rahim, standing silently during the call, nodded approvingly. "Thank you Major, for your assistance."

Rahim left without another word, and Sadi felt the muscles in shoulders begin to relax. It was his policy to keep on VEVAK's good side, but having one of them ask a "favor" of him had been traumatic.

Back in Natanz's VEVAK office, Rahim told his assistant, "I need to speak to the VEVAK office in Shiraz."

9

THE HARD WAY

4 April 2013
0810 Local Time/0510 Zulu
Southeast of Bandar Kangan, North of Highway 96

The sound jarred Jerry out of a deep, intense dream. Whatever the dream had been about was blasted away by a raucous *Waah Waah Waah* that filled the small cave.

Several of the group, like Jerry, had been sound asleep, but as he sat up, he saw Ramey and Fazel already awake and almost running to the sleeping Iranian couple, also stirring. Before Yousef or Shirin could sit up, the SEALs tore off the blanket and quickly searched the two. Fazel answered angry, confused shouts from Yousef with firm, sharp words in Farsi.

On the fifth or sixth *Waah*, Ramey pulled a cell phone out of Yousef's pants pocket. Holding it as if it was a venomous insect, he studied it for a moment, then tugged at the bottom of the case. Removing the cover, he pulled out the battery, silencing the device.

Yousef spoke rapidly to Ramey, but the lieutenant cut him off with a gesture and ordered Fazel, "Tell him I'm going to have Pointy check this out to make sure it doesn't have any tracking device in it, and ask him if he or his wife have any more cell phones or pagers—anything that pushes electrons."

Ramey gave the phone and battery to Lapointe, adding, "And see who was trying to call him."

Jerry stood, still processing the event. Someone had tried to call Yousef Akbari. He hadn't answered, of course, but what did it mean for them? Fazel was speaking in soft but urgent tones with Shirin and Yousef. Ramey had taken the lookout post just outside the cave, and Jerry moved to join him.

"It's a good thing he didn't answer," Jerry remarked.

"He's not stupid," Ramey answered. After a moment, he added, "But he wasn't smart enough to turn it off."

Ramey seemed uneasy, and shifted his position several times, not to get comfortable, but to improve his field of view.

"You're trying to decide if we need to bug out."

"It's crossed my mind," Ramey answered casually. "A lot depends on what Harry and Pointy find out."

It took Fazel another few minutes to finish his conversation and join them. "He bought it in Isfahan about six months ago," Harry reported. "He's required to have one whenever he's off base, and thought it would be suspicious if he turned it off."

Jerry nodded. "It would have been."

Ramey wasn't as kind. "He should have told us about it. He's put us all at risk. If they can track it, then they know where he is, where we are," he reasoned.

"But this is where they're supposed to be—on vacation." Fazel answered.

"Let's hope they still think that he's on vacation." Jerry's mind filled with other possibilities, but it all depended on whether Yousef and Shirin's deception still held.

"Dr. Naseri also had a cell phone; she says she uses it to talk to her handler. The phone is registered in a fictitious name and they use the Skype function so they can't be traced. It was off when she showed it to me." Fazel handed the phone to Ramey.

Lapointe made his report next. "It's a commercial model, made in Germany. It's low-end, with no GPS capability, which made it simple to check out. As far as I can tell, it hasn't been modified. There's also no tracking device, but that doesn't mean they don't have the ability to localize an active cell phone. If you're looking for one specific phone, it can be linked to the closest tower, whether someone is talking on it or not.

"I put the phone under a couple of thermal blankets and slipped the battery back in just long enough to get a list of the most recent calls. It's only been used once in the past two days: the incoming call this morning. Here's the number."

He offered a slip of paper to Jerry, who gestured to Fazel. "Find out if he recognizes the number."

The medic took the paper and turned to go to Yousef, but the captain had come to join them, concerned, or even fearful. The corpsman gave him the paper and spoke briefly. Yousef's face drained of color. Fazel translated his answer.

"It's Major Sadi's number. He is my superior at Natanz. They are looking for me."

4 April 2013
0950 Local Time/0650 Zulu
Natanz, Iran

Rahim gave them two hours, but the Shiraz office called ten minutes short of his deadline. "Captain Akbari's automobile is parked at Mehry Naseri's house. It has not been driven since they left on the excursion. I posed as someone interested in buying the car, and while examining it, verified that the tracker was in place. She maintains that the owners will be back tomorrow evening, 'probably late,' in her words.

"She also said their Cowin had developed mechanical trouble, so the couple took her car on their trip. It's a light blue 2001 Peykan. The license plate is Shiraz 21S347. We have e-mailed you all the details."

Rahim copied the information. "What did she say about their plans?"

"She was happy to pass the time. According to her, they are staying at a hotel in Bandar Kangan, and plan to visit a park in the area, and go to the shore."

"Good work." It was a simple task, but Rahim believed in recognizing competence. "Find out what the mechanical problem was. Watch her closely, and compile a list of her contacts. Monitor all communications—personal visits, phone, whatever, regardless of who it is with. This is your highest priority. And send everything you've discovered to the Bushehr office."

"Yes, Major." Rahim had not told the agent why he wanted the information, or who Mehry Naseri was. Traitor or witness, it didn't matter. Officers in VEVAK did as they were told.

It was still a few minutes before ten, but Rahim didn't wait. They'd changed their car. That was suspicious. Yes, there was an innocent explanation, but he'd need some convincing before he bought that story. He cursed his own complacency for not checking the tracker's location. It would have shown they'd changed cars. They'd given no sign of knowing they were being watched.

The office in Bushehr was less helpful. "Computer records show nobody has checked into a hotel in Bandar Kangan or anywhere else along the coast under either name. We have dispatched an investigator to Kangan with photos to make inquiries. It's a two-hour drive, and we expect him to arrive—"

Rahim interrupted. "Enough. Send their pictures to the local police in Kangan and tell them to search for the couple, with haste. And have them look for the car." He told the Bushehr agent about the Peykan.

"Yes, Major."

"This matter is urgent. I want hourly reports."

"Yes, Major."

Rahim hung up impatiently. So, a young couple, off on an excursion. They tell her mother they're going one place, and then they go somewhere else. They could have changed their minds en route, or gotten to Kangan and decided to go elsewhere. It could happen.

Or they could have lied to her. But Rahim didn't think so. Naseri was arrogant and far too intelligent for her own good, but she was close to her family. And she had no reason to lie to her mother. So if there was a lie, it was meant to deceive others.

A trip to the coast was innocent enough, but Rahim didn't see the gulf as scenic. Its waters had been a highway for smugglers and spies since time began. Had they met with a foreign agent? Were they trying to defect?

He made another call, this time to the VEVAK liaison at the Mobile Communications Company of Iran.

"Electronics."

"This is Major Rahim. What is the status of Yousef Akbari?"

"One moment." Rahim could hear taps on a computer keyboard.

"Subject Akbari, Yousef, Pasdaran Captain."

"That is correct."

"The subject was nearest to tower 1709, at Bandar Kangan, until the signal stopped this morning at 0810."

"Stopped?"

"The most likely cause is the cell phone being turned off or the battery running low."

Rahim searched for an explanation. "Is there any possibility he simply moved out of range of a cell tower?"

"He was receiving a call when the phone went dead."

"Who was calling him?"

The operator read the number. "It's assigned to a telephone at the Natanz Facility, an office assigned to a Major Sadi." Anger flashed through Rahim, and he fought to control it. He wasn't finished with the phone call.

"Send me a map with the area that the tower covers."

"I'll send it right away, Major."

"And notify me instantly if his phone turns back on."

"Yes, sir."

With the connection broken, Rahim placed the receiver back in its cradle gently, exactly the opposite of what he wanted to do. Sadi had called Akbari on his cell phone ten minutes after he'd had Sadi call the mother's house.

Rahim tried to build scenarios and possible courses of action. What did Sadi know, or suspect? A cautious man considers . . .

Screw caution.

Sadi was out inspecting the light antiaircraft emplacements when Rahim found him. Each twin 23mm or 35mm gun was emplaced on an earthen mound to give it a better field of fire. On top of the mound, the gun was protected by a ring of sandbags, and a ramp led back to ground level, where there was stowage for ammunition and a dugout shelter for the crew.

Sadi's jeep was parked next to one of the emplacements. The gun crew was lined up next to their weapon, at attention. Sadi was talking to them, while the captain in charge of the light antiaircraft guns stood to one side, taking notes.

Rahim's driver roared up next to the mound, the noise making Sadi stop and turn. When he saw who sat in the back, he spoke a few words to his subordinate and trotted down the ramp.

Rahim got out and started walking away from the jeep and the gun emplacement. The gun line was spaced several hundred meters out from the facility, and the individual emplacements were also several hundred meters apart, separated by open, bare ground. He walked quickly, forcing Sadi to run to catch up. They were forty or fifty meters away when he finally slowed and turned to face Sadi.

Purple with rage, Rahim spat, "You called Akbari! What were you thinking? Explain yourself!"

Sadi, horrified, reflexively came to attention. He didn't speak immediately, and Rahim could see thoughts flow across his face as the major tried to decide what to say. "Answer me!" Rahim demanded.

The other man swallowed, and said softly, "I . . . I remembered that I had Captain Akbari's cell phone number. I thought that if you were trying to reach him, I should . . . tell him."

"You mean warn him." Rahim's voice was made of metal. "You moron, you mistake of God! Don't you think I have his cell phone number as well?"

"I'm sorry, I didn't understand." A pleading tone filled his words. "I only wanted to help you find Akbari."

"And by calling him, you've interfered in affairs greater than you can possibly imagine. Matters of life and death for many, including yours, are at stake."

Rahim could see that it had finally sunk in. "I'm sorry, sir," Sadi repeated. "What can I do?"

"Nothing." Rahim spat out the word. "Attempting to correct your mistake will only increase the scope of the catastrophe. Since it wasn't clear before, I will say it now. Do not speak of either call you made to Akbari, now or later. Do not speak of my interest in Akbari, or repeat anything I ever have or will say to you in the future."

"Yes, Major." Sadi's face was as pale as milk. His breath was a shallow rasp, and his entire body trembled.

"Don't ever involve yourself in my affairs again!" Rahim turned and walked off without waiting for an answer from the terrified officer. Reaching his jeep, he looked back to see Sadi still standing, unmoving, where he'd left him.

It would have given him great pleasure to arrest Sadi, to question him until he admitted to being the Twelfth Imam, then execute him for blasphemy. But arresting the major would have drawn attention to Akbari's actions, and possibly to other events in play.

It didn't really matter. Moradi's plan was moving forward. In a short while, Sadi would either be killed in the raid or executed for mounting an incompetent defense. He would make a convenient scapegoat.

Part of Rahim's anger was also directed inward. Again, he'd depended on technology. The cell phone tracking had been so reliable that he'd taken it for granted. Technology was useful, but it couldn't replace human intellect. Returning to his office, he told his deputy, "Get me a helicopter for a flight to Isfahan, and then a plane to Bushehr. As fast as you can."

4 April 2013
1200 Local Time/0900 Zulu
Southeast of Bandar Kangan, North of Highway 96

They'd tried sleeping to pass the time, and were still worn out. Jerry had dozed, but it wasn't restful. In fact, he felt restless and uncertain. He'd spent much of the morning going over the logic of the cell phone call. What if it had been an innocent call? But answering would have allowed VEVAK to track the signal. It was also possible that their location was known anyway. In which case, turning the phone off might tell the authorities something as well.

Jerry watched Ramey, and knew he was working through the same process, with the same results. By rights, the two senior officers should be sharing their thoughts and looking for other options, but the SEAL lieutenant's demeanor made Jerry reluctant to approach him.

There was little to do, and a lot of time to do it in. Jerry remembered times on *Michigan* when he would have leapt at a chance to sit quietly and let his thoughts roam. Now they raced ahead, urging his body to follow. He wasn't bored. There was too much at stake. But the best course was the one they were following—hunker down and wait out the day.

They'd shared a breakfast of MREs. The SEALs had expertly prepared theirs. Fazel had tried to explain the package's contents to Yousef and Shirin, but it had not gone well. Jerry could not understand Farsi, but he'd seen Yousef almost snatch the rations away from the medic, then gesture impatiently at Fazel's explanation.

Fazel's expression had darkened, and he'd spat out something that left both Yousef and Shirin frowning.

An argument wasn't going to help anybody. But as Jerry had started to stand, Lapointe was already next to Fazel. He had one arm around the medic, resting on his shoulder, and spoke softly. Fazel's posture sagged a little, and the two SEALs retreated to their own side of the cave, where Ramey joined them. All three looked solemn, and spoke to each other with quiet voices.

After a while he caught Lapointe's eye and the petty officer came over. He didn't wait for Jerry's question. "Harry's just pissed, XO. He's pissed about Higgs and about being cooped up here in this cave, and right now he's especially pissed about having to breathe the same air as the captain over there."

"We're all cooped up, Pointy."

"Remember what I said about sympathy, sir." Lapointe grinned.

Jerry nodded, smiling. "I get it, but what about Akbari? The guy's on our side."

"Harry told me he considers the captain a double traitor, first to the Iranian people, then to his own service."

"That's a little harsh."

"I've known Fazel for a long time, and I'd heard about him before that. He's obviously the perfect man for this mission, but it's tearing him up. He told us about his family back in Cincinnati. How his parents got out of Iran, and what they'd lost. His family really suffered, and they didn't hide this from their children. Coming here is making it all too real for him.

"He's got a lot of relatives up north, near Tehran. They try to keep in touch, but too much contact and the secret police will come for them, too. That Pasdaran officer over there is exactly what he's been taught to hate."

"What about you, Pointy? Does your job include referee?"

"Priest, counselor, and batting coach, as needed, XO. You know the drill. The problem is, we've got too much time to think right now."

Jerry wasn't sure how much Ramey had slept. He'd been on lookout when Jerry fell asleep last night, and had been awake already when Yousef's cell phone had rung.

Whatever his fatigue, Ramey was full of pent-up energy. Jerry watched the team leader check the cave's camouflage and lines of sight. Then he double-checked his gear and each team member's equipment, one after another. He'd even explored the cave itself, which took an unsatisfyingly short time.

Finally, he'd sat down facing Shirin and Yousef, who'd stayed huddled under the thermal blanket, in spite of the day's warmth. The two had spoken softly, perhaps planning, or praying, for all the Farsi that Jerry understood. As he approached, they watched him silently.

"Ma'am, I think you should give us the encryption key."

Shirin's expression hardened. "What reason could I have for giving it to you?"

"So that if anything happens to you and your husband, we can still get the information you have to our people."

She nodded. "And that is exactly why we will keep it. Without us, you have nothing."

"Ma'am, we're not going to leave you behind. I thought you wanted the world to know about Iran's nuclear weapons program. Telling us the key increases the chance of that happening."

"No." Her tone was as hard as her expression. "Why was the boat canceled last night? The one that would have taken us to your submarine."

"Too many boat patrols. It was too risky."

"If you had been more willing to take risks, we would be aboard your submarine right now, not hiding in a cave."

"Ma'am, we took risks on this mission you can hardly imagine. One of my men is dead because of the risks we took." He sighed, a sound that mixed sadness and frustration. "There are good risks and bad ones. You have to judge them carefully."

"My husband and I know all about risk, Mr. SEAL. We have been stealing and sending secret information to your government for years, while VEVAK watched every move we made. Every day, every hour, I worried if we had given ourselves away somehow, if they were coming to arrest us. Can you imagine being afraid of every knock on the door, every phone call?"

Her voice rose. "And do you know what we were risking? Being called traitors by the ones we love would be the easiest part. Have you ever heard of Evin Prison? Do you know what would happen to Yousef and me in that hateful place? Yousef's brother was taken there and never came out. I have prayed that he died quickly. What a terrible thing to pray for."

"We'll get out of here, and I give you my word that we'll all get out together."

"But it isn't your decision, Mr. SEAL. Others have to take risks. They must want to come and get us. Us." She pointed to Yousef and herself. "Not the files. I have the baby to consider. And there are other things we know, not in the files, even more important."

"You've mentioned that before. What things?"

"Get us to your submarine, let them read the files. Then they will listen to us."

"I'm listening now."

"No. "

4 April 2013
1500 Local Time/1200 Zulu
Bandar Kangan

The helicopter from Bushehr landed at an athletic field near the edge of town. They were waiting to meet him. A police jeep in one corner headed toward his aircraft as soon as the engines spooled down.

A young man in civilian clothes hurried over as the helicopter's door opened. "Major? I'm Karim Dahghan, from the Bushehr office."

Rahim stepped from the helicopter and walked quickly toward the jeep. "You will be my assistant while I'm here."

"Yes, sir." Dahghan managed to look pleased and worried at the same time. As they approached the jeep, a young officer in a police uniform saluted.

"This is Lieutenant Rastkar. He commands Kangan's police."

Rastkar, standing next to the jeep, offered his hand. "We've made space for you and Mr. Dahghan at the barracks."

Rahim climbed in back, with Dahghan next to him. Rastkar sat in front, next to the police driver, and said, "Go."

Turning in his seat to face Rahim, he explained, "Kangan is a small town. We will be at headquarters in just a few minutes. We have already made progress. The couple you asked about was seen in several places yesterday."

Dahghan continued, "We found the hotel they were staying at, registered for two nights. They used the name 'Fardid.' They did not return to their room last night. The last sighting we have of them is in the early evening. We are still assembling a time line of their movements."

Kangan really was a small town, little more than a fishing village. The police barracks was a jumbled one-story structure that had seen several additions, but was in need of renovation. The barracks was full of activity, and Rastkar explained, "Normally we deal with a little smuggling, some domestic cases. A manhunt is much more interesting."

The space they'd set aside for Rahim and Dahghan was clean, if run-down. Several documents were waiting on one corner of a desk, and Rahim set down his valise and quickly skimmed them. The others waited patiently.

"Their car was seen outside town." It was a flat statement to Dahghan.

"Yes, sir. We interviewed the two Basij soldiers who found the vehicle. It was parked just off Highway 96. It was locked, with nobody in the vehicle or nearby. There was nothing suspicious, so they noted the license plate and continued their patrol. When they returned on the next leg of their patrol, an hour later, the vehicle was gone."

"And this was in the early evening, yesterday."

"A short time after sunset, Major."

Rahim sat down, looking thoughtful. Rastkar asked, "May I know what offense these people have committed? My officers have asked if they may be violent, or armed."

The major answered, "Their specific offense is not your concern. Akbari is a Pasdaran officer, and most likely is armed. Our first priority is to find them. Once we do, it is important that they be taken alive. There are many questions I want to ask them. Your officers must not shoot them, no matter the provocation."

"Yes, sir." Rastkar didn't look pleased, but he knew where Rahim's authority came from.

"I am concerned that these people may have contacted foreign agents. They may be meeting one, or may have met one last night. It doesn't matter if that foreigner is still with them, or if they have exchanged items or information. Whatever has happened, our first priority is to find them. Everything else will follow from that.

"Lieutenant Rastkar, were any boats out last night? Did you make any arrests near the water? Any unusual reports?"

"I'll find out, sir."

"Contact the local Basij commander. I want the two men who found the car to guide some of your officers to the exact spot they saw it. Search the area for any trace of activity. Move quickly. You only have a short time before sunset."

"Yes, sir."

"Also, tell the commander that I want to see him immediately," Rahim added. "I have other work for them. Go." Rastkar left quickly.

"Dahghan, search the hotel room. You know what to look for."

The agent nodded.

"How are your relations with the police? Their commander?"

"They have been very helpful, Major. I have no complaints."

"Good. Then go over the police reports on their movements. It's possible that someone here in Kangan was the agent they were supposed to meet. Or they may have left something in a dead drop somewhere along their route. Follow their path and investigate anyone or any place you think is worthwhile."

The agent nodded again, taking notes.

"And take one of the police officials along with you. He may see something that you wouldn't know is unusual, and I don't want you getting lost. Time is critical. The faster we work, the closer they'll be."

A large map of Kangan covered one wall. "Where is the cell phone tower? I assume there's only one."

Dahghan had to ask a police sergeant, who came in and marked a spot near the center of town.

"Akbari was within thirteen kilometers of this point when his phone went dead at 0810 hours this morning. Since their car was found east of town, along the highway, we can begin our search in the eastern half of that circle."

A police sergeant knocked. "Sir, the Basij commander is here."

Dahghan opened the door and stood back. A small man wearing a black turban and a brown, sleeveless cloak over his white robe waited for a moment, then came in, smiling. He was only a little older then Rahim, but his white beard gave him an air of great dignity. The black turban marked him as a descendant of Mohammed.

Rahim stood.

"I am Mullah Hamid Dashani, leader of the mosque and commander of the Kangan Brigade of the Basij."

"Thank you for coming, Mullah Dashani. I am Major Rahim, from the Ministry of Intelligence and National Security." Shaking the cleric's hand, Rahim bowed his head slightly, and motioned to the chair on the other side of the desk.

Sitting, Dashani smiled broadly. "You have created quite a stir, Major.

My Basij are at your service. In fact, they are already mustering, in advance of your orders. I think we may even have a few new volunteers."

Rahim sighed. "I had hoped to investigate this matter quietly."

"This is a small town, Major. Word spreads like lightning. A helicopter? A missing Pasdaran officer? I saw the pictures of the couple when Dahghan questioned my two men from last night. Are they mixed up with smugglers? Murderers? Or are they spies?" The cleric was still smiling.

"Please, Mullah Dashani. I cannot tell you any details, for obvious reasons, but I need your help."

The major's manner became more serious. "And please, no more speculation. I need checkpoints set up along the coastal highway and other major roads, as well as an increase in the number of patrols along the coast highway. I will also need, dedicated teams walking all the beaches north and south of the city. They should look for signs of a recent landing, or boats in unusual places. All foreigners must be stopped and questioned."

"We could give you several checkpoints, each manned by four men. And four-man patrols walking the beaches. And we can ask the police for more vehicles."

The cleric paused, and Rahim could see him calculating. "Normally we have just one patrol on the beaches, and another on the highway. We can do what you ask for a short while, but my brigade can only muster about fifty fighters. Many of them will have to miss work while we are mobilized. Should I ask some of the other brigade commanders for assistance?"

"No, please do not. It should only be for a few days. And tell your fighters that they are not to speak of this matter."

Dashani nodded knowingly. "I understand."

"And we need to increase the number of boat patrols, with some in close to shore, and others farther out."

"This can be done. I am on very good terms with the Pasdaran naval commander here. I will coordinate closely with him."

"If your men do find this couple, they should apprehend them, but it's important that they be taken alive. Can they do this?"

"Of course. My boys are energetic. What they lack in skill, they make up in devotion."

"There will be no pitched battles, I promise."

They arranged the locations of the checkpoints and communications procedures, and the mullah left, excited and eager to "send his fighters into action."

4 April 2013
1700 Local Time/1400 Zulu
USS *Michigan*, Battle Management Center

Captain Guthrie had been expecting to get a final brief on the rescue mission, but the plan was to wait until sunset to make a go/no go decision.

Instead, Frederickson had summoned him early, and he hadn't sounded happy.

"We started to hear increased traffic on the naval circuits earlier today. It took some time to find out if they were reacting to something specific, but there hasn't been any mention of a specific contact or an intercept." Frederickson sighed. "But boat patrols have stepped up their coverage by over fifty percent."

"Any pattern?"

"Yes, sir. But it's not one we can exploit. There are too many boats out there now."

"What if we shorten the run—say, close to six nautical miles?"

Frederickson fought to hide his surprise. "And disobey a direct presidential order?"

"It's merely a *hypothetical* question, Mr. Frederickson," remarked Guthrie quietly.

"Oh, well, in that case—it wouldn't help, sir. There are way too many patrol boats. Besides, that isn't our only problem."

He gestured to an operator, who called up images on the briefing screen. "This is why I called you. This is the beach where the rendezvous took place."

The UAV image showed the now-familiar beach, but Guthrie saw men in a ragged line, slowly walking over the landscape. "They're searching for something," he said.

Frederickson smiled grimly. "I don't think they're looking for seashells."

"This is seriously not good. Why that beach?" Guthrie asked, but the answer was obvious. "Correction— Is there any way that this is *not* connected to our people?"

The SEAL lieutenant frowned. "There has been no activity in that area since our people left last night."

"Other areas?"

"Nothing that we've seen, yet. They drove up in a couple of vehicles and began systematically searching the beach. We've got traffic on the road, people moving near structures, but this is the only organized activity near the shore within the UAV's field of view."

"Well, whoever they are, it's obvious we can't execute the pickup on that beach, or the secondary one down the coast."

"They can't stay there forever. My bet is that they'll leave when they've finished their search, sunset at the latest. It's really hard to search in the dark."

"That's not the real issue." Guthrie countered. "Why are they there? Are the Iranians looking for our people? If so, how much do they know? How hard will they look?"

"Increased boat patrols, search parties?" Frederickson asked. "Less than a day after our guys landed on that beach? There is no other logical conclusion. The Iranians are looking for our people."

"Then can we afford to have them sit tight? How safe is their hiding place?"

"Matt Ramey's good, Skipper. I've walked within a few meters of his position and I didn't spot him. But hiding's what you do while you're waiting for something to happen. If we can't go in to get them, then hiding's not the right thing to do."

"We need a new plan," Guthrie concluded.

"We're improvising at this point, Skipper, but we'll work up something."

"I know a few things about staying covert myself. This is just like submarine warfare, but on land. The enemy has a datum, and they're searching. The tactic is to clear datum quickly and quietly. Don't let them get a better whiff of you, and get outside their search radius."

Frederickson nodded. "Understood. Give me fifteen minutes with the rest of the platoon."

4 April 2013
1745 Local Time/1445 Zulu
Southeast of Bandar Kangan, North of Highway 96

The call came early. They weren't supposed to make a go/no-go decision until after sunset, and that wasn't for another half hour. Jerry knew it had to be trouble. He took the handset from Lapointe.

It was Guthrie. "XO, we have to scrub the recovery mission. There are people carefully searching your beach, and the boat patrols have increased this afternoon. *Dramatically* increased. We can't get a CRRC in to you, and even if we could, they'll probably be waiting for us at the rendezvous site."

Jerry's heart sank. Automatically, he answered, "Understood, sir. Do you have a recommendation?"

"Get out of there. Head northwest to Bushehr and find a boat. It's Frederickson's recommendation and I agree. Put Lieutenant Ramey on and I'll give him the details."

Jerry had turned the handset so that Ramey and Lapointe, both now close by, could hear. The others had seen his face and heard his tone. He passed the handset to Ramey and said to the rest, "The recovery mission's scrubbed. They're looking for us."

Shirin gasped and spoke quickly to her husband. His shocked expression matched hers, and they tried to ask questions, but Phillips and Fazel both motioned for silence while the lieutenant quickly made notes. He signed off, almost matter-of-factly.

"Mr. SEAL, Jerry said they were looking for us. Is it true?" Fear was wrapped around Shirin's question.

Ramey nodded. "This afternoon, more patrol boats came out, and there's a search party working the beach where we met. Only an idiot would think otherwise."

He let that sink in, then said, "They won't find anything, but they will expand their search tomorrow. It's what I'd do. I'd also watch that beach. That plan is gone. We'll head toward Bushehr and find a boat."

"Bushehr is over a hundred kilometers from here," she protested.

"Almost one eighty, according to the map. We'll cut north, away from the water for a while, then overland until we can find transport. For the moment, we walk."

"Stay off the roads?" Shirin asked.

"They've seen the car. They have its license number, and they'll be watching the highway. We'd never make it past the first roadblock. We'll have to steal something once we're past Kangan."

Yousef spoke softly but urgently to Shirin. She replied, and the conversation almost became an argument. Fazel listened, but did not translate. Finally, she seemed to remember that he could understand them, and spoke in English. "It might be better if we went to Bandar Charak. My uncle lives there. If we get to him, he will help us."

"How trustworthy is your uncle?" Jerry asked.

"He is the one who passed my information on to the Americans. He's opposed the government since the Revolution, and is a member of the Mujahedeen-e-Khalq, in your language the People's Mujahedeen Organization of Iran. My uncle was going to send us out with a smuggler, but something went wrong. Then he arranged this meeting with you."

"Which hasn't worked out so well, either," Ramey finished. He folded a map. "Bandar Charak is half again as far, in the other direction, and it's near some medium-sized Pasdaran bases, but on the other hand Bushehr has the largest naval base in this part of the gulf . . . and it's always good to know somebody in a strange town." Ramey went silent as he weighed the possible enemy forces and the terrain, choosing their destination.

"All right, we head southeast. Pointy, call our friends back and tell them there's been a change in destination. We'll need a new route. Philly, this is as good a place as any to bury the swim gear. Doc, put dinner together. We should eat before we start out. We are gone at last light."

"One other thing," Ramey added. "The twenty-four-hour weather report has a storm coming in from the northwest sometime tomorrow morning. The forecast called it 'a typical spring shamal pattern.'"

Yousef understood the word, and spoke urgently. Jerry didn't. "A shamal?" he asked.

"Sandstorm," Fazel explained. He nodded toward Yousef. "The captain thinks we should wait here until it passes." The corpsman's tone was full of contempt.

"They can't search in a sandstorm," Jerry reasoned.

10

COLD, WET, AND SANDY

4 April 2013
1900 Local Time/1600 Zulu
Southeast of Bandar Kangan, North of Highway 96

Ramey, Lapointe, and Phillips dug like rabid badgers. With the scrubbing of the second CRRC mission, the SEALs had to dig a hole big enough to bury all their scuba gear; and there was a lot of it. Jerry initially tried to help while Fazel stood guard, but he soon found himself more of a hindrance, getting in the way of the three human backhoes.

"I still can't believe that idiot had his cell phone on," grumbled Ramey, as his spade bit into the sand. "They gotta have a good idea of where we are by now."

"Not necessarily, Matt," added Lapointe. "All they'll get is the tower his phone was linked into. That could be five to eight miles away. That's a lot of territory to cover, and a fair chunk of it is rugged terrain. They'll search the easy stuff first."

"Pointy's right, Boss," Phillips chimed in. "Kangan probably only has one cell phone tower, but once they match that with the Basij report on the car, they'll be all over this place like a swarm of bees."

"Which means we need to get the hell out of Dodge, and soon," concluded Ramey, throwing his shovel on the cave floor. "This will have to do. Grab the gear, tanks first, Philly."

Phillips and Lapointe leapt out of the four-foot-square, three-foot-deep hole and started handing Ramey the air tanks, followed by the fins, masks, rubber hoods, and gloves.

"Hand me the garbage, too, while you're at it," said Ramey. Phillips tossed him the two bags with the remains of the MRE pouches. "Is that everything?"

"Yes, sir, I made two sweeps of the cave."

"Good," Ramey replied, as he jumped out of the hole and picked up his shovel.

"Start filling, guys. XO, you can lend a hand here, too, if you don't mind."

"Certainly," responded Jerry, as he joined the other three men throwing dirt into the hole. Ramey was still tense, but his overall demeanor seemed to have improved, at least Jerry thought so. He couldn't tell if the platoon leader was actually dealing quietly with his grief, or merely keeping it in check, storing it up for release later.

After fifteen minutes of shoveling and stomping, the hole was filled and the remaining sand kicked around the cave. A quick glance by an untrained eye would not see anything amiss. But if a professional did a thorough inspection, the soft spot in the ground would be quickly discovered. And while the SEALs were hoping the distance from the cave to the car would be enough to prevent the discovery of their equipment, burying it was a little extra insurance.

"Okay everyone, huddle around for a planning session," Ramey announced, as he put on his battle gear. Motioning Phillips toward the cave entrance he added, "Philly, take the watch. I need Doc's linguistic skills for this. And keep a sharp eye out on that road." Phillips nodded his head as he grabbed his weapon and went outside.

"I can translate for my husband," protested Shirin.

"I'm sure you can, ma'am. But we can't afford any misunderstandings. Doc here will only assist when necessary to make sure Mr. Akbari has a clear picture of what we are trying to do," responded Ramey coldly. Yousef was not happy with the lieutenant's tone, and he clearly heard and understood the word "mister"—as opposed to rank—that Ramey used before his name.

Ramey unfolded his map and placed it on the ground. Shining his flashlight on to the map, he pointed to their location. "We are here, in these foothills approximately ten klicks from Bandar Kangan. Our destination is way the hell down here, just shy of two hundred and thirty-five kilometers to the southeast." His finger swept down the coastline until he tapped the map at Bandar Charak.

"Given our untenable position, we have to start this trek on foot. My intention is to use this dirt road as our evasion and escape route. It parallels Highway 96 and is roughly graded and fairly flat, which will make it easier for us to maintain a reasonable pace. The closest we get to the highway is three hundred meters, and the farthest is one-and-a-half klicks, so we'll have a good field of view to watch out for anyone coming from the highway. There is good ground to the northeast, with plenty of hills and shallow ravines, so we have excellent cover in case anyone does go off road. My goal is to make Akhtar by 0400, forty-five minutes before twilight begins. There are some hills to the west where we can hide out until later in the evening. Hopefully, we can find a small van there that we can requisition." Ramey paused as Shirin relayed the plan to Yousef. A frown quickly formed on his face.

"Matt, I'm not all that great with land navigation. What kind of distance are we talking about here?" asked Jerry, noticing Akbari's reaction.

"Almost fifteen kilometers, XO."

"That's a bit of a hike, don't you think?"

"In eight hours? That should be very doable. I specifically chose a route to accommodate Dr. Naseri's condition."

Yousef leaned over and asked Shirin a question. "My husband wants to know what we should do about the car? A Basij patrol has seen it."

Ramey nodded. "I was just about to get to that. On our way down to the road, we will stop and remove the license plates and then damage the car so that it looks like it has been vandalized. We can't use it without drawing a lot of attention, and one of the patrols will eventually find it. By removing the identifying plates and damaging it, it will take the Basij and police longer to figure out that the car is yours. They'll work it out sooner or later, but the longer it takes them, the better it is for us. Are there any other questions?"

"What about the weather, Matt? What do we do if we are out in the open and a shamal hits?" Jerry rarely trusted the accuracy of weather forecasts, and the worst possible time for a storm to hit would be while they were out navigating an unknown route in the dark.

"If the storm hits before we reach Akhtar, we'll shift to a column formation and everyone will be tied together with a line. We'll then seek immediate shelter. Anything else?" No one spoke.

Ramey stood up and tucked his weapon under his right arm. "Okay people, diamond formation just like before. Pointy on point, Doc has the backdoor. We move quickly, we move quietly. Let's go."

"Hooyah!" responded the SEALs. Shirin and Yousef looked on with confusion, while Jerry felt even more alone.

As they filed out of the cave, Phillips bumped up against Jerry. "Good question, XO. You're starting to think like a SEAL."

"God forbid," Jerry replied with a slight smile. "I prefer my own brand of insanity."

Phillips shrugged his shoulders as Ramey slashed a "knife hand" across his throat, motioning for them to knock it off. Idle chatter would not be tolerated.

Once out of the cave, Jerry and the Iranians were placed in the center of a loose diamond. Lapointe and Fazel were already scanning the horizon with their night-vision sights. After they reported "All clear," Ramey whispered over the radio circuit, "Forward."

If climbing up the hill in the dark was bad, going back down was worse. The loose rock and sand made finding good footing treacherous. Shirin slipped several times during the early phase of the descent. She just couldn't keep her balance.

"XO," Ramey's voice came softly over the radio. "Get in front of Dr. Naseri."

Jerry did so, while Ramey motioned for Yousef to grasp his wife's waist. Ramey then grabbed Shirin's right arm and placed her hand on Jerry's shoulder. The stability Shirin gained from the two men made the remaining trek down the hill smoother, but it slowed things down. Half an hour later, they had reached the car.

Lapointe and Phillips took watch positions on the crest. They were still a few kilometers from the highway; there were no signs of any Basij patrols. The lights of Bandar Kangan could be seen glowing on the horizon. The sky was overcast, with only a slight breeze coming from the sea.

"No signs of any patrols," reported Lapointe. "We're good, Boss."

"Roger that, Pointy. You and Philly keep a sharp eye. Things are going to get a little noisy in a minute."

Ramey asked Yousef for the keys. He unlocked the door and quickly put the vehicle in neutral. "XO, Doc, push the car forward a little."

Jerry and Fazel started pushing, but the car was sitting in some soft sand and it resisted their efforts. Yousef came over and the three were able to get the car moving. After about four feet, Ramey said, "Whoa. Good enough. Doc, get the rear license plate."

The two SEALs quickly removed the identifying plates and Ramey stored them in his backpack. He then opened the glove compartment and carelessly threw the contents on to the front seat and the floor. He found nothing of particular value, but saved what looked like official documents for Fazel to inspect.

Ramey tossed the keys to Fazel and said, "Doc, force the trunk open. Make it look sloppy."

The corpsman took the keys and opened the trunk. He found the tire iron, closed the trunk, and then proceeded to pry and bend open the lock. The creaking and screech of torn metal seemed particularly loud. Placing the tire iron back in the trunk, Fazel rifled through and shifted the contents all around. He threw some on the ground as well.

"Sprinkle some sand in the trunk, Doc. Not too much though."

As Fazel worked on the trunk, Ramey slashed the seats and tore them open. He then found the identification plate on the door and began rubbing it with a handful of sand. A brief inspection by flashlight showed that the vehicle identification number was badly scratched, with parts of the number unreadable, but not totally eliminated. Checking the doors, he made sure they were all unlocked.

"Done here, Boss," called Fazel.

"Okay, Doc. Take a quick look at these documents and make sure there are no names or addresses. Then have everyone back off. Stand by for some noise," he announced. With that Ramey took his rifle, and using the butt, completely smashed all the windows. Shirin jumped at the sound of crushed glass. Jerry winced with each strike, convinced that the noise would be noticeable down on the highway. He glanced over at Yousef who looked on approvingly. He took that as a good sign.

After Ramey had thrown some sand inside the car, he stepped back and declared with satisfaction, "There. The car looks sufficiently vandalized."

"We're still good, sir. Nothing is moving out there," spoke Lapointe without prompting. Phillips also reported that all was clear.

"Awesome," Ramey replied. "Diamond formation. Positions as before. We'll follow this path down to the road. It's one and a half klicks to the south-southeast. Maintain a careful sweep of your sectors, just in case someone did hear all that noise. Everyone be quiet. No talking unless the tactical situation requires it. Form up."

Lapointe and Phillips scampered down the small hill and took their positions. Once Ramey was satisfied everyone was in his or her proper place, he ordered, "Forward."

Slowly, the group began their long trek down the Iranian coast.

Ramey was true to his word. The dirt road he chose was more or less level, firm, and free of big rocks and other obstructing debris. The soft crunching of boots on the sand was the only sound made by the party, interrupted by the occasional truck that passed by on the highway less than a kilometer to the south. Jerry initially thought they were doing pretty well pacewise, but after a couple of hours, Shirin started slowing noticeably. Yousef tapped Jerry on the shoulder and gestured that she had to rest. Jerry relayed the request to Ramey who sighed audibly. "Hold," he commanded over the radio. Phillips directed Yousef and Shirin to rest behind a small ridge; Fazel came up to check on Shirin. He gave Yousef a bottle of water and instructed her to drink as much as she could.

Ten minutes later, they were on the march again. But this time, Shirin barely walked for an hour before she had to stop and rest. Frustrated, Ramey called Jerry and Fazel over to discuss the situation.

"We've got to pick up the pace if we are going to reach Akhtar before first light," complained Ramey impatiently. "We can't keep stopping like this."

Before Jerry could respond, Fazel spoke up. There was an edge to his voice. "Boss, the lady is on the small side to begin with, she doesn't have a whole lot of muscle mass, and she's almost five months pregnant! She's not barfing her guts out, but fatigue is still a major issue at this stage of her pregnancy. She's moving about as fast as she can."

"Honestly, Matt, I think we need to reevaluate our goal for tonight," suggested Jerry.

"Ya think?" Ramey snapped. "Thank you, Captain Obvious!"

Jerry didn't even bother to reply to Ramey's angry outburst; he just looked at him sternly. Fazel's expression showed he disapproved of the lieutenant's behavior as well. Ramey rubbed his neck and huffed, trying to get his emotions back in check.

"All right, Doc. Do what you can. I'll look for a place for us to bed down that's closer."

"Hooyah," replied the corpsman as he went over to check on Shirin.

Ramey pulled out his map, placed it on the ground, and shined a small red light on it. He found Bandar Charak and started working backward.

Jerry said, "Matt, I'd like to talk with Dr. Naseri for a moment." Ramey's expression made it clear he wasn't pleased with the idea.

"Look, they don't trust us, and for good reason from their perspective. She's given us a peek into the treasure trove of information she's carrying, but she's holding something back, something big. We need to understand why they are so damn eager to prove their worth to us."

"I already asked her, XO. She said 'no.' She either doesn't think we would believe them, or they're still scared we'll take the data and run. She was emphatic that we had to see the value of the data they had, before we would accept whatever they are holding so damn close to the chest," responded Ramey impatiently.

"All the more reason for us to find a way to break the ice. Five minutes, and I'll keep it down."

Ramey sighed deeply, and after a short pause, nodded his reluctant approval for Jerry to go have his talk.

Jerry walked over and sat beside Shirin. Even in the dim light he could see she was exhausted. "We're looking for a closer place to stay. There is no way you can make it to Akhtar."

She looked confused, and then glanced in Ramey's direction.

"It's okay. I got his approval for us to talk. Just keep it down; whisper."

Naseri smiled. "Thank you. I'm sorry that I am slowing you all down."

"Can't be helped. You're not exactly in the best shape for a long distance hike."

"We didn't plan on having a baby just now. But Allah's will has gently pushed us down this path. Do you have any children, Mr. Jerry?"

"No, no, I don't have any children. We aren't quite ready for that yet."

"You are married though?"

"Yes, Dr. Naseri. My wife is a university professor, a teacher."

Shirin nodded as she took another drink. "Dr. Fazel is insistent that I drink much water."

Jerry chuckled softly. "Petty Officer Fazel is not a medical doctor." Naseri looked confused again. "He's a hospital corpsman, more like a nurse. Although, I think he'd be mad if he heard me calling him a nurse. The title 'Doc' is a nickname. A friendly title given to a person, usually associated with one's occupation."

"Ahh, I understand," said Naseri. "My mother told me that my father was called an 'Ali-Cat' because he was a pilot."

Jerry's expression changed instantly, becoming more intense. "Your father was a Tomcat pilot?"

Shirin seemed embarrassed, and looked away from Jerry. Yousef saw her reaction and spoke in Farsi. She put her hand on his arm and put him at ease.

"Yes, Mr. Jerry. My father was a fighter pilot in the Imperial Iranian Air Force."

Jerry's broad smile had a soothing affect. "I've read a lot about the bravery of Iranian fighter pilots, and F-14 pilots in particular. I was once a fighter pilot myself, but I had an accident that forced me down another path. Did your father fight in the war?"

Shirin's eyes began to water, and she choked as she spoke. "They imprisoned him after the Revolution. He was too Westernized for their liking. The Pasdaran beat him. But after the Iraqis attacked us, they let him go. And despite all that they had done to him, he flew to defend Iran from Saddam Hussein." Tears were now falling from her eyes as she wept softly. Ramey looked over at Jerry, wondering what the hell was going on. Jerry waved him off.

"He died on the eighth of October, 1986, defending Khark Island from an Iraqi raid. An Iraqi Mirage shot down his plane, his body was never found. I . . . I was less than a year old when he died. He had so very little time with me as a baby. This is all that I have to remember him." She reached into her pocket and pulled out a piece of folded green material and handed it to Jerry.

It was a piece of a flight suit, with an F-14 Felix the Cat patch, showing a gray cat decked out in Persian garb, complete with slippers and a scimitar. The words "Ali-Cat" on the lower border were in bold, italicized letters. Jerry held it as if it were made of pure gold.

"I'm sorry," he said sympathetically, as he handed the precious memento back. "I didn't mean to bring back sad memories."

"No . . . no, you do not understand. That is why I have been a spy for you. The leaders of the Revolution are leading us back to war. A war that will cause the deaths of many tens of thousands." Her hands started to gently rub her abdomen. "I want my son or daughter to know their father. I want him to have time to cherish his child. The war that is coming threatens us all."

Jerry saw his chance to ask her to be more specific, but before he could speak, Ramey's voice popped on the radio. "Okay, people, time to get moving again. Form up."

Annoyed, Jerry got up and started walking toward the young SEAL when suddenly, Phillips exclaimed, "Ooh snap! Boss, look to the northwest."

Ramey and Jerry both looked up and saw the flashes over the horizon. A storm, a big storm, was coming straight at them from off the Persian Gulf.

"That don't look good," Jerry said dryly.

"Nope, XO. It don't look good at all."

4 April 2013
1200 Local Time/1700 Zulu
White House Situation Room

General Duvall rose swiftly as Joanna and her boss entered the briefing room. "Dr. Kirkpatrick, Dr. Patterson, thank you for making time to meet with us. This is Mr. Gene Cooper, the head of the Weapons Intelligence, Nonproliferation, and Arms Control Center at CIA."

"It was no inconvenience at all, Gordon. Truly. Please, sit down. I presume this has something to do with the file that *Michigan* sent us yesterday?"

"Yes, sir. But I'll let Gene explain," said Duvall, as he motioned for Cooper to start.

"Dr. Kirkpatrick, we've been going over the technical details in the Natanz centrifuge accident brief sent by *Michigan*, and we're convinced that it's accurate; it matches what little we have from COMINT and imagery. The file also provided a lot of background material behind the accident that makes a great deal of sense."

Kirkpatrick raised his hand, stopping Copper. "When you say 'we,' who is the 'we' specifically, Mr. Cooper?"

"Sir," interrupted Duvall. "The analytical work was done by an intelligence community working group that I had formed back in March. They work for me. I picked Gene to lead the effort."

"Ahh, I see. Thank you, Gordon. It's not that I don't trust the CIA. I'm just leery of single agency positions. I trust the results of this analytical effort reflect an intelligence community consensus?"

"Unanimously, Dr. Kirkpatrick," Cooper stated firmly.

"Go on."

"The bottom line, sir, is we believe, with high confidence, that the uranium enrichment program has suffered yet another technical setback. In February, a prototype fifth-generation centrifuge cascade blew itself apart when some of the centrifuge rotors started delaminating while spinning at high speed. The root cause was assessed by the Iranians to be a manufacturing flaw, probably during the curing process of the carbon fiber rotors."

"February, you say?" Patterson observed. "Mr. Cooper, can you correlate this Iranian briefing with the recent IAEA report?"

Cooper smiled broadly. "Yes, Dr. Patterson. Here is an imagery shot of the Pilot Fuel Enrichment Plant at Natanz taken on the third of February. Note this empty area behind this building to the west. Now, the same location three weeks later; see the pile of debris? This imagery is from 10 March; as you can see, the debris is still there. But by 13 March, two days after the inspection, the area is clean as a whistle. We have good information that these are the same centrifuges the IAEA took their samples from."

Patterson looked closely at the series of pictures, before handing them to Kirkpatrick. "You said a prototype cascade. How many machines?"

"Sixty-four, ma'am."

"Were they being fed uranium hexafluoride?"

"Yes, Dr. Patterson. The initial feed was at three percent enrichment," answered Cooper.

"How long had they been operating?"

"A little over six days."

"Six days? That's all?" pressed Patterson, surprised.

"Yes, ma'am. The centrifuges were working on their seventh day when the accident occurred."

She turned to Kirkpatrick. "Sir, there is no way they could have achieved an eighty-five percent enrichment with so few machines over such a short period of time."

Kirkpatrick's brow scrunched as he evaluated the data. "Gordon, is there a chance we're being deceived by the information provided by Opal?"

"Dr. Kirkpatrick, it is my belief that we are being deceived, but not by Opal. The data has been vetted through multiple groups, each looking at the information from a different angle. It's been 'Red Teamed' and dissected by technical experts. Opal's data appears to be accurate and authentic. The uranium enrichment path is almost certainly not going to provide the Iranians with the necessary material for a test device any time soon."

"What about the plutonium path then?" countered Kirkpatrick.

"It's nowhere near ready, either, if our information is accurate," answered Patterson. "All indications are that the reactor has had difficulties of its own and only went critical a few months ago. That's not nearly enough time to produce a sufficient quantity of weapons-grade Plutonium-239."

"Gordon, are you seriously suggesting that the test preparations are the deception? For what possible purpose?"

"Sir, I believe the test preparations are real. Every piece of data says the Iranians are following the correct steps to conduct a test. The problem is, we can't find anything to test!"

"General Duvall, this makes absolutely no sense at all. Why would the Iranians do something so blatant, unless they had a device to test?" The national security advisor's tenor showed his growing impatience with Duvall's cryptic theory.

"We don't know the answer to that yet, sir. We are looking at all the possible options, to include the remote possibility that they procured a weapon from another nation. But what I can tell you, is that the Iranians' actions are having an effect."

"In what way?"

Duvall pulled a short report from his briefcase and handed it to Kirkpatrick. "As of this morning, the Israeli Air Force has grounded the 69th and 107th squadrons at Hatzerim Airbase, as well as the 119th, 201st, and 253rd squadrons at Ramon Airbase. In addition, the Saknayee Boeing 707 tankers of the 120th squadron have backed out of an exercise with the Sixth Fleet, because of 'maintenance issues.'"

Kirkpatrick looked solemn as he read the report's key judgments. Patterson didn't understand the significance of the NIC chairman's statement.

"Forgive me, General. But what does this mean?" Patterson asked.

"Dr. Patterson, these squadrons are composed of F-15I and F-16I tactical aircraft. They are the only aircraft in the Israeli inventory that can, with in-flight refueling, reach Iranian targets."

"Oh my," she said.

Duvall leaned forward, his face showing intense concern. "Sir, we need more of the information that Opal possesses to help us nail down this problem."

"I'd like to accommodate you, Gordon. But that isn't possible right now. Opal and company left their hiding place an hour ago and are out of touch for the next several hours, at least," replied Kirkpatrick. "Furthermore, the young lady who is the true source of the information is reluctant to provide more until she and her husband are out of Iran. It seems they're afraid we'll leave them high and dry once we get the information."

"Then let's ask her for just one more file," suggested Patterson. "Have Captain Guthrie ask her to give us a report on the status of the Arak reactor. The file inventory list says she has one, and if it's in line with what we know, odds are General Duvall's assertion is correct, and we can warn the Israelis."

"They'll want to see the proof themselves," warned Kirkpatrick. "Are we ready to release this kind of information?"

"Normally, I'd be very reluctant to provide such sensitive data to anyone but the Brits," admitted Duvall. "But given the circumstances, I think it's in our best interest to share this with the Israelis. But that may not be my boss's position."

"Very well," Kirkpatrick replied as he stood up. "I'll make the recommendation to the president, after I discuss this with the director of national intelligence."

"Dr. Kirkpatrick, General Duvall, I'd also like to request that you consider bringing my husband in on this."

"Senator Hardy? Why, Joanna?" Kirkpatrick actually looked surprised by her request.

"Lieutenant Commander Mitchell, the senior officer of the group that is stranded, served under my husband on *Memphis*. Lowell also knows Captain Guthrie reasonably well, and he is well versed in covert submarine operations. He's also on the Senate Armed Services Committee, which gives you a knowledgeable point of contact on the Hill."

Kirkpatrick thought it over for a moment, and then looked at Duvall.

"I have no objections to reading Senator Hardy in," Duvall remarked.

"Alright, Joanna, I'll raise this with the president as well. But I make no promises."

5 April 2013
0330 Local Time/0030 Zulu
Three Kilometers North Northwest of Akhtar

Phillips and Lapointe burst through the door, their weapons at the ready. Ramey followed right behind them. Only after a hasty inspection to ensure the building was abandoned were Jerry and the others allowed to stumble in. Fazel shut the door and anchored it against the howling wind with an empty cabinet.

The shamal had hit them a little under an hour earlier with twenty-five-mile-per-hour sustained winds, driving rain, and a ten-degree drop in temperature. While the shamal was on the mild side, everyone was thoroughly soaked, chilled to the bone, and covered with sand.

Phillips was the first one to get his mouth cleared. "Okay," he gasped, as he spit some sand out of his mouth. "That officially sucked!"

"I haven't been this miserable since Hell Week," agreed Lapointe. His reference to the fifth week of the Basic Underwater Demolition/SEAL training, or BUDS, is the standard metric by which SEALs compare the relative unpleasantness of a situation. If it's "like" or "worse" than Hell Week, it's really, really bad.

"I don't know, Pointy," Phillips argued. "I've been cold, wet, and sandy before, but never sandblasted! Hey, maybe I should suggest adding a driving wind to Hell Week."

"You're a sadistic bastard. You know that, Philly?"

"Can it, you two," Ramey barked. "Since you're so full of energy, Phillips, you can take the first watch."

"Yes, sir," responded Phillips coolly. Jerry noticed Lapointe's jaw tighten.

"Doc, report. How's our favorite spy?"

"She's really cold, Boss," replied the corpsman.

"We all are, Harry," observed Ramey. His voice was cynical, uncaring.

"No, sir, I mean she's dangerously cold," Fazel repeated more sternly.

"Her body temperature is low, and she's showing symptoms of mild hypothermia."

"What can you do about it?" injected Jerry. Ramey's head snapped around at the sound of his voice.

"We need to get her out of those wet clothes and under some warm blankets. I've already asked her husband to strip her down as much as possible."

"I bet that didn't go over well," Jerry noted with a little sarcasm.

Fazel snickered. "No. It didn't. But I think I got my point across."

"What else can we do, Doc?" asked Ramey impatiently.

"I'll start making dinner or breakfast, or whatever, and get her some hot tea, but we need to get her off this concrete slab. Any insulating material that you can scrounge up would be really helpful."

"I think I can handle that," Jerry volunteered. "You guys have more important issues to deal with."

He started walking toward the back of the building, when Lapointe called over, "Hey, XO, I think I saw some cardboard boxes in the back left-hand corner." Jerry thanked him and started rummaging through the junk. The building looked like it had been used for shipping, and was filled with all kinds of miscellaneous packing material. He found the boxes Lapointe had referred to and started breaking them down. Jerry also found a canvas covering and some twine. Out of the corner of his eye, he could see Lapointe and Ramey having a quiet, but animated conversation. Neither looked very happy.

Jerry stacked the flattened boxes, along with something that looked like rough packing paper, into the canvas and tied the corners together with the twine. It wasn't fancy, but it would keep both Naseri and Akbari off the cold floor. As he tugged it toward the Iranian couple, Fazel came over and helped him carry it. The corpsman was impressed. "Great work, XO. This will do nicely."

"Well, it isn't a Sealy Posturepedic mattress. But it should do the job."

Yousef had picked Shirin up off the floor, partly to make sure she stayed covered, but also because she was still shivering so hard it was questionable that she could even stand. Jerry and Fazel positioned the makeshift bedding in the center of the building, and Yousef gently put her down. Shirin's face, still darkened by the sand, showed a weak smile. It was all she could offer as a thank-you. Fazel reassured her that she would start feeling warmer soon, then suggested that Yousef should snuggle up close to her and transfer some of his body heat to her.

After their meal, Jerry sat down with Ramey and Lapointe. The two had been poring over a map and taking stock of their situation. Ramey appeared to be calmer, but Jerry detected concern in Lapointe's voice.

"Boss, we could be stuck here for days if this storm is really bad. And we're almost out of MREs and water. We'll have to start foraging soon."

"I know, Pointy. I know. We really should leave and move on tonight, but I doubt Doc will support it. Dr. Naseri probably can't handle another night out in the open with that kind of weather."

"How long does a spring shamal normally last?" asked Jerry. He'd heard about the summer storms that could go on for days, sometimes for an entire week.

Ramey let loose with a deep sigh. "The spring storms aren't as intense as the summer ones. Typically a spring shamal can be as short as several hours, or as long as a day. Maybe a day and a half."

"This one is on the weak side, XO. Not that anyone here would likely agree with that after the hour we spent in it." Lapointe's wry smile told Jerry that he was back to his old self. "But if I had to guess, twelve hours. Eighteen tops."

"More worst-case planning then?"

"Exactly," said Lapointe, as he touched his nose with his index finger and pointed in Jerry's direction. "And it don't look too good, if you ask me."

"What Petty Officer Lapointe is trying to say, XO, is that we are running short of provisions and we'll need to start looking for food and water as well as trying to evade capture." Ramey was still a bit snippy, but he had definitely improved.

"This shouldn't be a problem, gentlemen," Jerry said nonchalantly. Both SEALs looked confused; convinced that he just didn't understand the dilemma they were in.

"Once the weather clears, we contact *Michigan* and have them send in one of the Cormorant UAVs with supplies and any gear you think we might need. Since they're stealthy, it should have no problem avoiding Iranian early warning radars." But as Jerry started to describe how this aerial resupply theoretically would go down, he ran into an assumption that he hadn't thought of initially.

"The only trick is that *Michigan* will have to stay at periscope depth and guide the UAV to us. If the patrol boat activity is still heavy, this could seriously complicate matters."

Now it was Lapointe's turn to look cocky. "*Michigan* won't have to, XO. I have the portable remote control terminal in my pack. I can guide the UAV straight to us and then send it back on a different preprogrammed course. All *Michigan* has to do is launch and then retrieve the UAV. We just have to be careful how long we use the terminal. It uses a low power, frequency-hopping signal, but it is an omnidirectional transmission and is more detectable than the 117 SATCOM radio."

"Okay. We'll contact *Michigan* tonight and give them our shopping list, which needs to include more blankets and a SCAR for the XO, as well as food and water. We can arrange a drop location once we have a better idea of how long it will take for the weather to clear," concluded Ramey. "Now, I strongly suggest you guys get some rest. I'll take the first watch with Doc."

As Jerry laid down his head on a pile of boxes, he realized just how exhausted he really was. In that fuzzy state between consciousness and sleep, Jerry looked at the Iranian couple. Both were sound asleep, with Yousef holding Shirin close to keep her warm and to reassure her that, for now, everything was all right. As Jerry finally drifted off, his last thought was, *I miss you, too, Emily.*

11

UNEXPECTED REUNION

28 September 2009
0745 Local Time
Naval Postgraduate School
Monterey, California

It was the first day of class, and he was going to be late. Jerry grumbled to himself as he walked as fast as he could, given the deep mist. The day had not started out well. It had been a very long weekend, with late nights on both Saturday and Sunday to unpack his household goods, and he had overslept. Then there was the fog. Jerry had been warned about Monterey's bumper crop of fog days, but this was ridiculous. Visibility was a quarter mile at the very best, usually less, and it made the commute painfully slow. He was fortunate to find a parking spot along the fence line, but he still had a short hike to the nearest gate.

Jerry flashed his military ID as he entered the gate and began walking in the general direction of Spanagel Hall. He had spent most of the previous week getting acquainted with the Naval Postgraduate School campus, locating all his classrooms and getting to know the general lay of the land. But all his landmarks were now totally obscured by the pea soup the Pacific Ocean had served up for breakfast. A faint dull shadow was all Jerry could discern of a building in the swirling gray around him, and he made a beeline toward it.

He bounded up the steps and flew through the front doors. He paused

momentarily in the foyer to gain his bearings, *left stairwell or right? Right!*
Again he took off, taking two stairs at a time. As he approached the second
floor, Jerry glanced at his watch—8:03. Damn! He had just reached the top
of the flight of stairs when suddenly, *POW*!

He had run into something, and hard. Jerry reeled to his left following
the collision. Papers were strewn in the air and he heard a body hit the floor.
A woman's voice squeaked out a surprised "*Ohh!*" followed immediately by a
more guttural "*Umph.*"

Jerry steadied himself against the wall, cursing his stupidity. He looked
down and saw a small woman sitting on the floor, her papers and books
scattered around her. Mortified, Jerry got down to help her pick them up
and began apologizing, "I am so sorry. I didn't see you at all. Are you all
right?"

The young woman seemed shocked when she heard his voice, and then
spun her head about quickly. When Jerry saw her face, his heart stopped.

"Jerry?"

"Emily?"

"What are you doing here?" they both said simultaneously. Dr. Emily
Davis laughed, obviously pleased to see him; Jerry felt awkward.

"I work here, Jerry. I'm the Deputy Director of the Center for Autonomous Vehicle Research," she said with a huge smile.

"I'm just a lowly student," replied Jerry, stunned, trying to figure out
just what the hell was going on. "Who happens to be late for his first class."

"Can we meet for lunch? I'd love to talk to you," asked Emily. It was
more of a plea than a request. "I'm free at eleven o'clock."

Jerry pulled out his schedule and saw he had a conflict. "Can't, I have
physics at eleven. How about one o'clock?"

Emily sighed. "Can't, I'm teaching Intro to Unmanned Systems and
then I have office hours at the lab."

Jerry shook his head. *Here we go again*, he thought. Then trying not to
sound too interested, he asked, "Since our schedules aren't cooperating, how
about dinner?"

"That would be lovely."

"Fisherman's Wharf, say six-thirty?"

"Absolutely. Where should we go?" she asked. Jerry was sure he saw her
eyes welling up.

"How about Crabby Jim's?"

"My favorite! It's a date!" Her face darkened immediately after she spoke, as if she regretted that last sentence.

There was an awkward silence as Jerry helped Emily collect the rest of her papers and books. His stomach was doing barrel rolls.

"Thank you," Emily whispered. "It's *good* to see you." Those eyes again.

Jerry nodded his head. "I'm sorry that I bowled you over. Not very gentlemanly of me."

Emily hesitated, then leaned over and gave Jerry a peck on the cheek. "I'll see you this evening. Now, you'd better get to class, Mr. Mitchell."

"Yes, ma'am," he replied with a mock salute. Jerry watched as she walked down the stairs. Dazed and confused he wandered off to class.

Jerry was hard-pressed to remember anything from that first day. His class notes were minimal, little more than the contact data for the instructor and a few scribbles on the syllabus. His thoughts were elsewhere—in the past—and they were haunting him.

At his apartment that afternoon, he struggled through his homework and reading assignments, but managed to complete them, sort of. He still had an hour before his dinner with Emily, so he plopped down in a lawn chair on the apartment's balcony and forced open Pandora's box.

Everything had seemed to be going so well between them. Emily Davis and Joanna Patterson were on the pier when USS *Memphis* returned to New London in July 2005. And after unloading Davis's precious remote operating vehicles, they stayed for Jerry's dolphin pinning ceremony and the party afterward. With *Memphis* in the dry dock for repairs, Jerry had plenty of opportunities to drive up to Boston and spend time with Emily. Those were good times.

The cracks in the relationship first showed up at Patterson's and Hardy's wedding that October. Emily was the maid of honor, and that seemed to throw a switch in her head. She began to talk about the two of them being more than just a couple, and even though she didn't mention the word *marriage*, it was abundantly clear that was what she had in mind. Initially, Jerry didn't see any harm in her talking about the idea. He wasn't against the concept in principle; he just felt it was a bit premature. The two of them needed more time to figure out who they were as individuals, before trying to make a marriage work where the priorities weren't necessarily about oneself.

The following year was more turbulent, with more than the occasional hard conversation about the future. Jerry was trying to figure out where he wanted to go next in his submarine career, while Emily gave mixed signals about moving on to academia or the corporate sector. She wanted them to be together, but she also wanted to keep her highly successful career going. Jerry appreciated her desires, but made the mistake of being blunt in telling her that he didn't see how they could work all of the "wants" out.

In November 2006, at the victory celebration for Lowell Hardy's election to the House of Representatives, the tectonic plates of their relationship suffered a major quake. Jerry told her that he had submitted a request for his next set of orders. He planned to skip the traditional shore tour and go straight to the Submarine Officers Advanced Course, and then back to sea. This would allow him to completely catch up with his peers and put his career back on a proper course. He added that his first choice was a *Seawolf*-class attack submarine, so he would hopefully be staying in the New London area. Emily seemed to take the news well, and said she was happy for him. But thereafter things never seemed to be quite the same.

By February 2007, the relationship was strained to the breaking point. Emily wanted everything. Jerry just couldn't see how that was possible. He believed he had an obligation to the Navy leadership to pay them back for their investment, even if it had been forced. Emily had attractive offers from academic institutions across the country, none of which were near a submarine base. Jerry saw their situation as a classic design problem; you have three parameters to maximize, choose two.

The vexing part of it all was that he truly loved Emily, and wanted to make her happy. He analyzed the "data" and concluded that her career seemed to be more important at the time. Jerry was fine with the idea, they could wait until she had established herself academically, and he encouraged her accordingly. Unfortunately, Emily interpreted his willingness to put her career ahead of their relationship as a sign that he was no longer interested in a relationship. Frustrated, confused, and angry, Jerry lost his temper and suggested that they both might be better off with some time apart. His bad choice of words, coupled with unbelievably poor timing, Valentine's Day, reinforced Emily's belief that Jerry wanted to move on. They broke up a couple of days later; and while the parting was amicable, that didn't do anything to soothe the pain.

Now, two-and-a-half-years later, Emily Davis had suddenly popped back into his life. It was clear from their collision that morning that she still had strong feelings for him—the enthusiastically spoken word *date* echoed in his head.

With a deep, resigned sigh, Jerry reached for the phone and called his sister, Clarice. For fifteen minutes she listened to her younger brother as he poured out his heart. When he finally asked what he should do, she encouraged him to not try and solve the problems, but to just listen. And, she added, to listen to the voice behind the words, as much as the words themselves. With his confidence shored up by his elder sibling's wise counsel, Jerry quickly ran a brush through his hair and grabbed his jacket.

He paced impatiently back and forth at the foot of the wharf; stopping only to look at his watch, it read 6:43. She was late—again. Jerry took an odd solace from the fact that Emily's lack of punctuality hadn't been affected by the years. Or had he been stood up? He quickly dismissed the thought, ashamed that he had even considered Emily was capable of such cruelty. He had just purged his brain of that notion, when he heard her call out to him.

"Jerry!"

He turned to see her almost running down to him. She was modestly dressed, almost business casual, but it didn't hide any of her physical charms. He had forgotten how beautiful she was.

"I am so sorry to be late," she gasped. "The staff meeting went on forever, all we talked about was the budget and the impact the continuing resolution would have on our department. It just dragged on and on. I thought I'd never get out of there."

Sounds just like my classes, thought Jerry. But there was no way he would say that. "I'm afraid I can't help you with the fiscal planning process of our government," Jerry remarked cynically. "It's pure frickin' magic as far as I'm concerned, and requires a bubbling cauldron and a pointy black hat to even begin to understand it." He offered her his arm; she gladly took it.

"I don't want to understand it. I just want those *politicians* to do their job, that's all."

"Be careful, now. You know one of those *politicians* personally," admonished Jerry as he mimicked her tone.

"True," Emily agreed tersely. But before she could say another word, an audible grumbling sound came from her midsection. She blushed with embarrassment.

Jerry laughed as they walked up to the restaurant's entrance. "Now, that problem I do know how to take care of. And the solution is right here." He opened the door and gestured for her to enter first.

They took a table by the large windows that overlooked the harbor. The view was impressive. A group of sea otters were frolicking in the water right in front of them, while on a nearby dock, sea lions were napping between expensive yachts. The tide was coming in, bringing with it the heady aroma of the sea.

Jerry ordered a bottle of white wine and two cups of Crabby Jim's world-renowned clam chowder as an appetizer. He then lost himself in the menu. Like most of the restaurants on Fisherman's Wharf, there was an abundance of choices. So much food, so little time.

"So what are you going to have?" inquired Emily. She was starting with the obvious small talk.

"I think I'm going to go with the chicken piccata tonight."

"What!?! Chicken!?!" Emily appeared shocked. "Jerry, this is one of the best seafood restaurants in town, and you're going to have chicken?"

"Emily," Jerry replied defensively, "my household goods only arrived this last weekend. I've been eating out ever since I reported to NPS and I'm up to here," he put his hand up to his neck, then moved it over his head. "Correction, up to here with seafood. I've got a serious hankerin' for a terrestrial critter, okay?"

"Heathen," she said playfully.

A waitress took their entree orders, while another delivered the wine and clam chowder. Both sipped at their soup in awkward silence.

"What field of study are you pursuing at the postgraduate school, Jerry?" Emily finally asked.

"Huh? Oh, I'm in the engineering acoustics track," he replied nonchalantly.

"Acoustics? I would've thought someone with your experience would be more interested in the unmanned systems curriculum." *Was that hurt in her voice? Or just disappointment?*

Jerry wiped his lips with his napkin, giving him time to think of how to word his response. "I seriously thought about it, Emily. I admit that I have more experience than most in the submarine force with unmanned underwater vehicles, but I also lack the equivalent experience in more traditional submarine missions and systems. The postgraduate school's Undersea

Warfare Curriculum seemed like an excellent way to bridge that gap, and the acoustics track will give me a better understanding of a submarine's main sensor."

"I hadn't looked at it that way," she responded thoughtfully. "From a big picture career perspective, it sounds very reasonable."

It was also a lie. He had originally intended to pursue an emphasis on autonomous systems, but after his first class he went straight to the chair of the undersea warfare group and explained his concerns over an earlier relationship with a current faculty member in his chosen curriculum. Jerry then requested that he be moved to the acoustics track. It was his second choice when he applied to the postgraduate school, and this would preclude any perception of impropriety by moving Jerry out of Dr. Davis's academic chain of command. He wanted to protect Emily, as well as himself, from any unpleasant investigation that could seriously impact their careers once their prior relationship became known.

"Would you be willing to come and talk to my class?" asked Emily. "You're a bit of a celebrity in the unmanned systems lab after *Seawolf*'s collision with the Russian sub."

"Who? Me? Seriously?" Jerry was both surprised and uncomfortable with the idea.

"Certainly! You've done innovative things with UUVs and the resupply concept you thought up was sheer brilliance."

"It wasn't all me, Emily," protested Jerry. "*Seawolf*'s torpedo officer and I basically came up with the idea at the same time, and we implemented it together."

"Regardless, you came up with a new function for an established UUV on the fly and made it work. The thought process behind executing the concept is what is important to pass on to my students. Besides"—Emily leaned forward, a slight grin on her face—"you're here and *Seawolf*'s torpedo officer isn't."

Jerry opened his mouth to speak, but then closed it. His lips pursed into a frown. He couldn't think of a good rejoinder. Recognizing that he had been checkmated, he sighed and said, "It's hard to argue with that kind of logic."

Her reaction wasn't quite what he expected. She became somber, swallowed hard a couple of times, and spoke quietly. "I wouldn't force you to do anything you didn't want to."

Alarm bells went off inside Jerry's head. While the words he heard were directly related to her request, the tone implied something else. Hopeful, but still cautious he replied.

"It's not that, Emily. It's just . . . well, I'm not very good at public speaking. Correction, I'm only slightly above abysmal. But, if your director and the undersea warfare chair have no objections, then I guess I can come by and share some insights with your class. Nothing formal, mind you, just some thoughts about what we did and how we did it."

Her expression lightened only a little, but she sounded appreciative. "Thank you, Jerry. I'm sure there won't be any problems from Dr. Hunter or Commander Evington. And I know my students will enjoy hearing how you worked through the problem."

"I'll settle for not boring them," Jerry replied flippantly.

"Jerry Mitchell! I have never found you boring!" exclaimed Emily angrily. Her sudden emotional outburst took them both by surprise. At first, Jerry just sat there, bewildered. Then he noticed the tears welling up in her eyes, and that she had started trembling. He reached across and gently placed his hand on hers. She began crying, muffling the sobs in her napkin, and clenching his hand tightly. It was a little uncomfortable when the waitress brought their food. Emily only nodded as the plate was laid in front of her. Jerry said, "Thank you."

After what seemed like an eternity, her sobbing finally slowed down. Jerry leaned forward and softly asked her, "Are you going to be all right?"

Emily sniffed and ran the napkin across her cheeks and eyes. "I think so. I'm so sorry, Jerry."

"About what, Emily?" His heart was beating rapidly. "For crying?"

"No. No. About what I did over two years ago! I was frustrated, disappointed, and I acted foolishly."

"Yeah, well, I seemed to recall that I wasn't any better. No, actually I was worse. I was the one that got angry, not you."

"But I made you angry. I . . . I drove you away." Emily paused to breathe and wiped her eyes again. "And that hurt you. I know it did. I'm so very sorry!"

Jerry pulled his hand away from hers, and gently lifted her chin. "Enough of that, Marcie," Jerry's use of her nickname on *Memphis* caused Emily to smile. "Our food is getting cold. And besides, we are breaking one of the unwritten rules of getting back together. No 'sorries' until after dessert."

Jerry then took his wineglass, raised it, and offered a toast. "To a second chance."

9 March 2012
Hilton Minneapolis Hotel
Minneapolis, Minnesota

Jerry's feet were killing him. Thank God the reception line was almost done. How Emily could stand there for so long in high heels mystified him. As if she had been reading his mind, she leaned over and whispered in his ear, "I don't know about you, but I'm ready to sit down."

"Ditto," remarked Jerry. "I've been regretting breaking in those new hiking boots for the last half hour."

"Told you so," she said sweetly, as she greeted another well-wisher.

"Thanks . . . dear," growled Jerry.

The wedding ceremony had gone off perfectly, with everything happening, as it should, when it should. Jerry wasn't surprised. The joint chiefs of staff could learn something about coordination from his mother and his sisters, who were absolutely thrilled to help Emily with all the planning. All he had to do was nod sagely, and stay out of the way.

Emily had been relieved to find the entire Mitchell family so loving and accepting; her own parents had been divorced for many years and they still had issues. As the only child, she constantly found herself as the rope in a never-ending game of tug-of-war. Emily had already been leaning toward Jerry's home state for the wedding, more as neutral ground than anything else, but once she found all those "enchanting" hiking trails up on the North Shore, the deal was sealed.

Finally, the last couple approached them. Jerry and Emily had both been waiting patiently for this reunion.

"Emily, you look radiant!" exclaimed Patterson, as she rushed up to hug her. "I always knew this day would come." She turned to Jerry and gave him a big hug as well. "Even when the two of you were too damn stubborn to admit it!"

"I'm so glad you could make it, Joanna. We were surprised by your RSVP, we know how busy you and Representative Hardy are this month," Emily replied.

"Nonsense! We wouldn't have missed this for the world!" beamed Patterson. "Besides, we both needed a break from the campaign trail. I'm just glad the Minnesota caucuses were last week. Very convenient."

"Congratulations, Emily, Jerry." Hardy smiled broadly as he gave the bride a hug. "I have to admit I wasn't as prescient as my wife, but I am just as pleased that the two of you woke up and pulled your heads out of your rears." He slapped Jerry on the shoulder as he shook his hand.

"Is it true you're going to be an executive officer?" asked Hardy with disbelief.

"Yes, sir. I'm slated to be the XO of USS *Michigan* blue crew."

"Good Lord, I suddenly feel old. I think I need a drink," Hardy moaned. Jerry thought he did look much older, but was too polite to say so.

"Congratulations on winning the primary in Connecticut, sir," he said, instead.

"Thank you. The senatorial race has been rougher than I expected, but we did well," He tilted his head in Patterson's direction. "Joanna is a force of nature in such matters. I doubt I would have won without her insight and dogged determination."

"You see, Jerry. Lowell has mellowed over the years," teased Patterson, as she wrapped her arms around Hardy's neck. "What he really wanted to say was 'nagging.'"

Hardy rolled his eyes, while Emily and Patterson laughed. Jerry struggled to maintain a neutral composure. It's not nice to laugh at a former skipper.

"Moving on," Hardy demanded. "Where are you lovebirds going to spend your honeymoon?"

"We're heading north, sir. Emily has discovered Superior National Forest and she really wants to do some winter hiking," replied Jerry enthusiastically.

"You're kidding, right?" Hardy was skeptical.

"No, sir. Emily is quite the hiker," answered Jerry. "Truth be told, she's walked my butt off in California. We're hoping to get in some good old-fashioned walking on the Gunflint Trail, and maybe some cross-country skiing. I doubt I'll get her on the slopes at Lutsen though."

"That's not a honeymoon!" barked Hardy. "That's a forced march, in Siberia no less! Please tell me you aren't planning on doing cold weather camping?"

"No, no, no. Emily has some very strong opinions on that," stated Jerry firmly. "Her idea of roughing it is confined strictly to the trails. The accommodations have to have a warm bed, a hot tub, a good restaurant, and a well-stocked bar. Tents and dehydrated food are right out."

"Thank God, for that tattered shred of sanity!" responded Hardy, amazed.

"Now, darling, not everyone wants to be a beach bum," chided Patterson sternly. "It's their honeymoon, let them do what they want."

"Oh, oh, I know that voice. I'd better go get that drink, before I end up sleeping on the couch. We'll talk more later." It was Hardy's turn to chuckle at his wife's expense. The two walked toward the bar hand in hand.

The dinner was exquisite. Lenny Berg's toast as the best man was unexpectedly gracious. The first bites of the wedding cake were exchanged without incident, and Jerry launched the garter into a sea of eligible bachelors. When it was Emily's turn to throw the bouquet, she positioned herself before a throng of unattached young women and lofted the bunch of lavender roses over her head.

Jerry watched as the tidy bunch of flowers slowly flipped end over end, almost in slow motion. Flowers? Flowers! . . .

He awoke suddenly, his mind racing, triggered by the vision of flowers floating in the air. Did the florist remember to send Emily the card and flowers? As his groggy head started to clear, he remembered getting the familygram from his wife, thanking him for the flowers and the beautiful card. He had left the handwritten card with the florist to accompany the roses. The message was short and simple, "each petal a thought of you." It was the best he could do since he would be at sea during their first anniversary.

Jerry shivered as he looked around. The wind was still howling; he could hear sand pelting the building's thin metal walls. Lapointe and Phillips were standing guard, while everyone else appeared to be asleep. He laid his head back down and tried to snuggle deeper into the thermal blanket. Cold and sore, Jerry desperately wanted to go back to sleep. He wanted the dream to continue, he wanted to be back home.

12

BAD COMPANY

5 April 2013
1730 Local Time/1430 Zulu
Three Kilometers North-Northwest of Akhtar

They'd ridden out the shamal, which had thankfully ended about 1700. It had been a long, uncomfortable wait. Even with rags stuffed in cracks around the doors and windows, the air in the shed had been filled with fine dust. They'd all worn improvised masks, but the grit still found its way onto their teeth. Clothing offered little protection. This made staying bundled against the damp chill more unpleasant as the gritty cloth rubbed up against their skin.

It wasn't all bad news. Any trace of their passage last night had been obliterated, and with luck, the old Peykan was buried under a new sand dune.

Jerry had slept, but he didn't feel rested, and he'd kill for a shower. Still, he felt better. There would be no shamal tonight, and just knowing what to expect helped his attitude. He also blessed the day he'd joined the Navy. He liked the outdoors, but this was taking it too far.

After the shamal ended, they managed to push open a door on the lee side of the storage shed. The SEALs secured the area, Lapointe set up the satellite antenna, and Jerry called *Michigan*.

"We're ready for resupply. When do you plan on launching the Cormorant?"

Guthrie's voice was almost cheerful. "We'll launch at 1900, just before last light, so we can hide the plume of the booster rockets. Everything you've requested is being loaded as we speak."

"Thank you, sir. This drop will help boost morale." Jerry knew the re-supply effort would solve their immediate needs, but it didn't deal with the larger issue. "How's the surface picture looking?"

"Worse. The number of surface patrols has increased steadily; you'd think there was a regatta up there. Fortunately, they haven't wandered too far from Kangan, yet. But you are less than forty kilometers from the IRGC naval base at Asaluyeh, which means we still can't come in and get you. By the way, we've had a request. Our friends back home examined the material you sent and would like one more file. Tell Dr. Naseri it's a confidence building request." Guthrie read off a string of letters and numbers.

Shirin was still dozing, so Fazel quickly explained and Yousef roused her while Pointy used his laptop and found the file Guthrie had asked about. Yawning, she typed in the decryption key, then again when it didn't work the first time. "This is the last one," she warned.

1815 Local Time/1515 Zulu
USS *Michigan*, Missile Compartment

Guthrie had tried not to hover, but now it was time for a last check. Sim-mons could get *Michigan* to the right location, depth, and heading without the captain looking over his shoulder.

The missile compartment was crowded when he arrived. The two sup-ply capsules had already been loaded and secured inside the Cormorant's fuselage. Lieutenant Frederickson, Chief Yates, and several enlisted mem-bers of the SEAL platoon were watching with interest as the missile techs performed the prelaunch checks while Lieutenant (jg) Pat Doolan, one of the assistant weapons officers, supervised.

The captain had served in *Ohio*s before as a junior officer, when the boats carried twenty-four Trident II missiles. Now, the "Sherwood Forest" of double cylinders was loaded with other things. And while their general appearance hadn't changed, Guthrie could see the details: the equipment added to recharge the scuba tanks and the added workspace for the SEALs to maintain their gear. And for two tubes, twenty-three and twenty-four, the equipment that supported the Cormorant UAVs inside. The access hatch was open, with Doolan and his chief making the final inspection. The shape of the UAV was hidden, wrapped inside its own folded wings.

Lieutenant Frederickson offered the captain a clipboard. "Here's the final list, Skipper—four hundred and seventy pounds."

"Is that all? The Cormorant can carry more than twice that."

"But our people can't. If they split the load equally, it's over sixty pounds per person. And I don't think the woman's going to be carrying much at all. My guys have been working on this list since Matt and the others got stuck on the beach."

Behind him, the missile techs closed the access hatch to the tube and began checking the seals. "Captain, can we watch the launch in the control room?" asked one of the techs. "The Tomahawk weapons control center is going to be packed, and we'd like to see our bird fly."

"I don't need a lot of bystanders in control during this evolution. But, I'll authorize your team to go to the BMC for the launch. That way those of you who are not on duty can watch."

The young missile technician smiled. "Thank you, sir."

Half an hour later, *Michigan* was at UAV launch stations. Sonar reported no nearby contacts, and the diving officer was ready to compensate for the absence of nine thousand pounds of robotic aircraft. The launch procedure was ridiculously simple.

The sound-powered phone talker reported, "TWCC reports Cormorant shows ready."

Guthrie ordered, "Open the hatch on missile tube twenty-three."

"Open the hatch on missile tube twenty-three, aye. Launcher, Control. Open the hatch on missile tube twenty-three." After no more than thirty seconds, the petty officer reported, "Hatch on tube twenty-three indicates fully open and locked." The chief of the boat, standing watch as the diving officer, could see the indicators on the ballast control panel. He nodded confirmation.

"Elevate the platform," commanded Guthrie. The phone talker relayed the order to the launch control station in the missile compartment. The Cormorant was perched on a launch rig that would lift it clear of the missile tube hatch. Since the UAV was uncontrolled during its ascent, it had to be clear of any obstacles before it was released.

"Captain, launch platform is raised."

"Very well. Release Cormorant."

"Release Cormorant, aye. TWCC, Control. Release Cormorant." Seconds later, the phone talker relayed, "Sir, Launcher indicates Cormorant has been released."

"Good," Guthrie answered. "Lower the platform and close the hatch on tube twenty-three. Increase speed to five knots, come to course one five zero."

The helmsman echoed his order and began turning the sluggish sub onto its new course. The Cormorant was still rising, although it would break the surface in moments.

"Up periscope." *Michigan* still had an old-style Type 8 optical periscope, along with the newer photonics mast that didn't need to penetrate the pressure hull. Coached onto the UAV's bearing by Simmons, the BVS-1 photonics mast would be pointing straight at the Cormorant when it cleared the surface. Monitors in the control room showed the two images side by side; natural light and low-level light from the photonics mast's cameras. Guthrie used the older Type 8 to conduct a safety sweep.

"Thar she blows!" Simmons announced. "I can see the boosters." On the natural light monitor, a brilliant spark flashed, but was quickly enveloped by a cloud of backlit exhaust. The vehicle itself was only visible on the low-light monitor, a bent arrowhead at the top of the cloud. Two shapes fell away, and the vehicle arced over from vertical to level flight. The petty officer monitoring the UAV console narrated the action as he reported the telemetry. "Booster separation, engine start. Speed is good, following preset course and altitude."

Lieutenant Frederickson's voice came over the intercom. "Control, BMC. We've notified the team the vehicle is in the air."

Guthrie acknowledged the reports. "Understood. Good work, everyone. Mr. Simmons, give me the best course to the recovery position."

The Cormorant UAV was built from gray angles. A triangular intake in the front was attached to two gull wings and a triangular lower fin that looked like the keel of a sailboat. The cylindrical cargo containers were hidden inside two angled bumps on the fuselage, to maintain the vehicle's stealthy radar signature.

This was a short trip for the unmanned aircraft, even including the doglegs Guthrie had ordered to conceal *Michigan*'s position. Cruising at 450 knots, it covered the twenty miles of its flight plan in just less than three minutes.

Halfway to its destination, the vehicle sensed a coded signal. The controller operated by Petty Officer Lapointe refined the location of the drop point, and the vehicle automatically made a minor correction in course.

Lapointe barely had time to acknowledge Frederickson's transmission before he had to use the remote control terminal. Jerry and the others waited inside for the supply drop. Lapointe had to be in the open so the terminal's signal wouldn't be blocked, but Ramey wanted everyone else under cover. "We can't see it coming, and the thing's dropping two canisters two feet in diameter and five feet long. If the chutes don't deploy, I don't want anyone exposed."

Although curious to see the vehicle in flight, Jerry agreed. Besides, at night there would be little to see.

The UAV slowed as it approached the programmed waypoint. Lapointe could see their building through the sensor feed, and verified the Cormorant wasn't about to dump its cargo on top of them. It climbed slightly, to give the chutes a chance to open, and released the two cylinders. Feeling no pride in a job well done, the vehicle immediately turned to the next programmed course, which started it on a dogleg track back to the recovery point near *Michigan*.

Lapointe gave the "all clear," and everyone piled out of the storage building. Looking through his nightscope, he was pointing to the north. "I saw two chutes. They're not far, in that direction."

The capsules had landed within a dozen meters of each other. At almost three hundred pounds apiece, it took two trips, with four men to lug each container, two SEALs for security, and Shirin carrying the rolled-up parachute.

A five-minute flight following a different path brought the Cormorant to its splashdown point. It orbited, at low altitude and slow speed, waiting for *Michigan* to reach the spot, farther away from the coast and well away from the launch point.

After reaching periscope depth, Captain Guthrie made a sweep with the optical scope while the photonics mast and the electronic surveillance sensor made their own checks. "No close contacts. The area is clear. Send the splashdown signal."

Mindlessly circling, the Cormorant cut its engine and deployed a para-chute, settling gently into the water. By the time Jerry and the SEALs were opening the supply capsules, an ROV from *Michigan* had attached the haul-down cable to the Cormorant. It would be reeled back into the missile tube, where it would be refueled and prepared for the next time it was needed.

With darkness, Ramey was impatient to get moving. The remote chance of someone observing the supply drop provided additional incentive to clear the area. Like all SEAL evolutions, they had planned what each man would do as soon as they opened the capsules. Their contents were quickly distributed. In addition to obvious things like food, water, and ammuni-tion, there was a SCAR rifle and tactical vest for Jerry, additional thermal blankets and camouflage suits for the Iranians, handheld night-vision gog-gles, a more comprehensive medical kit for Fazel, and spare batteries for everything.

Phillips helped Jerry rig the vest and reviewed basic procedures for the rifle. Even though he'd had the session with Ramey on *Michigan*, it was a lot less academic now. "Bottom line, XO, if you see us shoot, you shoot at that. If you see something that you think needs shooting, talk to us first. There may be a reason we haven't."

There were a few surprises. Fazel found a plastic jar with a note attached. Reading it, he smiled and opened the jar. Taking out two pills, he offered them to Shirin along with a bottle of water.

"What are these?" she asked suspiciously.

"Compliments of the ship's doctor," he replied. "Vitamin pills. For your pregnancy."

Five minutes later they were walking southeast.

5 April 2013
1400 Local Time/1900 Zulu
The White House

He wasn't making headway. Andy had always been stubborn. Myles wouldn't have won the nomination without his friend's pigheaded drive. But once made up, unmaking Andy's mind was nearly impossible.

"Mr. President, it's my job to give you my best advice, and in this case, it's a warning. The Iranians are selling us a load of organic fertilizer, and the sooner we recognize that, the better off we'll be."

Secretary Lloyd was pacing back and forth, the length of the Oval Office. Myles could feel his frustration. They'd known each other for thirty years, and he knew Lloyd regarded himself as the practical one, and Myles as the idealist.

The president asked, "Why didn't the Arak file change your mind?"

"Because it's no different than the first one. If the Iranians can create one file, why not two? Others have done it to us, and we've done it as well. Forged documents are an established part of intelligence tradecraft."

"So it comes down to whether you think this file is authentic or not."

Lloyd stopped pacing to stand in front of Myles's desk. "Sir, as secretary of state, my official judgment is that we have been deceived by a long-term Iranian disinformation campaign. Their true status is now being revealed as they prepare to test a weapon, an overt but necessary step. Not only does a test allow the bomb designers to gain critical information, it shows the world that one more nation has joined the nuclear club."

Lloyd pressed his point. "An Israeli attack within the next few days is inevitable. The argument about whether or not the Iranians have the bomb is moot. The real question is, What do we do when the shooting starts?"

Myles shook his head. "I want to stop the shooting before it even begins. Another war in the Persian Gulf won't solve anything."

Lloyd spoke slowly, picking his words. "I will remind you, sir, that our intelligence people have always called an Iranian nuclear test the "starting bell" for an Israeli attack. Our people also said that because of that, the Iranians wouldn't test the first device, but the third or fourth one. If the Iranians already have two or more nukes, then war may be the only way to stop Iran from using the bombs on Israel, or us."

Myles's intercom buzzed. "Dr. Kirkpatrick has arrived."

"Thank you, Evangeline. Please send him in."

"Reinforcements, Mr. President?"

Myles laughed grimly. "New information, Mr. Secretary."

The national security advisor was hardly in the room before announcing, "The Israelis said, 'Thanks, we'll look at it carefully.'"

"And this is Mossad's official response?" Myles prompted.

"I spoke to Yitzhak Harel, Mossad's number two, personally," Kirkpatrick answered. He sounded tired, and disappointed. "He said it would be considered as part of their total intelligence picture."

"Which is politespeak for giving more weight to the test site and the IAEA findings."

"As they should," Lloyd added. He turned to Kirkpatrick. "Doctor, which type of intelligence is more reliable, HUMINT or physical evidence?"

"You're allowed to disagree with our findings if you want to, Mr. Secretary. We're trying to find a solution that accounts for all the data. A responsible analyst—"

"Did you get any idea of their time line?" Myles interrupted. As vital as the Opal files were, getting a sense of Israeli intentions was even more important. And the last thing he needed was a fistfight between his national security advisor and the secretary of state.

Lloyd bristled. "My people will tell me, if and when the Israelis tell us."

"By which time it will be too late," Myles answered impatiently. "They've already written us off. We won't hear about it until planes are in the air."

Kirkpatrick answered, "I asked him flat out what their official assessment was. He said, 'They have the bomb. We are trying to find out how many and where they are.' After that, Harel paused for a moment, and added, 'We must give Laskov our best estimate in less than two days,' and then he hung up. By the way," Kirkpatrick added, "General Laskov commands their air force."

Myles sighed. "Good work, Ray. That's what we needed to know. We've got less than two days to stop them."

Lloyd acted surprised. "Sir, I don't believe that's wise. It may not even be possible."

"More 'official judgments,' Andy?"

"Sir, I say again, the Israelis are going to attack, and we'd best be prepared with our own response. There's a lot we can do behind the scenes to help them. And frankly, Mr. President, if you want a short war, with a favorable outcome for our interests, our best course is to join them."

"Mr. Secretary!" Kirkpatrick almost rose out of his chair, shock in his expression as well as his words. "A combined U.S. and Israeli attack—"

Myles held out a hand, cutting off the rest of Kirkpatrick's outburst. "I've been waiting twenty minutes for you to say that, Andy."

"Iran's been a bleeding sore in the region since the Revolution—

assassinations in foreign countries, exporting terrorism, attacks on Israel through Hamas and Hezbollah, helping the insurgents in Iraq. The only reason they haven't done more is because they can't. If Israel's going to attack, I say help them to do a good job of it, then we can all relax."

Myles's temper started to show in his voice. "First you take over General Duvall's job, now you want to replace Ray here as well? 'Relax' is the last thing we'll be able to do." The president gestured to Kirkpatrick. "Ray is right. A war between Israel and Iran is bad enough. Israeli bombs can start a war, but heaven knows how it will end, or where it will spread. And you want us in that mess? That's not judgment, that's emotion."

Myles stood and walked to the windows. It was springtime in Washington, but the view didn't calm him. "Mr. Secretary, it's the State Department's job to help me keep the U.S. out of trouble. Are you sure you're being objective?"

"Mr. President, if you have lost confident in my judgment, then it's best if I resign. I can have—"

"No, Andy. You don't get to take your ball and go home. We're in a crisis, and I need you at state, but working with me. My official position is that the Iranians are not close to finishing a weapon and that if the Israelis attack, they will be making a mistake that will cost everyone dearly. Your task is to communicate our deep desire for peace throughout the region, while protecting the rights of each nation to live without fear of destruction."

"Weasel words," grumbled Lloyd. "It's an impossible situation."

"As long as nobody's shooting, nothing's impossible," Myles answered.

"And I know how this town works," the president continued. His voice became hard. "Do not repeat your opinions of either our intelligence assessments or possible courses of action outside this office. If I read about any dispute between state and the Oval Office in the days to come, I won't fire you, not right now, but you will lose my trust and respect."

Myles continued, "I will make sure you are included in the distribution of all relevant intelligence and are present at all the national security council meetings. You can give the State Department's input at those times."

Lloyd started to speak, then stopped and nodded. He left without saying another word.

After a moment, Kirkpatrick said, "I'm sorry, Mr. President. I know you were close friends."

"And still are, I hope," Myles answered. "What good are friends you can't argue with? . . . Although we've never been this far apart." He sighed, but then his tone changed. "And that goes for you, too, Doctor. If this dispute appears in the media, I'll come looking for you first. I've known Andy a lot longer than I've known you."

Nodding, Kirkpatrick got up to leave, but Myles had one more item to discuss. "Have you read Hardy into Opal yet?"

"No, sir. I was going to see who else we could find who's served with Guthrie. I'm a little uneasy about bringing in someone from the legislative branch—even if he is from our party."

"I understand the complications, but let's brief the senator into the program. I think I have a job for him."

6 April 2013
0300 Local Time/0000 Zulu
3 km Northwest of Bandar Tahari

Ramey had promised lots of short breaks during the walk that night, but had still set an ambitious goal: fifteen kilometers.

As before, they were in the now-familiar diamond. They walked quietly, Shirin and Yousef sometimes speaking softly, the radio headset so silent that Jerry checked occasionally to make sure it was still working. After each break, Ramey rotated the SEALs' positions. Jerry stayed in the center.

The road was deceptive. Probably built to support construction of a pipeline that paralleled it, it was wide enough for two cars (or more likely trucks) to pass, but it was still just graded earth. It was definitely better than walking cross-country, but the uneven surface kept him alert. Ruts from tires or rocks in the surface could make him stumble. He imagined the effects of a sprained ankle on their progress.

A fair portion of Jerry's attention was on Shirin Naseri. She trudged along next to Yousef, who concentrated on picking the smoothest path. Jerry followed. Shirin didn't move quickly, but she seemed to be pacing herself, and never had to wait too long for a short respite.

The moon had just come out, which helped a little with their navigation. To his night-adjusted eyes, a quarter moon seemed bright, especially on the bare, brown landscape. There were lights to the right, either from scattered buildings on the far side of the highway or occasional vehicles passing. The glow from Bandar Tahari could be seen over the ridge past the highway.

Of course, the bare ground also made them more visible, but the SEALs took extra care to limit that vulnerability. Whoever was watching the road would spot the approach of a car by the glare of its headlights, and call a warning. Everyone would go to one knee and freeze until it had passed. It seemed extreme, given that they were several hundred meters away from the highway, but it was best not to take chances. Traffic had trailed off after midnight, but never stopped completely. Highway 96 tied Iran's Persian Gulf coast together, running all the way from Bandar Mahshahr, near the Iraq border, to Bandar Abbas.

Highway 96, Just North of Bandar Tahari

Corporal Molavi had drawn three new men for the patrol. Men? None was older than nineteen. One of them was still trying to raise a beard, and Molavi's five-year-old nephew could follow instructions better.

They were covering a twenty-five-kilometer section of Highway 96, ten kilometers on each side of Bandar Tahari, as well as the city itself. The highway ran nearly a kilometer north of the city, between two large ridges; with little light it required boots on the ground to be patrolled properly. The Tahari Basij Brigade did not have enough vehicles for the increased number of patrols, so they were using a panel van loaned by Private Salani's employer. Local business support of the Basij was considered an act of piety, and with Salani mobilized, there was nobody to drive it, anyway.

The van only had room for two in front, the corporal and Private Salani, who drove. The other two privates had to ride in the back. Salani's employer ran a cleaning service, but even with most of the cleaning equipment left behind, the privates were uncomfortable in the windowless van. Molavi wasn't too concerned about the privates' comfort; but they were useless in the back.

"Here's a good spot." The corporal pointed to the left. "Pull off there." He could hear Salani sigh as he slowed and turned off the pavement. The ground was hard-packed and smooth, and led up to a cement factory. Molavi had him drive about a hundred meters north, until the surface was too rough for a civilian vehicle.

The van sat in a relatively flat area between two high dunes. The land rose sharply to the north, and the dunes were fingers of higher ground shaped by erosion and wind into north-south ridges. The bare ground was graced with a few dark green shrubs, but there wasn't enough greenery in sight for a decent garden, even if it had all been brought together in one spot.

Molavi pounded on the metal partition between the cab and the rear of the van. "Out! Wake up back there!"

Salani seemed reluctant to get out of his seat. "Qassem, we did this just thirty minutes ago. Isn't this too soon?"

"It's 'Corporal,' to you, Private, and unless we're out of the car, searching the ground, we're not patrolling, we're just driving. Now get moving." Molavi grabbed his rifle, an Iranian-made copy of the AK-47, dubbed the KLF. It had a folding stock, which allowed him to carry it in the confines of the cab. The three other members of the patrol were similarly equipped.

The rear doors of the van swung open as Molavi approached, and two privates slowly emerged from its depths. "Get your butts out here!" the corporal roared. "Are you two sharing a goat back there? No, wait. You wouldn't know what to do. And where are your weapons?"

The taller of the two, Private Jebeli, answered, still stretching. "We had to get out of the back, first."

"As useless as you two are with a rifle, you're more useless without them, if such a thing is possible. Move!"

While the two quickly fetched their weapons from the back of the van, Molavi harangued them. "A weekend on the range and a green headband doesn't make you soldiers. Listen to what I tell you. I was getting shot at by Kurds while your father was teaching you how to wipe your ass.

"We are searching for smugglers, spies—people who are breaking the law. Nighttime is when they are out and up to no good. They will not wait while you lazily retrieve your weapon. When we pull to a stop, you will boil out of the back, alert, armed, and looking for trouble."

He surveyed the three and sighed. "By now, any lawbreakers nearby have left, but we are still going to search the area for evidence of illegal activity: footprints, tire tracks, evidence of digging, unusual trash."

He handed Private Jafari, the other militiaman riding in the back, a pair of binoculars. "Your turn." Molavi pointed to a large dune to the west.

"Get up there and see what you can see. Report any movement off the highway, no matter how innocent it looks. Stay there and watch until I come and get you."

The skinny private nodded and trotted off. "You two," he ordered, "we are going to systematically search the area." He gestured with his arm. "Salani to the left, Jebeli near the road, and I'll take the center. Go."

They started quartering the ground. Molavi didn't expect to find anything, of course, but that was when you were most likely to actually find something: a cache of weapons, drugs, or maybe those two fugitives they had been warned to look for.

Molavi divided his time between searching his own sector while watching the other two privates. He was sure they could screw up walking. They had flashlights, but were under orders not to use them. It ruined their night vision, and besides, with the moon out, there was enough illumination for a simple search.

They'd been looking for about ten minutes when Jafari, up on the dune, called out, "Corporal, I see something!" Molavi turned to see the private on his knees waving to him. "There's something out there." The private pointed to the west, the far side of the dune.

"Get down, you moron!" Molavi took off at a trot, but he turned his head and called to the other two as he ran. "Keep searching your sectors."

Shirin thought about her uncle while she walked. It kept her mind off her feet, and besides, there was a lot to think about. Seyyed Naseri was Mehry's younger brother, and was as bold and outspoken as Mehry was quiet and thoughtful. Their similar temperaments were one reason she'd always been close to Seyyed, who bragged about being Shirin's "favorite uncle." Of course, he was Mehry's only sibling.

He would be delighted to see her, and doubtless willing to help her and Yousef, but a mob of Americans? And getting two people out of Iran had to be easier than smuggling out seven.

How would they go about contacting him? They'd have to hide somewhere while Shirin or Yousef made contact. But if VEVAK agents were looking for her and Yousef, would they be watching Seyyed? They might be watching him anyway. Maybe she'd have Harry go into town with her. She didn't normally go veiled, but wearing one would keep her from being recognized. That seemed like something from a spy novel, which meant it was probably the right answer.

Shirin was trying to figure out where they could get the clothes for the American when Jerry, from behind her, whispered, "Down." Almost without thinking, with Yousef's help, she dropped to one knee. Yousef knelt beside her, both of them keeping perfectly still and holding hands. They'd done this over a dozen times as they marched, and she watched the highway for the headlights from a passing vehicle. Once it passed, they'd start walking again.

Instead, Jerry leaned closer to them, and said softly, "Philly saw something move on the crest ahead of us, to the right." In the moonlight, she could see the ground ahead of them, and the sharp line between land and sky, but otherwise she couldn't see a thing. She hadn't expected to. The Americans had night-vision scopes, though. What had he seen? Men? An animal? She tried to remember what creatures lived in this part of Iran. She wasn't frightened, not with Yousef next to her and surrounded by commandos, but she was curious.

Molavi was slowed by the loose surface of the rise, but he took the time to drop to all fours, and then crawled to the crest line. Jafari was prone, binoculars glued to his face. Even in the dim light, Molavi could see the private straining to pull detail out of the dark landscape. If anything was there.

The corporal eased in next to the private, trying to keep as low as possible. He reached over, and Jafari handed him the glasses without being asked. Molavi used them to scan the area, a stretch of ground turned by the moonlight into pale gray and dark gray shadows.

Patiently, he studied the construction road that paralleled the highway closely here. He looked for lines, shapes that seemed out of place. Nothing moved.

"Where?"

Jafari pointed to a patch of rocks to the left, some distance away. "I saw motion over there, near the dirt road. It looked like someone holding a rifle."

There was nothing there now, and most likely there'd never been anything. But dismissing the private's report would make him less likely to report the next time.

He handed the binoculars back to Jafari. "Keep watching. I'll send Jebeli up to you. Call if you see more movement, or anything at all." Backing away from the crest, Molavi kept low until he was well clear, then double-timed to the bottom, motioning to the other two privates.

They hurried over, and Molavi pulled them into a huddle. "Jafari's seen movement on the other side of this rise. We're going to investigate." He pulled out three magazines from the pouches on his vest. He handed them to the privates, their eyes wide as saucers.

He handed one to Salani, and two to Jebeli. "Here's one for Jafari as well as you. Go ahead and load, and for the sake of the Prophet, keep your selectors on 'Safe!'"

Molavi's weapon was already loaded. He watched them insert the magazines, then said carefully, "Salani and I will go around this rise on the left while Jafari and Jebeli cover us from above. Remember trigger discipline. Nobody shoots unless they see a person with a gun. Even if I shoot, you don't shoot unless you have a clear target, and anybody who shoots me had better kill me, or they'll wish they were dead. Clear?"

Both privates nodded nervously, and Molavi sent Jebeli up to join Jafari on the crest. "And for pity's sake, stay low near the crest!"

The corporal blessed the good fortune of having not sent Salani up the hill. He was the only one of the three that had anything on the ball. "You and I will circle around this rise. We take turns moving in rushes while the other one watches from cover. Just like that weekend practice. All right?"

Jerry listened to Phillips's report of movement on the crest, suddenly feeling exposed. There was little cover, and he'd known better than to look for some when Ramey had told them to freeze.

Jerry knew which misshapen shadow was Phillips. Like Jerry, he was also on one knee, but probably was looking through his night-vision scope. Jerry had frozen in place with his rifle lowered, and dared not move now to raise it. Phillips had also managed to stop near a scrubby-looking bush. Combined with his camouflage, he was nearly invisible from Jerry's position ten yards away. The ridge was much farther ahead, sixty or more yards.

"More movement, the same location." Jerry studied the crest line carefully. There might be something near the top of the crest, but he couldn't see it. He divided his time between watching the suspicious location and making sure Yousef and Shirin didn't move.

Phillips was in front, with Lapointe nearest the highway, and Fazel on the left. Ramey was in the rear, and probably itching to move up. Fazel and Lapointe reported their sectors as clear, and Ramey told them to all hold in position. "XO, keep our friends very still."

Jerry told Shirin about the sighting, and Ramey's instructions. He could hear her relaying them to Yousef, who replied softly. Jerry could see Yousef's right hand resting on his pistol.

How long would the SEALs stay like this? Motionless. Exposed. What were they waiting for?

"More movement. A second man just joined the first." Jerry thought he saw them now, or imagined that he saw their location. And he understood. Ramey was waiting for whoever else was on the far side of the rise.

"I see a rifle barrel, now two." Not civilians, then. Jerry's urge to find cover was almost uncontrollable. Whoever was up there had clear shots at all of them. Did they have night-vision gear?

Phillips's latest report seemed to make up Ramey's mind. "Harry, shift to Philly's targets. Philly, cover to the left. Pointy, cover the right."

As the sniper, Fazel's scope was more powerful, and his SCAR Heavy rifle had a longer barrel and a bigger round for better accuracy and greater range. The ground also rose on the left side of the construction road, which gave him more height. His reply came in seconds. "I have them. Two men prone, one with binoculars. Confirm rifles. It's not a great angle, but I have a shot on both."

"Understood. Wait."

Jerry wished Ramey had given him a target. It wasn't that he felt left out, but with nothing to concentrate on, his mind raced. Without moving, he tried to look for cover. There was precious little, just shallow depressions that didn't offer protection from above. If the men on the crest started shooting, where would he go? What about Yousef and Shirin? He was sure that Yousef would shield his wife and unborn child with his body.

"Movement on the right." Lapointe's report was so quick, Jerry almost missed it, but this time he could see what Lapointe was warning them about. A shape appeared on the right of the crest's slope, near the ground. Ramey's instruction came immediately. "Wait. Hold. XO, do not fire. Tell our friends to stay still."

As Shirin translated the lieutenant's order, a second shape that could only be a man running came into the open and dove down behind a fold in the ground. After a moment the first shape left its hiding place and sprinted, falling behind a piece of low brush.

"I see them," Ramey said, almost casually. "Wait."

Yousef weighed their chances. They and the Americans were exposed, and if the others had indeed put two men on the hill, then Shirin, he, and the Americans were in a lethal crossfire. He didn't think much of their chances.

It was five against four, but the Americans' senior officer was inexperienced. The others had cover, and were on guard. They were still, what? Forty, fifty meters away? When the SEALs opened fire, the others would reply. There would be a gun battle. He and Shirin were not directly in the line of fire, but he knew how far and how wide stray rounds could go.

They would need his weapon after one or two of the Americans went down. He resolved to draw it the instant Shirin was flat on the ground. He would hold his fire until the others advanced. They would not see him until he fired, as they came into range of his pistol.

Jerry listened to his headset. Were there more coming? He was sure now that they didn't have night-vision gear, or they'd already be shooting. Jerry wondered how close they'd have to get before they'd see him.

"Philly, keep watching your side. Harry, are you good?" asked Ramey.

"Yes for both."

"XO, on my mark, drop flat and freeze."

"Understood." Jerry softly passed Ramey's order to Shirin, who relayed it to her husband.

"XO, drop. Open fire!" Ramey commanded.

Yousef heard the American's call. As he helped Shirin to lay flat, a flurry of single shots erupted from the Americans' weapons. Each SEAL popped off two rounds at their respective targets, then stopped just as suddenly as they began. He saw the two men on the right fall. One fired a burst, the muzzle flash almost blindingly bright, but the shots were wild, into the air. As Yousef protected Shirin with his body, he waited for the soldiers on the crest to return fire. Instead, he heard the Americans calling to one another.

The SEALs then charged forward. In moments, they were at the fallen Iranian soldiers's positions in the ravine and on the dune crest. In the next moment, two of the SEALs were around the rise, gone from view. The other two at the top of the rise fell prone, facing south.

Yousef waited, but there were no shots. Was that it? He'd never been in combat, and was relieved the shooting was over, but shocked at the ease with which the Americans had prevailed. No gun battle, not much return fire from the others at all, just a single random burst from one man, dying as he fell. Yousef still thought they were undisciplined, and he didn't know if the Americans could get them out of the country, but by Allah they were good shots.

Telling Shirin to stay down, he rose to his knees and then stood, ignoring Jerry's calls behind him. Walking quickly to the two soldiers he'd seen fall, he bent down and checked. Both were dead.

They wore Basij uniforms. One of the bodies was distressingly young, a boy still in his teens. Yousef had been ready to kill his countrymen for Shirin and the baby's sake, but he was glad he hadn't had to use his pistol. It was still in his hand when one of the SEALs came back around the rise.

Shirin, watching Yousef as he stood over the bodies, saw the American first, and screamed, "Don't shoot!" as Yousef lifted his head and the SEAL leveled his weapon.

Jerry added his own voice. "It's Yousef!" and the SEAL snapped the barrel up and clear. After pausing a moment, Lapointe reported, "All clear. It looks like it was just these four."

Jerry stood, then helped Shirin to her feet as her husband came back, holstering his weapon. Lapointe followed him, then went over to Jerry and spoke urgently. "Sir, we needed you to keep them down and in one place. I thought one of the bad guys was getting back up." His tone was earnest. Nodding toward Shirin, he said, "If she'd waited half a second to speak, she would have been a widow."

Beside them, Shirin had heard Lapointe and stifled a small cry. She grabbed Yousef's arm and pulled him close, also speaking earnestly.

"I understand, Pointy. Next time I'll tackle him if I have to."

"Tackling is good. Using the headset to warn us he's moving is good, too."

Jerry stood quietly, absorbing Lapointe's remarks. This was the real deal, with live ammunition. His first firefight, and he hadn't done anything, except almost let Yousef get shot.

Shirin didn't stop talking until she'd gotten a promise from Yousef to stay right next to her from then on, especially if there was any shooting. In the darkness, she'd seen and heard little except the flashes of gunfire, and she wasn't sure she wanted to see any more than she had.

Ramey came back a few minutes later. Ignoring the near-disastrous meeting between Lapointe and Yousef, he announced, "We've got transport. Let's get out of here."

With the others, Jerry walked around the southern edge of the dune. Fazel was searching the two bodies there and collecting their uniforms and weapons. Shirin stopped just long enough to ask him a question in Farsi. He nodded and answered, first in Farsi and then in English. "Yes, they will face Mecca."

He handed the results of his search to Ramey, which included a set of car keys. There were two rifles, and the lieutenant offered one to Yousef, who paused for a moment before taking the weapon and slinging it over his shoulder. There were also magazine pouches, flashlights, and cell phones, which they quickly disabled.

The transport was a white panel van. "There's room for everyone, but it'll be crowded," Ramey announced. We've got to police the area and get out of here ASAP."

He put everyone except Shirin to work. While Phillips kept watch, the others, including Yousef, dug a grave big enough to hold the four bodies and deep enough to satisfy Fazel and Yousef. They had to pause several times as vehicles passed, but with so many digging, the work was done quickly.

The four corpses were gathered from where they fell and placed with care in the grave so that they faced southwest, toward Mecca. While three of the SEALs policed the area for spent brass and any other remnants of the fight, Fazel joined Yousef and Shirin, standing by the graveside and reciting the *Janazah Salah*, the prayer for the dead.

Half an hour after Phillips's first warning, the van pulled back onto Highway 96, heading southeast.

13

CONVERGENCE

6 April 2013
0730 Local Time/0430 Zulu
The Persian Gulf Coast, West of Deyyer

A jeep met Rahim's car at the first checkpoint and led it down to the beach. They had to stop when the ground became too soft and proceeded on foot down to the water's edge.

The police lieutenant volunteered, "Fishermen spotted it this morning when they came down shortly after dawn. High tide was two hours before sunrise." The body lay under a blanket, guarded by a pair of policemen. The police lieutenant escorting Rahim and Dahghan gestured to them, and one gingerly removed the covering.

A man's body lay half-buried in a mudflat, facedown. He was wearing brown-patterned camouflage fatigues. It wasn't an Iranian uniform, or from any of the Gulf countries as far as Rahim could tell. And in spite of the beard, he was sure this man was European or American.

Rahim stepped closer and examined his face. Matted black hair partially hid his features, but ugly wounds and discolored areas on his face and neck showed that he hadn't died of natural causes. The major had seen enough injuries in his time to recognize burns. An accident? He'd also seen enough drowning victims to know he hadn't been in the water long—two or three days, most likely.

Rahim said, "You say he washed ashore this morning. And nothing's been touched? Nothing taken?" There could only be one right answer.

"Absolutely nothing." The police lieutenant glanced at the two officers. Either they had clean consciences, or they were good actors.

"Get a dozen men, more if you need to. Search the shoreline for ten kilometers in either direction. Collect every piece of trash or debris you find. And then help Dahghan sort through it."

"Yes, sir. I'll have my forensics people help him."

"Good. And do it again tonight and tomorrow morning as well." The lieutenant nodded as he made notes.

A military ambulance had driven up, and two men carried over a stretcher. "Dahghan, go with them and oversee the autopsy. I want a preliminary report by noon and a final one by tonight. Nobody is to speak of this." Rahim raised his voice enough so that everyone could hear him, and he met each man's eyes as they nodded their understanding. "Lieutenant, in your report simply record this as an unknown corpse, too badly decomposed to identify."

"Yes, Major."

6 April 2013
0000 Local Time/0500 Zulu
Georgetown, Washington, D.C.

Lowell Hardy was hardly surprised by Joanna's call. She'd been keeping crazy hours, and of course hadn't been able to tell him anything except that she was an action officer, and it was national security work. She'd managed a few hurried calls, and he'd been patient with her absence, and secretly proud.

He'd been hoping she'd say she was coming home, and could he please cook her something? They could have a quiet meal together and not talk about work.

Instead, she wanted him to meet her at the White House. A car was already on the way to pick him up. When asked why, she said she'd tell him when he arrived.

The limo took him from their Georgetown apartment straight to the visitor's entrance; his name was on the VIP access list and he was expeditiously processed through security. A staffer collected him and he was quickly escorted first to the West Wing and then down to the situation room.

Joanna was waiting for him by the door, and after he'd passed through another security check, they quickly hugged. She pecked him on the cheek and whispered, "We'll be able to talk shop, now."

He'd never been in the White House Situation Room, and was frankly a little envious of his wife. Of course, she'd never gotten to command a nuclear submarine, so that was probably fair.

It was less impressive than he'd thought, and actually a little cramped. There was the obligatory long conference table, wood paneling, and computer screens and maps lining the walls. Several civilian staffers and service members worked at desks in one corner. It wasn't really about the room. It was about who came here and the decisions they made.

He'd taken all this in as he was almost hustled to one end of the long table. He recognized Alison Gray, the deputy chief of staff at the White House. A man sitting next to her rose as they approached. "Senator Hardy, I'm Steven Weiss, a collection management officer with the National Clandestine Service at CIA. I'm here to brief you into the Gemstone sensitive HUMINT compartment." He offered Hardy a classified nondisclosure form.

"Senator, you're being read into the Opal subcompartment of Gemstone. By signing this form, you agree not to discuss or divulge any information within this subcompartment with anyone else unless that individual is also read in, and their status has been verified by the National Clandestine Service. There is no termination date on this agreement and it will remain in force for the rest of your life. Please check your social security number, then sign and date here." Hardy quickly scanned the form and signed it, while trying to process the news.

He handed the completed form back to Weiss, but looked at Joanna and then Gray. In a dark gray suit, with her hair pulled back, she looked every inch a White House official. "I'm here to oversee this brief and address any questions that Joanna can't answer." She checked her watch, and then said, "We're a little behind, Doctor. Please tell him what you've been working on."

His wife began what was clearly a well-rehearsed brief, complete with graphics on her laptop. As she called up maps and photographs, she described *Michigan* and her mission, the Iranian assets, now known to be a married couple, the information they had provided, and the information they claimed to have. Then she described what had gone wrong.

Hardy took it all in silently, although he winced when Joanna mentioned the battery fire on the ASDS. When she finished, Weiss asked him if he had any questions regarding security or access procedures. Hardy shook his head "no," his mind was halfway around the world, comparing what he knew with what he'd just been told. It didn't compute.

"So the public bluff and bluster by Iran is just for show? Am I missing something?" Hardy asked.

Gray answered, "A lot of people don't think it's a bluff." She outlined the Israelis' actions of the past few days. "And there are some people over here who agree with them."

"But our intelligence community says exactly the opposite."

"The second file we received, about the reactor in Arak, confirms our information from independent sources," Gray answered. She glanced at her watch again. "Senator, your wife has been managing the recovery of our people, but that is now one part of a much larger problem."

"Which is why I need your help," a new voice added.

Hardy turned to see President Myles, followed by Chief of Staff Alvarez and National Security Advisor Kirkpatrick. Old reflexes kicked in and the retired naval officer snapped to attention. Everyone else also rose and Myles reached out to shake Hardy's hand. The junior senator from Connecticut sensed a photo opportunity, but there were no cameras present.

Myles seemed to read his mind. "Lowell, I've got a tough job for you. If you can make this happen, you will save a lot of lives and make me very grateful—much more grateful than a mere autographed photo."

"I'm at your service, sir." Hardy braced himself.

Myles sat down at the head of the table, with the others on either side. Weiss had disappeared, and Hardy tried to remember what form he'd just signed. "First, tell me about Captain Kyle Guthrie."

Hardy smiled. "I served with Kyle on USS *Kentucky*. I was the main propulsion assistant, he was an assistant weapons officer. We've seen each other since then, occasionally. He's a good officer. Thorough, takes care of his people. Not as independent as some submarine captains, but there are different opinions on the value of independence."

Myles nodded. "And his executive officer, Lieutenant Commander Mitchell?"

Hardy hesitated for a moment, then answered, "One of the best, sir. I'm sure he's keeping *Michigan* running smoothly." Why was the president interested in *Michigan*'s XO, Hardy asked himself. Subs were largely one-man shows, and Guthrie was the decision maker.

Myles saw the puzzled expression on Hardy's face and turned toward Patterson. "You haven't told him about Mitchell yet?" questioned Myles.

Joanna saw Hardy's expression change from confusion to concern. "I was going to tell him about that later, sir." She faced Hardy and took a deep breath. "He's okay right now, Lowell, but Jerry's in trouble. He was one of the pilots on the ASDS when it sank. He's on the beach with the SEAL team and the two Iranians."

Myles asked, "How will he do in that situation, Senator?"

Hardy hesitated as he absorbed the news. "Well, sir, he's definitely out of his comfort zone." He paused again before answering. "I meant it when I said Jerry's one of the best. He's intelligent, resourceful, and doesn't give up."

"Good." Myles's smile seemed genuine. "Now for your mission. Alison briefed you on the Israeli preparations?"

"Yes, sir. It sounds like they'll be ready to strike in a day or two at the most."

"You and Joanna are going to change their minds. The Israelis don't give the files Opal sent the same weight we do, and I need you to convince them to wait. Buy us enough time to get at the rest of the information that the Iranian scientist is carrying."

"What did they say when you showed them the two files?" Hardy asked.

"They pointed to the IAEA report and imagery of the test site. Our ambassador didn't make a lot of headway, and Andy Lloyd didn't push him very hard." The president paused for a moment, and added, "While Andy and I get along on many things, this isn't one of them. I must depend on your discretion."

Hardy wasn't a political animal, but Joanna was, and had spoken of Lloyd's long relationship with the president. He asked, "How closely do we work with the State Department?" The nature of their trip was becoming clearer.

"Not at all. You are my personal envoys with sensitive information that is to be discussed with their intelligence people. With luck we can keep this below the Cabinet level on both sides. If Mossad or Military Intelligence can be convinced that the Iranians are not close to assembling a weapon, they can convince their leaders to wait."

"What do you think about the other evidence: that the Iranians are getting close?"

Myles leaned back in his chair. "I agree with Dr. Kirkpatrick. There's a mystery, but I'm not ready to throw away everything we've done before. Normally I'd wait and let the intelligence agencies sort it out, but we can't sit on the fence, not with the Israelis ready to fly."

Alison and Alvarez were both looking at their watches. Alvarez started to lean forward as if to speak, but Myles waved him back.

"If the intelligence supported it, I'd wish the Israelis Godspeed. But I'm convinced it doesn't, and we"—he pointed to Hardy and Patterson—"meaning you two, have to convince them they're wrong."

The president stood. "You two are going to stop a war before it starts. Go home and pack. You leave in eight hours."

6 April 2013
1200 Local Time/0900 Zulu
Kangan Police Barracks

"It's confirmed, Major, he didn't drown." Deyyer was only twenty kilometers by road from Kangan, so Dahghan had chosen to give his report to Rahim in person. "There was no water in his lungs, and the doctor said he died from electric shock and severe burns. There are traces of exotic chemicals on his skin and clothing, which they are analyzing. He carried no identification. He was wearing an American-made watch."

Dahghan was smiling now, and Rahim asked, "What else did you find?"

The young agent unwrapped an object. It was a thin piece of red plastic the size of a large book. One side was ragged, where it had been torn from a binding or notebook.

Rahim spoke English, and could easily read the lettering:

Deck Log

Advanced SEAL

Delivery System Hull 1

"They found that two kilometers southeast of the body's location. I called our headquarters in Tehran. The Advanced SEAL Delivery System is a U.S. Navy minisub that can be used for commando missions. It has a crew of two and can hold at least six passengers. It's carried by a larger sub. There is only one vehicle known to be in service. It is currently carried by USS *Michigan*, a Special Operations and cruise missile submarine, which was reported to be exercising with the Pakistani Navy last week."

The major worked it through. "So an American submarine entered the gulf and sent a minisub in to contact two traitors on a beach southeast of Kangan. They wouldn't send a sub unless they intended to exchange something or someone. Some time during that trip, the sub experienced an electrical fire"—he pointed to photos of the corpse—"killing at least one crewman and"—holding up the cover of the logbook—"likely causing it to sink."

Rahim smiled. "Allah is good to us. But now he gives us another test. Where is the wreck of the submarine? Did survivors make it ashore? What was their business with the traitors?"

The major sat silently for a few minutes, got up and paced, studied the map, then started firing orders to Dahghan. "Expand the search. Alert every police station, Basij unit, and VEVAK office along the coast and from here north to Shiraz. Increase the number of checkpoints.

"I'm changing the traitors' status as well. They are no longer to be captured. Pasdaran Captain Yousef Akbari and the nuclear engineer Shirin Naseri are dangerous traitors and should be shot on sight. *If* they are taken alive, they are to be held incommunicado until they can be turned over to VEVAK."

The major continued, "The captain's only living family member is his mother, but she is in a vegetative state. Naseri's father is dead, but arrest her mother and uncle. Question them both thoroughly."

"Yes, sir. The mother lives in Shiraz, but her uncle lives in Bandar Charak. We don't have an office in such a small town. They'd have to come from Bandar Abbas."

"We can't wait," Rahim insisted. "Go ahead and tell the Bandar Abbas office to send a team, but tell the local Pasdaran to make the arrest immediately. He should be held incommunicado until our people arrive and take custody. We know where these people live," he added. "I want them both in our hands an hour from now. Move."

After Dahghan left, Rahim placed a secure call to Moradi. He'd briefed the general earlier about the discovery of the body, but the new evidence confirmed his suspicions, and raised new concerns. The general answered immediately.

"They have been in contact with the Americans," Rahim reported. He described the cover to the logbook. "If nothing else but to arrange a meeting. There is no way to know what information the traitors have passed to the Americans. At a minimum, they could provide a great deal of information on the actual status of the program."

"Which could delay an attack," Moradi concluded.

"The greater risk is if they had knowledge of our immediate plans." Even on a secure line, Rahim was circumspect.

"Have you found any evidence that they do know?" Moradi's tone was carefully neutral. They both understood the implications if the couple had revealed their plan.

"I am concerned that the date of their disappearance coincides with the commencement of our operation. I never assume coincidences."

"Once they are captured, we will know how much they told the Americans."

"I disagree, General. That is irrelevant. We are on a short time scale, and there is nothing we can do to reverse what has been done. Our best course is to limit any further spread of the information. If they have the secret, it will die with them. I'd also like to withhold information about the discovery of the body."

"You're asking a lot. There are several ways we could publicize this that would badly damage American prestige."

"I understand, sir, but it also warns the other side. I don't like telling them what we know."

"Concealment is not always the best course."

"General, this is about more than merely embarrassing the United States. Because the Americans were meeting with Akbari and Naseri, there may be a link to our operation. Questions will be asked by both sides. If we can find them before news is released, then that link will be broken."

"All right. I am convinced, and while we wait, I will use the time to plan how to use our dead friend to the best effect."

"Another question arises. Was he alone?" Rahim asked.

"You think there was more than one American aboard the submarine?" Moradi asked.

"Two is likely, more is possible. But are they entombed within the wreck, or will they float ashore tomorrow? Or are they already on our shores, and alive?"

"In which case our traitors would not be traveling alone. Live Americans would look even better on television than a dead one," Moradi observed wistfully.

"If there are Americans here, then their sub is still offshore, waiting for them," Rahim said. "They will be trying to reach it," he reasoned. "We must find it and sink it."

"Only Pasdaran units can operate in gulf waters," Moradi reminded him. "The navy operates east of Hormuz."

"I understand that, sir. But only the navy can find and kill an American submarine, which, you can remind them, they let slip through the Strait of Hormuz unmolested."

"If you're suggesting we ask the navy for assistance, that will not sit well with my colleagues," Moradi said, "I'm sure you remember how hard the Pasdaran had to fight to get sole control of the Persian Gulf."

"Yes, sir, I do. But can you think of another way to find and kill an American submarine? No disrespect, sir, but the Pasdaran Navy is not equipped to hunt down a submarine. And finding that submarine not only helps us find their friends on land, but will interfere with their attempts to escape."

"All right," Moradi conceded. "You've made your point. I'll speak to the commanders of both navies immediately."

The Outskirts of Bandar Charak
1215 Local Time/0915 Zulu

Highway 96 left the coast halfway to Bandar Charak, bending north, then east again, skirting around a mass of rough rocky hills between the highway and the coast. Following Shirin's instructions, north of Charak they turned right onto another paved road that would take them straight into town. The road lay between the hills to the west and an eroded flat plain to the east. Neither showed many signs of man.

They stopped a couple of kilometers north of town. A grove of trees on a low hill gave cover, and after they'd unloaded everything from the van,

Ramey and Phillips drove it back north half a kilometer. A dirt road ran at right angles into the hills from the paved highway, and they hid the van there, sanitizing it like they had the Peykan.

Yousef and Shirin had wanted to take the van into town, but both Ramey and Jerry had decided against it. "By now the patrol's been missed, and they're looking for their vehicle." That meant Shirin and Fazel would have to walk into town, and her uncle's house was at the southern end of town, near the water.

While the two SEALs hid the car, the others under Lapointe's guidance worked on setting up what would be a layup position at least until that evening, and quite possibly for a day or two. It was nearly 1230 by the time Ramey and Phillips returned. After inspecting their newest home, Ramey pronounced it acceptable. "Time for phase two."

Shirin looked at Harry in the stolen Basij uniform. They had a pair of pants and a uniform shirt that more or less fit him, but they hadn't taken any boots from the corpses. "I wouldn't change these anyway," he told her. "Nobody will notice the difference, especially after we've been walking for a while."

The American had left all his equipment behind, except for his radio, which he'd hidden in a pocket. Reluctantly, Yousef handed him the Iranian-made pistol and gun belt. They had the rifles they'd taken from the Basij soldiers, but they'd all agreed a rifle might draw unnecessary attention from the authorities. Basij normally wouldn't carry one unless they were on duty.

The American also had the identity papers for the dead Basij corporal, a Qassem Molavi. The photo, height, and weight were wrong, but they might pass casual examination.

Together, they worked on a legend, with "Corporal Molavi" escorting his sister-in-law "Miryam" to visit her family in town. Shirin's husband was away on duty with the Pasdaran, and no self-respecting Iranian woman, especially a pregnant one, would travel unaccompanied by a male relative. It was also true that no self-respecting Iranian husband would let his wife be accompanied by a stranger, but Yousef could see no alternative.

"I wish you didn't have to do this," Yousef had told her. He was looking at the American while he said it.

"I don't want to do this either," she'd answered. "I hate the thought of walking that far. But it won't be bad. And I'm looking forward to seeing Uncle Seyyed. I know he will help us."

"I also wish I knew something about the Charak Basij Brigade," Yousef complained. Looking directly at Harry, he warned, "Remember, you're wearing an Iranian corporal's uniform now. Show some discipline. If you act the same way you do with your own officers, they'll either spot you as an impostor or throw you in jail for insubordination."

Anger flashed across Fazel's face and into his voice. "You don't have a clue about what it means to be a professional soldier. It's going to be easy to pretend I'm Basij. I'll just act like a thug. Oh, no, wait, that's if I want to be Pasdaran."

Shirin threw herself between the two men, and while the other Americans may not have understood Farsi, they knew trouble when they heard it. Lapointe and Phillips were closest. They managed to move so that while they discouraged Fazel from saying anything else, they stood with their teammate, facing Yousef. "That's enough," Lapointe ordered. Looking at Ramey and Jerry, he said, "It's time to go." Both officers nodded.

Embracing Yousef one last time, Shirin sighed and followed "Qassem." They waited briefly, made sure the highway was empty, and hurried out to the roadside. Although it was early April, in the south it was already in the low twenties of degrees Centigrade. This close to the water, the southerly breeze was humid, but thankfully cool.

The Bandar Charak Road ran almost straight north-south here, two lanes of asphalt bordered by wide shoulders that blended with the surrounding landscape, sometimes almost seamlessly. It seemed flat, but as they walked, Shirin could see that the road cut through a series of low, gently sloping dunes.

Harry explained, "It's a little less than two kilometers to the edge of town. We should get there in half an hour or so."

"Fine, Qassem. So tell me about yourself. How old are you? Do I have any other in-laws?" Her tone was humorous, but she knew she was right. They were supposed to be family, even if only by marriage.

They walked in silence for a few minutes before the American answered. "We are not supposed to share personal information with the people we meet, but we are also taught that if we have to construct a legend, it's best to stay close to the truth. I am twenty-eight."

"So you're Yousef's older brother. Yousef is twenty-four. You have"—she paused for a moment—"had another brother, three years younger than Yousef, Ali. He was at university, but protested the 2009 elections and was arrested. He was killed in prison, by the Pasdaran."

"I'm sorry. That must have been hard on Yousef and our parents."

"Your father passed away several years before that. Your mother was diagnosed with Alzheimer's disease earlier in 2009, and the loss of her younger son accelerated her decline. Ali was the only family Yousef had. That is why it is so important that the two remaining brothers should get along." Her plea came from her eyes, as well as her voice.

Harry walked silently for several minutes. "Alright. Thank you for telling me about Ali. But why would Yousef join the Pasdaran if he felt that way?"

"He was already in, and stayed because of me, and because leaving the Pasdaran without good reason is not always easy, or safe."

They walked and worked out several more details of his life. She and Yousef had met in Shiraz, so it made sense that "Qassem" lived there. He was an army veteran who had joined the Basij, and was studying to be a paramedic.

"I'm probably in charge of giving first aid classes to my fellow Basij fighters."

"Don't take them lightly," she warned sternly. "They don't, and they're a law unto themselves. Yousef wasn't wrong about being careful."

She was telling Harry about Shiraz when they reached the edge of town, with scattered houses stretching away from the road. The city limits were officially marked by a small traffic circle, busy but not crowded with traffic in the middle of the day. The center island was filled with carefully tended greenery.

A policeman stood at the edge of the circle, watching the traffic. He noticed the couple and waved. Fazel waved back and Shirin nodded politely.

Another road headed east from the circle, and they turned that way, doing their best to look like locals. Walking east past a soccer field, they turned south again. One- and two-story buildings, all built from the same tan brick, lined the street. The bare ground was dotted with dark green scrub, but no grass. Trees often grew in the houses' courtyards, with the houses built to surround them.

She discussed the route as they walked, with the American always steering her toward the largest crowds. It was well into the lunch hour, and her stomach complained.

On a street lined with shops and small businesses, they bought kebabs at one stall, and fruit drinks at another, always alert for anyone following or even showing interest in them. There were places to sit and eat, and Harry offered to let her rest, but she was too impatient to see Seyyed. And they couldn't linger. Yousef and the others were depending on them.

As they headed south, Shirin began to see familiar places, and told Harry stories about Seyyed and the rest of her family. Her feet no longer hurt, and she began to rehearse how she would introduce the American to her uncle. "Uncle, this Basij corporal is actually an American commando." There had to be a better way to say that.

Only a few blocks from his house, they saw a traffic barrier across the street, and two policemen waving traffic away. Like the one at the traffic circle, they were dressed in dark fatigues and ball caps, and carried submachine guns. Pedestrians tried to pass or spoke to them, but they were all turned away. Nobody argued with the officers, but several small groups had congregated across the street.

Alert for any sign of authority, they'd both spotted the police at the same time. Shirin's cheerful mood vanished. "What do we do?" she whispered. Already walking south, they were in a residential neighborhood. Stopping or turning away would look suspicious.

The American simply said, "Peace, Miryam. We'll turn at the corner. Our destination is to the east of here, remember?" They were so close. She could almost see Seyyed's house from where they were.

"Yes," she answered mechanically. Then she remembered something from her visits. "The old Al Ali Castle, down near the water."

"And I forgot the camera again."

His response almost made her laugh, and she relaxed a little. But why was the street blocked?

As they neared the intersection where the barrier was placed, Harry surprised Shirin and spoke to an elderly man standing at the corner. "He didn't let you pass?"

"No," the old man grumbled. "I wanted to visit my friend Farrokh, but they are not letting anyone by. They won't tell me why, or how long it will be there. I don't have a car, and my home is six blocks from here. We play chess every day, and smoke together. . . ."

Another man came up, followed by a pair of women in burquas. He asked Fazel, "Do you know what this is about?"

"No, no," he answered. "We're just visiting."

The two quickly moved on before they could be drawn into the discussion. Now that she could see down the cross street at the intersection, Shirin saw barriers at the streets on either side of this one, also manned by police, all blocking passage south. They walked quickly east. "Qassem, I'm worried. This can't be a coincidence."

"We're still walking to the castle," he reassured her. "See, the next intersection is not blocked off. We can use that street to head south."

When they turned south, they did find more barriers, this time blocking access back to the west. Again, three streets were blockaded, and the center one passed near Seyyed's home.

"We can turn west down there," she said, as they walked by the barriers.

"No," he replied. "We can't risk showing too much interest. . . ."

The gunfire interrupted him. It came from their right, where Seyyed's house should be. She heard a single shot, then a burst of fire, followed by several more. Then an explosion. All the fear and worry inside her wrapped itself around her heart.

The pedestrians on the street, and even the policemen at the barriers, ducked at the sound. The police kept their positions, but went to one knee, and kept turning and looking behind them. The civilians, some calling or shouting, fled.

Feeling Harry's grip on her arm, Shirin let herself be hurried south. The shooting continued, and even Shirin could distinguish the sounds of different weapons. Single shots with different sounds, perhaps from pistols and rifles, mixed with a deeper boom. A shotgun? And laid over them was the chatter of automatic weapons. It was a full-blown gun battle.

They'd crossed two or three streets when Shirin stopped, leaning against a wall, almost gasping. "No farther. Please." She drew a few breaths, hearing the sounds of battle and wishing Yousef could tell her what was going on. But Harry was a soldier, too. "What's happening?" she asked.

Harry shook his head. "A barricaded neighborhood." He nodded toward the firing. "And Seyyed's house is in that direction?"

"Yes," she answered unhappily.

"They may have tried to arrest him. It looks like he decided to put up a fight."

The ice around her heart remained, but she said, "I have to see. I have to know what's happening."

The streets were virtually empty now, and she started west. "Nahil Street is almost straight. We may be able to see."

Harry's expression told her he wasn't happy with the idea, but she was already walking, and he reluctantly turned to follow. A few fast steps and he took the lead, hugging the walls of any buildings, looking around each corner before crossing any gaps between buildings.

A loud explosion, then another, made the American flatten against a wall, but Shirin hardly slowed. "Those were RPGs. Rocket propelled grenades," he said softly.

The gunfire slowed, then stopped, and she started to walk faster, afraid that she would not know, and afraid of what she would find out.

One street over from Nahil, Harry paused to look north toward Seyyed's house, and pointed. A tangled column of smoke was rising, its source still hidden. It had to be a fire. She felt numb. What had happened?

They crossed the next block quickly, without fear of stray rounds, at least. Again, Harry looked around the corner first, then turned and nodded to Shirin. They stepped around the corner and began walking north. "If anyone stops us, we were curious about the smoke," he said.

That made sense to her, but her mind only noted it in passing. The roadblock at the intersection ahead was unmanned, which allowed them to get closer without fear of being questioned. Bullet holes in the wooden barriers explained why the post was vacant.

Her uncle's house was visible, but only between two army trucks. Soldiers in Pasdaran uniforms stood in clumps, weapons slung or held casually.

She heard sirens, and one of the trucks moved, giving a clearer view of the structure. The front of the building was a jumble of blackened brick, and smoke streamed out of both the front and the roof.

"It's his house," she confirmed, almost to herself more than the American.

Two white ambulances pulled up and soldiers in green fatigue uniforms were loaded inside. The paramedics worked on one for several minutes before putting his stretcher inside.

She watched the activity. "I don't see my uncle," she told Harry. What did that mean?

"I only see uniforms," the American replied. "I see three lightly wounded, two incapacitated."

The ambulances pulled away, and for a moment she could see more activity. A uniformed figure, probably an officer, was pointing and giving orders, while other soldiers did things with their weapons.

"There, on the right. Between those two men." Harry couldn't point, but she saw two soldiers standing, with their rifles held at the ready, as if guarding something. Between them, on the ground, were bundles that she'd seen earlier, but dismissed as debris. Now she saw they were man-sized. There were four of them, partly covered with blankets, but she could see civilian clothes beneath.

Tears blurred her vision, and she started crying. Harry tried to shush her, and even put his arm around her shoulder, but he was not Yousef, and it held no comfort.

"Are you people all right?" Absorbed in her grief, she hadn't noticed the policeman's approach. Harry seemed surprised as well. "Is your wife injured?"

"She's my sister-in-law," Harry answered softly. "She's just upset."

The policeman nodded. "Women should not see such things. Why did you bring her here?"

"We were on our way to visit the Al Ali Castle when we heard the shooting. After it stopped, we were curious about the smoke."

"And look what it got you," the policeman's tone was critical, almost angry. "This is none of your business, anyway. Go now."

"Yes, Officer," he answered, and Shirin let herself be led away. They walked through town back west and north. Fighting for control, she stopped her voice, but not her grief. The walk back seemed shorter. They were not stopped or questioned again.

Along the way, Harry tried to get her to talk, but she waved off his questions, thinking and trying to deal with her grief, and new fears. How would they get out of Iran now? Could they even get out? And if they didn't, what about what they knew?

They reached the layup in late afternoon. She didn't realize how exhausted she was until she saw Yousef, and almost collapsed in his arms. She began weeping again, completely losing the control she'd worked so hard to maintain.

While Yousef tended to his wife, Fazel explained to the others what had happened. Ramey took it hard, suddenly sitting down like he'd had the air let out of him. "We are so screwed," Phillips complained.

"They're hunting us for sure; chasing us," Lapointe observed. "They're rolling up her family, maybe people they know."

Jerry felt badly for Shirin and her husband, and he really wasn't sure what they'd do next. "We need another plan. What if we find a really good spot to hide and wait for a few days?"

"For the 'heat to die down?'" Ramey asked. He started to say something else, but Shirin interrupted.

"No. There is no more time." Wrapped in a blanket, holding a nearly empty water bottle, she looked like an accident victim, but her voice was strong. "I had hoped that Seyyed would be able to get us out soon, even tonight."

Yousef said something to her, and she nodded, answering him in Farsi. "We must tell you something. I know it will sound fantastic, unbelievable. That is why we wanted to prove ourselves before saying anything, but that is not possible now. You must set up the radio and warn your government. The people in charge of the nuclear program, maybe the Iranian government itself, is trying to provoke an attack by the Israelis on Natanz."

Jerry heard the words, but they didn't make sense. "You're saying they *want* the Israelis to attack? That's insane! Why?"

"Because they are impatient for the confrontation, and the weapon isn't ready. We won't have it for years, if we get it at all. A public admittance of failure would be a colossal embarrassment for our leaders. If Natanz is destroyed, it's not Iran's fault anymore."

Nobody said anything for a minute, and finally Shirin continued. "We don't have proof—none of the files on the flash drive say anything about this, but what we know, what the files prove, is that their recent actions are completely at odds with the facts. There is no bomb to test."

"Hundreds of my friends and coworkers will be killed, and a war will start because of pride and greed and fear of what will happen if they fail."

"How soon?" Jerry asked.

"I don't know exactly. The contingency planning I saw assumed that once we prepared to test a weapon, America, the Israelis, or both would attack within a week, or less. That's why we weren't going to test the first device we built, but the third or fourth. Any attack on us would be followed by the destruction of Israel by nuclear-armed ballistic missiles."

Jerry told Lapointe, "Get the SATCOM radio set up. This is way beyond my pay grade. We'll send this on and let the higher-ups sort this one out."

"No," Shirin insisted. "Do not just pass this on to someone else. We risked everything to get this information to the West."

"And that's what we're going to do," Jerry answered. "It's all we can do, that and try to find bus tickets back home."

14

ROUND TWO

VEVAK agent Hafez Omid surveyed the chaos with contempt. It was a typical Pasdaran operation, a frontal assault with no planning, no reconnaissance, and no thinking. Omid fumed as he took stock of all the opportunities those idiots in the bright green uniforms had cost them. And to make matters worse, the bumbling Pasdaran captain was touting this skirmish as a great victory! Victory? What did they have to show for this "great victory"? Four dead traitors whose knowledge was lost forever? Whatever secrets they had had were smoldering in the fireplace. Papers, laptop computers, cell phones, electronic storage media, all of it charred to uselessness by the flares the traitors had thrown onto the pile. *Damn those incompetent Pasdar fools,* cursed Omid to himself.

The air was still thick with smoke from the byproducts of gunfire, explosives, and burned-out flares. The acrid atmosphere assaulted his eyes, nose, and throat, worsening his already foul mood. He'd collect the burnt remains of the electronics. There was a slight chance that some of the data might have survived, but everything else was gone. Angrily, Omid stormed out of the house. He needed to find his partner, and he needed a cigarette.

Passing through what was left of the front door, Omid saw Teymour

Sattari across the street taking the Pasdaran unit commander's statement. *No doubt elaborating on his military brilliance*, Omid thought. He motioned for Sattari to get rid of the officer and join him. Pulling the pack of cigarettes from his jacket pocket, he withdrew one and lit up as Sattari approached.

"That bad?" Sattari asked. He could read the sour expression on his partner's face.

"Worse. It's probably a total loss. I'll have the remains of the computers and cell phones sent to Tehran. We might get something if we are very lucky. But the discs and paper are nothing but ashes," replied Omid, as he took another drag. "The traitorous bastards used magnesium roadside flares, six of them, to torch their information. They were quite effective."

Sattari winced and shook his head; flares like that could easily get over one thousand degrees Centigrade. They would be lucky indeed if they recovered any useful information. Gesturing toward the battered house, he asked, "Do you think they were mujahadeen?"

"Of course they were MEK," snapped Omid as he threw the last of the cigarette on the ground and stamped it out. "But there is absolutely no way we can benefit from that knowledge, because of that arrogant imbecile!" He pointed vigorously in the direction of the Pasdaran commander. "We lost our best chance to trace the network Naseri belonged to when that Pasdaran jackass stormed the house!"

"They were only following their orders," counseled Sattari quietly. "The Pasdaran are a blunt instrument. Don't expect a hammer to do the job of a screwdriver. If there is negligence, look to the carpenter, not the tool."

"Rahim?" Omid literally spat the name out. "Trust me, my patience with our esteemed colleague is all but spent. He has become too close to that Pasdaran general and has lost sight of his true duties."

"He certainly has been stingy with his information," Sattari admitted. "He could have alerted us much earlier about the missing traitors. And why was he in such a hurry to arrest her uncle? With just a little more time, we could have conducted a proper operation here. The outcome would have likely been very different."

"And my report will say as much," Omid said determinedly. "Rahim routinely oversteps his authority, and this time I will have him held accountable." The finality of his statement seemed to appease the senior VEVAK agent and he relaxed. Pointing again in the direction of the Pasdaran captain he asked, "So what did our hero of the battle of Bandar Charak have to say?"

Sattari smiled. He was relieved that Omid had calmed down. While his anger in this case was completely justified, Omid's short-fuzed temper had gotten him in trouble before with his superiors. The last time was over an altercation with Rahim concerning an investigation of a possible MEK informant at Isfahan. Omid had presented a superior investigation plan, but Rahim knew all the right buttons to push, and Omid eventually lost his patience. His furious denouncement of Rahim's suggestions cost him the position of lead investigator. And even though his recommendations were ultimately accepted, Omid was "exiled" to Bandar Abbas, while Rahim became the VEVAK liaison to the Iranian nuclear program. Needless to say, there was no love lost between the two men.

"He actually had little to say." Sattari opened his notebook and walked down the time line. "They received their orders at 1255. Mobilized two squads of Pasdaran soldiers by 1318, and began their assault at 1333.

"Resistance was much greater than expected. The occupants had automatic weapons and grenades, and they repulsed the first assault. He regrouped his men and with the use of RPGs, succeeded in storming the house. The objective was secured by 1355. Seyyed Naseri, his wife, and two unidentified males were killed in the attack. Pasdaran casualties were three dead and five wounded; two seriously."

"Hmph, I expected their losses to be greater," Omid remarked cynically.

"Hafez, you need to learn to be more gracious. The Pasdaran may be blunt instruments, but they still serve the Islamic Republic and their sacrifice deserves our respect," chided Sattari.

Omid sighed deeply, acknowledging his partner's rebuke. "You're right, Teymour. My apologies. Was there anything else?"

"Uh, yes, one last item. It seems our captain was not impressed with the barricade established by the Charak police force. One officer in particular allowed two civilians to get too close. Fortunately, the fighting had already ended."

Omid looked at Sattari intently, intrigued. "Did he give you any details?"

"Just that it was a man and a woman. They left before he had a chance to speak to them. The captain then claimed he became occupied in disciplining the officer and didn't see where they went," answered Sattari.

"Find that police officer, Teymour." Omid's voice was hard. "I want to question him personally." The junior agent initially considered asking why, but the stern look on Omid's face suggested that would be a bad idea. He left quickly to find the policeman.

It took only fifteen minutes for Sattari to lead a very nervous police officer into the sitting room of the Naseri house. Omid was seated behind a desk busily labeling plastic bags with the charred remains of the computers and cell phones. He looked up as his partner cleared his throat.

"Sir. Police Officer Golzar reporting for questioning as ordered."

Omid stood and pointed to the chair in front of the desk. "Excellent, Agent Sattari. Officer Golzar, please be seated."

The man sat down stiffly. His face was pale, and he swallowed hard. There was fear in his eyes.

"Be at ease, Officer Golzar. You are not under any suspicion. I only wish to ask you some questions concerning the two civilians that managed to get past your barricade."

Golzar relaxed noticeably, but his voice still wavered. "I will do my best to answer your questions, sir."

"Excellent." Omid smiled as he opened his notebook. "Would you please describe the two civilians?"

"They weren't both civilians, sir," Golzar answered warily. "The man was a Basij soldier, a corporal. The woman was properly attired in a full, dark-colored burqua. He claimed she was his sister-in-law."

"I see," responded Omid. "Can you describe this corporal in more detail?

"He was about my height. Approximately 1.8 meters tall, stocky build. His uniform was typical for Basij, ill-fitting and a little dirty. He was also armed. The weapon appeared to be a standard-issue sidearm."

"Did anything appear unusual about this man?" probed Omid.

"No, sir. He appeared to be a typical Basij militiaman. Although"—Golzar paused momentarily, a brief grin flashed across his face—"he was unusually respectful and obeyed my command to leave immediately without question."

"And the woman?"

"She was much shorter, perhaps 1.6 meters tall. She seemed slight of build, but it is difficult to say with certainty as she was wearing a full burqua. She was visibly distressed by what she saw. She was sobbing uncontrollably."

Omid wrote down the salient points, and then continued, "Exactly where did they cross the barricade?"

"I can't say for sure, sir." Golzar was getting nervous again. "I found them twenty-five meters inside the perimeter. They appeared to have come up from the south, from the direction of Bandar Aftab Road."

"What time did this occur?"

Golzar checked his watch. "Just over an hour and ten minutes ago, about 1405."

"Did they say why they were there?"

"Yes, sir. The corporal said they were on the way to the old Al Ali Castle when they became curious about the noise and smoke. I criticized him for bringing the woman there and told them that it was none of their business and that they had to leave."

Omid leaned forward; his gaze was intense. "Did you observe their departure directly?"

"Yes, sir, at . . . at least initially." Golzar audibly gulped as he spoke. "They headed north on Bandar Charak Road, and then the Pasdaran captain diverted my attention. When I looked back, they were gone. They could have headed west on Nahil Street, but that would be a guess on my part, sir."

The VEVAK agent slowly closed his notebook and rose. Golzar sprung to his feet, standing at attention. Omid smiled and offered his hand. "Thank you for your cooperation, Police Officer Golzar. You have been most helpful."

Golzar hesitated at first, but he took Omid's hand and shook it. Sattari then led him outside and cautioned him to not speak about the interview. When Sattari returned, he found Omid sitting in his chair, a satisfied expression on his face.

"Do you believe the two were Naseri and Akbari?"

"Yes, Teymour, I do," Omid's tone was calm and confident. "The old castle is on the other side of town, over a kilometer away, and yet they approached from the south or the east? The descriptions Golzar gave are about right. Naseri wore a burqua to prevent being recognized and Akbari changed his Pasdaran uniform for Basij. This deception would fool the police and probably any Pasdaran officer, but her reaction to the fighting gives them away. They are here, Teymour! In Bandar Charak!"

Sattari grinned, pleased that things seemed to be turning their way, "We should report this immediately."

"Absolutely not!" shouted Omid. "Provide an initial report of the out-come of the raid, but do not mention my suspicion that Akbari and Naseri are here. Then I want you to find the local Basij commander. We need eight of his men to support us in the search."

"Hafez, I know you don't like Rahim, but procedure demands we re-port this," argued Sattari.

"Actually, I despise the man," Omid shot back forcefully. "But my feel-ings for that jackal only play a small part in my decision. Time. Time is what is against us. If we report in, we'll have to wait for Rahim to get the message and respond. And since we don't have the authority to mobilize the entire Basij brigade ourselves, we'll have to sit here with our fingers up our ass waiting for him, doing nothing. Every minute we delay gives those two traitors more opportunity to escape. No, Teymour, we'll grab some Basij and go find them ourselves."

"Akbari is a Pasdaran captain, and he is armed," warned Sattari. "He won't go down without a fight."

Omid's laugh was laden with contempt. "Bah! If you and I, with a little help from the Basij, can't apprehend one Pasdaran captain and a pregnant woman, then we have no right to be in our line of business."

Although apprehensive, Sattari reluctantly nodded his agreement. Omid gave him a reassuring slap on the back as the junior agent departed to find the local Basij brigade commander. *Omid is one of the best field agents in VEVAK*, he thought. *He knows what he is doing.*

6 April 2013
0900 Local Time/1400 Zulu
U.S. Air Force C-37 Gulfstream V

They'd barely taken off when an Air Force tech sergeant said, "Ma'am, Senator, I've got an urgent video call from the White House Situation Room. They're in contact with some people in Iran."

Joanna almost leapt from her seat, with Lowell close behind her. The communications tech guided them to one side of a conference table in the midsection of the cabin. "The video conference camera will see you both," he said, pressing a key. Then, speaking into his headset, he said, "Dr. Kirk-patrick, they're both here."

The communications tech pointed to one of the video screens. It showed Kirkpatrick in the situation room. A screen next to it showed her and Lowell, and she fought the urge to fix her hair. Men never notice anyway.

With Joanna on the move, Kirkpatrick had taken her place in the situation room. It was appropriate, considering that the problem was now much larger than a simple intelligence op. A war could start in the next few days, and the U.S. had to stop it, or be ready if they couldn't.

"This is a secure line," the technician announced.

"The president is still en route, but we're going to start anyway," Kirkpatrick announced. "Commander Mitchell's position is not completely secure. Commander, are you still there?"

"We're still here, sir." Jerry's disembodied voice wasn't as strong as Kirkpatrick's, and was overlaid with a little static.

"Jerry, it's Joanna. What's your status?" she asked. She tried, and failed, to hide her worry.

"We're safe for the moment, but our source's contact was killed by the IRGC. We're going to have to work up a new strategy to get out with *Michigan.*"

"We're working with them as well," Kirkpatrick added. "Joanna, I've explained your role to Commander Mitchell, and why I thought you should hear his information."

President Myles appeared in the screen, and sat down next to Kirkpatrick. "Commander Mitchell, the president just joined us. Please tell him and Dr. Patterson what you told me a few moments ago."

Jerry's voice sounded intense, almost desperate. "The Iranians are deliberately provoking Israel into bombing Natanz. Our Iranian friend confirms that they aren't even close to assembling a weapon. An Israeli attack gives them an excuse for their failure, and makes Israel the bad guy."

Patterson didn't respond immediately. In her mind, she walked through what they knew; it was entirely consistent with Jerry's report. It made sense. "It explains Iran's behavior, including several things that have happened in the last few days. I'm assuming you've been too busy to follow the news."

Kirkpatrick shook his head "no" and added, "And there's no hard proof, Commander? No files?"

"No files, sir. They have nothing that directly substantiates it. We've been transmitting for some time, now, sir," he reminded Kirkpatrick. "There is some risk of detection."

"Jerry," Patterson interrupted. "Lowell is with me; we're going to try and convince the Israelis to wait. To give us time to get all the data together that shows this is a deception."

"So I've been told. Just don't beat them bloody with the facts, Skipper," joked Jerry. "We kind of need their cooperation."

Patterson and Hardy both snickered at Jerry's affectionate poke at his former commanding officer's personality. "We'll do our best, Jerry. But I won't make any promises I can't keep," Hardy replied.

"Fair enough, sir."

After a brief moment of silence, Kirkpatrick asked, "Joanna, any other questions? Mr. President?"

She shook her head, and then realized Jerry couldn't see that. "God-speed, Jerry."

President Myles said, "Getting all of you and the information you have out of Iran is vital. Stay alive."

"Aye, aye, sir. Out here."

After Jerry signed off, Patterson spoke hurriedly. "Mr. President, before we break the connection, I have a question."

"Yes, Joanna."

"How much can we tell the Israelis?"

"Use your good judgment, Doctor," Myles answered. "But also use your discretion. Like Ray said, we don't have direct proof, and Opal's information only makes sense if you believe they don't have a weapon to test. Their intelligence plays by different rules."

Hardy nodded. "They've got a lower threshold of proof. If they make a mistake, they could cease to exist as a nation. With an outcome like that, they are far more willing to shoot first and ask the hard questions later."

Myles added. "And they've got an attitude as well. Their intelligence people are good, and most of them think we're not as good."

"At least this validates your decision, Mr. President," Kirkpatrick observed.

"Only if you accept that they're not close to assembling a weapon," Myles insisted. "There are people in my own administration who won't buy this theory. And the only way we can prove it is to get our people out of Iran. Make it happen, Ray."

6 April 2013
1715 Local Time/1415 Zulu
Bandar Kangan Police Barracks

Rahim paced impatiently in his makeshift office. He was starving for information. It had been over five hours since he ordered the coastwide alert and
arrests of Seyyed and Mehry Naseri. The Shiraz office had responded quickly.
Naseri's mother was in custody and pleaded ignorance. Her questioning was
underway.

Despite numerous calls to Tehran, all he knew about Seyyed Naseri's
arrest was that the Pasdaran had been ordered to raid his home. What were
the results? Was the uncle in custody?

His last call to headquarters, an hour and a half earlier, had been a
waste of time. All the desk officer could say was that two agents from the
Bandar Abbas office, Omid and Sattari, had left for Bandar Charak shortly
after the alert had been received. They had to drive to Bandar Charak and
the earliest they could have been on the scene was sometime around 1500.
No reports as yet had been received, but the desk officer assured him that he
would be contacted as soon as any information was available. Rahim had
slammed down the phone into its cradle, cursing the overly centralized
command structure of the Iranian security services.

In a way, it was worse than no news. Rahim was not pleased to hear
that Omid had been sent to Bandar Charak. The man was far too emotional
and his legendary temper had affected his judgment in the past. He was also
known to hold grudges against those who crossed him, something Rahim
had done on numerous occasions.

Would Omid put his feud with him ahead of his duties to the Islamic
Republic? It was a possibility, but Rahim didn't think so. For all his faults,
Omid was also passionate about protecting the homeland of the Islamic
Revolution. He would fulfill his obligations, Rahim thought, and work
with him, even if Omid really didn't want to.

Dahghan had the misfortune of walking into Rahim's office soon after
the phone call, to deliver the final autopsy report. Without warning, the
major exploded on his assistant, venting his frustration, and ordered him to
personally contact the local Basij militia commander and demand a progress report. He would not tolerate being ignored any longer. The surprised

young agent was highly motivated to carry out his new orders, and hurriedly left the office, the autopsy report still in his hands.

Sometime later, a knock at the door snapped Rahim out of his brooding. "Sir, I have the report from Mullah Dashani that you wanted," Dahghan said warily.

"About time," growled Rahim. "What does our venerable Basij commander have to say?"

Dahghan ignored the sarcasm and read the report as received over the phone. "Mullah Dashani says the additional security checkpoints have been established on both sides of Bandar Kangan, as well as on the eastern side of Deyyer. All vehicles traveling on Highway 96 have been stopped and searched since 1400 this afternoon. There has been a constant Basij presence at both harbors since Thursday, and every vessel is searched before being allowed to depart. There has been no sign of Akbari or Naseri at the checkpoints, or in Kangan or Deyyer. There has also been no trace of their vehicle. Extensive searches of the beaches along a forty-kilometer front have not produced any additional bodies or debris."

Rahim rested his head in his right hand as he listened to Dahghan, analyzing the information he was hearing. The trail had gone cold. The two traitors were no longer in Kangan, of this he was certain, but where did they go? Were they on board the American submarine when it sank? Oh, if only Allah would be so gracious.

Dahghan concluded the report with a request from Dashani, asking how long Rahim would like the security checkpoints to be in place.

Annoyed by the mullah's request, Rahim ignored it and shot back, "Is that all?"

"Ah, no . . . sir," replied Dahghan, his voice sounded nervous. "Mullah Dashani admitted that he discussed coordinating checkpoints with Mullah Bahar, the commander of the Tahari Basij Brigade yesterday afternoon."

Rahim stifled a groan, and rubbed his face as Dahghan relayed the Tahari Brigade's report. He'd asked Dashani to keep this whole thing quiet, but that discussion had been overtaken by events. Still, it irritated him greatly that people didn't seem to take him seriously when he asked for something. He was considering what "corrective guidance" he would administer, when Dahghan said something that suddenly caught his attention. ". . . and Mullah Bahar is concerned that one of his patrols has failed to return. The men did not show up for their muster this afternoon, and inquiries showed they had not returned from their patrol earlier this morning. A search is underway to try and find them."

"What? Repeat that last part," demanded Rahim. The assistant read again the part about the missing patrol. Rahim was more than curious. Could it be merely a coincidence that a Basij patrol disappears during the same time frame when the two traitors may have fled the area? He didn't believe in coincidences.

"When was this patrol taking place?" he asked, his voice was tense.

"Between midnight and 0600 today, sir," replied Dahghan.

"Where?"

"They were patrolling a twenty-five-kilometer section of Highway 96 north of Bandar Tahari."

"How many men?"

"Four, sir. One corporal and three privates."

"Why wasn't this reported earlier?" Rahim asked with disdain.

Dahghan gulped quietly. He was afraid to answer that question. "This brigade's policy is that if the patrol does not discover anything significant, the members can go straight home and sleep, then report when they muster in the afternoon."

Rahim rubbed his face again, desperately fighting the urge to laugh. Such laxness was simply incomprehensible, almost comical. "Militia," he finally whispered to himself. After a brief pause, Rahim straightened and spoke firmly. "Dahghan, get a vehicle. We leave for Bandar Tahari immediately."

"Yes, Major. At once," responded the young agent, who literally ran out of the office.

Rahim grabbed his holster, jacket, and cap and quickly put them on. He had just started walking toward the door when the phone on the desk began ringing. Grabbing the handset, he answered tersely, "Major Rahim."

"Major, Agent Mahdipur at headquarters. I have the initial report from the Bandar Abbas agents."

"Excellent. Is Naseri in custody?" asked Rahim impatiently.

"Agent Sattari reports that the Pasdaran raid was a 'bungled disaster.'"

"Go on," he prodded. Rahim's expectations sank with every word Mahdipur spoke.

"Two squads of Pasdaran soldiers responded to the arrest order. The oc-

cupants violently resisted arrest with automatic weapons and hand grenades. The first assault was repulsed. The second assault was successful and
the house was taken at 1355." Rahim closed his eyes, a deep sigh escaped
from his lips. He already knew what Mahdipur was going to say next.

"Seyyed Naseri, his wife, and two unknown male accomplices were
killed during the battle. Sattari further reports that Naseri had destroyed
two laptop computers, several mobile phones, as well as his papers and electronic media with magnesium flares. They were recovering the remains of
the computers and phones on the off chance that some information could
still be salvaged, but Senior Agent Omid does not hold out much hope for
that. They are continuing their investigation and expect to file a more complete report later this evening. Sattari also mentioned that they had a lead
that Omid wanted to run to ground before submitting their final report."

Rahim's curiosity was immediately piqued. "A lead? Did he say anything more specific about this 'lead'?"

"No, Major."

"What time was the initial report filed?"

"About 1530."

"Very well. If there are additional reports, call me on my mobile phone.
I'm leaving for Bandar Tahari momentarily and will be away from this
phone for an unknown period of time." Mahdipur acknowledged Rahim's
order and hung up.

As Rahim placed the handset in its cradle, his eyes caught sight of a
local map pinned up on the wall. He walked over and examined it, focusing
his gaze on Bandar Kangan. Something just didn't seem right. He picked
up a ruler and measured the distance from the beach where the traitor's car
was last seen to Bandar Tahari; twenty-four kilometers point to point,
thirty-two by road. Two days.

Akbari's cell phone was at Kangan on the morning of the fourth. Two
days later, a Basij patrol disappears. Suddenly, it struck him. *They're on foot.
In two days, even in her condition, Shirin Naseri should be able to walk twenty-
four kilometers. And the recent shamal would have obscured any trace of their
passage.*

With growing excitement, Rahim followed this line of thought, building on his theory step-by-step: *They're traveling at night to avoid detection,
probably paralleling Highway 96 to ease navigation.*

But could Akbari take on four Basij? True, he was Pasdaran, better trained and more disciplined, but all the reports had him armed with only a pistol. His combat specialty was in air defense; he was not a professional infantryman. Surely he couldn't defeat four more heavily armed men by himself, could he?

A cold feeling descended on him as he came to the inevitable, but disturbing conclusion—*Akbari and his pregnant wife were not alone. Americans had to be with them. American commandos, soldiers of some sort were in Iran.* He bolted for the door, reaching for his cell phone. He had to tell General Moradi immediately.

6 April 2013
1730 Local Time/1430 Zulu
The Outskirts of Bandar Charak

They were packing again, getting ready to abandon the layup position as soon as it was dark. The only things they were waiting on were the transmission from *Michigan* and for the sun to go down.

The entire group had heard Jerry's radio conversation with Washington, and the president. Shirin had whispered a translation to Yousef as Jerry made his report. Both had been disbelieving, then impressed when they heard President Myles identified. "Is this commonplace in your military?" Shirin asked.

"No, it's a sign of just how much trouble we're in," Jerry replied with a slight grin, "and also how important you two are to our country. They need you to help stop a war."

Later, as they discussed what to do next, the debate circled and shifted around the idea of getting a boat. The Iranian Persian Gulf coast was lined with small harbors. Most supported small fishing villages. But they could also accommodate smaller speedboats as well.

"But what about the guards?" Shirin asked. "Every harbor is surely being watched."

"We could take them out," responded Ramey. "But if we can't kill them quietly or sneak past them, they'll sound the alarm, and there goes any head start we might have had."

"We'll need a boat fast enough to outrun the IRGC patrol craft. That may be hard to come by," Lapointe remarked.

"And how do we get aboard *Michigan* with patrol boats on our tail?" Jerry asked.

"What if it didn't have a full gas tank?" Phillips wondered aloud. "That would be very embarrassing."

The other SEALs and Jerry stopped talking and stared at Phillips, a look of mild irritation on their faces.

"What!?" pleaded Phillips defensively.

Ramey just shook his head. "Here's how I see it. Bandar Charak is not an option; there's too much attention focused on this town right now, and that was a long phone call we made. Even though the SATCOM is hard to detect, we have to assume that the military units in the town are still at a heightened state of readiness. And then there's the IRGC naval station on Kish Island, eighteen nautical miles to the northwest. We'd be cut off before we even reached the twelve-mile limit. Backtracking to the northwest is a nonstarter, so we continue to head southeast, but to where?"

They attacked the problem throughout the rest of the afternoon, looking at the various ports, building scenarios, trying to find weaknesses in the Iranian defenses, or at least ways of reducing the risk. And they had to move; they couldn't just wait out their pursuers. The longer they took getting out of the country, the more resources the Iranian authorities would add to the hunt. And then there was the big picture issue of getting the information out so that Washington could rein in the Israelis.

But every time, their exploration wound up in the same rut. Which harbor was the best bet? Would there be a boat big enough and fast enough for them to even attempt an escape? Would they have to split up to have a decent chance? What about security checkpoints along the way? Where and how many were there? And then there was the inevitable pursuit.

To a man, each SEAL was convinced they'd have to fight their way out. Their chances of success depending entirely on the type of patrol boat, or boats, they ran into. In other words, a total crapshoot.

There were just too many unknowns. The secret to success of any SEAL mission lay in exhaustively researching the target, planning for as many contingencies as possible, and leaving little to chance. This operation would be entirely ad hoc, opportunity driven, trusting to luck. And the odds just weren't in their favor. To the SEALs, and Jerry, the small boat escape idea looked like suicide. But what other option did they have?

"Maybe we should just head southeast and figure this out on the fly,"

Jerry suggested wearily. "We can task *Michigan* to get us real time UAV imagery on each of the ports, and maybe some shots along the highway. We can also see if the Rivet Joint aircraft can help us nail down the locations of some of those checkpoints. We evaluate each opportunity as it occurs and go with the one that looks promising."

Ramey frowned, clearly unimpressed with Jerry's haphazard approach to mission planning, but he remained silent as he had little to offer in return.

The discussion was beginning to die out, the participants frustrated with the seemingly insurmountable problem before them, when suddenly Yousef had a funny look on his face. Turning to Shirin, he spoke rapidly, with a note of excitement in his voice. Shirin seemed confused, but Yousef was adamant and gestured for her to translate.

"What kind of plane can XO Jerry fly?" Shirin relayed.

Surprised, Jerry answered, "Well, I flew the Super Hornet, a jet fighter."

When Shirin translated, Yousef quickly asked another question. "Is that the only kind of airplane you can fly?"

"I flew trainers before that, and I have a current private pilot's license. Why do you want to know?"

Shirin explained for her husband. "Iran has small airfields all along the coast. If we stole a plane, we could be across the gulf within a few minutes' flying. There would be no time for pursuit."

"Well, that's a novel idea," Ramey observed, encouraged.

"I can't fly a helicopter, but I could fly most fixed-wing aircraft well enough to take off and head south. I can read the owner's manual once we're in the air," Jerry added, smiling.

Lapointe was already looking at the maps stored in his laptop. "The nearest airport is at Bandar Lengeh, about sixty klicks to the southeast as the crow flies, seventy-five by road."

Ramey moved to look over his shoulder. "I like it. The runway is just over a klick from the beach, and Highway 96 runs right past it so we can take a quick look as we drive by. There's a good road net, and no major obstacles if we have to go cross-country. And there is a harbor just five kilometers away, just in case. Sweet!"

"Highway 96 runs right along the coast line from Bandar Divan all the way into downtown Bandar Lengeh," noted Lapointe. "We should be able to get a good long stare at the road if CENTCOM gets one of their UAVs up."

Their critical need for information prompted an early call to *Michigan*.

While the team members on the sub vetted the newest plan and the intelligence requirements, the group ate a quick dinner and prepared to move.

Michigan's response came just after sunset. Lapointe downloaded detailed photos for the team to study, as well as analyses of military radio transmissions along their intended path. Once he was done, Lapointe gave the handset to Jerry.

"XO, we can see two Falcon 20s sitting on the tarmac at Bandar Lengeh," Frederickson reported. "Can you fly one of those?"

"That's not a polite question to ask a pilot," Jerry answered with feigned offense. "Twin-engine bizjet. Yes, I can fly it."

"Then the skipper says get it in the air and head for Saudi Arabia. CENTCOM is working on a fighter escort the instant you're clear of Iranian airspace."

"Understood. We'll be moving shortly. Out here." Lapointe took the headset and had just started to fold the PRC-117 antenna, when Fazel called out.

"Boss, XO, I think we may have a problem."

The covered truck pulled to a stop on the side of the road. Omid jumped out and hit the speed-dial number for Sattari on his cell phone. "Teymour, Hafez. How is your investigation going?"

"Not bad, Hafez. I have several reports that indicate our two suspects were proceeding north on Kalat Road."

"Excellent, Teymour. I have only two reports, but one witness is certain he served them kebabs earlier in the afternoon. It looks like they came into town by way of Bandar Charak Road, cut to the east, and then back south. I think I like this Akbari guy. He took different, indirect paths in and out. Very professional."

"Where are you now, Hafez?"

"We're a couple of kilometers north of town on Bandar Charak Road, I'm checking out the last report. It had several people walking north, possibly including our two traitors."

"It's getting dark, Hafez. The sun is already down. Do you think it's wise to go wandering in those hills at this time of day? You can't see much."

"You worry too much, Teymour. I'm just going to verify that they didn't go toward the hills. We drove all the way up to 96 and back, but we didn't see anybody. So, either they went over the dunes, which is what I suspect, or they took to the hills. There is no evidence of a vehicle. If I can eliminate the possibility of them going into the hills tonight, we'll be able to better focus our search tomorrow."

Sattari hesitated, he hated to bring the subject up again, but he had to. "Hafez, since we haven't found them, I really think we should—"

"Yes, yes, yes, Teymour. You're as bad as an old woman, always nagging," interrupted Omid, with resignation in his voice. "Go ahead and report back to Bandar Abbas that we suspect the traitors were in Bandar Charak earlier today, and that they appear to have departed on foot northwards. We are attempting to pick up the trail, but units nearby should be put on high alert. There, are you satisfied?"

"Yes, Hafez. I really do believe it is the proper thing to do," replied a much-relieved Sattari.

"Fine. I'll meet you at the rotary just on the outskirts of town on Bandar Charak Road in about fifteen minutes, okay?"

"Got it. Till then."

"I'll see you shortly." Omid responded to his partner's farewell and then turned his attention to the four apprehensive young men with him.

"All right, my Basij fighters," announced Omid. "We'll form a line, four meters between each man, and we'll walk along the roadside looking for any evidence that someone headed toward those hills to our left. Since the light is waning fast, we'll make one quick pass up and back and then we'll call it a day."

The five men stretched out with four off the road, and one just at the edge. They each turned on their flashlights and slowly began walking toward the clump of trees near the hillside.

"Shit," cursed Ramey. "They're coming this way."

"I think they're looking for our tracks," Fazel guessed. "I'm sorry, Boss, but I didn't do a great job of hiding them."

"Couldn't be helped, Doc. You were practically carrying Dr. Naseri back up the rock ledge. Okay, people, listen up; column formation along this ridgeline. Pointy is in the lead, with the XO, Dr. Naseri, and then Captain Akbari behind. Philly has the rear while Doc and I cover our withdrawal. Move quietly, but move quickly. Go!"

Jerry helped Dr. Naseri to her feet; she was exhausted from the hike into Bandar Charak and back, but fear fueled her legs now. Yousef helped her to keep her footing as they moved slowly away from the advancing Iranian soldiers.

It took only a couple of minutes for Jerry to realize that the soldiers were gaining on them. They were at best one hundred meters away and closing. "Boss, they're getting closer," Phillips said over the radio net. Ramey made a vigorous motion with his hand, pointing for Jerry to keep the two Iranians moving.

Shirin was having difficulty climbing the ragged rock line. Shadows from the last light of the day hid loose rocks and low spots. Coupled with her fatigue, her movements were unsure and halting. Yousef quietly prompted her to move forward by gently pushing her waist. She stepped up on to the next rock, but when she put her weight down on it, a portion of the rock slipped away and rattled its way down the hillside. Ramey whispered urgently over the radio, "Everyone down! Don't move!" Jerry froze in an awkward position, half perched on a bolder.

"Sir!" shouted a young Basij private. "Over there, I heard some rocks fall!"

Omid quickly motioned for the private to be quiet; he, too, had heard the rocks, but falling rocks weren't unusual in this part of the country. Still, just to be safe, Omid had them approach more slowly, their weapons at the ready. Two Basij kept trying to scan the ridgeline with their flashlights. They hadn't gone another six meters when the sergeant called him. "Agent Omid, I believe these are the tracks of two people."

"I'm coming over," he said quietly. Unfortunately, the other three Basij followed him over as well. Moving as a group, they walked toward the ridge where Jerry and the others had been.

"They're on to us, Boss," Fazel concluded over the radio. "I have a good shot on the lead guy."

"Not yet, Doc," Ramey whispered. "I'm not convinced they know we're here. Let's be patient and give them a chance to back off."

"Hooyah, sir."

Ramey looked to his left, and with hand signals, ordered Phillips to assume a firing position. Running away was no longer an option. Jerry felt useless. He couldn't raise his SCAR, as he needed both hands just to keep him on the bolder. If he tried to move, he'd undoubtedly make more noise and likely give away their position. All he could do was hold still and watch as Phillips snuck quietly toward the ridgeline. But as he stepped down, his left foot started slipping on some loose sand. He instinctively threw his hand up to brace himself against the rock, and for a fraction of a second, his hand was exposed.

"Sir!" screamed one of the militiamen. "Movement, over there!" The soldier immediately raised his weapon and cut loose with several bursts.

The rounds ricocheted off the rock wall just above them; shards of rock and dust fell down from the impact points. Yousef pushed Shirin to the ground and covered her body with his. Shirin was shaking violently from fear. Jerry grasped the rock he was laying on even tighter. He couldn't see the soldiers, so theoretically they shouldn't be able to see him. Theoretically.

"Take them out," ordered Ramey calmly. The three men took careful aim, and fired together as if they were one man.

Omid was furious. He grabbed the soldier's weapon and shoved it toward the ground. "What the hell do you think you are shooting at? Shadows?" he asked angrily. The young Basij didn't have time to answer the VEVAK agent as a 7.26mm round pierced his chest. Two of the other Basij militiamen were also hit before Omid heard the cracks of the rifles. He dove for the ground, rolled toward the clump of trees, and hid behind one of the fallen men, seeking cover, as bullets whizzed above him. The fourth Basij soldier just stood there, stunned by what he had seen. A fraction of a second later, another single crack signaled his demise. Confused and terrified, Omid searched for his cell phone. He needed reinforcements.

"Last man down," declared Fazel. "I got two, sir."

"I got one, Boss," Phillips added.

"I'm pretty sure I only got one, as well," said Ramey. "One of those guys is playing possum."

"I can't tell which one, Boss. No one is moving and their IR signatures all look the same. Do you want me to put a round into each one again?"

Fazel asked. Before Ramey could respond, the corpsman saw a slight light appear in his scope. The man behind one of the fallen soldiers had opened a cell phone; Fazel now knew his target. "Oh no, you don't," he whispered as he squeezed his trigger for the third time.

Omid moved slowly. With the flashlights on the ground, his assailants probably couldn't see him clearly. If he moved very slowly, maybe he could fool them into thinking he had been hit. He gradually brought the cell phone up to his chest and carefully slipped open the face, trying desperately to hide the light. He managed to push the speed-dial number for Teymour's phone, and even heard it ring once. But that was the last thing he heard as a bullet sliced through his skull. The phone dropped onto the sand, a concerned voice emanating from its speaker, "Hafez? Hafez? Hafez, can you hear me? Hafez!"

By the time Sattari arrived eight minutes later, the Americans and their precious Iranian cargo were almost five kilometers down the road. Fazel drove with the lights off, using the night-vision goggles they had obtained from *Michigan*. He turned right onto Highway 96, and it wasn't until they had gone another twenty kilometers before he turned on the headlights and slowed to a more normal speed.

15

TASKING

6 April 2013
1830 Local Time/1530 Zulu
Bandar Tahari

"Would you care for more tea, Major?" asked Badar. The elderly cleric lifted the teapot and offered to pour more steaming liquid into Rahim's cup.

"You are most gracious, Mullah Badar. Yes, please," replied Rahim politely. What he really wanted was more information on the missing patrol, but he had to be patient with the old man who insisted on being a good host to one as important as himself.

The drive to Bandar Tahari, while short, had been exceptionally pleasant. The sun hung low in the cloudless sky, an accompanying soft warm breeze from off the gulf beckoned him to stop and appreciate life. Under different circumstances, Rahim would have allowed himself the luxury of enjoying the trip. As it was, he barely noticed the ancient castle of Sheikh Nosouns, an eighteenth-century fortress seated high up on a hill that dominated the village's skyline. His mind was elsewhere. All his abilities and energy were focused on killing the traitors and their likely American allies.

Rahim's phone call to Moradi as he left Kangan was short and to the point. The Pasdaran had to be mobilized. If American commandos were indeed on Iranian soil, as he strongly suspected, the Basij were not adequately trained or equipped to handle such an adversary. General Moradi was not keen on ordering the mobilization without just cause. If he didn't have a good reason, he had said, it would only draw unwanted attention, attention that could interfere with their operation. There had to be a tangible justification to declare a mobilization. One based on a clear threat to the Islamic Republic.

Rahim knew exactly what Moradi was hinting at over the unsecure phone. If he wanted the Pasdaran to become fully engaged, Moradi needed a bone to throw to the rabid bureaucratic dogs. One that would get their gaze focused in a different direction, away from Natanz. Reluctantly, Rahim acquiesced and agreed that Moradi could display his prize.

The general sounded extremely pleased, and said he would order the mobilization immediately. He also reassured Rahim, saying that it would take a little time to arrange the proper media spectacle. It wouldn't be until tomorrow morning before the world would learn of the foreign invaders. As the signal weakened, and almost as an afterthought, Moradi informed Rahim that the navy had agreed to send one of their Kilo-class submarines into the Persian Gulf to try and find the American submarine.

Content that all the pieces were being put into play, Rahim concentrated on how to deploy them to best effect. To do that, he needed to find the enemy. To find them required information on where they had been, and when.

"I do not wish to seem rude, Mullah Badar, but time is of the essence. What additional news have you found concerning your missing patrol?" prodded Rahim, as he took a sip of tea.

"I see that you are a man of action, Major. My apologies for not sensing the urgent nature of your visit. Here is my brigade's report on this incident." Badar handed Rahim a folder with several sheets of paper and a folded map. The report was neatly written and referenced the local map that had been liberally annotated. "We have found no trace of the patrol led by Corporal Molavi. He is an army veteran with some combat experience and is one of my best fighters." Badar spread out the map and highlighted their patrol route with his wrinkled hand.

"They were one of three patrols along a twenty-five-kilometer front on Highway 96. These patrols roamed between two established security checkpoints, here and here, ten kilometers on either side of the village. Molavi and three new privates had the early morning shift."

"Were there any reports of suspicious activity from the checkpoints or the other patrols?" queried Rahim.

"No, Major. Everything seemed very quiet."

"What measures have you taken to locate this patrol?"

"Molavi's patrol started their shift promptly at midnight. When they failed to muster at 1600 the next day, we went to each of their homes and verified that they had not returned after their shift was done at 0600. We then conducted a thorough search of the village and along the highway. We found no trace of the four men or their vehicle."

"Their vehicle?" Rahim asked with interest.

"Yes, my Basij only have two small cars available, so we asked for help from the local people. Private Salani's employer had a medium-sized van that could easily hold four, and he graciously allowed us to use it. It has also vanished. The details on this van are on the third page of the report," explained Badar.

Rahim turned to that page and noted the van's make, model, color, and license plate number. There were also several photographs. Excellent.

The mullah's description of Molavi also reinforced his suspicion that Akbari had help. He glanced at his watch. They could have had up to eighteen hours if they'd jumped the patrol early in their shift. *If they were bold, and traveled during the day, they could be past Bandar Abbas by now*, he thought. But that seemed unlikely; he knew that American Special Forces were creatures of the night and preferred to hide by day. This limited them to five, maybe six hours of travel time at the very most. Heading northwest was also unlikely; the security checkpoints in that direction had been established the day before. So assuming a southeasterly direction would put them somewhere between Bandar Tahari and Bandar Abbas. Naseri's uncle had lived in Bandar Charak. Rahim felt he was getting closer. Then he remembered the report from Tehran, and the lead that Omid was tracking down.

"Major? Major, I asked if you have any other questions?" Badar had apparently repeated himself.

Startled by the loudness of Badar's voice, Rahim was pulled from his musings. "My apologies, Mullah. I was just evaluating the information you provided. I have no further questions, but should some come up in the future, I will be sure to contact you immediately. You've been most helpful, and a most gracious host. However, I fear I must depart so that I can analyze this information further. May Allah's blessing be upon this house."

"May Allah guide you in your investigation, my son," responded Badar, pleased by Rahim's compliments.

* * *

Dahghan was sitting across the street, watching the last bit of sunlight fade, when he saw Rahim emerge from the house. He quickly jumped to his feet and trotted over to the car.

"Was the meeting with the mullah useful, sir?" he asked.

"Actually, yes. Yes it was. I want you to put out an alert for the van that is described on page three of this report. I believe the traitors commandeered the van after eliminating the Basij patrol that was using it," answered Rahim, satisfied. He handed the folder to his assistant and climbed into the car.

Dahghan took the folder and placed it in his case. After getting into the car, he turned to Rahim and said, "Where to next, Major?"

"Back to Kangan. I have a lot of thinking to do, and I need to speak with Tehran again."

"Sir, you've had almost nothing to eat today, and you ate sparingly yesterday as well. I suggest you get something to eat here. There is a nice café up the road. I can order us something while you make your call to Tehran."

Dahghan's suggestion made Rahim realized that he was indeed very hungry, and the chickpea cookies the mullah had served with tea only reminded his stomach that it was empty. He paused to think through the impact of staying in Tahari a little longer. By nature, Rahim analyzed everything, even with something as mundane as deciding when to eat. His primary concern was getting the data on the van to headquarters; a task he could do just as well from a café table as his desk. "You make a reasonable observation, Dahghan. Proceed."

The café was only a few minutes away and while Dahghan ordered lamb stew with rice and flatbread, Rahim walked across the street for some privacy. He made the call to the headquarters in Tehran, read off the specifics on the van, and ordered that the information be disseminated widely. He emphasized, however, that the Basij, Pasdaran, and VEVAK units to the southeast were to have priority. Rahim also instructed the desk agent to issue a warning to alert the police and security services that Akbari and Naseri were probably not alone, and that their accomplices were likely well-armed and dangerous. After confirming there was nothing new from Bandar Charak, Rahim closed his cell phone and returned to the café.

Upon entering the small restaurant, his sense of smell was inundated with savory aromas and his stomach growled with anticipation. Dahghan was seated at a small table, already laden with steaming dishes. Rahim was pleased with the promptness of the waiter, and he eagerly began piling food onto his plate. He had only taken a couple of bites when his cell phone rang. Glancing at the display, he didn't recognize the number.

"Major Rahim," he answered.

"Major, this is Agent Sattari."

"Yes, Agent Sattari, I'm surprised to hear from you. Is Omid still so mad at me that he won't speak to me personally?"

"Sir, Senior Agent Omid is dead." Sattari's voice wavered as he spoke.

Rahim almost dropped his fork when he heard the news. Gently, he placed it on the plate; his hunger had suddenly vanished. "What happened?"

"We were investigating the Naseri raid when Omid became suspicious that the two traitors may have shown up at the house soon after the fighting. We grabbed some Basij fighters and split up to search the northwestern quarter. We received reports that led Omid to believe the couple had used different routes in and out of the city. He took his Basij and headed north of town along the road that runs in to Highway 96. I continued eastward to cover the other possible options. I received a call from him at 1834, but he didn't respond when I answered. I proceeded quickly to his location and found him, and the four Basij fighters dead from gunshot wounds."

"I see," replied Rahim flatly. "What actions have you taken, Agent Sattari?"

"I've secured the scene and I have Pasdaran patrolling along the road and in the dunes to the east. There was no sign of the assailants, but the truck that Omid and the Basij were using is missing. There were no witnesses and we didn't see any vehicles on the road."

Rahim looked down at his watch, it was 1913. The traitors had nearly three-quarters of an hour head start. "You mean you didn't see any lights, correct?"

"Yes, Major. I sent Basij patrols twenty kilometers down both ways on Highway 96. They returned moments ago and reported seeing nothing on the road."

Rahim sighed with frustration; Sattari was young and inexperienced. He didn't realize that his quarry was almost certainly using night-vision devices. "Any other observations?"

"Only one, sir. Whoever the murderers were, they were excellent marksmen. Agent Omid was found lying behind a Basij fighter, a single gunshot wound to the head. Two of the Basij fighters also had only one wound. Captain Akbari couldn't have done this alone, Major. He must have had accomplices."

"Your observation is correct, Agent Sattari. I've only recently issued just such a warning, as it would appear that the same criminals are responsible for the loss of a Basij patrol in Bandar Tahari."

"What are your orders, sir?" Sattari asked. There was a note of determination in his voice.

"Have you alerted your home office yet?"

"Yes, sir. But given the circumstances I felt it was wise to call you directly."

"I commend your initiative, Agent Sattari." Rahim was genuinely impressed. Most agents had the bad habit of following the rigid command structure without question; this young agent had jumped the tracks when he had to. "Continue your investigation. I will leave for Bandar Charak immediately. It'll be several hours before I can get there, and I will want a detailed report as soon as I arrive. Is that understood?"

"Clearly, Major."

"One more thing, Agent Sattari. Have your search parties keep an eye out for a medium-sized, white panel van with Tahari plates. I suspect you will find it nearby."

"Yes, sir. Do you have a license plate number?"

Rahim passed on the information, signed off, and slowly closed his cell phone.

"What is it?" asked Dahghan. He witnessed Rahim's abrupt transformation and was curious, as well as concerned.

"Senior Agent Omid and four Basij were just gunned down outside of Bandar Charak. Pay our bill. We leave immediately for Bandar Charak."

"Yes, sir." The young man shot out of his chair and flagged the café's owner.

Rahim sat there stunned; his feelings mixed. Omid wasn't a friend, but he was a talented and loyal agent who had served Iran well. His death would be one more reason to justify the elimination of the traitors Akbari and Naseri, as well as the now certain Americans.

Out of the corner of his eye, Rahim saw Dahghan head for the door. As he left the café, he hit the speed-dial number for Moradi. He would only have a little time before they would be out of range of the cell phone tower. The general answered on the second ring.

"General Moradi."

"Sir, Major Rahim. I have little time, so I will be brief. There are Americans on our soil. They have just gunned down a senior VEVAK agent and four Basij fighters at Bandar Charak. I'm on my way now to lead the manhunt."

"You're sure of this, Hassan?"

"Positive. The initial report from the field clearly indicates excellent marksmanship and the likely use of night-vision devices. These are trademarks of U.S. commandos. When added to the body and the binder cover we found, there can be only one logical conclusion, sir."

"I'll issue an alert to all Pasdaran units. I will make it clear that the two traitors have well-armed, foreign military accomplices," responded Moradi.

"Another thing, General. They left Bandar Charak on Highway 96. We need to establish more roadblocks along that road. We don't know which way they went, but they have been heading consistently southeast."

"I've already ordered additional security checkpoints based on your previous report, Major. But I will reemphasize that all roadblocks need to have some sort of heavy weaponry to counter this threat."

"Thank you, sir. That should suffice. I will keep you apprised of any further developments," Rahim replied. The general's forethought to establish more checkpoints encouraged Rahim. The pieces were in place, the general whereabouts of the enemy were now known, it was time to spring the trap.

"May Allah guide you, Hassan," Moradi concluded.

"Thank you, sir. I have faith that He is doing so as we speak. Good-bye."

6 April 2013
1930 Local Time/1530 Zulu
Kilo-Class Submarine, *Yunes*, SS903
Bandar Abbas Naval Base

Commander Ebrahim Mehr rubbed his eyes and stretched, pops and crunches came from his neck and shoulders. Only three more reports to go, then he could go home and sleep for the next two days. He hated paperwork with a passion, but it was a necessary evil. If he wanted to take his boat to sea, he had to ensure that all the forms and reports were done properly. His first officer had actually done most of the work, and done it well, but any captain worth his salt takes a personal interest in how well his ship performs, even when it comes to paperwork.

He grabbed the next report off the stack and looked at it. It was the boat's maintenance and repair request. Shaking his head, he read the depressingly long list. Even though *Yunes* was the youngest of Iran's three Kilo-class submarines, she was well past the point for her midlife overhaul. As with most things in life, equipment tends to break down more often with age. Still, his crew had done a fantastic job keeping the old girl running. They'd just completed a seven-day patrol in the Gulf of Oman, and it went off without a hitch. Mehr signed the request and hoped that half of the items would be approved.

A knock at his cabin door drew his attention away from the cluttered desk. A junior officer poked in his head and said, "Pardon the intrusion, Captain. But you are needed topside."

Mehr closed his eyes and took a deep breath; he really didn't need this distraction right now. "Lieutenant Kashani, you are the duty officer. I'm sure you can handle the situation."

"Yes, sir. I tried," Kashani complained. "But the man refuses to leave. He says he's under direct orders to load the weapons he brought tonight."

"What!? What weapons?"

"He just drove down onto the pier next to us with ten torpedoes and demanded that we help him load them."

"But we just unloaded all our weapons this afternoon," exclaimed Mehr, confused.

"Yes, sir. I told him that."

"Surely they must be for *Nuh*." Mehr gestured in the direction of their sister ship berthed behind them.

"No, sir. The transfer documents clearly list *Yunes*, hull 903, as the recipient. Here is the manifest." Kashani handed the clipboard to his captain, who thumbed through it quickly. A sudden frown appeared on his face.

"These are all antisubmarine torpedoes," Mehr remarked. "And this is over half again what we normally carry."

Kashani nodded hesitantly. He was just as bewildered as his captain.

"And he wants to load them now? In the dark?"

"Yes, sir, he was very clear about that. Now you understand why you are needed topside."

Mehr tossed the clipboard back to the lieutenant, and with one smooth motion he stood and snatched his ball cap from off its hook. "All right, Kashani, let's go see what form of madness possesses this individual."

The lieutenant moved out of the way as his captain headed aft toward the ladder well. Mehr leapt through the watertight door and then swiftly climbed the steps into the control room. The bridge access trunk was close by, and with little effort, Mehr scampered up the ladder to the bridge. After threading his way around some masts, he emerged from a hatch on the starboard side of the sail. Walking around the sail, Mehr returned the salute of his quarterdeck watch and strode down the brow.

On the pier was a truck and five weapons dollies, each one bearing two torpedoes. An impatient-looking lieutenant commander was pacing in front of the truck. Before Mehr could address the officer, a voice greeted him from behind.

"Good evening, Captain."

Mehr turned and saw his squadron commander, Captain Aghassi, approaching him. He snapped to attention and rendered the proper honors. "Good evening, sir."

"I'm sorry to spring this on you without warning, Ebrahim. I need your crew to begin loading these torpedoes immediately. In the meantime, you will come with me," Aghassi ordered.

Surprised, Mehr hesitated for only a few seconds. "Yes, sir. I'll get my men started at once." Pivoting smartly, he faced his duty officer and issued a string of commands. "Lieutenant Kashani, find the first officer and inform him I've been called to an unexpected meeting with the squadron commander. He is to begin loading these torpedoes immediately. Have him ensure extra safety precautions are taken, as we will be loading in the dark. I don't want anyone to get hurt. Also, have him begin preparations for getting underway. Understood?"

"Yes, Captain!" exclaimed the young officer. Filled with excitement, he turned around and ran back up the gangplank.

Aghassi smiled as they walked toward the squadron building. "You're very perceptive to assume that you'll be ordered to sea soon, Ebrahim."

Mehr chuckled. "With respect, sir. A blind man could see that one coming. Why else would you have me load weapons in the dark, unless I was to put to sea early in the morning. I am confused though about the loadout. Why only antisubmarine torpedoes?"

The expression on the squadron commander's face changed abruptly. His tone as he spoke was stern. "Captain, the mission briefing you are about to attend will be politically charged, but also vital, I repeat, *absolutely vital*, to the security of the Islamic Republic. Do not say the mission cannot be done. Do not say there is little chance of success. In fact, my advice to you is to say as little as possible."

The submarine captain stopped suddenly and faced his superior, a feeling of dread welling up within him. "Are you saying I can't give my professional opinion or ask questions about this upcoming mission, sir?" Mehr asked pointedly.

Aghassi shook his head. "No, Ebrahim. You are my best submarine commanding officer, and your words will have considerable weight. I'm merely suggesting that you use as few as possible. You can say the mission will be a challenge. You can even say it will be difficult, but you cannot say it is nearly impossible."

"Even if I believe it is?" asked Mehr, seeking clarification.

"Even if you believe it is," replied Aghassi.

The two men finished their walk to the squadron headquarters building in silence. A guard opened the door and saluted as they entered. Aghassi led the way down the corridor to the conference room, the sounds of a heated debate spilling out into the hallway. Mehr's feeling of apprehension grew with each step. Just what sort of mess was he getting into?

As they passed through the doorway, Mehr saw two admirals, one Pasdaran, one Artesh, or regular navy, seated at the conference table along with a few staff officers. The Pasdaran and Artesh were two separate armed forces serving the same nation. They competed for scarce funds and political power. And each service thought the other was an ineffective joke. *Politically charged indeed*, thought Mehr. The two admirals sat at opposite ends of the long table.

"Admirals," said Aghassi, "may I present Commander Ebrahim Mehr, commanding officer of the Islamic Republic of Iran Navy submarine *Yunes*." Pointing to his right, toward the Artesh, or regular navy admiral, he continued the introduction. "Captain Mehr, I'm sure you remember our commander of the first naval district, Rear Admiral Zand."

"Of course. It is good to see you again, sir."

"And you, Captain," replied Zand haughtily. "I must compliment you on the completion of another successful patrol. Your reputation as one of our best commanders gives me great confidence that you will be able to carry out this next assignment with equal success."

Mehr bowed politely, accepting the compliment, but also noted how the admiral was raising the expectations on a mission that was still a complete mystery to him. "Thank you, sir. I will pass on your sentiments to my crew."

"And this," Aghassi continued, "is Rear Admiral Varamini, commander of the Pasdaran first naval district."

The Pasdaran admiral said nothing, but merely nodded. Mehr offered a bow in return.

Aghassi then motioned toward the chairs and said, "Please be seated." Mehr noted with some irony that he was positioned exactly in the middle of the table.

"Captain Mehr," Zand began, "we have been asked by our Pasdaran brethren to lend assistance in dealing with a dire threat to our country. Admiral Varamini will explain the nature of this threat and give you your orders." The sentence concluded on an icy tone.

Varamini stood, walked over to a chart, and pointed to a box off the coast to the north. "Captain, we have good reason to believe that a U.S. submarine is operating in close proximity to our coastline. Its last known location was here, near Bandar Kangan on or about 4 April. It is likely heading southeast at slow speed. We want you to find and sink this submarine."

The Pasdaran admiral offered no additional information, but simply walked back to his chair and sat down. Mehr fought to keep a poker face. *That's it?* he thought. A host of questions began racing through his mind as he grappled with the enormity of his orders. The room fell into an awkward silence. Both admirals were definitely unhappy with part, or all, of the mission, which meant it had been directed from on high.

"Well, Captain, what are your thoughts?" demanded Zand.

"Finding a submarine in the Persian Gulf, sir, is a difficult challenge," Mehr explained carefully. "The geography and physics are against the searcher; this is made even worse the closer one gets to land."

"So, you are saying it is impossible," Varamini blurted out.

Mehr looked across the table and saw Aghassi's facial expression, reinforcing his earlier advice. "No, Admiral, I am not saying it's impossible, but it certainly won't be easy either. Do you know what type of submarine I'm to hunt down?"

Varamini hesitated, his face contorted into a scowl. It was clear he was not pleased with Mehr's response. "We believe one of their SSGNs is in the gulf."

"A converted *Ohio*-class missile submarine?" Mehr asked, surprised.

Varamini nodded stiffly. The Kilo captain leaned back in his chair and took a deep breath. "That's a whale of a submarine, Admiral. An *Ohio*-class is at least five times larger than my boat. Size like that has definite advantages and disadvantages."

"Explain, Captain," Zand growled, but less intensely than before.

"A submarine of that size has considerable room for noise reduction measures. An *Ohio*-class boat is one of the quietest submarines in the world. This will complicate things considerably. However, once found, her size restricts her ability to maneuver. This is particularly true in shallow water. If I can find her, I have the advantage in a close-in fight."

"So, provided you can find the American, you feel your odds are good," concluded Varamini.

"Yes, Admiral. But finding her will be the trick. The Project 877EKM submarines we bought from the Russians were designed to hunt surface ships. They have a fair antisubmarine capability, but it is mainly for self-defense. An *Ohio* has a better passive sonar suite than my boat, however, her systems will be affected at least as badly as mine by the environment, perhaps more so since they are more sensitive. I have a superior active capability. If I can get a whiff of her, I'll be able to quickly transition to the attack." Mehr tried to look as confident as he sounded. What he had said was true, but he doubted either admiral appreciated just how hard it would be to get that initial whiff.

"Well, Captain, I must admit I'm encouraged by your succinct explanation of this complex problem," remarked Zand, clearly impressed. "Is there anything we can provide to assist you?"

"Yes, sir. I need the best torpedoes we have. I'm assuming that some of the weapons on the dollies are TEST-71ME-NKs?" asked Mehr hopefully.

"All of them are the newer torpedoes," Aghassi replied, smiling. "I've given you all of the available TEST-71ME-NKs that I have."

"Thank you, Captain. They will improve our odds."

"Anything else?" Zand asked.

"Any information I can get on the American's location would be of considerable value. I will begin constructing our search plan, but the more I can focus it, the better my chances of finding her."

"I will ensure you are given all available information," Varamini responded pleasantly. The Pasdaran admiral was even smiling.

After the well-wishing and farewells, Aghassi escorted Mehr out of the conference room. He whispered, "Well done, Ebrahim!" and shook his hand. Mehr reiterated that the tasking he had been given was a significant challenge, but he would do the best he could to find this American submarine and put it out of their misery.

But as confident as he was in the conference room, Mehr was troubled by a story he recalled from the Koran. The story was about the Prophet Yunes, Arabic for Jonah, who also had to face a whale. Mehr prayed that his boat would fare better than their namesake, and that when they grappled with their whale, it wouldn't swallow them.

16

ROUGH ROAD

6 April 2013
1800 Local Time/1500 Zulu
Highway 96, Between Bustaneh and Mollu

Lieutenant Sistani looked at the map and then pointed to the right. "Here."

Corporal Afshar pulled the big Zil truck off the highway. Before Sistani could get out of the cab, Sergeant Zahedi was out of the back and shouting, "We're here! Everyone out! Start unloading! We're losing daylight!"

Sistani asked the sergeant, "Who should take the first turn?"

Zahedi looked at the squad and spotted one small soldier struggling with a case of ammunition. "Ostovar. He's no use to me setting up."

"Fine, I'll take him and Corporal Afshar. I want to pick the spot myself."

Zahedi saluted. "Yes, sir. I'll keep them busy here."

"Be sure you get that truck far away from the road, and camouflage it well," Sistani ordered. Under Zahedi's direction, the corporal and Private Ostovar shouldered several pieces of red-and-white-striped wood and followed the lieutenant.

The three headed west along the side of the highway while Sistani studied the ground.

Along this part of the coast, Highway 96 was a two-lane asphalt road, pushing through a sandy brown landscape dotted with dark green scrub and trees. Although dry now, the ground showed signs of water and erosion everywhere, with dry streambeds cutting into the earth from north to south as the land sloped gently toward the gulf. A few hundred meters from where the truck had stopped, the lieutenant said, "Here. This is good."

The two soldiers quickly assembled a wooden barrier, blocking the road. They placed battery-powered lanterns on each side, reflecting brightly off the painted wood. There wasn't a lot of room on the shoulder, and the ground on both sides was uneven and rutted.

While the soldiers worked, Sistani checked a portable radio and flashlight, then handed them to Ostovar. "Repeat your orders."

Ostovar came to attention and recited, "Stop all traffic and check identity documents. I'm supposed to watch for two fugitives—" He stopped and pulled a paper from his shirt pocket. "—named Akbari and Naseri. They may have accomplices and are dangerous."

The private had read the last part off the paper, but Sistani was satisfied. "And if you spot them, or have any trouble?"

"Use the radio," Ostovar answered.

"And when do you use your rifle?"

"Only if I'm shot at."

Sistani nodded. "Good. You'll be relieved in an hour."

The lieutenant and the corporal walked back to where the rest of the squad was working. Looking back, he could see Ostovar, nearly dwarfed by his KL assault rifle, standing alone with an oversized sawhorse across the highway.

"Sir, shouldn't we leave two men at the roadblock? He can't stop anybody by himself."

"Let me worry about that, Corporal."

"Yes, sir."

Sergeant Zahedi had already set up one man on a low hill as a lookout, while others organized equipment or made positions for themselves in scrapes in the rocky ground.

Sistani climbed to the top of the rise. The lookout lay prone, reasonably well concealed, under a camouflage smock that would keep him warm while it masked him from observation. Using his own glasses, the lieutenant could see the highway for several kilometers in either direction. It ran almost straight east and west here, and while the ground was uneven, there was no place that offered a covered approach on his position. Aside from the paved road, there was no human mark on the land—no buildings, not even a power line. Private Ostovar's checkpoint was as bright as a lighthouse in the darkening landscape.

"Lieutenant, headlights." Private Peyman was on lookout duty, and he pointed east. The lights resolved into a civilian car, slowing to a stop as it approached the checkpoint. Ostovar, rifle slung, leaned over the driver's side window for a minute, then stepped back and swung the barrier out of the way. According to headquarters, the fugitives they were watching for would come from the west, but they had ordered all vehicles to be checked, whatever direction they came from.

Sistani walked back down and called to Zahedi. "That's a good position up there. Take Alizadeh off the rotation and put him up there along with the lookout. Having our best shot on overwatch should make whoever's on duty at the roadblock happier. And make sure his position is as well camouflaged as the others."

"Yes, sir," Zahedi said, then continued by asking, "Sir, how long will we be here?"

"Third squad will relieve us at 0600 tomorrow morning, and first squad will relieve them at 1800 tomorrow night. We'll take our turn again at 0600 the morning after that."

"And how long will this last?"

"Until they tell us to stop, Sergeant." As they talked, the two walked the squad's positions, pointing out small tasks or praising a soldier's work. Sistani smiled. "I've never seen the major move so fast as when he got that order. We drew this post because we were the squad on duty. Right now the major is mustering the rest of the battalion and passing out the rest of the assignments, all with the colonel gone. I'm glad to be away from that circus."

"Is it true that these are American assassins? That they've wiped out two platoons?"

"More rumors, Sergeant? Don't repeat them. Whoever the fugitives are, a Basij patrol is missing without a trace. Headquarters said to be ready for anything."

Sistani looked around. "And tell the squad to get this place organized. What if the major saw this? We've been here half an hour and already it looks like we lost a battle."

South of Baverdan, near Highway 96
1900 Local Time/1600 Zulu

Harry was driving, a pair of night-vision goggles draped over his eyes. Shirin still rode up front, with Yousef on the far side. The windows were open enough to keep the air from getting stuffy, as well as to help Harry stay awake. Yousef was dozing, as much as the bumpy ride allowed.

They'd turned off the highway fifteen minutes earlier, and slowed to a crawl as they felt their way along an unpaved track. Ramey, navigating with Lapointe's assistance, was taking them around a roadblock south of the town.

At *Michigan*'s direction, CENTCOM operators were using a UAV to scout ahead of the truck. The UAV's images were streamed directly to Lapointe through the remote video-receiver function on the laptop. This God's-eye view gave enough warning to let them avoid the roadblocks.

Unfortunately, that meant using some secondary and a lot of tertiary roads. The UAV had spotted roadblocks near most towns, a sign that the hunt for them had gone to a much higher level.

In the back, while Ramey and Lapointe navigated, Jerry and Phillips cleaned weapons and reorganized their gear. Phillips even drilled Jerry again on the SCAR rifle. With the rough ride, sleep was impossible. Dinner had been cold MREs, Harry and the two Iranians having theirs passed up to the cab.

Shirin, squeezed in between the two men, chewed mechanically on something she hadn't bothered to identify. It might have tasted better hot, but she didn't care. Beyond exhaustion, she didn't dare close her eyes. Even with them open, images from the fight flashed in front of her, as if projected onto the dark windshield. What would her dreams be like?

The first battle had been over in moments. But this time, there'd been enough time to be really afraid. She and Yousef had lived in fear for years, but that had been an abstract thing. This had been immediate. She'd heard bullets snap overhead, felt pieces of rock and dust fall on her.

This was Yousef's first time in combat, as well. He looked thoughtful, maybe a little sad. "Yousef, I thought you were very brave today."

"I'm glad we are safe," he responded in Farsi. "I keep on thinking about the men we killed. They had families. They were doing their duty."

"You can't do that," Harry told him. "Whoever they were, when they fired a weapon at us, they had to die. We didn't want the fight. They could have walked away and we would've let them. They got what they deserved, no more, no less."

"You mean I should ignore my feelings." Shirin was surprised. Yousef's tone was thoughtful, certainly not hostile.

"I mean, put them in perspective. If we hadn't killed them, they would have killed you and your wife, which would have led to many more deaths when the Israelis attack. Taking those soldiers out was necessary to our mission. It's as simple as that."

Shirin asked, "Have you killed many men?"

The American paused for a moment before answering. "That's not how I think of it. I don't keep count. I've been on two other deployments, and both involved combat."

"How long is a 'deployment'?" Shirin asked.

"Usually five to six months. It depends. We spend a lot of our time training and on exercises, then deploy for a while."

"So you've seen a lot of fighting," Shirin said.

"It doesn't matter how many fights someone's been in. What matters is being ready for the next one."

"And the feelings? Do they go away?" Yousef asked.

"They become more familiar. They never go away."

Memories of those dead Basij soldiers merged with the forms Shirin had seen outside Uncle Seyyed's house. She was a fugitive, and her uncle had paid the price. . . . Suddenly, a frightful thought burst into her mind.

"Yousef, I have to find out if mother is all right!"

The urgency in her tone shocked her husband. "Yousef, is there any way I can call mother? If they tried to arrest Seyyed, VEVAK will take her, too." As she spoke, her tone changed from urgency to horror at the thought of her own mother in their hands.

"We can't use a cell phone, or stop to use one somewhere," he said flatly. "You know that."

"There has to be something we can do to find out," she pleaded.

Yousef shook his head and held her hands gently. "What if we could call? Would you warn her? Tell her to run away? And if they were not interested in her before, that call would only draw their attention to her—give them a reason to question her."

"I had accepted that I would never see mother again, but I hoped we could find a way to keep in touch. But if they've taken her like your brother, Ali . . ."

Leaning against Yousef, grief swallowed her. "They are destroying my family," she wept. Eventually, she slept, giving herself over to whatever her dreams would hold.

Second Squad Position, Highway 96
1930 Local Time/1630 Zulu

Lieutenant Sistani had walked out to the roadblock. Binoculars were useless now, but he'd taken Alizadeh's nightscope and carefully studied the scene. The hills on the left blocked any view of his squad's position from the road, as he knew it would. He'd banned any fires, and the squad had grumbled but obeyed. All of them were in their positions, but he'd allowed some of them to sleep.

Telling Private Yadegar, now manning the post, to stay alert, he walked the four hundred meters back to the squad. The walk helped wake him up. They'd put in a full day's work before the alert message had arrived, and now with the rush to get in position over, and the enforced inactivity, fatigue was their enemy.

Sergeant Zahedi's voice echoed across the empty ground. "Lieutenant, urgent call from battalion!" It didn't sound like good news, and the young officer double-timed back to the command post.

The two noncoms had dug a circular position well back from the road, building it up in front with the spoil and rocks and covering it with a camouflage net. It wasn't as deep as Sistani would have liked, but oncoming darkness had limited their digging, and he didn't expect the fugitives to have artillery.

"Sir, it's the colonel," Zahedi reported softly, and the lieutenant took the handset.

"Sistani here."

"Report, Lieutenant. Has there been any sign of trouble?" the colonel asked, as if he were expecting bad news.

"All quiet here, sir. We've seen moderate traffic from both directions. They've all stopped and nobody has matched the names or descriptions of the fugitives."

"Any trucks?"

"Yes, sir. We searched them with no results."

The signal was clear enough so he could hear the colonel sigh. "There's been another incident just north of Bandar Charak. Four soldiers and a security agent were killed, and there's no sign that any of the fugitives were hurt. Headquarters says they may have accomplices, and are heavily armed. And an army truck is missing." The colonel read off a license number.

Sistani had been holding the handset so that Zahedi, standing next to him, could hear as well. He saw Zahedi's eyes widen, and knew his expression must be similar. The sergeant pointed to his watch, and Sistani nodded.

"When was this, sir?"

"About 1830, an hour ago."

"Which means if they're heading southeast on the highway, they could be here at any time."

"Exactly," answered the colonel.

"Do we know they're heading southeast?"

"Not for certain, but that's the direction they've been going."

"Understood, sir, I'll take every precaution."

Sistani turned to the two noncoms. "You heard?"

Both nodded.

He ordered, "Make sure every man is awake and alert. There are to stay hidden at all times. Zahedi and I will check each position every half hour. Afshar, stay by the radio. If you hear firing, report immediately. Do not wait for my order. I don't know what's coming, but they won't catch us off guard."

Highway 96, West of Second Squad's Position
2015 Local Time/1715 Zulu

They'd been back on the highway for ten minutes, just long enough for Jerry to get comfortable. He was dozing when Lapointe called out, "Roadblock ahead. Ten klicks."

Ramey shook off his fatigue and opened his eyes. He turned to look at the screen, while Jerry leaned forward to see.

A barrier lay across both lanes of the highway. The foreshortened figure of a man stood next to it. Lapointe was noting the coordinates. He switched to an area map and marked the spot.

Ramey checked his watch, then called forward to the cab. "Another roadblock in ten klicks. Pointy's working on a bypass."

Fazel responded, "Right, I'll slow to sixty to give him a little more time." They'd been traveling at up to eighty kph on the highway when they could.

Lapointe was still fiddling with the map, zooming in and out, shifting to different sections. The light from the screen lit his face from below. His expression showed he wasn't pleased. "Boss, XO, we got a problem. There's no bypass this time."

"What? Nothing?" Ramey said, unbelieving. They'd used dirt roads, even gone overland once to get around checkpoints.

"No roads at all. This is the boonies, even for southern Iran. I even looked at using streambeds, but they don't run anywhere useful. Here's the problem." He pointed to some rough terrain on the map. "A little over a klick to the north of the highway is a bunch of steep hills, real rough country. It completely blocks travel on the north side of the highway."

"And if we head south, we get wet really fast. The beach isn't even five hundred meters away. A natural bottleneck. . . . All right. How far do we have to backtrack?" Ramey sounded resigned.

"We'd have to pick up a side road at Baverdan." He slid the map northwest. "See? Almost all the way back to Charak. Then we go east and north to Lavaran, then Armak. That keeps us on the north side of the hills, but the road net only goes to Berkeh Jangal. We can get to Bandar Lengeh and the airfield from there, but it will be from the north and east. And we'll lose our UAV coverage if we go that far inland."

Ramey frowned. "The really long way around. How many roadblocks will we hit while we take the scenic route? And without our advance scout, we'd have to run them blind." The platoon leader rubbed his jaw; his options were between bad and worse. "Show me the UAV image of the checkpoint again."

Lapointe brought up the picture, a thermal image in false colors. Jerry could easily make out the bright figure leaning against the barrier. One of the man's arms was bent as if he was holding a cigarette.

"It's just the one guy," Lapointe observed.

"He's gotta have friends," Ramey countered. "It makes no sense for him to be alone. What else can you see off the UAV feed?"

Lapointe called up several other images, small-scale ones of the highway on either side and one with a larger field of view. He then transitioned over to the live streaming video, watching a pan of the area around the lonely sentry. "Nothing. It's only four kilometers from the checkpoint to either of these two small towns. Maybe the garrison there is just sending this one man out."

"Boss? Any word on when to turn?" Harry's voice sounded calm, but time was passing, and they were closing on the roadblock at sixty kilometers an hour.

Ramey looked at the image of the roadblock for another few seconds, then answered, "We're not turning. We have to run this one."

"That'll save us some time," Phillips observed. "Is there room to go around on the shoulder?"

"Some, but the shoulder could be mined. We go right through. They can bill us for it." Ramey knocked on the partition between the cab and the back. "Harry? Did you get that?"

"Understood, Boss, we're crashing the barrier."

"The airfield is only fifteen klicks away. We'll be there before they can react."

"What about the sentry?" Jerry asked.

"Harry will have to take him," Ramey decided.

"Hey, Boss! I know I'm good, but I'm driving, remember? Yousef is on that side."

"Yousef," Ramey called. "Can you take out the sentry?"

Shirin, awakened by the conversation, answered for him. "Yes. He says his rifle is in the cab and it has a folding stock, so he will use that. Harry should tell him when to shoot."

Ramey said, "Start to slow down, but don't let your speed get below thirty. When you get about a hundred feet from the barrier, have Yousef shoot, then floor it."

"Understood, Boss. Slow to thirty, shoot at a hundred feet from the barrier, then punch it."

Lapointe announced, "We're five klicks away."

"Let's get ready, just in case," Ramey ordered.

There wasn't a lot to do, but Jerry made sure his rifle was at hand. They piled everyone's packs in the back, since any shots would most likely come from that direction.

Shirin had heard the resignation in Yousef's voice. He had tried to avoid harming his countrymen. Now he had little choice. He'd have to kill so they could live. Yousef prepared his rifle, but held it out of view, in his lap. Harry's was in back. There was no room for it in the cab.

We are going to shoot the sentry and crash through a roadblock, she thought. After everything else they'd done, this seemed almost pedestrian. And the airfield was close.

The moon wasn't up, so the only visible parts of the landscape were the pools of illuminated highway that preceded the truck. Everything else was a featureless black. She watched the truck's odometer, figuring the distance to the roadblock.

Ahead, the horizon could only be seen as an absence of starlight, but a bright spot appeared directly in front of them.

Harry knocked on the back of the cab. "Boss? Tallyho."

"We're ready," came Ramey's answer. "Do it."

"Think pure thoughts," Harry said in Farsi. He held his speed for as long as possible, then gradually slowed from sixty to fifty, then forty, then thirty. Shirin readied herself, but then forced her muscles to relax. All she had to do was duck down when Harry pressed the gas. Simple.

The light became a shape, then expanded into a red-and-white barrier across the road. She hoped it wasn't made of metal. A soldier was standing to the right, waving a flashlight.

Shirin saw him take a few steps. "He's walking toward the road."

"Idiot," Yousef commented. "You never step in front of a moving vehicle."

"Never mind that. Shoot."

Although she should have ducked, she had to watch. Yousef brought the rifle up from his lap, leaned out of the passenger side window, and fired a long burst. Inside the cab, the noise was deafening, and the smell of burnt propellant made her gag. She didn't see any bullets hit the soldier, but he went down in a crumpled heap.

Harry was shifting gears, although she couldn't hear the engine until Yousef stopped firing. Lightly loaded, the truck quickly picked up speed and Harry shifted gears again, just as the front bumper hit the barrier. The engine almost howled as he accelerated. It flew up and to one side, and then she felt and heard pieces breaking under the truck's tires.

Second Squad's Position
2025 Local Time/1725 Zulu

Alizadeh, on the hill with the squad's night-vision scope, had seen the truck and called out. "It's an army truck, approaching from the east!"

Sistani, standing near the base of the rise, didn't have to sound the alert. After hearing about what happened at Charak, he was more concerned about the squad firing on a real army vehicle. Probably full of officers, with his luck.

Then it crashed the barrier and they heard the gunfire.

"Squad, open fire!"

Shirin saw tracers flying across in front of them, and heard a sound like hail on the left side of the truck. Harry yelled, "Fire from the left!" and floored the accelerator. But even as the truck sped up, explosions sprouted from the pavement a few car lengths in front of them. In the truck's headlights, some flashed red and gray. Others spat out billows of white smoke.

Yousef called out, "Fire from the right!" and Shirin saw tracers, a lot of them, coming through the smoke, from the right side of the highway. Were they surrounded?

The explosions seemed closer, and Harry shouted, "We've got to get off the road!" He jerked the wheel to the right and downshifted. The problem was that the ground sloped away on that side, and was cut by streambeds and gullies.

Only one headlight was working, Shirin noticed, as the truck swerved off the pavement. Harry left it on, needing the light more than the concealment. She saw the driver's side window crack in a star pattern, then the windshield.

A line of flame, much brighter and thicker than tracers, flashed from behind and to the right, missing them by a foot and disappearing into the darkness. "RPG!" Harry shouted. "I'm going to try to get us into a streambed!"

The truck was rocking violently from side to side, the result of Harry's driving and the uneven terrain. Shirin gripped Yousef's left arm with both hands, probably tightly enough to hurt, but she saw him hanging on to the door handle with his right hand so they wouldn't be thrown around. She wondered if any of the truck's tires had been hit.

It was hard to make out anything through the damaged windshield. The ground in front of them seemed to heave as the truck lurched and bounced. The tracers didn't improve the view, either. Shirin hoped the truck's wild motion would spoil their attacker's aim.

Harry certainly wasn't slowing down. It wasn't clear whether he was still heading for cover or just fighting for control when their wild ride came to a sudden end. A sharp jolt threw them all forward, and then to the right side of the cab. The SEAL's grip on the wheel was the only thing that kept him from landing on top of her. The truck stopped moving forward, but the right-hand tilt increased until she was sure they were going over. She tried to curl up in a ball, to protect the baby, but there was not much room to move.

They landed with a messy crash. Harry, hanging onto the steering wheel, shouted, "Cover your eyes!" and kicked with both feet. From her viewpoint, each looked as big as the truck itself. On the third kick, the windshield broke and fell away. "Get her out of here!" the American ordered.

Harry took Shirin's arm and pulled her up and clear. Yousef untangled himself, standing on the side door and then crawling out. While her husband stood up outside, Shirin worked her feet onto the edge of the opening, then let go of Harry's hand and fell forward into Yousef's arms. Shouting, "Stay down!" Harry stopped long enough to pass out Yousef's rifle, and then climbed out himself.

Jerry had heard the gunfire and felt the bullets striking the side of the truck even as he'd heard Harry's call and felt the truck's engine rev. Crouching as low as they could on the floor, the four men in back could do nothing but hang on for dear life as the truck sped up, then suddenly slowed, and swerved right.

The truck's downward progress off the road threw everything into the air or against the sides or ends of the space. Even Jerry became airborne when he lost his grip on the bench, landing heavily on Phillips.

Ramey, sitting near the front, had reacted by grabbing the seats on each side with his hands and extending his legs under the benches, bracing them against the supports. Relatively secure, Jerry could still see him strain to hold his position, and Ramey took hard impacts from several flying objects.

It got worse when the truck tipped over. The sudden deceleration threw everything and everyone to the front, with the lieutenant under it all. It spilled to the right as the bed went vertical, then a little past vertical on the downward-sloping ground.

Jerry coughed, tried to move, and realized his legs were entangled with Phillips, while one arm was pinned under Lapointe and several knapsacks, which now seemed to be loaded with rocks.

"Out! We have to get out!" Lapointe shouted. The petty officer was nearest the open end of truck, and struggled out from under a tangle of gear. He snatched the closest rifle and half-staggered to the opening.

Jerry flexed his liberated arm. Once assured it was working, he pulled himself clear of Phillips and helped him to stand on what had been the truck's side, now the floor. "Look after the boss," Phillips shouted as he grabbed a rifle and joined Lapointe by the back.

Ramey was unconscious, and Jerry forced himself to carefully check the lieutenant's pulse and breathing. He was alive, and moaned as Jerry checked for broken bones or other trauma. "Ow. All right, I'm awake. Ahhhh," he groaned, as he moved his arms then untangled his legs from the bench seats. Pulling himself to a kneeling position, he called, "Pointy, Philly, somebody tell me what's going on."

"Lot of fire from both sides of the road, Boss. It's died off, now."

"They probably think we're dead," Ramey answered. "Let's see if they send someone to check out the wreck."

"We'll keep out of sight."

"What about Harry and the Iranians?"

"I'm here," Harry reported. "No casualties. I need my weapon. The precious cargo is under cover, next to the truck. There's a machine gun fifty plus meters away on this side of the road, and I saw RPG fire. I had to get off the road because they had a mortar zeroed on it."

They grabbed weapons and packs. Lapointe handed Harry his rifle, and then passed Jerry the night-vision goggles. "Give these to Yousef."

Ramey ordered, "Harry, Philly, XO, go up front by the cab. Harry, see what you can do about that machine gun. Pointy and I will stay back here and see if we can put some fire down. They could rush us any time. Move."

The group had been huddled down, half inside the truck and the others behind. Lapointe and Ramey moved first, turning to lay prone on the sloping ground facing toward the enemy. As they moved into position, Jerry heard several single shots, spaced a few seconds apart.

Dirt and pebbles kicked up near Lapointe, and he cried out. "*UGH!* I'm hit, my leg!" Another shot quickly followed, but Ramey had already backed down the slope and avoided being struck.

Jerry and Phillips moved Lapointe to safety by the simple expedient of grabbing his feet and pulling. Fazel joined them, but as he reached for his first aid kit, the far side of the road erupted with gunfire, tracers converging on the truck. The machine gun to the right of the road also laced the area. A moment later, a pair of explosions ripped the ground a dozen yards away. "Well, they know we're still alive," Jerry said.

They all understood what was happening. "Get way from the truck!" Ramey shouted. "Head toward the beach!" he ordered. "Philly, XO, help the Iranians."

Jerry headed behind the fleeting cover of the truck to find Shirin and Yousef huddled against the canvas top. "We've got to get away," Jerry urged, and pointed down the hill.

The couple stood and hurried down the slope, with Jerry in front and Phillips covering their rear. Tracers flew over their heads. Another pair of mortar shells landed closer to the truck. They could hear fragments ripping through the metal body. Behind him, Jerry could hear Lapointe trying to stay quiet as Ramey and Fazel carried him, his wound still untreated.

Jerry heard a different-sounding explosion, and had just enough time to register the whoosh preceding it when the truck fireballed, briefly highlighting them in orange-red light as they struggled down the slope.

Jerry almost fell into a fold in the ground that appeared as a dark chasm in front of them. It was deep enough to kneel behind, but he found that out by landing badly on the bottom. He helped Shirin down and then called to Ramey and Fazel. Carrying Lapointe, they turned toward Jerry and the others, and sped up as much as they could, given the uneven terrain.

The instant they put Lapointe down, Harry opened his first aid kit and started to work. Jerry quickly crawled over and began taking off Lapointe's backpack. "Leave it," the corpsman said tersely. "It's not in my way."

"I want the radio," Jerry insisted. "Gotta make a call." He fumbled first with the pack, then with the radio. He'd seen Lapointe set it up plenty of times, but it was dark, and the edges kept getting caught on the fabric of the backpack.

Jerry said, "I'll get us some help. Just keep us alive for ten minutes," he told Ramey.

The lieutenant set about organizing their defense.

* * *

Lieutenant Sistani had taken a position on the rise, next to Private Aliza-deh. His night sight was proving vital, both for spotting the enemy and guiding the mortar. The sight had a built-in laser rangefinder, and he'd fed range data to the 60mm mortar Corporal Afshar and Private Kiani were firing.

The second volley of fire had driven the fugitives down the hill, which was good, but where were they now? "What can you see?" Sistani demanded.

"I saw motion down the hill, sir, but nothing now. I think they've gone to ground."

"Give me a range to where you last saw them."

The private checked his sight. "Three hundred and sixty-five meters."

Sistani hurried down the hill to the mortar position. "Afshar, get ready to put six rounds down at three seven zero meters, in line with the truck." As the corporal nodded, Sistani called to the nearest private. "Ostovar, tell Jahveri to put machine gun fire down wherever he sees mortar shells ex-ploding. Stay there and be ready to advance when I give the word. Go." The lieutenant watched him trot out of sight, counted another thirty seconds, then told Afshar, "Now."

USS *Michigan*, Battle Management Center
2033 Local Time/1733 Zulu

Guthrie's voice boomed out of the intercom. "BMC, Conn. We'll be ready to launch in a minute or two. Any updates?"

Frederickson answered, "They're still getting mortar fire. Lapointe is stable."

A new voice came over the intercom. "Control, Launcher. Missile com-partment manned and ready." Doolan's voice was almost breathless. "We're making the final checks now."

"No shortcuts, Mr. Doolan," Guthrie cautioned.

"We're good, sir. I double-checked the seals myself." There was a short pause, and he reported, "Tube two four is ready."

The SEAL lieutenant keyed the radio. "Launch in two minutes, XO." He heard two clicks in response.

Fortress of Solitude
2038 Local Time/1738 Zulu

Jerry wasn't getting a lot of help from Lapointe. The petty officer had refused to take any painkillers so he could stay awake, but he'd lost a lot of
blood, and half the time Jerry couldn't hear his answers, especially in the
middle of a firefight.

With Lapointe treated, Fazel had gone into sniper mode, concentrating
on the PKM machine gun that flanked them. He'd hit the gunner at least
once, but after a short pause, it had started up again. The SEALs picked
their shots carefully, no more than two rounds at a time, both for maximum
effect and to avoid revealing their location.

In between mortar bursts, Phillips had spotted movement along the
highway, then the others saw it as well—soldiers lining up along the road.
"They're positioning themselves for a charge, once the mortars have soft-
ened us up." Ramey and the others picked off a few who didn't stay low
enough, and tried to keep the others' heads down in between mortar bursts.

Jerry held the controller so Lapointe could operate it, and followed the
petty officer's hands as he powered up the device and tested the controls. It
was designed for use in the field, but Jerry had never trained on it. Lapointe
was breathing hard, but ran Jerry through the procedure.

As Jerry started to ask a question, the controller beeped twice, and
Lapointe said, "Time's up. Take it, XO."

Jerry fitted the visor over his eyes and adjusted the strap. The visor was
size of a pair of safety goggles, but heavier. Inside Jerry saw bright symbols
and numbers surrounding a black rectangle. In the center of the display, the
word "Signal" blinked, and Jerry could feel Lapointe guiding his fingers on
the hand controller. Lapointe placed his index finger on a switch, and the
image came alive.

He was flying over a dark, featureless surface. A bright, irregular landscape lay in the distance, but he was closing in at high speed. The numbers
and symbols started to change, and he recognized readouts for airspeed and
altitude. "I've got the signal," Jerry reported. He was over the water, approaching the coast.

Guided by Lapointe, Jerry's finger pressed another switch. "You've got
it," the petty officer told him.

Jerry gingerly moved the controller, and saw the landscape fall away as the UAV climbed. That suited him fine. Aviators get nervous too close to the ground, especially in an unfamiliar aircraft.

"I'm slowing down," Jerry stated. The speed readout was over five hundred knots.

"Stalling speed is one twenty," Lapointe told him, "but you're loaded, so try not to drop below one forty."

"Understood, bringing it down slowly," Jerry replied. "Five hundred, four fifty . . ."

The vehicle slowed quickly, and Jerry experimented with a left, and then a right turn. He quickly brought the UAV back on base course, though. A cursor at the top of the display indicated the direction to the controller, bringing it straight toward him.

Jerry brought the Cormorant in overhead at five hundred feet and two hundred and fifty knots. On the thermal imager, he could see the bright flare of the burning truck, and the line of soldiers lying prone along the highway. "I've got them!" he announced.

"Find that goddamned mortar!" Ramey ordered impatiently, and Jerry, already past the battle, turned the Cormorant to the right, trying to time the turn so he ended up over the highway. He was off, with the highway to the left of center, but as he flew overhead, he saw two human figures well back from the highway, working with something even brighter and hotter than they were.

"Got it," Jerry reported. He was past the target by that time, but he risked slowing a little more to focus on making a crisp one-eighty. This time, as the Cormorant passed over the mortar's position, he used the hand controller to mark its precise location. Increasing power, he said, "Climbing." He was getting the hang of this thing. He was sure a pilot had a hand in designing the visor. The readouts looked just like his Hornet's heads-up display.

At a thousand feet, he made a wide circle, constantly informing the impatient SEAL lieutenant of his progress. "I'm ready," he told Lapointe, and felt his hand guided to another pair of buttons. "Left to lock them up, right to fire," Lapointe reminded him.

He pressed the left button, and a bright "L," for laser, appeared in one corner. Then he pressed the right button twice. The image shook for just a second, and two streaks of light leapt from the foreground toward the two figures and what was hopefully the mortar.

He heard the double explosion at the same time as the screen flared. It was much louder than the mortar shells, and Jerry could see the figures were no longer together, and lay sprawled and unmoving. The laser-guided Hydra rockets had found their target.

"That's what I'm talkin' about, XO! Now get that machine gun off our backs."

Lieutenant Sistani lay with his men along the highway, trying to gauge the enemy's status. They were pinned down by fire, had at least one casualty if Alizadeh was to be believed, and were virtually surrounded. He had men to the north and east, the ocean was at their adversaries' backs to the south, and if they tried to break out to the west, he'd cut them down.

He'd been willing to wait and let the mortar work on them when he heard an explosion from behind him. It had come from the direction of the mortar crew. Had there been some sort of accident? He'd almost gotten up to go find out before remembering the enemy in front of him.

He was still low, crawling to a place where he could get up safely when another pair of explosions ripped the landscape near— No, it was at the PKM's position. It didn't fire again. He hadn't seen anything but rifle fire from the enemy. The range was too great and the explosions too large for a grenade launcher. He thought of a helicopter gunship, but there was no noise. Was it a stealth bomber?

Would there be more explosions? He was losing men, and the battle. His only hope was to close with them so that they couldn't drop any more bombs.

"By opposite numbers, advance!" Sistani's only thought now was to finish this quickly.

Jerry heard Ramey's shout just as he was lining up for a shot on the soldiers on the highway. In the display, he saw them moving, and pressed the right button twice, quickly, even though he hadn't marked their position. He kept the crosshairs centered on the middle of the line and watched explosions knock three men off their feet.

But they were coming now. Lapointe helped him find the autopilot key that would send the Cormorant into a circular orbit at a safe altitude.

"Help me up," Lapointe asked, and pushing up with his good leg, Jerry got the petty officer faced forward, then handed him his rifle.

Jerry grabbed his own weapon and looked for a place. Ramey motioned for him to go to the far end of the line, near the Iranians, and staying low, Jerry joined Fazel and Yousef, both firing.

The Pasdaran soldiers were advancing in pairs, taking turns firing while the other ran forward for the next bit of cover. Fazel was having the best luck sniping at the shooters, who were stationary at least, even if they were under cover. Kneeling next to Shirin, Yousef used his rifle to give Harry covering fire.

Jerry concentrated on the advancing soldiers, trying to guess when they'd spring up and run forward. He might actually hit one, or at least make him stop sooner than he'd planned. The trick was keeping them from getting too close.

Fazel dropped another one. As Jerry tried to count how many were still out there, he saw the soldiers nearest them raise their arms. He shouted, "Grenades!"

They ducked as the grenades fell short, but Jerry felt the blast on the back of his neck. Knowing the explosions would signal a general charge, Jerry came up firing, holding the trigger on full automatic and emptying the magazine.

Yousef was doing the same. Only the SEALs took the time to squeeze off aimed shots. Three soldiers had charged their position, firing as they came, but they all died. Jerry didn't know who had hit whom, and he didn't cared.

He was putting in a fresh magazine when another grenade went off in front of them. Suddenly, he heard Shirin scream and saw Yousef falling. Calling "Harry!" as he leapt over her, Jerry rolled Yousef face up and felt something warm and wet on his hand.

Somebody grabbed the back of his vest and yanked him away from Yousef, and Fazel said, "I've got him. You keep firing."

Jerry quickly turned and brought up his rifle, searching with the night-scope, but didn't see any movement. The firing had stopped on the other side as well. Several bodies lay sprawled a dozen meters in front of them, but remembering his past experience, Jerry didn't move forward.

"It's an artery," Harry said softly to Shirin, but Jerry was close enough to hear it as well. "Probably a grenade fragment."

Ramey asked, "Is the Cormorant still up there?"

"We've got another fifteen or twenty minutes on station."

"Can you use it to see if there are any stragglers?"

Jerry reluctantly turned away from Yousef, but knew he was in good hands with Harry. Finding the visor and controller, he took control of the orbiting UAV and had it fly straight overhead. "I see us, I see at least ten bodies, including three by the machine gun and two . . .

"Wait. I've got movement. One figure is running. I can see him heading for a vehicle—a truck."

"You've got to take him out," Ramey ordered.

"Doing it," Jerry said. It was eerie. Jerry could see the front of the vehicle grow brighter as the motor started. Before it could start moving, he put the UAV in a shallow dive and fired. The last two laser-guided 2.75-inch rockets hit the truck, and when the display cleared, the vehicle was on its side, burning. Jerry couldn't feel good about it.

"It's near bingo fuel," Jerry reported.

"Then send it home." Ramey answered. "Can you give a UAV a medal?" he asked, smiling.

As Jerry was telling the autopilot to head for the rendezvous point, Phillips walked up and spoke softly. "Boss, Harry's been working on Yousef, but it looks bad."

Jerry's heart sank. Ramey just said "Shit," and went over to kneel down by Yousef.

Fazel explained, "I've stopped the arterial bleeding, but I think the fragment did more damage internally. He's sinking, and I've run out of things I can do."

He was so pale, and Shirin did her best to smile and hold his hand, which was cold as ice. "My brave soldier," she repeated over and over again. She wasn't sure he could hear her, but he finally smiled, and coughed. He looked at her, then Harry, and said weakly, "Now you will say the *Janazah Salah* for me."

Shirin tried to speak, but tears stole her voice. "I promise," Harry finally said. "If we did it for our enemies, how much more will I do for my own brother?"

"Take care of her, then, brother." Yousef rasped. As he finished speaking, he exhaled—a long, slow, gurgling breath, and he was gone. Harry reached over and closed Yousef's lifeless eyes. Shirin began to weep uncontrollably, saying over and over again, "No, Baba, no!"

* * *

"We've got to get moving," Ramey ordered.

"I saw a truck, but one of my rocket strikes wrecked it," Jerry reported.

"Then we walk," Ramey answered. "Right now. Column formation. It will help hide our numbers."

Ramey then turned to Fazel and handed him a dead tree branch. "Harry, do what you can to hide our footprints. I don't want the Iranians to see us heading toward the beach."

Phillips and Jerry, the designated stretcher-bearers, rigged a litter and carefully moved Lapointe onto it. Once Fazel had dosed the petty officer with much-needed painkillers, and was sure Lapointe was settled, he asked Jerry, "Can you take my pack, XO?"

After Jerry took the backpack, at least as heavy as the fifty pounds he was already carrying, Fazel took a blanket and tied it around Yousef's body to hold it in place. Hoisting the limp form with Ramey's help, he balanced Yousef on his shoulders. "I'm ready," Harry announced. He saw the surprise in Jerry's expression. "You didn't think we were going to leave him, did you?"

"We could bury him here," Jerry suggested. He didn't say it, but he was a little worried about Harry's load. He'd traded a fifty-pound pack for two hundred-plus pounds.

"I'm good," insisted Fazel.

"We don't have time," Ramey said firmly. "And we don't leave our people behind."

Without another word, Ramey led off on point. Jerry and Phillips followed, carrying Lapointe, then Fazel with his solemn burden, and Shirin walking at his side.

17

AFTERMATH

They'd been walking for about half an hour when Jerry saw what had to be a convoy. Even from three hundred meters south of the highway, he could hear the diesel engines, and instead of one or two sets of headlights, he counted at least four or five, traveling as a group, and heading west, toward where they'd fought the battle. "If those trucks are carrying troops, that's at least a company," Phillips observed softly.

They'd frozen, of course, taking a knee and waiting for the lights to pass. There was enough vegetation along this part of the coast so that they were usually able to find cover when they needed it. The gulf lay just a hundred meters to the right. Ramey kept them closer to the water, where the brush was thicker and would hide their tracks.

Jerry was grateful for the frequent stops, even if it meant having to stand up again after the traffic had passed. Sometimes, Ramey would let them rest for an extra minute, using the time to check Lapointe or adjust someone's load.

They were all weighed down. Jerry carried Fazel's pack, Philips carried Lapointe's, in addition to both of them carrying the stretcher. Fazel of course carried Yousef, and now Shirin had a hand on his arm to help steady her. Even she did her part, carrying Harry's rifle slung over her shoulder.

The SEALs were absolutely silent as they withdrew from the scene of the skirmish. Besides the occasional snap of brush, or the sound of tottering rock, the group made little noise. Ramey led the way, but also would scout ahead, or to the side, or fall back and watch for any pursuit. For every step Jerry and the others took, Ramey took three.

The platoon leader pushed them hard, not just because they had to clear the area of the battle, but because they had to reach a good layup position before dawn. Their best option, a grove of trees close to the airfield, lay on the far side of the small village of Mollu, a little over four miles from where they'd had the fight. It was hard to estimate their progress, and the pauses didn't help. Jerry knew they were moving more slowly than they had two nights ago, but Ramey insisted they'd be there before dawn.

In another hour, they'd have to start angling south, toward the gulf, so they could cross behind the southern portion of Mollu along the beach. The nearest structure was over 150 meters away, but Ramey wanted them to traverse the one kilometer behind the village as fast and as quietly as possible.

7 April 2013
0000 (Midnight) Local Time/2100 Zulu on 6 April
Bandar Charak

They met at the town's hospital, which was also a morgue. Sattari was still there, bleary-eyed, and waiting for the final autopsy report. Still numb after the death of his partner, he greeted Rahim with little more than a handshake.

Rahim did not pretend to be sad at Omid's passing. The man was an ass, and by early accounts, had managed to engineer his own demise. But Rahim did honestly tell Sattari, "I'm sorry you've lost your partner. We will find out who did this and punish them for their crime."

"And you need to know what I've found out," Sattari replied mournfully. "Forensics went over the area as best they could in the dark. They found a position where the enemy had hidden while Akbari and Naseri went into town. There are signs of several men wearing an unfamiliar-patterned boot, as well as one man wearing Iranian-issue boots and a woman's civilian shoes. They picked up their spent cartridges and there was no sign of other trash, so we can assume they are professional solders with good field skills."

Sattari paused for a moment, then reported. "That's all we could find out in the dark. Their forensics man will be back out there tomorrow morning at dawn."

"One man?" Rahim asked. "Let's get him some help."

"Yes, sir," Sattari answered tiredly. "I'll call the police captain."

"No, I'll have Dahghan make the call." The young agent behind Rahim nodded and hurried off.

"Are you officially taking over this case, Major?"

"This has always been my case, Agent Sattari. Omid didn't want to work with me. He wanted to humble me by making an arrest himself. I don't know if he deserved to die for that, but it was obviously not the correct approach. Will you work with me to catch these traitors and whoever's helping them?"

Sattari nodded. "For Omid's sake, if no other. I don't know their exact crimes, but now they've killed my partner and four Basij soldiers."

Dahghan came back. "The police commander says he will get more forensics people from the surrounding towns. I also have the coroner's report." He offered it to them. Sattari took it, but Rahim said tiredly, "Just tell me what it says."

"All five died of gunshot wounds." He held up a small plastic bag. "This is one of the bullets he recovered. It's 7.62mm, but not from an Iranian-issue rifle. Without seeing one of the cartridges he can't be certain, but he thinks it a NATO-standard round. And ballistics indicates at least three different rifles, although some of the bullets were too damaged to be properly examined."

"That's good work, Karim." The information was useful, even if it was bad news. At least three professional soldiers were with the two traitors. It reminded him of that old joke about lion hunting: It wasn't hard to catch one; the problem was, what did you do after that?

Sattari's cell phone had beeped during Dahghan's report, and now he checked the display. "It's the Bandar Abbas office," he remarked as he called back. Any call from them was VEVAK business, and at this hour, had to be important.

His expression had been serious, but as he listened, it changed to shock.

After only a few moments, he said hurriedly, "Wait. Just tell Major Rahim. He won't believe me."

He handed the phone to Rahim, who looked to see if anyone was nearby, then pressed the speakerphone button. "This is Rahim," he said quickly.

"I've received a radio message from Colonel Yavari. He commands the Pasdaran garrison at Bandar Lengeh. He says that he received word of a battle at one of the roadblocks earlier this evening on Highway 96, near Mollu. Proceeding to the roadblock, he found many of his men killed, along with a burned-out army truck that matches the description of the one you are looking for."

Rahim felt his spirits rise, but when the speaker didn't continue, they dropped just as quickly. "Let me guess. There was no sign of other bodies— foreigners, or a woman's?"

"I'm sorry, sir, that was the whole message."

"Where is Mollu?" Rahim asked Sattari.

"It's a very small town. Ahh, I'd have to look at a map. No more than eighty kilometers," he stammered.

"And the roadblock is closer than that," Rahim said. "Come on. We can be there in an hour." He looked at Sattari's expression. "Dahghan will drive."

7 April 2013
0130 Local Time/2230 Zulu on 6 April
Between Bustaneh and Mollu

It was sixty-eight kilometers by the odometer when they were waved to a stop by a pair of heavily armed soldiers. Rahim's uniform and identity card quickly got them past the barrier, and directions to the colonel's command post.

Colonel Yavari was young for a colonel, almost too young for a lieutenant colonel. His hair and beard were jet-black and cut short. His headquarters tent was set up a short distance from the "battlefield," where there was room to park the troop trucks and ambulances that were still being loaded.

"Who are you? What are you doing here?" Yavari demanded angrily. Rahim's identification didn't impress him, and actually made him even angrier.

"Are you the one who sent my men out to their deaths? An entire squad is dead, and it's your fault." Yavari reached for his sidearm as he spoke, taking a step toward Rahim.

"You lost an entire whole squad? Twelve men?" Rahim's tone was incredulous, but he added enough contempt to make it clear who he thought was at fault.

"If you'd bothered to tell us who or what we were fighting, my men would be alive right now." Yavari actually had his weapon out of its holster, and was bringing his other hand up to work the slide.

"Colonel, please," Dahghan almost ran over to stand in front of Yavari. "We've just come from Charak, where we've been investigating the last attack. We still don't know everything, but we've got a few answers."

"Who attacked my squad?" demanded the colonel. Curiosity joined anger, but he didn't put away the pistol.

"We know at least three professional soldiers, probably with NATO rifles of some kind, are traveling with the two fugitives, one of whom is a Pasdaran captain."

Yavari, eyes wide, almost laughed. "Four armed men—wait, you said 'at least' four men. Well, that explains everything!" His sarcasm was biting. "Come with me!" Striding out of the tent, the three VEVAK agents hurried to keep up. Almost running, the colonel reached the pavement and walked west.

They'd set up work lights on either side of the highway, but the harsh beams showed only debris and destruction. Yavari pointed to a splintered traffic barrier. "This is where they set up the checkpoint. We knew any lawbreakers would ignore it, so the ambush was laid out beyond, with a mortar registered on the road, and a machine gun set up there."

Still walking, he pointed to the right, past the hulk of a burned-out truck, still smoking. "A marksman was up there with a sniper rifle." He pointed to a hill on the left. "Sistani's men were arranged here." He swept his hand in a line along the road. "See where they dug fighting positions?"

"After the truck ran the roadblock, Sistani's men opened fire, driving it off the road. My men have counted over a hundred bullet strikes on the vehicle. Somehow, whoever was in the truck survived an RPG hit, and got out after it tipped over. We found tracks down to a depression where the enemy took cover. Sistani's men charged them, but were defeated. Look at this."

The colonel led them to the left, behind the squad's firing line, to a shallow pit, which Rahim realized was actually a crater. A shattered 60mm mortar lay in the depression. "The dead soldiers, may Allah grant them peace, have been removed, and most of the weapons have been collected, but I told them to preserve the entire area until we can examine it in the daylight. Remember the machine gun I mentioned? It looks much the same. Sistani's transport"—he pointed—"is over there, also destroyed."

He turned to face Rahim. "Tell me again how only four armed men did this. They must have possessed heavy weapons."

His face was half-shadowed, but Rahim could still see Colonel Yavari's anger plainly. "I personally called Sistan"—he growled while pointing to himself—"and warned him when I heard about the fight at Charak. He was a good officer. We received a radio message from him when the shooting started, but nothing after that." When he'd started speaking of his lieutenant, the anger began to fade. By the time he was finished, the colonel was drained, the anger replaced by an equally strong sense of grief and loss.

"Missile strikes," Rahim said abruptly.

"What?" Sattari had asked the question, but they all looked at the major with the same puzzled expression.

Rahim explained, "You are right, Colonel, I apologize. I have not told you everything about this case because I did not make the connection. There is an American nuclear submarine off the coast, right out there somewhere." He pointed toward the water. "The traitors attempted to contact it several days ago. It could have fired missiles to support its countrymen when they were attacked."

The colonel straightened up a little. "It is nice to know we are not fighting supermen. A soldier's most dangerous weapon is a radio." Dahghan and Sattari were silent, more surprised by Rahim's apology than his idea of a submarine firing missiles.

"We can find them and beat them," Rahim insisted. Looking around him, he said, "We have to, after this."

"Colonel, I'd like to come back to your headquarters with you. We must plan how to reestablish the roadblocks. We will bring in reinforcements, and I want security increased throughout the region."

7 April 2013
0500 Local Time/0200 Zulu
East of Mollu, West of Bandar Lengeh

Jerry called it an oasis, though there weren't any palm trees. It was still the most verdant spot he'd seen since coming to Iran. The trees and shrubs were thick enough so they could walk into them and not see the other side.

Ramey had already worked through what they would do when they reached the layup. There would be no rest—not for a while, anyway.

The SEALs and Jerry picked a spot in the densest part of the vegetation and stowed their belongings. The others helped Yousef off Fazel's shoulders and laid him in a sheltered spot, then made up a pallet for Shirin close by. She gratefully collapsed onto it.

For half an hour, they set up fighting positions, added camouflage to the existing foliage, and did their best to remove evidence of their approach to the location. In the early morning twilight, Ramey surveyed their positions to make sure they were invisible.

With their location secure, they examined the place, finally picking an area open toward the water, but completely hidden by trees from the landward side. While Jerry, Ramey, and Phillips dug, Heydar Fazel washed the body. There was no white cotton for the shroud, so he dressed Yousef in his Pasdaran uniform, complete with his pistol and gun belt, and wrapped him neatly in blankets. The four then laid him in the grave facing southwest.

After the body was in place, Jerry and the others added Yousef's rifle. "When you get to Paradise, you'll have an honor guard," Ramey said.

They filled in the grave while Shirin and Fazel prayed. Clutched in Shirin's right hand was one of the epaulets from Yousef's uniform, along with the fragment of her father's flight suit.

7 April 2013
0700 Local Time/0400 Zulu
1st Regiment Headquarters, 47th Salam Brigade, Bandar Lengeh

There was no love lost between VEVAK and the Pasdaran, but Yavari had accepted Rahim's authority, especially after a 0400 call from the general commanding the southern region. The general was placing two additional regiments and a mechanized infantry company under Yavari's command. Advance elements would arrive by that afternoon. Helicopters, both transports and gunships, would start arriving tomorrow. This was all because of orders received from Tehran, the general explained.

There'd been no time for sleep. The colonel's staff and the VEVAK agents created a new net of roadblocks, centered on the site of the last battle. While they presumed that the fugitives were still headed toward the east, roads leading west were guarded as well.

The colonel's deputy, Major Seddigh, brought welcome news while they were still finalizing the plan. "Two of the fugitives are wounded, at least."

All work stopped and they turned to hear his report. "When the sun rose, our men searched the battlefield and found bloodstains on the ground. One patch was by the burnt-out truck, and another, larger one, was in the depression where they rallied. They also found wrappers from bandages."

"Were there any indications as to which way they went?" asked Rahim impatiently.

"Not that we could tell, sir," answered Seddigh. "We didn't find any tracks heading to the south or the east, and there has been too much traffic to the north and west making it impossible to identify boot patterns."

"Any evidence that they concealed their tracks?" pressed Rahim. The thought of losing his prey again was maddening.

"We didn't see anything suspicious, Major. Unfortunately, the terrain on either side of the highway is very rocky. It wouldn't take much to eliminate their footprints."

Rahim rubbed his hand through his hair; the enemy had been wounded, but they had also disappeared right before their eyes. Again.

"So, what you're telling me is that we've lost them?"

"It would seem so," conceded Seddigh.

7 April 2013
0900 Local Time /0600 Zulu
Bandar Lengeh Airfield

The airfield lay almost in sight of their hideout, but everyone, even Ramey, agreed that they had to get some sleep. After a small meal, the three ambulatory SEALs each took an hour of lookout duty while everyone else slept.

It wasn't completely refreshing, but Jerry had heard enough stories about SEAL training to know it would help.

Jerry asked to stand watch as well, but Ramey turned him down without explanation. Given their fatigue and frayed nerves, he didn't push it.

After they'd rested, Ramey helped him prepare for their reconnaissance. In addition to leaving their packs behind, the SEAL lieutenant had Jerry take off anything that reflected light, and double-checked Jerry's tactical vest for items that might make noise. As they prepared, he drilled Jerry on patrol techniques. "Watch me. When I crouch, you crouch. If I drop to the ground, you drop. Don't wait for me to tell you, sir."

"Understood, Boss," Jerry answered. There was no warmth in Ramey's tone, but that was okay, because this was business. He was in his element, and the lieutenant was indeed "Boss" for this patrol.

Jerry knew that Ramey didn't really want him along, but he needed to get a pilot's eyes on the airfield. They couldn't make a plan without it.

Ramey was especially cautious leaving the layup. While getting spotted at any time would be disastrous, being seen now would reveal everyone's position, and with Lapointe wounded, it would be almost impossible to escape pursuit.

The lieutenant moved slowly, and Jerry did his best to copy his movements, even stepping where the lieutenant stepped whenever possible. They hugged the line of trees and bushes for as long as they could.

Just east of the copse was a small farm, with cultivated fields just turning green with new crops. They moved to the north, bypassing scattered buildings, some looking abandoned, others occupied.

Jerry spent a lot of time on his stomach behind trees or low brush. When they crossed open ground, they sprinted, but only after Ramey was convinced the coast was clear. Twice they had to detour around farmers out in their fields. They crawled, climbed, and dashed from cover to cover. Finally, Ramey found a dried-out streambed that wandered through trees up to Highway 96. Although he was in good shape, Jerry was almost breathless when they reached their goal some four kilometers away.

Luckily, they didn't have to go all the way to the airfield. There was a rise to the west that provided enough cover, as long as they low-crawled their way to the top. The hill not only saved them some time, but as far as Jerry was concerned, the only decent way to look at an airfield was from above.

They'd studied the satellite photos so often he knew it as well as the field at Pensacola, where he'd learned to fly. This one was a lot smaller, though. A single strip, twenty-seven-hundred-meters long, it ran almost straight east-west. There was a single taxiway from near the middle of the runway to a wide apron where aircraft parked, and sure enough, he could see a pair of Falcon 20 jets, their white paint almost sparkling in the sunshine. Other aircraft, a mix of helicopters and what looked like civilian light aircraft were parked to either side. He looked for the fueling arrangements, and spotted several fuel trucks parked by an admin or maintenance building. The control tower was a three-story affair, with few antennas on its roof. There was no sign of traffic control radar or instrument landing aids. Of course, the weather here was usually clear.

Ramey, using his own glasses, gently nudged Jerry's shoulder and said softly, "XO, look about ten o'clock, near this end of the runway."

Jerry hadn't paid much attention to the runway itself. Looking to the left, at the near end, he saw an earthen mound, then spotted a ring of sandbags on top. Inside, a pair of soldiers was working with some sort of heavy weapon on a tripod.

"That's a DShK heavy machine gun," Ramey told him. "It's like our .50 caliber." Jerry felt his body go cold. Ramey continued, "This complicates things, but we can cope. While you're getting the plane ready, I go over with a knife and slit their throats, just like in the movies."

Jerry started checking other parts of the airfield. "Ahh, it looks like they're setting up a machine gun at the other end of the runway, too. These weren't on the overhead imagery we saw. This is recent. This is today." Jerry could see where they were still carrying sandbags to the top of the mound.

"Okaaay," Ramey answered. "So I get one, and Philly gets the other. That leaves Harry and you to carry Lapointe. Maybe Shirin carries one end so Harry's free to move. We can make this work." He paused. "Or maybe not. Look next to the hangar. In the shadow."

One large hangar dominated the cluster of buildings that lay on the south side of the runway. It was big enough to take a small commercial airliner, although they couldn't see what was inside. Parked in the shade, probably to avoid the sun as much as for concealment, were a pair of armored vehicles. Each had a flat top that led to an angled front, and a small circular turret with a gun barrel sat in the middle.

"Those aren't tanks, are they?" Jerry asked.

"They're armored personnel carriers, some variant of a Russian BMP. The gun on top is a 73mm. It's not as big as a tank gun, but bad enough. They each carry half a squad of infantry."

"Okay, so we use a Cormorant to take out the heavy stuff and distract them while we steal the plane," Jerry suggested.

"No good," Ramey argued. "Once that UAV starts shooting, we can give up sneaking onto the field. They'll go to general quarters and we're out of luck. Let's go around and look from a different angle."

They worked their way farther east. This entailed another half hour of creeping and dashing, then low-crawling up another hill. Now more concerned with the airfield than the aircraft, Jerry spotted trouble the instant he used his binoculars. "I see more BMPs," Jerry reported. He almost pointed, but remembered in time to stay low.

"I see them, too," Ramey answered. "The rest of a platoon, five altogether."

"And there will be troops for them, as well," Jerry concluded.

"Oh, yeah, probably setting up more emplacements all over the airfield. They'll use the vehicles as strongpoints." The SEAL lieutenant backed down away from his position, then rolled onto his back.

"Do the math. We took out a squad last night. This morning the airfield is alive with troops. Maybe they're afraid we might try to steal a plane."

"Not anymore we're not," Jerry answered.

"Never say die, XO. Let's keep looking."

7 April 2013
1000 Local Time/0700 Zulu
1st Regiment Headquarters, 47th Salam Brigade, Bandar Lengeh

Rahim and the others had managed to find a meal, but had returned to find no news. It really was too soon to expect any developments. But he was impatient, and set Dahghan and Sattari to work calling every barracks and headquarters between Kangan and Lengeh to make sure there was no new information. He'd learned the hard way. He wouldn't wait for them to report.

Overflowing with nervous energy, he started to organize the chaos they'd left behind. As he sorted through the documents, he found one pile laid to the side, from the Pasdaran Navy headquarters. "Did either of you see these?"

Dahghan shook his head. "No, Major."

They were reports from last night. None of the boats had seen any hostile vessels, of course. There were reports of a distress flare being fired, and extra boats had been called in. They'd searched the area between the Farur and Lesser Tunb Islands, starting at 2045 hours, but no further signals were received, either visually or by radio. Because of the darkness, aircraft had not been used.

That was close to where the second squad had been wiped out last night. The timing was also about right. Had the fugitives found a boat and escaped to the sea? But the patrols hadn't found anything. And if they had been on a boat, why would they attract attention by firing flares into the air?

As soon as he asked himself the question, Rahim understood. The image of a flame rising filled his mind. It wasn't a flare, it was a missile.

He had a message to send.

18

PERSUASION

The C-37 was fitted for VIP transport, and they both managed a little sleep after talking late into the night about Iran, Israel, and Jerry. There'd been no new information since his last report, and the conversation swirled in her mind.

"I keep thinking about Emily," Joanna complained. "I know we can't tell her a thing. Even if we told her, all she could do was worry."

"You're worrying enough for the two of you. He's been in bad spots before," Hardy reassured her. "Don't let it distract you."

"I understand, Lowell. Is this what you felt when you commanded *Memphis*?"

"Sort of. You didn't send Jerry into this mess, but you know him, and of course you care. There are seven people on the beach, and I try to worry about all of them, even the Iranians. Go read the writeups on the SEAL team. Learn their names. Look at their faces."

She'd fallen asleep with her tablet open to a webpage entitled "SEAL missions."

One of their security detail had awakened Hardy an hour before landing, and he woke Joanna immediately. By the time they'd washed, dressed, and had some breakfast, the plane was ready to land at Ben Gurion Airport in Tel Aviv.

As they buckled in their seats, an Air Force staff sergeant handed them their message traffic. Most of it was classified. None of it shed any more light on Iran's activities or Israel's preparations.

The morning news summary was useful only for gauging the world's stress level. Several nations had already taken sides, either urging Israel to act against Iranian aggression or supporting Iran's right to develop its own nuclear capability. An interesting side discussion was underway about Israel's own nuclear capability, which the country had never publicly admitted having. If a conventional attack failed to derail Iran's nuclear ambitions, would Israel use its own weapons?

There were also articles on America's role in the crisis. Some criticized the U.S. for not allying openly with Israel. The threat of a two-nation strike would surely deter Iran. Others complained about "American indifference," and its refusal to restrain their ally. Many assumed Israeli compliance would be automatic if the U.S. gave the order.

As much as the U.S. tried to stay on the sidelines, it was already a major player in the crisis, based on past decisions and policies. If Israel attacked Iran, they would use U.S.-made planes and many U.S.-made weapons. Even if America did nothing, the country was involved.

And the Iranians made it clear they would do their best to involve the world if the Islamic Republic was attacked. Statements came from either General Moradi himself, or a government spokesman in Iran, and they seemed to be in a competition to see who could make the wildest claims or the darkest threat. Iran would make the Strait of Hormuz an "iron barrier" to the world's oil tankers, and would "drown Israel in its own blood."

Iran's rhetoric wasn't doing a thing to calm the situation. It fit with what Jerry had told them, but the Iranians routinely trash-talked their enemies. Still, with Israel hypersensitive about its national security, and Iran dedicated to a policy of confrontation and provocation, Patterson wondered if there was any way it could end well.

The pilot's voice interrupted her reading. "We'll taxi to the military terminal. The tower says we will be met."

They had to wait after the door opened while the head of their security detail met with the Israeli security personnel, performed the proper rituals of greeting, and gave the "all clear."

Hardy and Patterson stepped out into brilliant, almost blinding sunshine. A small, compact-looking man introduced himself. "My name is Adir Ben-Rosen. I'm Dr. Harel's assistant. He cannot meet with you until later today. In the meantime, we've made arrangements for your lodging." His English was heavily accented, but understandable.

Hardy shook his hand, but did not smile. "I hope Dr. Harel understands the urgency of our visit."

"Two presidential envoys? In normal times, the deputy director would be here to greet you, but these are not normal times, Senator. Dr. Harel is not in Tel Aviv at the moment, and neither is the director. Dr. Harel is expected back this afternoon, and will meet with you as soon as he returns."

Ben-Rosen greeted Patterson warmly but did not shake her hand, and gestured toward the waiting cars. As they got in, Joanna whispered, "Orthodox Jew?" to her husband, and he nodded. "Likely, unless you've got some history with Israel you haven't told me about."

The half-hour drive through Tel Aviv's center was accompanied by a fascinating description of the sights along the way and the city's history. Neither of them had been in the city before, and Ben-Rosen recommended restaurants, museums, shops, even plays that they might want to see.

Joanna answered for them. "Tel Aviv has many things we'd love to see, but that will have to be on our next visit. Like your boss, we have a tight schedule."

The Daniel Hotel was on the west edge of town, almost on the water. The lobby was modern and almost tropical with lush greenery and a stunning view of the Mediterranean. It was located in Herzliya, a suburb north of Tel Aviv that was also the location of Mossad's headquarters.

They were met by the Daniel Hotel's manager and welcomed warmly. "Rooms for you and your security staff have been arranged. Your luggage is on its way up to your room. It has a lovely view of the Mediterranean, and there is an excellent outdoor breakfast buffet."

Ben-Rosen was ready to leave, pleading a pressing schedule, but both Hardy and Patterson forestalled him. "You still haven't told us when we'll be able to meet with Dr. Harel," she reminded him.

The assistant held up his smartphone. "I'm very sorry. I'd been hoping for an update on the deputy director's arrival while we were driving to the hotel, but it hasn't arrived. I'll be back at my office in fifteen minutes, and I will send you a schedule as soon as it's ready."

Ben-Rosen hurried off, and Patterson and Hardy headed for the elevators.

7 April 2013
0215 Washington, D.C. Time/0715 Zulu/0915 Tel Aviv Time/
1015 Tehran Time
Daniel Hotel, Herzliya, Israel

Still unpacking, they'd turned on the TV as soon as they'd gotten into the room and found a news channel.

CNN had picked up the live feed from FARS about five minutes after the press conference began. English subtitles scrolled across the screen, but the Israeli news service relaying the CNN broadcast had added their own Hebrew subtitles. The two lines of text partially covered what was not a high-fidelity image.

Patterson recognized General Moradi at once. *What else could he possibly say?* she wondered.

Now, he stood in front of a battery of cameras and reporters, patiently answering questions. The press conference, according to FARS, the official Iranian news agency, was taking place at a hospital in Deyyer, a town on the Persian Gulf coast, where an unidentified body had washed ashore.

Without even thinking about it, she sat down and called to Lowell. "You need to see this."

The questions, all from Iranian reporters, were prearranged setups. "When did you find the body? What injuries had it sustained? Have you identified it?"

Moradi was careful with the last question. "We do not know the individual's identity or nationality. He was wearing an American-made watch, and his uniform is American issue."

"What do you intend to do next?"

"We are sending his fingerprints and a copy of the autopsy report to the Red Cross in Geneva, to be passed on to the United States so they can determine if this man is one of their service members. He must have a family, and I'm sure they would like to know what has happened to him."

Behind her, Lowell muttered cynically, "What a considerate guy." She shushed him.

"There are also questions that must be answered about how he came to be in our territory. Certainly we cannot release a body to anyone until this mystery is solved."

"What if he is not American?" a reporter asked.

"If the Americans do not claim him, then in several days we will post all the information: fingerprints, photographs, and the autopsy report, on the Internet so that others can examine it, and perhaps tell us who he is. Again, our first consideration is his bereaved family members, and understanding the circumstances of his death."

Moradi continued, "We have a sketch of his features." He paused and looked to one side, and a hospital worker held up two poster-sized drawings of a young man, one with a beard and one without.

"It's Higgs," she confirmed. She felt a pain in her chest. "I recognize him from the briefing." She tried to remember what it said about his family.

"Lovely," Hardy said grimly. "We can get the body back and explain why we were there, or disown him."

"We can't do that," she protested.

"We won't," he answered, "but until we get Jerry and company get out of Iran, we can't answer questions. And thanks to the kindness of General Moradi, Higgs's family may have just gotten word that he's dead. How long will it take for the news media to swoop in on them? Suddenly, I want to bomb Tehran."

The secure phone rang, and Hardy answered. "Yes, Dr. Kirkpatrick, we saw it, too. I can't predict how the Israelis will react, but it doesn't reflect well on U.S. capabilities."

Hardy listened for a minute, then answered, "The best way to fix it is to get Jerry and his people out, then have our own news conference, with an Iranian nuclear engineer and a boatload of files about a weapons program the Iranians say doesn't exist."

7 April 2013
1500 Local Time/1300 Zulu
Daniel Hotel, Herzliya, Israel

They'd had an excellent lunch, Hardy had called his congressional office, and they'd had a brisk exchange of e-mails with Kirkpatrick confirming that the body Moradi described was indeed Lieutenant Vernon Higgs. They'd reviewed possible scenarios, and researched some finer points of the Israeli governmental structure.

And Ben-Rosen had finally called, at 1500, to explain that the doctor had been delayed en route. They were waiting for a new ETA and would have the schedule quickly after that. He asked for their forgiveness, and patience. The hotel had a pool, a spa, and offered guided tours of the historic parts of the city. Perhaps they could refresh themselves while they waited.

Hardy almost slammed the phone in the receiver when he hung up.

Joanna fumed. "They're trying to distract us. They think we're so self-indulgent we'll happily wait while they prepare their attack."

"I wonder how many times it's worked," Hardy mused. "So let's relax. Want to take a walk on the beach?" He put his finger to his lips.

The outside temperature was seventy-two degrees Fahrenheit, with a light breeze. The Mediterranean could have been an oil painting. It was hard to be angry or impatient in a setting like that, and Patterson felt a little of her tension fade. She looped her arm through his and slowed to his pace.

Once they were away from the hotel, Hardy said, "I know our detail swept the room for bugs, but the Israelis are good. Let's not take chances."

"What if they call while we're out here?" Patterson asked.

"They won't call until we make them call," he answered. "If they can stall us for a day, maybe just overnight, they can say 'It's too late now, we're committed.' They're that close to being ready."

"When, do you think?" she asked.

"As early as tonight. It doesn't affect them as much as the Iranians. The Israelis can fly and fight in the dark as easily as the daytime. It reduces the chances of agents here spotting all the activity, the Iranian air defense crews will be tired, and it gives more time to rescue aircrews if any get shot down. I'd start provoking false alarms around midday, start messing with their minds. . . ."

"But how do we force a meeting?" she asked.

Hardy smiled. "How did you get that meeting with the Russians on *Peter the Great*?" In negotiations with the Russian Navy, she'd connived suspicious, almost hostile Russians into listening to her by publicly announcing that a meeting had been scheduled. It was risky, but it had worked.

"I came at them from a different direction, through the media. Can we do that here? The Israelis don't care about what the press says. Their national survival is at stake. Can we apply pressure somewhere?"

Hardy almost laughed. "They don't want what we've got right now." He paused for a moment. "But they will want what we've got later, after the strike."

"Political support," Joanna said.

"Right. We can promise to abstain from any Security Council vote. We can threaten to limit arms sales in the future. The Israelis have to convince us that they are using the stuff we sold them for legitimate self-defense. If the Iranians don't have the bomb, and the Israelis won't listen, then they're just bombing Natanz because it feels good."

She didn't look convinced. "We can't say that on our own hook. Sure, you're on the Senate Armed Services Committee, but you're the junior member. We need to get approval from State."

"Or from someone higher in the chain. We'll ask. The Israelis know that acting against their ally's wishes will have a political cost. Maybe they need to see what the price tag actually says."

Patterson spoke softly. "And what about the data Jerry's group has? When we get it, we'll release a lot of the files. It would prove the Israelis were played—that there never was a bomb. It would embarrass both the Iranians and the Israelis."

Hardy did laugh out loud, but lowered his voice to answer. "You mean make Mossad, the world's greatest intelligence agency, look like monkeys? Would we do that?"

She just smiled, envisioning the scene.

"Let's go write some e-mails," Hardy suggested.

"But we should play nice," she added. "We could say that we're willing to listen to their analysis. We have the president's ear. This is one last chance before the shooting starts to convince the U.S. and get our support."

"And to think I married you for your looks," he answered.

7 April 2013
2100 Local Time/1900 Zulu
Mossad Headquarters, Herzliya, Israel

Given their reception, a casual observer could not guess that the U.S. and Israel were allies. Mr. Ben-Rosen was waiting in the security lobby at Mossad headquarters. He didn't smile, and didn't offer his hand to either Hardy or Patterson. Once they'd signed in and gone through the scanner, he simply said, "Please come with me." At least they didn't have an armed escort.

The headquarters was busy, even hectic, but in addition to all the activity it looked to Patterson like security had been beefed up as well. One expected security guards in the lobby, all armed with Uzis of course, but there were additional checkpoints as they moved through the building. And when Ben-Rosen pulled out his identification so they could get on an elevator, she spotted the shoulder holster under his suit coat. So they did have an armed escort after all.

The elevator took them straight to the top floor. The previously voluble assistant didn't utter a word until they stepped out. "They're waiting for us in the conference room." He opened a door on the left.

Joanna went in first, followed by her husband. She expected the long table, the Israeli flags, and paintings on the wall. What she didn't expect was the Israeli Minister of Defense, Michael Lavon, seated at the far end of the room. He'd been in the news enough to be instantly recognizable.

A second man stood next to a coffee urn at the far end. He was about the same age as Lavon. Ben-Rosen introduced them. "Senator Hardy, Dr. Patterson, this is Dr. Yaniv Revach, our Director, and General Lavon, our Minister of Defense."

So instead of meeting with one deputy director, they were speaking directly with the two most powerful, and probably the busiest men, in Israel.

Neither was smiling, and while they shook hands with the Americans, there was no warmth in their grip. There wasn't any small talk either. While Hardy and Patterson took their seats, Ben-Rosen served coffee and then left the room. The two ministers took chairs on the opposite side of the table from the American envoys. They were the only people in the room, which was big enough to hold thirty. No secretaries, no briefers, no assistants.

Lavon spoke first. In his early fifties, his trim build and short blond hair hinted at his past. He still flew fighters when time allowed.

"We are hoping this meeting will be short. That's one reason for limiting its size. We also hope we can all speak frankly, without unfriendly, or even friendly ears overhearing the discussion. We will not take notes, and you will have to accept our guarantee that we are not being recorded." Lavon smiled a little, but it appeared forced.

As defense minister, Lavon outranked the head of Mossad. He took the lead. "We hope you will convey to President Myles our desire to resolve our differences and work together to face a common threat. You can also tell him we don't like being threatened by our friends."

As they had discussed, Joanna spoke for both of them. "Right now, we're the kind of friend who takes away your car keys when you've had too much to drink, or tries to warn you about the girl you're asking out. Our information proves the Iranians aren't close to having a nuclear weapon. Not only will your air force bomb a worthless target, you will give the Iranians exactly what they want."

"They want to be attacked?" Lavon sounded incredulous, then amused.

"To hide their failure to develop a weapon," she answered. "If you destroy Natanz, they can claim whatever they want, and you've destroyed the evidence. In fact, they want the world to agree with you, that they are about to get the bomb."

"This is the valuable intelligence you had to convey? Some speculation by an analyst to explain away the conflicting data?" snapped Revach angrily.

"This information came from the same HUMINT source as the two files we sent you recently. The individual stated with certainty that the Natanz facility is being deliberately set up as a target. The test site, the bomb assembly facility—it's all a sham."

Lavon and Revach leaned toward one another and spoke softly. Not only was it hard to overhear them, but Patterson was pretty sure they were speaking in Hebrew.

Revach, now calmed, said, "In the past, your government has told us that this individual is an Iranian national. From the information you've provided, they appear to be very knowledgeable in nuclear matters and the specifics of the Natanz operation. Can we interview this person?"

Hardy answered now. "No. Not yet. The source is a married couple trying to defect, but the operation to extract them has experienced difficulties. Several of our people are on the ground with them, and we are working to get them all out of the country."

Revach was chubby, almost fat, with a ring of white fuzz circling his bare scalp. His English was better than Lavon's, but he spoke slowly, as if he had to check each word before he said it. "This would explain the presence of USS *Michigan* in the gulf. Her minisub, the ASDS, it has a troubled history, does it not? Wait. General Moradi's press conference this morning. Was that the body of one of her crewmen?" Revach seemed surprised at his own conclusion.

Hardy answered, "Yes. The vehicle was lost and the rest of its crew is on the beach along with the people that were going to bring them out. The reason they decided to defect was their discovery of the plan to provoke an attack on Natanz."

Patterson added, "The source has a flash drive with stolen data—not just on Natanz, but the entire nuclear program. The file we gave you about the Arak reactor core failure was to show you the depth of information. It shows the Iranians are hampered by numerous technical problems and may never successfully develop a nuclear weapon."

The chief of Mossad sat quietly for a moment, then added, "We have picked up some plain-language police chatter about a hunt for fugitives along the southern coast. The intercepts imply a large-scale, high-priority search is underway."

Hardy nodded. "That confirms their story, then."

"It confirms nothing," Revach answered sharply. "The Iranian authorities could be searching for your couple or someone else entirely. Even if this is true, your source may be willing to say anything to get your help escaping Iran."

"What if you could examine the files they have? We have a list of the information the flash drive contains."

"You don't have the files themselves," Revach countered flatly.

"We will have them soon. A new plan is in place to get them out, as early as tonight. If you can delay your attack, you can examine the evidence with us, and prevent a war."

Revach sighed heavily. "That new data would still have to be considered in light of all the intelligence we have on Iran's activities. There is new data, from intercepts and other sources."

"We haven't seen that. What about our information-sharing agreement?" Hardy asked. There was a challenge, if a soft one, in his voice.

"This has been discovered in the past day. It will be passed to your agency in good time, but we are a little busy right now."

"And you didn't think we'd listen," Patterson concluded.

Lavon spoke carefully. "Many here believe that only the detonation of an Iranian nuclear weapon outside Iran's borders would force America to act militarily. It would be our bad luck if that detonation was also inside Israel's borders. The United States has made war on too many Muslim nations. Your government simply doesn't have the political will to take on this challenge."

Revach added, "We have made it clear to Iran and the world that we cannot allow them to have a nuclear capability, yet here they are about to execute a classic nuclear breakout. Mossad has spent much of its time trying to understand how they deceived us. Unlike the United States, we are willing to admit when we are wrong, and face the consequences."

"Our information explains both the old and the new data," Hardy responded.

"But it requires that we sit back and watch, hoping you are right. That is not acceptable." Lavon stood and paced. "We believe that Iran would not organize a nuclear test unless it already had the material for three or more weapons. A weapons test announces to the world, especially the Muslim world, that they can defy the West's sanctions. But that is only half their purpose. Their other, repeatedly stated goal is the destruction of the State of Israel."

Revach said, "Just today, we've detected increased activity at what we've identified as a bomb assembly facility established at Natanz. There is also increased security around several missile storage bunkers at the Sajjad ballistic missile depot near Tehran, and around one of the missile assembly buildings. The Pasdaran 5th Ra'ad Brigade is based there, and they operate the Sejil-2 and Shahab-3 missiles with the range to reach Israel."

The director's voice hardened. "How long would you have us wait? Until the missiles leave for their dispersal points? Until they are fueling the missiles? No, wait, the Sejil-2 is solid fueled. They don't have to wait. And actually, they could launch from pads located at the depot, with almost no warning at all."

Hardy said, "A carrier strike group is moving into the northern Persian Gulf as we speak. It has two Aegis ships with ballistic missile defense upgrades. We can position them to reinforce your own formidable antimissile defense systems."

"Untested in combat," Lavon remarked. "Both yours and ours."

Hardy conceded the point, but with a twist. "True, but the missiles that Iran would launch are very similar to those we've both tested against. And the SM-3 has been tested more often than your system." The two Israelis paused and looked at each other, silently evaluating Hardy's words. Sensing a chink in their armor, he played his last card. "The most likely scenario involves Iran launching two or even three brigade's worth of missiles at one time, perhaps as many as twelve or fifteen missiles, of which one or two would have nuclear warheads. The Iranians have never launched that many missiles at one time. Have you seen preparations for a simultaneous launch of that magnitude? We have not."

"This is true," Revach agreed.

"Then we have at least twenty-four hours. Let us get our people out of Iran tonight, and we will look at the data on the flash drive together. We can have the lot uploaded to us here or anywhere else within an hour of them getting out of Iran."

Patterson added her own arguments. "Imagine getting all this data, and what it will tells us. After we have reviewed it, we release it to the world together. It's a triple embarrassment for Iran: First, that one of their own engineers turned against them; second, that they have consistently lied about having a nuclear weapons program—no more political cover for their allies—and finally, that they just can't get it done. A humiliation like this could potentially bring down the government. On the other hand, an airstrike will only strengthen domestic support for their leadership."

Revach actually smiled, just a little, while Lavon remained neutral, but at least he wasn't frowning. "What if we find the information is false, or it doesn't convince us?" the general asked.

"We only ask that you examine the data before acting," Hardy answered. "We believe that if you see it, the information will convince you."

"You're going for broke," Lavon answered, but it's our money you're betting." He paused for another moment, and looked at Revach, who shrugged.

"All right," the general announced. "*If* we were intending to launch an airstrike against Iran, we will refrain from doing so for another twenty-four hours so that we may examine the intelligence on the Iranian nuclear program which you will provide once you obtain it yourself. And once we have seen it, Israel is free to act as it sees fit for its own self-defense."

"With the United States supporting your decision," Hardy completed.

"Then we have an agreement," Lavon said, offering his hand.

* * *

Back in their own car, Patterson first hugged Lowell in celebration, then reminded him, "You just promised Israel unconditional U.S. support, even if they do attack Iran." Her tone wasn't critical, but there was a note of warning in it.

"That's just Andy Lloyd's current policy," he answered, smiling. "Besides, we're already betting that the data on that flash drive will completely discredit Iran's nuclear program. Once you've gone that far, you might as well go 'all in' to convince the Israelis."

He smiled again. "Let's go shock the president and give him some good news."

19

OLD IDEAS

7 April 2013
1600 Local Time/1300Zulu
Kilo-Class Submarine, *Yunes*, SS903
South of Qeshm Island

Like all submarine fire control systems, *Yunes*'s Russian-designed equipment allowed the operator to create an artificial target on the displays. This feature enabled the sub's attack team to train as if it were fighting a real opponent. Everything about the target could be defined, from its acoustic characteristics to its own sensors and weapons.

Commander Mehr had started drilling his team while the torpedoes were still being loaded. It wasn't that they were ignorant of antisubmarine warfare tactics, but they were rusty. After all, Iran was the only Persian Gulf country with submarines. Most of their training was against surface targets, while the ASW training requirement was a twice-a-year canned drill against another Project 877EKM-class boat.

No more canned targets now. Mehr had started them out slow. Simply creating a very quiet synthetic submarine target had been enough of a shock. Radiated sound levels were a fraction of what they'd seen from surface ships, with initial detection ranges well inside weapons range for both sides.

That had spurred Mehr to add rapid salvo-firing training against targets that suddenly appeared. He might only get one chance, and seconds would matter. Choices had to be considered and made now, before the fight started. For example, the TEST-71ME-NK torpedoes had two speed settings. They could run at 40 knots for 15,000 meters, or the range could be extended to 20,000 meters by slowing to 26 knots. Given that this would be a close-in fight, he'd ordered 40 knots preset into the weapons.

His first officer, Lieutenant Commander Khadem, ran the drills while Mehr watched and thought about how he would fight this enemy. Once the team was used to a target that could change depth, he would start experimenting. Should he use active sonar before he fired? What was the best number of torpedoes in a salvo?

The latter one was not a simple question. The newer version of the TEST-71 torpedo was a more flexible weapon than its predecessors. It had an acoustic seeker that would either listen for the target or use its own active pulses to locate the enemy sub and home in. It could also be wire-guided, with a thin wire that connected the torpedo directly to *Yunes*. A wire cassette would reel out the guidance wire to compensate for the movement of the torpedo and the submarine, allowing *Yunes* to see what the torpedo's seeker saw and to control its movements.

Yunes had six tubes, but only two of them had connections for the guidance wires. The other four tubes would only allow the acoustic homing mode. The final complication was that he could only fire two TEST-71ME-NK torpedoes in active acoustic mode at a time. If he fired more than a pair of weapons, they would likely begin homing in on each other once they went active, like a cat chasing its own image in a mirror.

Mehr had one of his officers researching the *Ohio*-class and its torpedoes, the Mark 48. He would present a detailed brief in a little over an hour. Other parts of the crew were running emergency drills. Everyone understood they were going to war.

He stood up and stretched. His desk was cluttered with manuals, printouts, and scribbled notes. It was time to take a tour. The crew needed to see him.

Nikhad, the senior radioman, found Mehr as he left his stateroom. "Captain, urgent message!"

Mehr snatched the printout out of his hands and then cursed himself for showing too much excitement. He took his time reading the short message, then read it again to make sure he understood it clearly.

PASDARAN BOAT PATROLS AND CIVILIAN SHIPPING REPORT BRIGHT FLAMES
ON THE WATER IN THE VICINITY OF 26° 16' N/054°49'E ON THE NIGHT OF 6
APRIL APPROXIMATELY 2030 HOURS/1730Z. THIS CORRELATES WITH TIME OF A
SUBMARINE MISSILE ATTACK DURING A GROUND SKIRMISH NEAR MOLLU. IN-
VESTIGATE.

A skirmish? Missile strikes? Nobody ever told him anything. The message was signed by Admiral Zand. The routing was through the main headquarters at Bandar Abbas via Tehran. A sighting report from Pasdaran
units and civilians, no wonder it was so old. Mehr said, "Acknowledge the
message, and say, 'We are en route.'"

The radioman hurried off, while Mehr headed for control. Khadem was
still drilling the attack team, and the captain did his best to appear calm.

"How are they doing?" Mehr asked casually.

"Better," the first officer answered, "especially after I told them they could
improve, or die."

"Good, because we have a possible sighting of the enemy, about eighty
kilometers from here."

Like Mehr, Khadem fought to control his excitement, and didn't entirely succeed.

"Drill them for another hour, and feed everyone," Mehr ordered. "I'll
get us headed toward the reported location, and then we will work up a re-
vised search plan. The sighting is nineteen and a half hours ago, and it isn't
very precise, but it gives us one critical advantage over the Americans."

"What's that?"

"We know they're there."

7 April 2013
1600 Local Time/1300 Zulu
The Oasis, East of Mollu

Shirin had been looking at her watch since noon, and insisted on helping
keep watch for Jerry and Ramey. Harry had found a shady spot and made
her comfortable, expecting her to fall asleep. Instead, she'd laid patiently,
looking to the northeast as the warm afternoon hours passed. Nothing had
moved, neither friend nor foe.

In typical SEAL fashion, they had agreed before leaving on what to do if the two did not return. The first part of that plan was abandoning the layup and moving to a second spot they'd chosen earlier. Shirin was reluctant to leave, but it was all according to plan. "After 1600, they won't expect us to be here," Harry explained.

With Lapointe incapacitated, Harry was the next senior petty officer. He'd done what he could during the afternoon, checking their gear and improving their camouflage when he wasn't on lookout duty. Jerry and Ramey had left their packs behind, as well as other pieces of equipment. As it neared the cutoff time, Harry started to plan what the three would take and what they would have to bury.

Phillips had finally spotted them, just before the cutoff time. The pair was hurrying as much as they could while doing their best to stay concealed. With Ramey in the lead, they were as careful about being seen returning as departing.

When the two finally reached the relative safety of the layup, even Ramey was breathing hard. Jerry was gasping. "We pushed it," Ramey explained. "We were scouting their defenses."

With the last word, everyone's expression changed. Nobody said anything for half a moment, then Fazel said, "There weren't supposed to be any 'defenses.'"

"There are now," the lieutenant answered unhappily. "We watched a company of infantry—mechanized infantry, actually—set up strongpoints all over the airfield. There were machine gun emplacements and armored personnel carriers with fields of fire covering every open area, troops inside buildings making firing positions, and snipers on the roofs.

"The XO and I spotted them setting up as soon as we got to the field. We spent the rest of the time studying their defenses, looking for holes, something we could exploit." He took a gulp from a water bottle.

"And then the second company drove up, a little after noon," Jerry added. "Although they were only in trucks, not APCs. They expanded the perimeter, and then the officers started walking the ground around the airfield."

Ramey explained, "At that point, we just wanted to get away, but with so many eyes, we had to move carefully, and slowly. That's what almost pushed us past the cutoff time."

"There was nothing on the imagery," Phillips insisted. "This must have all happened this morning."

Ramey nodded emphatically. "Brand-new. We saw them making emplacements and filling out range cards. In a way, it was ideal. We watched
them set up. We know exactly where everything is. If I had the whole platoon, we could take that place apart." He smiled at the thought.

"It isn't happening," Jerry said finally. "We can't steal a plane." He hated
to say the words. He felt more than frustration. After so many failed plans,
being pursued and shot at . . .

"Well, that's why we reconnoiter a target before we go in," Phillips announced philosophically.

"We took out an entire squad," Fazel said. "They're pissed, and they're
scared. They won't take any more chances. They'll flood this area with troops. "

Shirin sat silently, the latest bad news simply impossible to absorb.
She'd lost so much, so quickly—her uncle, her mother, and now her husband. She was still trying to understand that Yousef was gone. His child
would grow up without a father, if the baby got the chance to grow up at all.
A wave of fatigue washed across her, and she felt cold, the same kind of cold
she'd felt holding Yousef's hand.

"I think I should tell you all the encryption key," she said quietly. "It's a
mathematical formula, a transform on each group of three numbers—"

"Wait a minute!" protested Jerry. "I agree we need to distribute the key,
but I don't like the reasoning behind it. You just can't assume it's hopeless
and give up. We are going to get you out of here," he affirmed. The others
all agreed emphatically.

Fazel said, "You have to believe we'll make it, that we can beat them.
They haven't found us yet, which means we are still in the game."

"What else can we do?" she asked him, almost in tears.

"Something. We just need to think it through, that's all," the SEAL
answered. "I've seen guys overcome terrible obstacles and still succeed because they were certain that they could. That's not arrogance; it's just the
will to keep on slugging until you win. You've suffered, but we're still with
you, and we won't let you down."

Harry took her hand. "Come over and lie down. I'll get you something
to eat." When she objected, he said, "Doctor's orders. You need the calories."

Keep on slugging. Fazel was right. Jerry tried to focus on what had to happen next. There was a prearranged comm window at 1630. Originally it had

been intended to review their escape plan with *Michigan*, but now he'd have to report that another plan had fallen through. Which one was this? Plan F? Plan G? The PRC-117 radio was already set up, and at exactly 1630, he reluctantly pressed the transmit key. At this point, Jerry was so familiar with the equipment it was almost like using a phone.

Lieutenant Frederickson acknowledged the call, and as soon as Jerry heard his voice, he knew something was wrong. "What's happened?" he asked.

"They found Vern," Frederickson said. "They've got Higgs." Even over the radio, Jerry could hear his grief and anger.

"Who's got him?" Jerry demanded. "The Iranians? How?"

Frederickson sighed. "He washed up on a beach. They had a press conference this morning, with drawings and fingerprints. The Iranians are turning all the information over to the Red Cross. If we say he's ours—tell them who he is, the Iranians say they'll give him to us—after we explain how he got there." The anger rose in his voice with the last sentence.

Frederickson's voice leapt out of the handset. "Damn it, Matt! Can you hear me? This is your fault. This is a major screwup! You left him, and this is what happens."

Jerry had been holding the handset so that Ramey and Fazel could listen in as well. Frederickson's words shattered the lieutenant. Jerry saw his expression dissolve into anguish.

"That was my decision, Lieutenant," Jerry spoke sharply, almost automatically. "I ordered him to leave Higgs in the ASDS. We had no choice."

"I'm not talking to you, sir! This is SEAL business. We don't leave our own behind, and this will be a lesson to future BUDS classes of why that rule has always been followed. Up until now."

"That's enough, Mister." Jerry heard Captain Guthrie's voice, first in the background, then more clearly as he took the handset from Frederickson. "Jerry, we watched a download of the press conference. The Iranians don't say where the body washed ashore, but it was sometime yesterday morning. They're playing the 'concerned citizen' act to the hilt."

"I'm sorry, sir. This complicates everything."

"Not for us. This is for the people in Washington to sort out. There's nothing you or I can do, or could have done differently." Guthrie said the last part with a hard edge. Jerry guessed the captain was looking at Frederickson while he said it.

"Sir, more bad news. The airfield plan is a total bust." Jerry quickly summarized the situation at the airstrip.

"And we can assume that the roadblocks have been beefed up as well," Guthrie concluded. "Moving is going to become more and more dangerous."

"I wouldn't want to have another fight like that again, with two fewer guns," Jerry said. Fazel, still listening, nodded emphatically.

"Do you have a new plan yet?" Guthrie asked.

"Sort of, sir, the backup was to look toward the harbor at Bandar Lengeh. We'll call as soon as we have something worked out."

"Understood," Guthrie answered. "Good luck, XO."

Jerry turned off the power and started to break down the radio for travel. Although they'd have to call *Michigan* again, and hopefully soon, SEAL practice, as Lapointe had taught him, was to keep it packed up, in case they had to move suddenly.

Ramey was nearby, just a step or two away from where he'd stood with Jerry while listening to the radio. Jerry studied his face. Lines of strain and fatigue lay under a layer of grime. Jerry was sure they all looked that way, but Frederickson's words had hit dead center. Ramey's features also showed pain, and Jerry could see tears streaking the dirt.

Ramey was working hard to keep it together. "You know, I tried to warn Vern away from Judy. I thought they were too much alike. I worried all they would ever do was butt heads. After they were married, she forgave me, then she started teasing me about how I didn't warn her."

Jerry started to say something, and remembered Lapointe's lecture about sympathy. It wouldn't help Ramey to hear how sorry Jerry was about Higgs. But just turning his face toward Ramey was enough to focus the lieutenant's attention on Jerry.

"Why did I listen to you?" Ramey shouted. "Why didn't I get him out of there?"

"Because I ordered you to leave him," Jerry said. He spoke softly, with as little emotion as possible. Yelling back at someone who was already angry was rarely a good idea.

"And if I'd had half a brain, I would have ignored you. All my training, all my instincts, said to get Vern out of there, and instead I screwed up. Look what's happened now: The mission's been exposed, and the only way we get Vern back is by telling how he got there, which we won't do."

"Trying to get Higgs out of the ASDS would have taken both of us, and the battery packs were already exploding as I pushed you out the hatch. It was the right decision then and it's even more so now," Jerry insisted forcefully. "Imagine the effect on the mission if one or both of us had been hurt, or lost."

"Oh, yeah, the mission," Ramey answered caustically. "And it's gone so well. We've lost half the precious cargo, my LPO is crippled, and we're trapped in enemy territory."

There it was. Loss of a friend, loss of a comrade, loss of a mission, all eating away at Ramey's insides. SEALs were all about control—controlling the situation and controlling their own feelings. But Ramey was a pressure cooker. Maybe he was trying too hard, or maybe he just had too much on his plate. That much emotion had to come out somewhere. Ramey's had come out aimed at Jerry.

"All I hear is bullshit," Jerry answered angrily, his patience threadbare. "You can grieve all you want once we're back on the boat. Right now we need to focus on getting out of here."

"Let it go, Boss." Lapointe's voice was just as hard, more critical than Jerry's. "The XO's right. It sucks big-time, but that doesn't change the fact that he's right." He turned to Jerry and asked, "Sir, could you please take over lookout from Philly?"

Wordlessly, Jerry nodded and changed places with Phillips. Lapointe, sitting with his back against a tree, started to stand, and with Fazel and Philly helping him, got up. All four SEALs headed away from Jerry, deeper into the trees. This was SEAL business.

Jerry kept his attention focused outside the grove. The SEALs spoke quietly, but they hadn't gone far enough away to mask the sound of their voices. The tone of the conversation was stern, with the occasional hard word, but sometimes challenging.

Seeing Ramey's grief brought back Jerry's own experience. He'd been navigator on a boat that had collided with another submarine. The fault lay with the other skipper, and Jerry's own crew had been completely cleared. Not only was it not their fault, there was nothing they could have done to avoid the collision.

But men had died on both vessels. Jerry had been present, with some small influence over the situation—but not nearly enough to prevent a tragedy. Was it pride that kept asking "What if?" even when the situation was beyond your control? Should you be punished for failing when there was nothing that could be done? For some people, being at fault was better than being helpless.

A few minutes later the SEALs came back with Ramey in the lead. Swallowing hard, his jaw was tense. He walked straight over to Jerry. "You were right. It was your call to make. I don't think I'll ever be happy about it, but this isn't about what makes me happy. I let you all down, and I apologize. It won't happen again." He made it a point to look at everyone as he said it. "Let's get the hell out of here."

7 April 2013
1800 Local Time/1600 Zulu
Mossad Headquarters, Herzliya, Israel

Dr. Yaniv Revach, the head of Mossad, met them in the hall. "I was in a meeting when word of your arrival reached me." He waved off the escort. "I have them from here."

A uniformed aide came to attention as they followed Revach into his office. He closed the door with a look to his assistant that made it clear they were not to be disturbed. Motioning toward a comfortable-looking couch, he sat down wearily. "This room is one of the most private places on Earth. We will not be recorded, and nothing you say will leave here, I promise."

Patterson didn't keep him waiting. "It's bad news, Doctor. We received word that our people in Iran had to abort their escape plan. They're still relatively safe, but they'll need a new way to get out of Iran."

Revach didn't say anything, but got out of his chair and walked over to a large map of Iran that almost covered one wall of his office. "After our talk earlier today I asked our signals intelligence people to report any unusual communications traffic in the area of southern Iran. You can understand that this meant reassigning resources that were involved in other tasks."

Both Americans nodded. "I'm sure your Iran section has been very busy," Hardy said.

"It didn't take them long," Revach told them. He ran his hand along the Persian Gulf coast of Iran. "Pasdaran and Basij units from Bushehr to

Bandar Abbas have been mobilized, and alerts for a"—he paused to look at a paper on his desk—"Yousef Akbari and Shirin Naseri have been circulated to every police barracks in the southern provinces. There are reports of firefights, with heavy casualties among the Iranian forces."

He sat down again. "In a way, it's helped. We saw so much signal traffic we were worried it might relate to our own activities, or to some asymmetric plan the Iranians were preparing, but it's just an all-out manhunt for your fugitives. This is them, isn't it, Akbari and Naseri?"

"Yes, that's them," Hardy admitted. He looked over at Joanna, and then explained, "They had hoped to steal an aircraft at an airfield near Bandar Lengeh, but at the last moment the airfield's defenses were heavily reinforced."

Revach nodded knowingly. "Our analysis indicates that they will find it the same anywhere they go. It is unlikely that we will be looking at the files on your flash drive any time soon."

"Our people are very resourceful," Patterson insisted. "I'm sure that they will have another plan very soon. Look at how long they've evaded capture so far."

Revach shook his head. "I must disagree. If they had trouble getting out of Iran before, it will be considerably harder now." He smiled. "Yes, they have stayed free, but also left destruction in their wake."

The director stood again, and paced, as if impatient. "This is disappointing news. This affair will probably end badly, for them, or the United States, and possibly for both. Your government should make the necessary preparations."

"As long as they're free, there's a chance," Patterson insisted. We'll keep you informed, every step of the way. . . ."

"No, Dr. Patterson. We agreed to delay any hypothetical operation, and there will be no operation today. However, preparations for tomorrow must begin soon. Hypothetically, of course."

Hardy stated, "Dr. Revach, if Israel attacks, you will be doing exactly what the Iranians want."

"So you said earlier, based on information you haven't even seen. Mossad has more rigorous standards."

"We can't let you do this," Hardy insisted. "Another war will not solve your problems."

"What will you do, take away my car keys?" Revach's voice hardened. "We are not drunk, and we are a sovereign nation. Many Muslim countries think we are your cat's paw. Don't believe the lie yourself."

"I cannot predict what the political cost to Israel will be in the U.S., how the U.S. public and Congress will react."

"More threats, Senator? We kept our end of the agreement. You failed to do your part."

Patterson and Hardy both absorbed the harsh words. Hardy's answer was just as harsh. "I believe we will get our people and the information out of Iran, and I believe it will prove that Iran does not have any nuclear devices. If we release the information after your raid, it will show Israel acted rashly, that Israel refused to listen. And with Natanz destroyed—nobody doubts that you can level the place—there will be no way to prove who was right."

"So if we act in our own self-defense, you would undermine us? Stab us in the back? Israel has stood alone before. Maybe in the end, we are always alone. Tell your president that Israel will act as it sees fit, and will remember others' actions as well."

Revach added, "Since your purpose in coming here has been accomplished, there is no further need for you to remain in Israel. Leave without delay." He opened the door, and his aide was standing outside, accompanied by two security guards.

Silently, the two Americans left, with the aide leading the way and the two guards in back. They stayed with Patterson and Hardy all the way to the lobby. Their car was waiting, and Joanna found herself glad to see her security detail, just to look at a friendly face.

As they drove away, a sense of failure washed over her. She grasped Lowell's hand. His face was a grim as she'd ever seen. "I've never been declared persona non grata," he said. "Doesn't feel very good."

"I don't like it either," she answered. "I've never had a whole country mad at me before." It was supposed to be a joke, but she could not make herself laugh. "What do we do now?"

"We tell the president we failed," Hardy answered bluntly. "That the Israelis are emotionally committed to attacking a blood enemy. That we have pissed them off, and that we'll probably have to make them even madder before they will stop. It's time for tough love."

7 April 2013
1900 Local Time/1600 Zulu
The Oasis, East of Mollu

Ramey wouldn't stop talking about the airfield, and despite his earlier assessment, kept looking for cracks in the defenses. "I've memorized the layout, and no defense is perfect. We find the hole and we're in and then gone. We use one Cormorant to create a diversion some distance away. That draws off some of them, then we use the second one to blast a hole in the airfield's defenses and get a plane out of here."

"Boss, the Cormorant can only carry eight rockets," Phillips said from his lookout position. "It's too big a fight even if some of the defenders are pulled. . . . *Everybody down and freeze!*"

They'd actually practiced what to do, and Jerry half-rolled into a hole right next to him, pulling a carefully selected branch over himself. The others did the same, except for Phillips, who was observing from a concealed position to begin with. "I've got a helicopter, low, to the northwest. It's going to pass by about a klick away."

"Type?" asked Ramey.

"It's a gunship. A Huey, of all things," Phillips answered.

"Iranians have a ton of them," Fazel added.

"Night vision or IR sights?"

"Not according to the specs, Boss, but anything's possible." Jerry could almost hear Harry shrugging his shoulders. Jerry agreed. Even if the helicopter didn't have night sights, the gunner could just use a handheld nightscope. He would.

The aircraft did not change course or speed. It flew off to the east, staying low. Within a few minutes the sound faded, and then the machine's navigation lights disappeared.

"I bet it was heading for the air base," Fazel suggested.

"I have never been this popular before, and I don't think I like it at all," Phillips observed.

"That's it, we're going for a boat," Jerry said.

"XO, are you sure about that?" Fazel asked. Concern filled his question.

"Absolutely not!" Ramey countered. "We go for the airfield."

"What does heading inland do for us?" Phillips asked. "They know we're trying to go south. If we go north, the net won't be as tight."

"But we're farther from *Michigan*. No help from the CENTCOM UAVs or the Cormorant."

"And there will still be roadblocks, tougher ones," added Fazel.

"And it would take too long," Jerry finished. "While I regard our personal survival as an important goal, there are larger matters at stake. I don't know Israel's time line, but we've got to get Shirin's information out of Iran as soon as possible. What if the war starts tomorrow while we're sitting here, or fighting another Pasdaran patrol?"

"The quickest way out of Iran is a boat," Fazel answered. "We go to the nearest harbor and swipe the fastest boat. There's a harbor two klicks from here. To quote T. E. Lawrence, 'It's just a matter of going.' "

Ramey smiled. "Did T. E. Lawrence mention how to deal with the Pasdaran patrol boats?" In spite of his smile, the lieutenant's tone was serious. "That's been a nonstarter since the first night."

"That's when we were trying to avoid a fight," Jerry countered. "We are going to have a fight no matter where we go. Can patrol boats be worse than a company of mechanized infantry?"

Jerry could see the SEALs calculating, and pressed his point. "The math is changing. The threat is increasing by the hour. If we stay here, we'll have to fight again, this time at reduced strength and against incredibly bad odds. Let's pick our next battle, before the Iranians give us one we can't possibly win. I don't want us to lose anyone else," he said, looking at Shirin.

Ramey started to object, but Jerry cut him off. "We go, and we go tonight." That got a rise out of all the SEALS, but Jerry was firm. "I've worked with you now for several days, and I see the value of planning, of reducing the risks as much as possible. We'll do what we can, but in the end, we will have to trust to luck."

"We're used to making our own luck," Fazel said, "but in addition to him being the senior officer, I agree. If we don't try to get out now, we may not be able to. From here on, the odds are only going to get worse."

Ramey had broken out the laptop and was looking at the UAV imagery. "Sorry to be the bearer of bad news, but that harbor you're in love with? It's got zilch." Ramey sounded almost happy as he showed them the overhead image. A curved breakwater jutted out from the shoreline near the village of Bandar Shenas forming a sheltered oval. Inside the enclosure, Jerry could see a total of four fishing boats. He was no expert on small craft, but none of them looked very fast.

"Check the next one down the coast. The larger one that was already part of the last backup plan," Jerry ordered. "The one at Bandar Lengeh."

Ramey typed in the commands. The image flickered, then spun, but in thirty seconds they were looking at the much larger harbor of Bandar Lengeh. It had a double breakwater, and the inner one was crammed with boats, including sleek-looking Pasdaran craft.

"That's exactly what we need," Jerry said.

"Too bad it's about twelve kilometers away," remarked Ramey, looking at the distance readout on the screen. "We can't use the highway. Most of the terrain is pretty rough, and it's probably patrolled. We wouldn't be able to walk that far with Shirin and Pointy and still have time to snatch a boat; without being seen, that is."

Jerry didn't answer for a moment, but then said, "That's why you and Philly and Harry are going by yourselves."

"What?" Ramey's question was echoed by the others. Even Shirin looked puzzled.

"How fast can you cover twelve kilometers? Could you do it in two or three hours?" asked Jerry.

"Hell, yes," Fazel responded indignantly.

"Then you get to the harbor along the beach. Come in from the water, steal a boat, and bring it back down to this nice little harbor where Shirin and I will be waiting with Pointy."

Jerry could see all of them, even Ramey, were thinking it over hard. How could they make it work? They started passing questions back and forth.

"How far do we have to swim?" Phillips asked.

"There's beach almost up to the harbor breakwater. And there's plenty of good cover in the cargo storage area," answered Fazel, looking at the screen.

"Isn't it all built up? This is a decent-sized town," asked Phillips.

Fazel took over the laptop and zoomed in on the shoreline. "But it isn't built up to the water's edge. The beach is fifty to a hundred meters wide in most places. It'll be dark, with no moon, and it'll be the small hours of the morning. If we're spotted, we go in the water. He shifted to a different section of the coast. "But here's a problem. Look at Gasheh. This little village goes almost down to the water's edge."

"Then we go in the water there, if we have to, and get out when we're past it. We can enter the harbor area here, at the western edge. There isn't a fence along the southern perimeter near the water," Ramey answered, pointing at the screen.

Phillips smiled. "Now it's starting to feel like a real SEAL mission. Run on the beach, get wet, run on the beach some more, get wet again. Ah, the memories."

"If you're a good boy, Philly, we'll let you roll in the sand." Fazel grinned, happy to see his team's attitude returning.

"How long will this take?" Jerry asked. Harry zoomed out the view, so that the entire route was visible, from their oasis to the harbor. He traced one route with his finger, then a slightly different one, and then looked at Ramey. "Boss?"

"Two hours to get there. We're in the water, sneaking in, then back out with a boat. That will take at least an hour, maybe a little more. Motor back at ten to fifteen knots. That will take half an hour. Call it four, maybe four and half hours."

Jerry nodded. "An hour and a half is a reasonable estimate for me to get Pointy to the other harbor. But he's going to need something to support that leg."

"I'll see to that, XO," volunteered Fazel.

That brought up another set of questions. Where the three would wait, what to do if they were seen. What to do if the others were delayed, or failed to return.

"I still do not get good vibes about splitting up," protested Ramey.

Fazel shrugged and nodded reluctant agreement. "There is a risk, XO."

"It's riskier to stay." Jerry insisted. "We need a boat, *now*."

"Yes, sir," Ramey answered. "We'll make that happen."

"Last question," Jerry said. "What about the pursuit?"

"I have a few things I can throw together. If we can keep the Iranians distracted long enough, maybe we can sneak away," Ramey answered.

"Okay then. Let's call *Michigan* and inform them of the latest plan. By now I'm sure Captain Guthrie has a useful suggestion or three to pass on. We can use all the help we can get," concluded Jerry.

20

HEAD FOR THE WATER

8 April 2013
0000 Local Time/2100 Zulu on 7 April
The Oasis, East of Mollu

Ramey inspected Phillips's camouflaged face, looking closely at the hairline and neck. The lieutenant frowned and motioned Fazel for the face paint compact. Dipping a finger in the dark hunter green, Ramey touched up a bare spot on the top of Phillips's forehead. He then checked the diagonal striping on the face and arms. A grunt signified his satisfaction.

Jerry had watched Ramey earlier as he applied his own face paint; it reminded him of an Indian brave putting on war paint, but the analogy ended there. Whereas war paint was more ceremonial, designed to enhance one's appearance and bring good fortune in combat, modern facial camouflage is all about hiding the face's features to the maximum extent possible. A base covering removed the inherent shine of the skin, while darker colored diagonal lines broke up the recognizable pattern of the eyes, ears, nose, and mouth. In the dark, the three men would be effectively faceless.

The platoon leader had instructed his men to go light; only mission-essential gear was to be carried. They had a long run and swim ahead of them, and Ramey didn't want them weighed down with unnecessary equipment. Each man had his SCAR, sidearm, ammunition, ka-bar, radio, and a small pack with distributed common gear such as water, rope, first aid kits, and explosives. Lapointe's pack was also emptied and then restuffed with the bare minimum, the PRC-117 radio, both laptops, ammunition, rope, and four bottles of water. The UAV remote control terminal was set alongside. Everything else was buried in the ragged wild shrubs that made up much of the grove.

While the other SEALs made their final checks, Shirin sat on a small dune next to Fazel. She was visibly unhappy, and told Harry in Farsi exactly what she thought. "This is a bad plan. How can we help each other if we separate?"

He answered gently, "There is a risk, but we discussed all the alternatives earlier; this gives us our best chance of getting outta here."

Almost crying, she said, " I've had enough of death. I don't want to see anyone else killed."

Turning and kneeling to face her, he softly said, "Every man here is a volunteer who knew what he had signed up for, even the XO. Besides," he added with a grin, "we don't plan to get killed."

Resigned, she scrunched herself up into a fetal position and pulled the thermal blanket around herself, her small body shaking with cold and sobbing.

As Harry reached out to adjust a corner of the blanket, she shook off his hand. "Just go," she said, weeping, "but please come back."

Before leaving, Fazel checked in on his patient. He had rendered Lapointe's damaged right leg immobile with a sturdy splint. It was the best he could do given the available materials, and he wanted to make sure it and the bandages were secure.

"Okay, peg leg, this should get you down to the beach. Just be careful how you transfer your weight and you should be good. But I do have to warn you, it's going to hurt like a son of a bitch."

"Well, at least you're an honest pain technician," replied Lapointe sarcastically. "Much more precise than the usual 'you may feel some discomfort' crap."

Fazel chuckled at the brave face Lapointe was putting on; he knew how badly the LPO wanted to go on this mission. "I'll be sure to add an extra honesty fee to my bill," he teased.

"In that case, belay my last," said Lapointe jokingly. Then he said more seriously, as he looked at Phillips, "Keep an eye on him, will you? He's trained, but he's also inexperienced."

"You worry too much, mother hen. He'll do fine. See ya later, dude."

"Later, Doc."

Ramey completed his checklist and then signaled Fazel and Phillips it was time to go. Picking up his pack and weapon, he came over to Jerry and Lapointe.

"Time check, Pointy. I have five minutes after midnight in five, four, three, two, one. Mark."

"Check, Boss," Lapointe replied firmly. He was still weak from his wound, but he didn't have to sound that way.

"Right. We'll rendezvous down at the Bandar Shenas breakwater in four hours. See to it you're on time."

"Hooyah, sir." A halfhearted salute accompanied Lapointe's response.

Ramey gave his LPO a rough slap on the shoulder, rose, and faced Jerry. His gaze was icy, his voice mechanical. "I'm leaving Petty Officer Lapointe in your care, sir. He's your responsibility. I expect to see him at the breakwater when we return."

Jerry could tell that the young officer was still struggling with their blowup earlier. But his message was crystal clear, even though he hadn't said the words—don't leave anyone else behind. "Understood, Lieutenant, and good luck."

Ramey didn't acknowledge Jerry's well-wishing and started to leave. But after a couple of steps, he stopped and looked over his shoulder. "Remember, if we aren't back by 0500, XO, grab one of those fishing boats and make a run for it."

"Hope for the best, but plan for the worst, Mr. Ramey?" questioned Jerry.

"Of course, sir," he said soberly. "If we aren't back by five, odds are we aren't coming back."

8 April 2013
0030 Local Time/2130 Zulu on 7 April
1st Regiment Headquarters, 47th Salam Brigade, Bandar Lengeh

Rahim pored over all the reports again, comparing each of the times and positions to those displayed on the map, looking for something that would tell him where the enemy had gone. *Nothing!* He threw the reports on the table with frustration and rubbed his face. It had been over twenty-four hours since the last attack and they hadn't come any closer to finding the traitors or the Americans. How could they move so fast with wounded members? Were they still on foot? Or did they manage to commandeer another vehicle? Did they head back to the northwest, breaking their pattern of the last four days? Or did they head into the hills to the north? Finding them in such rugged terrain would be extremely difficult. His questions seemed endless, and all of them were unanswered.

He yawned and stretched, fatigue was grinding his ability to think to a halt. It had been over thirty-six hours since he last slept, and he'd kept going by sheer force of will and an abundant supply of coffee. Most of the additional troops had arrived as promised, and the security at the airport, harbor, and all of the nearby checkpoints had been beefed up significantly. Dedicated search-and-destroy teams would be deployed later in the morning, supported by aviation assets. He'd reviewed the detailed search plan developed by Colonel Yavari's staff and deemed it acceptable. If the fugitives believed they could simply go to ground and hide until things calmed down, they were sadly mistaken. Rahim took some encouragement from that last thought, for if true, it meant the traitors were unaware of the plan that he and General Moradi had put into play.

Yawning again, Rahim concluded that any further attempts to keep working would be a waste of time; he really did need some rest. He had to be refreshed for the activities later in the day. After writing a short note to remind himself to discuss augmenting the command center staff with Colonel Yavari, Rahim slowly made his way to the cot put up for him at the back of the office. Collapsing onto the stretched fabric, sleep came quickly.

8 April 2013
0230 Local Time/2330 Zulu on 7 April
Port Cargo Storage Area, Bandar Lengeh

Ramey, Fazel, and Phillips leaned up against the stack of loading crates stored near the water's edge. This was the designated operational readiness position, or ORP they'd selected from imagery, the launching point for the water phase of their mission. The harbor at Bandar Lengeh, like many Iranian ports, was constructed using three breakwaters. The nearest one was a two-hundred-meter-long segment that ran straight out into the gulf. The second breakwater was farther away, and it was the longest of the three. Built in the shape of a crescent, it formed the back and side of the harbor. The last breakwater was an artificial island; offset about two hundred meters from the harbor entrance, it protected the mouth from any waves that came directly from the southwest. The platoon leader carefully surveyed the two breakwaters connected to land with his infrared sight and noted the guards walking their beat. A well-armed fast boat was just exiting the harbor, departing on patrol.

It had taken the SEALs longer than anticipated to complete the land portion of their plan; there had been a lot of patrols along the beach. A typical SEAL could have run the 11.5 kilometers from their layup position to the edge of the storage area in about an hour, but Ramey and company had spent a lot of time on their bellies crawling through the sand, rock, and short scrub. Twice, a Pasdaran patrol walked within meters of where the SEALs lay, oblivious to their presence. Travel got a little easier once they reached the edge of town, where the pathways and unlit streets enabled them to safely pick up the pace.

"Okay, gentlemen," Ramey whispered. "We hit the water here. I can only see one guard on the curved breakwater. It's much more likely there are two, possibly more, as that section is a lot longer. If you have to take them out, use your knives only. Clear?"

Both Fazel and Phillips nodded in silence.

"Pick a fast-looking boat and tow it behind the dhows. After I set the charges on the IRGC patrol boats, I'll meet you at the exfiltration ORP by the far breakwater. Any questions?"

Both shook their heads no.

"Alright, then, let's get ready," ordered Ramey.

As one SEAL removed his camouflage jacket, rolled it up, and stuffed it into his pack, the other two kept watch. The green t-shirt and darkly camouflaged arms offered less of a contrast against the water than the lighter jacket, and it would make swimming a little easier. One by one they crawled from behind the crates and down the rocks lining the harbor wall, slipping silently into the water.

During the planning session, it became clear from new imagery that the landward approaches to the harbor were just as reinforced as the airport. But unlike the airfield, which could only be approached by land, the harbor had another, more difficult to defend avenue—the sea, and that suited Ramey just fine. Unlike other Special Warfare soldiers that see water as an obstacle, to the SEAL it is a sanctuary. When SEALs find themselves in trouble and have the option, they always head for the water.

The trio swam quietly but steadily toward the closest of the three break-waters. The water was on the cool side, but definitely warmer than their earlier swim the night the ASDS sank. A light wind was at their backs, from the southwest as expected. The slight waves it generated could be heard breaking on the rocks, helping to mask what little noise the SEALs made. They traversed the open water swiftly, and then hugged the base of the break-water around into the mouth of the harbor.

Fazel and Phillips broke off at that point, swimming across the harbor entrance, after making sure no one was entering or leaving port. It was only 150 meters to the other side and they used the channel marker light as their guide. Ramey continued to follow the breakwater around, heading toward a small pier that jutted out from the rocky base. The harbor buildings were illuminated and he could make out the silhouetted forms of two IRGC pa-trol boats berthed at the pier. Following the breakwater, he inched slowly toward the small jetty. He was halfway there when he heard someone walk-ing above him; he froze. A guard was making his rounds. Ramey could see a flashlight being waved about as a Pasdaran soldier made a halfhearted search along the water's edge. Without a sound, the platoon leader slipped under the surface and swam away from the breakwater, toward the pier and his intended targets.

8 April 2013
0230 Local Time/2330 Zulu on 7 April
The Oasis, East of Mollu

"They're back," reported Jerry. "Four armed soldiers, walking along the beach, toward the east. About five hundred meters due south."

Lapointe dragged himself over, grunting every now and then when he rubbed his wounded leg up against the ground. Jerry handed him the night-vision goggles and pointed toward the ocean. The petty officer looked through the NVGs and scanned the entire area between them and the small break-water at Bandar Shenas. "Every hour, on the hour. Punctual fellows, these Pasdaran. Very commendable."

"Agreed, their consistency is a good thing. But I don't think an hour will be enough time for us to hobble across two kilometers," Jerry stated politely.

"Did I ever tell you that I dislike smart-ass officers, sir?" grumbled Lapointe, with a grin on his face. "Under normal circumstances I could kick your ass in a 10K run, XO."

"I don't know about that, Pointy. I'm pretty good at running, but the circumstances right now ain't exactly normal, are they?"

The enlisted man sighed. "No, sir. They most definitely are not. But don't think I didn't hear that challenge. After we get back and I'm all patched up, we're gonna have a race, you and I. And I'm going to enjoy all that beer you'll be buying me and my buddies after I win."

"You're on, Sailor," replied Jerry confidently, as he extend his right hand. Lapointe grasped it firmly, and shook it.

Jerry raised his SCAR and looked through his infrared sight; Lapointe was still using the handheld NVG. "I think they're leaving," Jerry said.

"Concur, sir. We should get going as soon as they clear the area. We'll cross to the north, over the sand dunes with the scattered scrub and trees. That should keep us well outside of their visual range. Where is Dr. Naseri?"

Jerry tilted his head back into the grove. "She's still sleeping over by Yousef's grave. She said it would be her last time to be near him."

"She's one tough woman, XO. She lost her uncle and husband in one day, but she's still fighting. You have to admire intestinal fortitude like that."

"She's lost a lot more than that, Pointy. Did you see the piece of green cloth she wrapped one of Yousef's epaulets in?"

"Yes, sir, I did. What's that about?"

"That's a piece of her father's flight suit. He was an F-14 pilot, imprisoned and tortured by the IRGC right after the Revolution. And yet, he flew to defend Iran during the Iraq war in the eighties. He died in combat. Shirin was just a baby, she never knew her father. You heard what she repeated over and over again after Yousef died?"

The petty officer nodded.

"Well, Harry told me that 'Baba' is kind of the Persian equivalent of papa. She was crying for her unborn child, as much as herself. On top of all that, her mother has almost certainly been arrested, and probably killed. She's lost everyone dear to her. That's a steep price tag in anybody's book," Jerry observed thoughtfully. "We owe it to her to get her out alive."

"I'm all for that," agreed Lapointe, as he continued tracking the Pasdaran patrol. "They're just about far enough away for us to get started. You get Dr. Naseri, I'll grab my new crutch and my weapon. It's time for us to catch our ride home."

8 April 2013
0300 Local Time/0030 Zulu
Harbor at Bandar Lengeh

Fazel emerged from the dark water like a creature out of a horror film, and carefully crept up the embankment. The guard had just walked by, interested more in searching the edge along the outer perimeter of the breakwater than inside toward the harbor itself. Silently and methodically, the corpsman climbed up onto the path, approaching the guard from behind. With one smooth motion, the SEAL covered the guard's mouth with his hand, pulled back his head, and plunged the knife between the collarbone and trapezius muscle into his heart; the guard didn't even have time to drop the flashlight he was carrying.

Grabbing the flashlight, and then rolling the body over onto the rocks of the outside wall, Fazel slowly began pacing along the path, pretending to be the Pasdaran soldier. Ramey had been right, there were two guards on that part of the breakwater, but the other one was easily over one hundred meters away and walking in the opposite direction. As long as he stayed that far away, he wouldn't be a problem.

"All clear, Philly. Check out the boat, but be quiet about it," Fazel advised over the radio.

"Understood," Phillips responded. He was already beside a speedboat that had caught his eye. It was about the right length, six or seven meters, and it had a respectable one-hundred-horsepower outboard. There were a couple of boats with larger engines, but they were in the middle of the nest. This one was the last boat in a long string, which meant its absence wouldn't be as easily noticed. Pulling himself up onto the transom, he was able to get a footing on the outboard and slithered inside. Phillips paused to listen for the guard, then peered over the gunwale to check on his location. The Pasdaran soldier was at the far end of the breakwater, walking away from him.

Crawling toward the open cockpit, Phillips could feel his heart pounding with excitement. This was his first deployment and it was everything he'd dreamed it would be. Being downrange, mucking about in the bad guys' backyard unseen and unheard, was what kept him going during BUDS. He relished being part of a selective group that was determined to succeed, no matter how tough the job was or how much it hurt.

Phillips pulled out a small red light and held it up high under the steering console. He quickly inspected the wiring. No security measures; they'd be able to hot-wire this boat in no time. Sliding back down to the stern, the young SEAL peered over the gunwale again. The guard was still far away, but had turned around, as the flashlight beam now pointed in Phillips's direction. He needed to finish up soon. Checking the after storage compartment, he made sure that the marine batteries were in place before looking for a fuel gauge. He found it on the starboard side of the below-deck fuel tank, near the fueling port. The tank looked hefty and the gauge read three-quarters full. "Score!" he whispered.

Slipping off the transom and back into the water, he moved quickly toward the boat's bow. Tracing the mooring line by hand, he cut it as close to the pier as he could. He didn't want a long piece of line floating in the water that could attract unwanted attention. Again he paused and listened for the guard. Nothing.

"Harry, I've got the boat. Where's the guard?" radioed Phillips.

"Still a ways away, but walking slowly toward us. I'm on my way back, start towing the boat out."

Phillips had already slid between "their" boat and the next one in the nest when Fazel gave the order. Slowly, carefully, Phillips pushed away the hull. The beast was heavy, but it soon surrendered to his determined shoving. Inertia did the rest. Once the boat was clear of its neighbor, Phillips returned to the bow, grabbed the line, and began pulling it along the inner edge of the breakwater. With two rows of nested dhows between him and the harbor lights, it would be virtually impossible for anyone, other than the guard that Fazel had taken out, to see him as he struggled to tow the boat out to sea.

It wasn't long before Fazel was back in the water with Phillips. And after stringing a second towline, he put his back into it as well. "Sweet ride, Philly," remarked the corpsman approvingly. "She certainly looks fast."

"And I made sure she has plenty of gas, Doc," huffed Phillips. Fazel could only smile and shake his head. Together, the two SEALs manhandled the speedboat toward the mouth of the harbor.

On the other side of the port, Ramey had just finished attaching two of his improvised explosive devices to the undersides of the IRGC patrol boats. The first boat was one of the notorious Swedish Boghammars. Very fast and armed with two heavy machine guns, this bad boy definitely had to be taken out. He tied the Mark 67 hand grenade, wrapped with half a pound of C4 plastic explosive, to the lowest step of the swim ladder using duct tape and rope. He made sure the explosive package was underwater to improve its effectiveness. He then looped line through the eye of the pin, straightened out the pin's flared end to ensure a smooth extraction, and secured the line to one of the pier's pylons. When the boat moved away from its mooring, the pin would be pulled from the grenade, followed four or five seconds thereafter by a loud *BANG*!

The second IED was attached forward, taped on the outboard side of the hull, just below the sharp chine near the waterline. And like the first grenade, he looped a line through the pin, straightened the end, and tied it off on a pylon. The booby trap would almost certainly be spotted in bright daylight, but by then it wouldn't matter. All Ramey cared about was that these boats didn't leave port for the next few hours.

The second patrol boat was a smaller Watercraft 800. Ramey didn't see any armament, but he knew it was fast and fixed two of his IEDs to it as well. He still had some time, so he took the two remaining bombs and rigged them to blow up under the pier's wooden deck. He took extra care to ensure one was directly under a fuel tank that was bolted to the deck—an insurance policy that hopefully would keep the Pasdaran busy while they made good their escape. With all his special packages in place, Ramey ducked underwater and swam away. When he surfaced he was over thirty meters away from the breakwater. He could see the guard's flashlight, and while it was unlikely he would be seen, Ramey wasn't taking any chances and went back under to put more distance between him and the Pasdaran sentry. When he came up the second time, in the middle of the port proper, he spotted the channel marker light and headed for the exfiltration point.

8 April 2013
0345 Local Time/0045 Zulu
Near the Breakwater at Bandar Shenas

Jerry struggled to keep Lapointe upright as they worked their way across the uneven, sandy terrain. They'd left the grove over an hour ago, but even though he was giving it his all, the wounded petty officer could only go so fast. While the crutch and splint enabled Lapointe to move, each step was agonizing. Jerry knew he was in considerable pain as the sweat was pouring off his shaking body, and yet all Jerry heard was his sharp exhale each time the splint hit the ground. Lapointe had insisted they take this route even though it would be tougher for him to navigate. It was not only the shortest path to the breakwater, but it kept them out of range of any passing patrol. It also would provide good cover for them to hide, just in case a Pasdaran patrol deviated from its observed route. The problem was they still had about half a kilometer to go till they reached the breakwater, and their pace was slowing.

It had been a difficult departure. While Lapointe got accustomed to the feel of his walking aids, Jerry went back to Yousef's grave to get Shirin. He found her there, kneeling, her hand on the freshly turned soil, speaking softly in Farsi. He knelt down next to her, cleared his throat and said, "Shirin, it's time to go."

"I know," she choked. "I was just saying my last good-bye. I won't be able to . . . to come back . . . ever. It's so hard, Mr. Jerry." She began weeping again.

· "He wanted you safe, Shirin. He'd be mad if you didn't leave." It was a weak argument, but it was the best he had to offer.

"Yes, I know," she replied quietly. "He often got upset with my stubbornness." Jerry watched as she bent down and kissed the ground where Yousef's head lay. He heard her whisper something before straightening up.

"XO," Lapointe's hushed voice came from the darkness, "we really need to get going now."

"We're coming, Pointy," Jerry replied. Reaching down, he helped Shirin to her feet and steadied her during those first few parting steps. They emerged from the shrubs to find Lapointe standing, his rifle over his shoulder. Jerry grabbed his weapon, the UAV remote terminal, and his backpack and started putting them on.

"Give me something to carry, Mr. Jerry," said Shirin. "You need to help Mr. Pointy walk, let me do something, *please.*"

Jerry was going to argue, but Lapointe was quicker. He removed his backpack and handed it to her. "Would you please carry this for me, Doctor? I think it would be safer for the XO if my weapon didn't swing around on my pack and bounce by his head every time I took a step."

Shirin took Lapointe's heavy pack and slung it over her shoulders; she tottered a little initially then defiantly stood upright, ready to go. Sighing, Jerry slung his rifle upside down across his back and propped Lapointe up on his left side. "Ready?"

"Ready as I'll ever be, XO."

"Forward, march."

They had paused for a short rest, Lapointe needed a break from the constant pounding on his leg and Jerry needed to use the night-vision goggles to scout ahead of them. Shirin sat down on a rock and carefully took the weight of the pack off her shoulders. She was breathing hard, but didn't complain.

"How's it look, XO?" grunted Lapointe.

"I think there's another Pasdaran patrol approaching from the other side of the breakwater. We couldn't see them before because of that dune we just crossed back there."

"I kind of expected that, sir. Help me up." Jerry helped the LPO stand; his grip trembled with pain as soon as he put weight on the damaged leg. Once up and steadied, Lapointe took a look himself.

"Yup, that's a different group. I count four soldiers, and they're heading toward the breakwater." There was a note of frustration in his voice.

"How much further do we have to go, Pointy?"

"I'd estimate three, maybe four hundred meters, XO."

"Can we beat them to the breakwater?" Jerry asked.

"Nope, not a good idea," answered Lapointe.

"Okay, what's next?"

"We keep moving and go to ground seventy-five meters from that first building. Then we wait for them to move on."

"We'll be late," warned Jerry.

"Sir, we're already going to be late."

A ghostly gray shape slowly materialized out of the darkness. Relieved, Ramey swam with renewed vigor toward the boat. It hadn't been a long swim by SEAL standards, but he'd been in the water for an hour and half and he was cold and tired. Phillips grabbed his platoon leader's arm and helped him over the gunwale; Ramey tumbled onto the deck. For a moment he simply laid there, catching his breath, then pulled himself up on to the console chair.

"Report," he commanded wearily.

"No problems getting the boat, Boss," replied Fazel. "One guard had to be taken out, but no one saw us leave."

Ramey nodded his approval and praised his men. "Well done, Gents! I've rigged the two patrol boats to blow should they pull away from the pier. And I left an extra special surprise, just in case."

"Sounds like you had all the fun, Boss," complained Phillips. "My shoulders are killing me from tugging this beast."

"Rank does sometimes have its privileges, Petty Officer Phillips," teased Ramey. Picking up his rifle, he took a quick look through his nightscope to get a better feel for their location. The island breakwater was less than ten meters away. Surprised, he exclaimed, "Damn! I didn't think we were that close. We'd better move away from those rocks. Philly, grab the other oar."

"Hold on," Fazel interrupted abruptly. "We've got company. A boat's coming in."

Ramey reached for his weapon again. "Where, Doc?"

"Off the port beam."

It took him a few seconds to sweep through the bearings, but Ramey soon had the boat in his sights. "Damn it! It's a patrol boat! And he's coming right at us! He's probably going to use the southeast channel. We need to get on the other side of this breakwater, but keep us as close as possible."

"Closer than we are now?" asked Phillips, as he dug his oar into the water.

"Yes, move us in so that we are just off the rocks."

"Is that a good idea, sir?" Fazel was uneasy with Ramey's chosen course of action.

"Think about it, Harry. We're at least a good hundred meters from the center of the channel. It's so dark out, they won't be able to see us. But if they have radar, which is highly likely, then our butts will be hanging in the air unless we can hide this bucket in the ground clutter of the breakwater."

"Got it," exclaimed the corpsman as he seized the other oar, and together with Phillips, began rowing the boat closer to the breakwater.

While Ramey kept track of the incoming patrol boat, the two enlisted SEALs pulled the boat to within an oar's length of the breakwater's base.

"It's got an enclosed cabin, a standard nav radar, two outboard engines, and what looks like a 7.62-millimeter machine gun on a pintle mount forward," Ramey whispered. "This guy could definitely be trouble. Let's hope he berths at the same pier as the others."

As the patrol boat entered the channel, it passed behind the breakwater and the SEALs lost sight of it. Ramey hustled over to Phillips and grabbed his oar. "Philly, get this puppy hot-wired ASAP. That boat's engine noises will mask our startup, then steer southwest at slow speed."

"Hooyah, Boss," barked Phillips.

In less than a minute, the outboard whined as the starter motor cranked the dead engine to life. Suddenly, it caught and a low grumbling noise broke the silence. Ramey and Fazel then pushed the boat away from the rocks, and after making sure they were clear, Phillips advanced the throttle slightly. Slowly, the boat pulled away from Bandar Lengeh.

While Fazel stored the oars, Ramey shuffled up to the console. "Okay, Philly, keep us close to the coast, but not too close. And keep our speed down, but not too slow."

With a look of irritation, Phillips replied, "Can you be a little more specific, Goldilocks?"

"Just drive the damn boat, will you?" countered Ramey. "We need to get back and pick up the others as fast as we can, but without getting spotted either from a patrol on land or a boat at sea. Capiche?"

"Yes, sir. I capichee."

Ramey looked at his watch and grimaced. It was already twenty after four, and it would take close to another half hour to get back to the breakwater at Bandar Shenas. They were going to be very late, but hopefully, not too late.

8 April 2013
0430 Local Time/0130 Zulu
Breakwater at Bandar Shenas

The four Pasdaran soldiers walked in a loose formation toward the break-water, and even though they were still sixty or seventy meters away, Jerry found himself holding his breath. The three of them had crawled to the very edge of the broken scrub; the Persian Gulf was less than a hundred meters to their right. The breakwater lay directly in front of them, not even two hundred meters away, across a nice soft, but very open, sandy beach. So close, yet so far.

"Are you serious?" hissed Lapointe.

"What's wrong, Pointy?"

"They're going out *on* to the breakwater, XO."

Jerry quickly took a look through his scope. Lapointe was correct, the Pasdaran patrol had continued down the road and was now heading out onto the breakwater. "Oh crap! Now what do we do?"

"We follow them out," Lapointe stated frankly.

"Come again?" Jerry was sure he didn't hear him right.

"I said, we will follow them out onto the breakwater. It's not like we have a lot of choices, sir."

"Why can't we just wait here for them to finish their job and leave?"

"Because the other patrol, you know the one we've been watching all night, will come over that rise to the south soon. We don't know exactly how far down the beach they'll come. My guess from what we've seen is they'll get close to the breakwater, if not right up to it. If we stayed we would be stuck here for far too long," explained Lapointe. "It's only about an hour till sunrise. We need to be on a boat and out to sea before then, preferably long before."

Jerry felt like smacking himself, he'd forgotten about the other patrol. Finding themselves stuck between two groups of Pasdaran soldiers was an unpleasant thought, but he wasn't thrilled with Lapointe's idea either. "Can't you radio Lieutenant Ramey and just have him swing by and pick us up here?"

"I don't know where Mr. Ramey and the others are, XO. I'd have to crank up the power on the radio to ensure I reached him, and the odds of the transmission getting picked up by the Iranians is pretty damn good. By going out onto the breakwater, Matt will be able to see them, and us. He can initiate contact when he thinks it's best to do so. Besides, I'd rather have those IRGC soldiers in a cross fire, than the other way around."

Jerry hesitated. He tried weighing all the variables of the tactical situation, but none of the options looked any less risky or more likely to succeed than the other. He didn't know what to do. This just wasn't what he was trained for.

"XO, we don't have a lot of time. You're just going to have to trust me on this." While respectful, Lapointe's tone was firm. And it was the confidence in Lapointe's voice that broke Jerry's mental gridlock. SEALs are trained to handle these kinds of situations, and they train hard.

"Alright, Pointy, we do it your way. But getting over to the breakwater quickly isn't going to be easy."

A wiseass smirk flashed onto Lapointe's face. "Well, you know, XO, the only easy day—"

"Yes, yes, I know," interrupted Jerry, annoyed. "The only easy day was yesterday. I got it. I got it."

"Then let's do this. Just get me moving as fast as you can, XO. Don't worry about my leg." The LPO then turned to Shirin and said, "Dr. Naseri, we're going for the breakwater. Just keep up."

"I understand, Mr. Pointy."

"Let's move, people," Lapointe commanded.

8 April 2013
0445 Local Time/0145 Zulu
At Sea, Near the Breakwater at Bandar Shenas

"You're right, Doc. Those are not our guys," remarked Ramey. They'd seen several flashlights earlier, but they couldn't tell how many people were standing at the end of the breakwater until they got closer.

"My bet is they're IRGC," Fazel commented. "But where are Pointy and the others?"

"If I know Nate Lapointe, he's nearby. Keep looking."

"Ahh, Boss, there's another group, right off the port bow, on the beach." Fazel pointed in the general direction of the new contact.

Ramey shifted his scope to the left and took a long look at the new contact. A frustrated sigh escaped from his lips. "Oh, bite me! It's another IRGC patrol. Four men in a single column."

"Where are you, Nate?" growled the corpsman through clenched teeth. The tactical situation was deteriorating rapidly. They had to find the others soon; otherwise it was going to get real messy, real fast.

Ramey continued scanning the length of the breakwater. All he could see were the four IRGC soldiers. Suddenly, a new contact emerged from around the curve in the outer breakwater wall. This contact was not on the road, but farther down on the wall. The platoon leader held his breath as he watched two more individuals round the bend. The lead person was moving stiffly—it was Lapointe.

"I have 'em, Doc! They're coming around the bend in the breakwater. Right off our bow," announced Ramey. He toggled his radio. "Pointy, it's Matt. I think I see you. Wave your right arm."

The lead person of the new group started waving his right arm.

"Confirmed your identity. Okay, Pointy, head for the water. We're coming in."

"XO, move toward the water," whispered Lapointe. Jerry reached out blindly with his foot for the next rock, found it, and slowly scooted down onto it. Planting his feet firmly between two large boulders, he reached back and guided Shirin down, supporting her weight. He then checked on Lapointe who seemed to be doing all right on his own. Turning about, Jerry repeated the process, inching closer and closer to the sea.

"They're almost down, Boss," reported Fazel. The boat was less than fifty meters from the breakwater, but as Ramey evaluated the situation, he was convinced it was going south fast; they wouldn't get away without a fight.

"Doc, the IRGC soldiers are heading back toward our people. We're probably going to have to engage. Pick your target, but don't shoot unless I give the order."

"Understood," replied Fazel, who sat down on the deck steadying himself.

Ramey raised his own weapon and set his sights on the lead soldier. He toggled his radio. "Pointy, you have four IRGC closing on your position.

We'll engage and draw their fire. Don't shoot until after we do, and only if you have a clean shot. How copy, over?"

Lapointe whispered back his orders, confirming he had heard them correctly. He could see through his scope that the speedboat was tantalizingly close, but what he couldn't see were the IRGC soldiers—the breakwater blocked his view.

"XO, hold my weapon while I get into a reasonable prone position. Dr. Naseri, get behind the XO. Mr. Ramey thinks it's going to get a little crazy here in a few seconds. XO, don't shoot unless I say so." Jerry handed Lapointe his weapon after he had slithered onto a large flat boulder. Jerry nestled down behind him. Once again he was to remain passive, the SEALs would do the shooting. Shirin moved behind Jerry and curled up into a ball.

Ramey and Fazel stayed fixed on their targets as they moved. If they so much as deviated one inch from their present path, the SEALs would drop them. *Just keep going, pay no attention to that man behind the curtain,* Ramey thought to himself.

The soldiers were very near. Lapointe could see three of them clearly as they got closer and closer. They seemed oblivious to the presence of the boat. That is, until one man abruptly panned his flashlight out to sea.

The flashlight beam momentarily blinded him, but Ramey could still make out his target. "Fire!" he commanded. Both he and Fazel squeezed off two rounds each and dropped their respective targets. Lapointe waited, then fired and hit the soldier with the flashlight that was illuminating the speedboat. The last remaining man, confused and terrified, hit the deck and began firing wildly out toward the sea.

"Move it, XO!" yelled the LPO. Jerry turned about and grabbed Shirin off the rocks. He could see the shadow of the boat and he moved as fast as he could toward it.

"Over here, XO," Fazel shouted, his hands outstretched. Seeing the corpsman, Jerry moved closer and literally tossed Shirin into his open arms.

"Get in!" yelled Ramey.

Jerry spun, ignoring Ramey's command. "Pointy!" he shouted. He heard a bullet whiz by his head.

"Keep your shirt on, I'm coming," Lapointe yelled back. He was sliding down a rock, when his wounded leg got caught in a crevice. *"Arrgh!"* he screamed as he fell.

"Boss, there's reinforcements coming!" Phillips exclaimed, pointing toward the rapidly undulating flashlights on the beach.

"XO! Move your ass, now!" shouted Ramey, still shooting.

Jerry staggered over to Lapointe, yanked him to his feet, and dragged him to the boat. Fazel reached out, grabbed his teammate, and unceremoniously dumped him on the deck while Jerry jumped into the boat.

"Punch it, Philly!" Ramey ordered.

Phillips wasted no time in slamming the throttle all the way forward and the small boat leapt away from the rocks.

As the coast began to fall away, they heard explosions over the din of the engine. Ramey looked over toward Bandar Lengeh and saw a huge fireball climbing into the dark night sky.

"Way to go, Boss!" shouted Phillips.

Ramey didn't smile. He had bought them time, but would it be enough? "Keep the pedal to the metal, Philly! We aren't out of the woods yet."

21

INTERCEPT

7 April 2013
1800 Local Time/1500 Zulu
Uranium Enrichment Facility, Natanz, Iran

It was nearly dark. Moradi finished the latest report from Rahim with disappointment. The major was almost legendary within VEVAK, both feared and admired. Was that reputation misplaced, or was his failure to capture the traitors an indicator of their own strength? If they had indeed wiped out a heavily armed Pasdaran detachment lying in ambush, then they might indeed escape, or at least take more lives and further delay their capture.

This was not good, and in normal circumstances would be a crisis of national importance, but Moradi and Rahim had worked to limit the spread of information, so far successfully. It had been difficult, and they couldn't keep it up forever, but after tonight it wouldn't matter.

The latest intelligence reports were more than encouraging. Last light would be at 1845, but the planes wouldn't come until later, in the early hours of the morning, or even just before dawn. But all indications were, it would be sometime tonight.

They'd run drills for the last three days, with the workers hustling into shelters while Pasdaran crews hurried to their stations. Over a thousand men were dedicated to defending the facility.

He expected the casualties to be light to moderate. The Israelis didn't fly all this way to bomb guns and SAM launchers. A few planes would use antiradar missiles on the SAM guidance radars, but the gun crews would be relatively safe. Likewise, workers in the shelters and at home would not suffer too greatly. The greatest losses would be in the underground centrifuge halls.

Unfortunately, there was no way to quickly shut down the centrifuges in an emergency. Nonessential staff would be evacuated during an air raid, but the machines had to be tended. Spinning at tens of thousands of revolutions per minute on magnetic bearings, it took hours to slow and stop them, and that was only after the cascades had been flushed with nitrogen gas.

The workers had emergency suits that they could put on when an alert sounded, but uranium hexafluoride gas was both toxic and corrosive. It would take a big bomb to penetrate the layers of earth and reinforced concrete that protected the halls, but that same protection would then contain the blast. A powerful explosion would send the delicately balanced centrifuges caroming off each other, spraying the lethal gas everywhere. He was sure the Israelis would use more than one bomb. In fact, he was expecting the halls to be so ruined that the only sensible course would be to cover them with even more earth and leave them as poisonous, radioactive tombs.

Moradi had decided to stay in his office in the main administration building until the alert sounded. After that, he would hurry to the command bunker with the others. It was possible that the Israelis would attack without the air defense system even detecting their approach. While their planes were not stealthy, he'd received briefings on the electronic techniques they had used elsewhere, and if the planes flew low enough, they could simply fly under the radar beams. Iran lacked the airborne radar aircraft that could track low flyers.

There was a risk that he could be a casualty himself, even with adequate warning, if the Israelis chose to hit the bunker. It was a logical target, and he could certainly find an excuse to be elsewhere, even away from the base entirely. But this was his plan, and he would risk his life along with the rest. He had brought this on himself; he would let Allah decide his fate. Whether he lived or died, his plan would succeed when the bombs fell.

7 April 2013
1130 Local Time/1630 Zulu
Oval Office, The White House

Saudi Ambassador Mutaib bin Khalid was wearing traditional Arab dress—the long white *thobe* with a dark *bisht*, or mantle, over it and of course, the white headdress. President Myles immediately wondered what message the ambassador was trying to send. Young for the post, in his mid-forties, and clean-shaven, Khalid was usually seen around Washington in fashionably tailored suits. Then Myles remembered that Arabs wore the *bisht* on formal occasions.

The request for a meeting had described the matter as "urgent and important," and Myles had treated it as such. In addition to Secretary of State Andy Lloyd, who would be present for any such visit, James Springfield, the Secretary of Defense, was also waiting to hear the ambassador's message. Aside from them, the only other person in the room was Chief of Staff Alvarez.

After Khalid greeted the four, Myles sat and invited the ambassador to join him. The center of the Oval Office was furnished with two long couches facing each other across a coffee table, where a tray with tea and coffee had been placed. Myles had taken a seat on one of the couches, leaving more than enough room for the ambassador. There was also an overstuffed wing chair at each end of the couch; the ambassador took one of these, facing the president.

After the others had taken their seats, Alvarez served coffee and tea while the president and ambassador exchanged courtesies and shared their concerns about the crisis. Myles thought he was offering a noncommittal pleasantry when he said, "I'm sure our two countries, working together, can be a powerful influence to preserve peace in the region."

Khalid quickly put down his coffee cup and said, with some intensity, "If that peace ignores a great danger, then peace is of no value, and may do harm."

Myles and the others were surprised, but when the president started to answer, Khalid spoke first.

"My apologies, Mr. President, but I've been watching a lot of American news broadcasts lately. Rarely has a disagreement between two countries' intelligence arms become so public. Actual news has been supplemented with many so-called experts and analysts explaining different aspects of the crisis. How much damage can Iran do with a nuclear weapon? How will they deploy it? What is Israel so worried about?"

He smiled. "I don't have to tell you why Israel is so hypersensitive. While we may not agree with the Jewish nation on many things, we understand their situation. A few nuclear weapons, delivered by ballistic missiles or terrorists, could destroy it. Such an attack would be a great victory for Iran, not only removing its greatest enemy, but giving the country a claim of being the most powerful nation in the Islamic world."

He paused for a moment, and when it was clear he was waiting for some response, Myles replied, "That is a nightmare we all wish to avoid, Mr. Ambassador."

Khalid nodded. "Yes. That would be bad enough, both for American interests and, I must admit, for the entire region. Have you thought about what would come after that? What will Iran do if its greatest enemy is destroyed? How would Iran use its new power? The Shiite leadership of Iran has made no secret of their hatred for the House of Saud. While our numbers are three times Israel's, a few weapons could also do our country great damage. In fact, we are not sure that Iran might not choose us as its first victim, aiming for Riyadh or Jeddah, or the greatest nightmare of all—Mecca."

The ambassador saw the surprise in their faces, and he reminded them, "What happens to the House of Saud if we fail in our duty as guardians of the holy city? Twelver Shia Islam is based on the return of the Twelfth Imam, who they believe is in occultation. He is prophesized to return in a time of chaos, which according to some writings, it is their solemn duty to create."

Khalid stood suddenly and removed an envelope from his robes. "My pardon for this long explanation, but it will help you understand our actions in the next few days." He handed the envelope to Myles and said carefully, "Under the existing Status of Forces agreement, in times of national emergency, we are allowed to close our air bases to American aircraft operations. We are declaring such an emergency. While your planes are not required to vacate their bases or leave Saudi Arabia, they may not fly from those bases until further notice. This includes all types of aircraft."

Shocked, the president and his two secretaries looked at the ambassador, and then each other. SECDEF Springfield finally gathered his thoughts and said, "Mr. Ambassador, planes from those bases support both our nations' interests. The information from our E-3 Sentry and RC-135 intelligence aircraft is shared with your government. Your air force trains at those bases. And in a time of crisis, like this one, our warplanes are ready to assist in your defense."

"Our own air force will deal with the current situation, Mr. Secretary, and we expect this interruption to last only a few days, maybe just one." He smiled. "Perhaps your mechanics can use the time to get caught up on their maintenance.

"Letters identical to this one are being given to your ambassador in Riyadh, the commander of U.S. Central Command, and the commanders of the five air bases involved. No further takeoffs or landings will be allowed except for those aircraft currently aloft, and of course, humanitarian missions, which must be approved by my government."

Myles, still shocked, understood the purpose of the Saudi action. "Without U.S. air presence, Israeli planes could operate over Saudi airspace without our knowledge. I'm surprised, Mr. Ambassador, that you would allow them passage."

"Do not read too much into our agreement with the Israelis. We may have found common cause with them on this particular issue, but that has more to do with the Iranian genius for creating enemies than our love for the Jews."

Khalid bowed. "Peace and Allah's blessings be upon you." The ambassador turned to leave, and Alvarez followed him out.

The instant the door closed behind them, the president's phone buzzed. Answering, Myles listened for a minute, then said, "All right, Ray, we'll be there in five minutes."

7 April 2013
1150 Local Time/1650 Zulu
Situation Room, The White House

President Myles's arrival created a ten-second pause in the commotion, but even Ray Kirkpatrick barely hesitated in his conversation. All the workstations on one side of the room were manned, and staff poured into and out of the room, bringing or taking away messages or assisting the operators. Myles noticed that the rank of the staff was slowly increasing. Officers replaced some enlisted personnel, and senior officers replaced the junior ones.

Nodding toward the president and the two secretaries, Kirkpatrick spoke encouragingly into the phone, "I understand, General, but turn them around as quickly as possible. We need those planes back in the air."

The national security advisor spoke quickly to an Air Force colonel, who hurried away, then turned to the three officials.

"The Saudis have caught us completely unprepared. We're going to get one E-3 and one RC-135 out of Saudi airspace to Iraq, but there won't be any support at Tallil or Baghdad. It will take hours to get more planes and people from Tinker in Oklahoma. I'm sorry, but I don't know just how long yet."

"At least twelve hours," Springfield said gloomily.

"By which time it will be too late," Myles concluded. "When is sunset at Natanz, Ray?"

"In Iran? About 1830 local time. It's dark over there now," Kirkpatrick answered.

"Then they could go at any time," Myles said resolutely.

"But, sir, the Israelis told Dr. Patterson they wouldn't go today," Springfield reminded him.

Myles chuckled quietly. "That was before we pissed them off. Still, you're probably right. But all bets are off at the stroke of midnight Greenwich Mean Time."

"I'm working with CENTCOM to use E-2 Hawkeyes from USS *Reagan* to take the E-3's place, but that means tying her strike group to the western half of the gulf. People might be able to take advantage of that. By the way, the Saudis are parking trucks and other large vehicles on the runways and taxiways at all five of their bases. We can't sneak anyone out."

"What do we know about the Israelis?" Myles asked.

Kirkpatrick invited them to take seats, and he gestured to a naval officer. "Commander Kennedy has been continuously updating the Israeli status, based on what little we know."

Kennedy was a big man, filling out his dress blues. The aviator wings were almost lost on his uniform jacket. He pressed a key on his laptop and the big screen lit up with a map of the area.

"Even when we know where to look, the Israelis aren't giving away much. There's been a complete communications blackout for several days, and they've timed aircraft movements to avoid our satellite passes. Our attachés have been barred from visiting any of the air bases or IAF headquarters. Normally, we'd at least get rumors from the local media, but they've put a lid on that as well. Our best bet is to look at their mission planning."

A line appeared, running from southern Israel almost due south into Saudi Arabian airspace. Once past the southern tip of Jordan, the line turned east-southeast across the Saudi Arabian peninsula, passing just south of Iraq and Kuwait. When it crossed the Saudi coastline over the gulf, it turned northeast, straight toward Natanz.

"This is our estimate of the Israelis' flight path. Until the Saudis made their announcement a short time ago, we had to consider three possible routes: north, then east across Turkey; straight east across Iraq; or south and east across Saudi. Now we know who they've gotten in bed with."

Distances appeared by each line segment, and the commander explained, "Knowing how far they have to fly tells us how many aircraft they're likely to send. They will have to refuel in flight, probably just before they turn the corner over the gulf. Given nine operational tankers, they can put four squadrons of fighter-bombers over Natanz, one of F-15Is and three of F-16I. If I was going to hit Natanz, that's how many I'd send. And remember, Israeli squadrons are double the standard size—twenty-four instead of twelve aircraft."

Secretary Lloyd asked, "How many will they lose?"

Kennedy hit a key, flashing past several slides. A map of Iran appeared, marked with symbols for radars, missile sites, and fighter bases. "This is Iran's air defense network. Their newest radars use 1980s technology and most of their surface-to-air missiles are just as old. The Iranians have two squadrons of early MiG-29 Fulcrums, but their pilots have limited air-to-air training. In an air battle, the Israelis outclass them in every category. It's first-rate air force against a third- or even fourth-rate one. There is a fair possibility that the Israelis will not suffer any losses. It's likely that they will suffer only a handful, five at the very most."

Kennedy zoomed in the map until the Natanz facility filled the screen. More symbols marked hundreds of light and heavy antiaircraft guns, six batteries of SAM launchers, and several low-altitude warning radars. "Natanz is the most heavily defended place in Iran, except for the capital, Tehran, but most of this is wasted effort. The biggest guns there, ten batteries of four radar-guided 100mms each, have a range of four-and-a-half miles."

The screen changed again, to show a plane's flight path from the side. Near the target, the plane's flight path climbed sharply and curved back the way it came. "The Israelis will almost certainly use GPS-guided bombs from high altitude. When they're ready to release, they'll go into a zoom climb and literally toss the weapon toward its target. The bomb arcs over and uses its own guidance, while the plane is now headed directly away from the target. They'll launch from eight to ten miles away, well outside the range of the guns. Jamming and antiradar missiles will deal with the SAMs."

Lloyd looked surprised, even shocked. "So the guns, the missiles . . ."

Kennedy shrugged. "Against a 1970s or 1980s threat, it's bad news. Now it's just a Pasdaran jobs program."

The commander highlighted different sections of the facility. "Here is the fake weapon's assembly facility next to the transformer building. These are the two buried centrifuge halls, about five hundred thousand square feet, give or take. This cross-shaped collection of buildings is the pilot enrichment plant. These will be the primary targets."

"And that takes nearly a hundred aircraft?" Lloyd asked.

"It's a long way to go, so the strikers can't carry a full load. The F-15I is rated for two GBU-28s, five-thousand-pound penetrators, but at that distance they can only carry one. That's twenty-four weapons, twelve for each hall. We estimate five weapons are needed to destroy each hall completely, and they will have to 'double-tap,' drop a second weapon into the hole made by the first one, if they want to get through the overhead protection. Of course, even one or two weapons penetrating into the underground facility will wreak tremendous damage.

"One of the other F-16 squadrons will carry smaller weapons, in the thousand-pound- or two-thousand-pound class, to attack the assembly facility and the pilot plant buildings. Those aren't armored."

"And the other squadrons?" Lloyd asked.

"Dual role, defense suppression and escort. Some will fan out and attack radars and SAM sites in the area, or launch decoys to confuse the defenses. Others will stay close to the strikers and do the same thing to the defenses at Natanz proper. And both squadrons will carry AMRAAM and Python 5 air-to-air missiles, just in case the Iranians do manage to get some fighters up."

"We always knew the Israelis could level the place," Myles said. "But what happens when the Iranians aren't prevented from building a bomb, because there was never one to build?"

Kennedy put up a new screen, with range circles centered on Iran. "Their first response will be conventional ballistic missile attacks. The missiles are inaccurate, but cities are big targets. If one hits a populated area, it will take out a city block. Iran will encourage Hamas and Hezbollah to make large-scale attacks, and it's likely they've stockpiled some unpleasant surprises. Iran's also promised to close the Strait of Hormuz if they're attacked. Iran's government has made it clear that they will spread the pain as far and wide as they can. They like to use the phrase 'increase the arc of crisis.'"

"But this was a war they wanted," Secretary Springfield protested. "What can they win?"

Myles sighed. "Israel's goal is to deter Iran from building a bomb that never was. It can't physically defeat Iran or occupy its territory. All they will do is give Iran a *casus belli*. If Iran can't become the leader of the Islamic world by building a bomb, how about by leading a war against Israel—a war Israel can only lose, because there is nothing for it to win."

"A war we can't stay out of," Springfield added. "We've declared that if Iran closed the strait, we'd use force to open it again. Europe has said the same thing. And we have to keep it open. So we all get pulled in."

Kirkpatrick added, "We've also seen some interesting things going on at Saudi air bases. Their Strike Eagles and Tornado squadrons may be preparing to make their own attacks."

"Joining the Israelis?" Lloyd asked, surprised at the idea.

"No, sir, they're taking advantage of the confusion." Kirkpatrick motioned to Kennedy, who changed the map to show the entire length of the Persian Gulf. More range circles appeared, centered on the Saudi airfields. "They're thinking ahead," Kirkpatrick explained. "If the Iranians do try to close the Strait of Hormuz, the Saudis will be hurt the most. We believe there is a good chance that the Saudis will preemptively strike antiship missile batteries that the Iranians have near the strait, both on the coast and on islands in the strait. They could also attack Iranian oil loading terminals and refineries, like the one at Bandar Abbas."

Lloyd smiled. "That's one way of removing your competition. But it also gives Iran justification to attack the Saudis, their other non–best friends."

"And another U.S. ally becomes involved," Myles observed. "That guarantees us getting sucked in. Anyone want to guess what will happen to the economy when energy prices spike? And it won't be just us. Everyone who brings oil through the strait will be hurt."

"And this is a win for Iran?" Lloyd asked. "I know how you feel, Mr. President, but sometimes I think that bombing Iran is the right call."

Myles shook his head and smiled. "Business before pleasure, Andy. We aren't going to defeat their military and occupy the country, either. Do you want to bet on how long it would take them to say 'uncle'? And what if they get support from other countries? China would love to keep us tied up in the Persian Gulf."

Myles turned to face the entire group. "Trust me, gentlemen. The first principle of the Myles doctrine is going to be 'Bombing stuff is not always a good idea.' But I may have to polish the language a bit."

7 April 2013
1230 Washington, D.C., Time/1730 Zulu/2230 Iran Time
Captain's Cabin, USS *Ronald Reagan* (CVN-76), in the Persian Gulf

Commander Gary, the carrier air group or CAG commander, almost ran into Captain Allen's stateroom. Breathless, he asked, "Skipper, tell me this is a practical joke."

Allen smiled as he shook his head. "No, Taz, and you've got one minute and twenty seconds to park it and catch your breath."

Complying, the CAG asked, "Aye, aye, sir, but why here? Why not in Combat or Flag Plot where we have videoconferencing facilities?"

Allen's answer was interrupted by Admiral Thomas Graves, the strike group commander. Although senior in rank to the captain, he was "embarked" on *Reagan* and technically a guest. He knocked on the open door frame and asked, "May I join you?" as if he hadn't been summoned as well.

"Of course, sir," said Allen, mentally shoving the admiral into his seat with seconds to go. Allen and Gary retook their seats and the captain nodded to a petty officer. "All right, it's time."

Precisely at 2230, the video screen in Allen's stateroom came to life. Facing the three naval officers, thanks to the wonders of technology, were President Myles, Secretary of Defense Springfield, and General Dewhurst, Chairman of the Joint Chiefs.

Dewhurst started the conversation. "Good evening, Admiral. What is your status?"

Graves didn't hesitate. "We've got two E-2Ds in the air with escorts, another two CAP stations covering any approach from Iran. We have strike aircraft and relief CAP on five minutes' notice. We ran drills all morning with excellent performance from the entire formation. I just came from Flag Plot. No subsurface tracks, six air tracks, all visually identified as commercial. The surface picture is much busier. We've had close passes from Iranian speedboats, most of them armed. They're testing our reactions, but they haven't pushed it. I told my escort skippers to play nicely until I say otherwise."

"Do you have any problems?" asked Kirkpatrick.

"Well, sir, gap-filling for an E-3 is a challenge. It would be nice to have some more E-2s. Running two stations instead of one with only four aircraft aboard means port and starboard duty."

"By the time we could get you any additional Hawkeyes, it wouldn't matter. If you can make do for tonight, that should be enough."

"Of course, sir," Graves answered. The admiral looked over at Gary, who nodded confidently.

"Anything else, Admiral?" Kirkpatrick sensed there was something else bothering the strike group commander.

"I wasn't happy about detaching one of my destroyers to head southeast, sir. That left a big hole in my screen. We've jiggled around the remaining escorts, but we're thinner than I would like. If the Iranians do try to execute a swarm attack, my defensive posture isn't as robust," complained Graves.

"I understand, Admiral. But the issue isn't about the Iranians," said Kirkpatrick, gesturing to the president.

Myles finally spoke. "Gentlemen, sometime this evening, or more likely early tomorrow morning, we expect the Israelis to launch a powerful airstrike against the Iranian facility at Natanz. It will pass through Saudi airspace and is likely to cross the western end of the gulf just south of Kuwait."

Graves answered, "Yes, sir, we're ready. We came to that conclusion as well after the Saudis shut down all our bases. We plan to be well clear of Iranian airspace."

"Admiral, when your E-2s detect that raid, you must intercept and prevent the Israelis from entering Iranian airspace."

"Intercept the *Israelis*?" Graves was dumbfounded. "Sir, with all due respect, let me confirm that you want me to *stop* the Israeli attack against Iran. That you want us to force the Israelis to turn around and return to base."

While Admiral Graves spoke, Captain Allen's mind spun in circles. He'd more than half-expected the presidential summons to be orders to join the Israelis in the attack, or attack other Iranian targets while their air defenses were tied up in knots.

"Admiral, without going into the background, Iran is intentionally provoking the Israelis to attack. If they succeed and the Israelis strike Iran, it will start a war that will tear the region apart and inevitably involve the United States, to no good end."

"Turning them back will take more than strong language, Mr. President. If I send armed aircraft to intercept the raid, what are my rules of engagement?"

Myles sighed. "If they refuse to turn around, shoot them down. But if either we or the Israelis shoot, the Iranians win. It would be best if you could turn them back without firing."

And that's why we're doing this in the captain's cabin, Allen realized. This was dynamite.

8 April 2013
0430 Local Time/0130 Zulu
USS *Ronald Reagan* (CVN-76)
VFA-147 Argonauts Ready Room

The pilots of Fighter Attack Squadron 147 were used to getting briefings on threat aircraft, everything from older MiGs like the Fishbed and Flogger to first-line aircraft like the Flanker. Nobody expected to fight the Russians anytime soon, but third-world countries had a lot of Russian gear. The Iranians had MiG-29 Fulcrums, for example.

But they also operated French Mirage F1s and even old American-made F-4 Phantoms, so Zipper, aka Lieutenant (jg) Allan Zirpowski, the air intelligence officer, had put together briefs for those aircraft as well. It was more than just data on speed, ceiling, and weapons carried. Tactics needed to be adjusted to match the opponent and the pilots. He gave good briefs, and the Argonauts listened hard and took notes. Sleeping though a threat brief was a good way to end up dead.

But this was too much. Zipper was displaying images of a brown-and-tan mottled F-16, an American-built Fighting Falcon flown by the Israeli Air Force. "They call the F-16I variant 'Sufa,' or 'Storm.' Note the 'shoulder pads.'" He pointed to two long bulges on the upper fuselage. "These conformal tanks give it the range, with refueling, to reach Iran and come back. Our Super Hornets have the APG-79 radar, which has a longer range than their APG-68. We carry the AMRAAM D model, which is smarter and has a longer range than their AMRAAM C-5s. But their Python 5 dogfight missile substantially outranges our AIM-9X Sidewinder. The Israelis like to tweak their gear, adding their own special upgrades, but our gear was buffed up before we came on this deployment.

"They're a hundred knots faster at high altitude than we are, and we expect they'll have over twice our numbers. But we have two engines, they have one. And they're a long way from home. In other words, gents, it's a fair fight."

The squadron commander, Tom "Heretic" Dressler, stood up. "I hate fair fights." His voice boomed in the darkened ready room. "The best fight is one where you sneak up on the other guy and he's dead before he even knows you're shooting. That will not be the case tonight. They'll know who we are, where we're coming from, and will get to watch us take the first shot, if it comes to that."

He gestured to Zipper, who changed the screen to show a map of the Persian Gulf, with the supposed flight path of the Israeli raid and the position of *Reagan* marked. "They will get their feet wet here, just south of Kuwait. We have to intercept them while they are over the gulf, in international waters. That's a space of just under a hundred and thirty nautical miles, which they will cover in fifteen minutes. We cannot allow them to enter Iranian airspace. This is straight from the CAG, Commander Taz, and he got it straight from POTUS himself. Everybody recognize that call sign?" Heads nodded.

"The skipper has orders from the 'Big Guy' to shoot them down, if we have to, and we'll go up ready to do just that. The president also made it clear to our boss that nobody wants to shoot anybody. If that happens, the Iranians will be the only ones smiling. So our boss is going to do his best to turn them back with no shooting. That's the happy ending we're looking for here."

He pointed to two airborne early warning stations over Iraq and the

Gulf. "E-2Ds are deployed here and here, and should pick up the Israeli strike about three hundred and fifty nautical miles away. As soon as they detect the Israelis, they will drop back, keeping their distance but staying in contact.

"We will launch, climb to co-altitude, and position ourselves directly across their flight path. We will be number two squadron in the barrier, with the 323rd on the left and the 146th to our right, and beyond them the 154th. Flights within the squadrons will be stacked at thousand-foot intervals, squadrons spaced one mile apart. Aside from a few hangar queens, every Hornet flies. Counting the escorts for the Hawkeyes, that will give us approximately forty-five fighters in the air.

"The Growlers will be back here and above us to provide jamming support, but like us, they won't send out an electron until Taz gives the go. He will be in the ready E-2 that will launch first. He intends to use the comm systems on the Hawkeye to talk to whoever's leading the Israeli strike."

Heretic paused, and one of the pilots asked, "Skipper, what if the Israelis fire first?"

"Maneuver defensively, but hold your position in the barrier as long as possible. The Growlers will jam their guidance links and seekers, but if it's a mass launch they won't be able to cover everyone. Force them to maneuver. They're tight on fuel, so if we can make them burn it up, then they have to go home. Do not return fire, even if you're fired on first, until the order is given."

That brought murmurs, if quiet ones, from the squadron. "I repeat, you will fire only if you hear the order from Taz or me, and I won't give it unless I hear it from Taz. I won't have to punish anyone who shoots without orders, because he'll have to answer to the president." He paused for a moment, and added, "I know you don't like what I'm saying, but if we have to take a few hits to get the Israelis to turn around, well, that's what they pay us the big bucks for. The only other option is to do nothing and let the Israelis start a war."

Reagan's 1MC announced, "ALL HANDS, FLIGHT QUARTERS," followed a moment later by the general quarters alarm. Zipper hit a key and the map changed to show the real-time position of *Reagan*, her battle group, and all known air contacts. A large number of unknown aircraft over Saudi Arabia were headed toward the gulf. Orders for each squadron flowed across the bottom of the screen.

"We launch in fifteen, Argonauts," Heretic announced. "Do it right."

As the squadron commander watched his people file out the door, one of the pilots approached him and spoke quietly. "Sir, permission to speak frankly."

Heretic nodded. "Of course, Smokey. This job is too important to leave any question unanswered."

The lieutenant sighed. "Sir, of course I'll follow your orders on this, but I'm not happy about risking my life to defend the Iranians."

"Taz says the Iranians want this fight, Smokey. They're on a downward slope and they want to pull everyone down with them. You are not defending the Iranians. And if you're risking your life, it's to stop a war."

22

PURSUIT

8 April 2013
0448 Local Time/0148 Zulu
1st Regiment Headquarters, 47th Salam Brigade, Bandar Lengeh

The ringing of his cell phone jolted Rahim out of a deep sleep. Not quite awake, he fumbled for the squawking device on the floor by his cot. Finally managing to grab it, he sluggishly opened the flip cover and answered, "Major Rahim."

"Major!" It was Dahghan, his voice was loud, excited. "A Pasdaran patrol on the Bandar Shenas breakwater has come under attack. An unknown number of assailants fired on the patrol from a boat and the shore."

"When?" shouted Rahim. He bolted from the cot toward the door, the surge of adrenaline snapping him from his lassitude.

"Within the last few minutes, sir. We've lost contact with the patrol leader."

"Are there any other patrols nearby? Can they confirm the presence of a boat?" Rahim thrust his hand into his pants pocket, searching vigorously for his keys.

"Another patrol is responding, but they are too far away to see anything," replied Dahghan. Rahim heard the sounds of a man running, breathing hard.

"Where are you, Karim?" he said, as he slammed the accelerator to the floor. The tires spun, spewing gravel behind them.

"I'm en route to the harbor at Bandar Lengeh. Two Pasdaran Navy patrol boats are preparing to depart immediately."

"Wait for me. I'll be there in a couple of minutes," ordered Rahim. His car was speeding through town at almost ninety kilometers per hour.

"Yes, Major. But please hurry!" Dahghan exclaimed, and then hung up. The last thing Rahim heard was the sound of boots pounding on a wooden deck.

Rahim's heart was racing as he roared through the rotary in the middle of Bandar Lengeh. *They were practically on top of us the whole time*, he thought. *Only fifteen kilometers away! Less than five from the airport, and with all those troops! How could we have missed them?!*

It was only four kilometers from the regiment's headquarters to the harbor, and it was right down Highway 96, which was mercifully clear of traffic at this early hour. He had to slow to make the hard left turn off the highway, but accelerated as he rounded the corner of the perimeter road. Two men jumped out of his way as he tore past the main harbor building. With the horn blaring, he came to a screeching stop at the end of the breakwater. Leaping from the car, Rahim sprinted toward the pier with the Pasdaran patrol boats. He could see Dahghan waving at him from the stern of the larger boat; urging him to run faster. The boats had just pulled away from the pier.

As he ran, Rahim saw a weird flash by the bow of the Boghammar. Sections of the forward part of the boat peeled away and were cast skyward. A second later, he saw another explosion, this time back by the stern. The rear end pitched up violently, throwing people and equipment into the air. He watched as Dahghan was catapulted over the superstructure and onto the now ragged bow. As the Boghammar settled and began sinking, the smaller patrol boat next to it also exploded. Only this time the blast seemed louder as its gasoline fuel ignited and erupted into flames, reducing the boat's small composite hull into tattered burning shards.

Rahim started slowing down, a stunned look of disbelief on his face. It was all so surreal. He just couldn't quite wrap his mind around what was happening. Nor would he have the time, for a split-second later he was picked up bodily and thrown to the ground by another, even larger explosion. An intense wave of heat hit his face as the detonating fuel tank on the pier sent a column of flames high into the air. Dazed by the powerful blast, Rahim slowly struggled to his feet. The pier was ablaze, as were the two patrol boats and the water around them. Shaken, he wobbled as he took those first steps toward the destroyed pier. A man rushed up and grabbed Rahim by his left arm, supporting him as his legs buckled. The man's lips were moving, but Rahim heard nothing. His ears were still ringing from the force of the explosion. Pointing toward the wrecked patrol boats, he could only mutter, "Dahghan?"

8 April 2013
0455 Local Time/0155 Zulu
Five Nautical Miles South of Bandar Shenas

"Get the hell off my leg!" shouted Lapointe through clenched teeth. Jerry and the poor petty officer had been thrown together into a contorted heap at the back of the boat when Phillips opened up the throttle and accelerated away from the breakwater. Ramey and Fazel untangled the two and laid Lapointe down along the gunwale. Jerry plopped down behind Phillips; the boat was up on plane, speeding away from the Iranian coast.

Lapointe was obviously in great pain, swallowing hard, with tears streaming down his cheeks. Fazel pulled out some ibuprofen caplets and a bottle of water. Lifting up Lapointe's head, the corpsman helped his teammate down the painkillers. "Sorry about the rough landing, Pointy. But we were in a little bit of a hurry," he apologized.

"Stow it, Doc," Lapointe shot back with a slight grin. "You just wanted to body slam your LPO. Admit it."

Fazel paused, stroking his beard, feigning deep thought. "You know, now that I think about it, I did find it strangely satisfying." Both men laughed, but Lapointe did so weakly.

The corpsman slapped his friend on the shoulder and said, "I can't give you anything stronger for the pain right now, Nate. It would make you too loopy. Just hang in there for another hour, then I can give you some of the good stuff. Okay?"

Lapointe nodded and tried to lie still as the boat bounced along.

Fazel took off his jacket, rolled it into a makeshift pillow, and placed it under Lapointe's head. He then shuffled over to Jerry. "You okay, XO?"

"None the worse for wear, Harry. Just a little tired, that's all," answered Jerry unconvincingly. Actually, he was exhausted. The hike from the grove, while short, had been tiring. Supporting Lapointe took a lot more out of him than he thought it would. Combined with the letdown from the adrenaline rush, Jerry felt like he could sleep for the next two days.

"You done good, sir." Fazel's compliment was sincere. Jerry acknowledged it with a nod.

Fazel took another quick look at Lapointe; he seemed to be resting as well as he could, given the circumstances. Seeing that everything was more or less in order, he leaned toward Jerry. "Excuse me, XO. I need to check on Dr. Naseri." A simple weary wave was Jerry's only response.

Tired as he was though, there was no way he could sleep. The constant jostling of the boat required him to maintain a firm grasp on one of the safety rails with both hands. Besides, they weren't clear yet. Ramey may have taken care of the patrol boats in the harbor, but there were still others out at sea. At least one had to be in hot pursuit, slowly closing the distance with them. Everything depended on how far away the other boats were when they got the call. If they were lucky, the Pasdaran patrol boats would find only empty water by the time they got here. Jerry snickered at that last thought; their track record with luck during the mission hadn't been all that great. "Hope for the best, but plan for the worst," he muttered aloud.

Hearing his voice, Lapointe slowly turned his head toward Jerry. The petty officer smiled and gave him a thumbs-up. "Thanks for coming back for me, XO," he said, struggling with the words, his voice laden with pain.

"You're welcome, Pointy. But I was just following my orders from the Boss," Jerry said, while motioning in Ramey's direction. "Now try and get some rest."

"Hooyah, sir," the weary SEAL replied.

Shirin was sitting in front of the control console, huddled up with one of the thermal blankets wrapped around her. She was too excited to be tired. They had made it. They had escaped from Iran. Soon she would show the world the terrible hoax that someone, whoever it was, was trying to play on Israel and her own people. Soon she would be safe. Soon she would be free. But she realized with guilt and sadness, she would also be alone. She'd lost everyone—her mother, her uncle, and her precious Yousef. She had sacrificed all so that many other innocent lives could be saved from pain and death. At that moment, a soft jab in her abdomen reminded her that she hadn't lost everything. She still had her child—Yousef's child. "I'm sorry, little one, I keep forgetting about you," she whispered softly in Farsi.

"Excuse me, Dr. Naseri," interrupted Fazel. "I just wanted to see how you were doing."

She looked up, startled to find Harry standing over her. "I'm fine, Harry. Thank you. How is Mr. Pointy?"

"He's in a lot pain. His foot got caught in the rocks and he badly twisted his damaged leg. He'll live, but he's going to be crankier than usual." The young Iranian-American smiled broadly.

Shirin suddenly became solemn; she fidgeted nervously as she tried to find the right words. "Harry, what will happen to us?" she finally asked.

Fazel witnessed her abrupt change in expression, and completely understood the emotions behind the question. His parents had gone through the same thing. A feeling of loss and isolation, coupled with uncertainty and some fear. He sat down beside her, and did his best to allay her anxiety.

"I don't know exactly what will happen, Dr. Naseri. I know you'll be taken care of, both of you. Initially, there will be a lot of work to go over all the data you have on that flash drive. But afterward, what you do is up to you. With your credentials, you could teach, work for a nuclear engineering firm, or do something entirely new. Like I said, its up to you. America is a free country."

"Where would I live? Are there many Iranians living in America?"

Fazel laughed heartily. "Absolutely! There are a great many Iranians living in America! Next to our mother country, no other country in the world has more of our people. And all of them are proud of their Persian heritage, as well as their allegiance to the United States. I can assure you, you will be most welcome in any community. If you wish, I can ask my father to put together some information on the various Iranian communities in America. He has many friends who'd consider it an honor to assist you."

Harry's confident response soothed and intrigued Shirin. She had no idea that the United States had so many Iranians living there, or that they would openly welcome someone who was guilty of treason. All she wanted was a quiet place to raise her child, meaningful work, and new friends to replace the ones she'd lost.

"Do you have any other questions, Dr. Naseri?" Harry asked.

"Yes, Harry, just one more. What is your real first name?"

Fazel was momentarily surprised, but in a way the question did make some sense. He had spent more time with her than any of the other SEALs or Commander Mitchell, and he was a fellow countryman. She wanted some assurance that he meant what he had said. It was a question of trust. She had no choice but to trust him, but did he trust her? It was a small thing, almost trivial, but it was an important gesture for her. While he pondered his response, she sat there quietly. Finally he let out a deep sigh, looked her straight in the eye, and answered her question. "Harry is my real name, but it would be more accurate to say it's my nickname. My given name, my Persian name is Heydar."

"Thank you, Heydar," she said politely.

8 April 2013
0505 Local Time/0205 Zulu
Harbor at Bandar Lengeh

Ten minutes. They seemed like an eternity. Rahim paced back and forth in the harbor master's office, agitated, seething, while he waited for the flames to be extinguished and for a tanker truck to bring more gasoline for the remaining patrol boat. They were refueling the boat now at another part of the harbor, but the fire was still raging around the damaged pier. The initial report said there were no survivors from the two Pasdaran boats. Dahghan was dead. The chase had just gotten personal.

A young Pasdaran first lieutenant approached him, saluting as he spoke, "Major Rahim, sir, I'm Lieutenant Qorbani. We will be ready to depart as soon as the fire is put out on the pier."

Rahim's hearing had partially returned. There was still a maddening ringing in his ears, but he heard the lieutenant well enough, and he wasn't happy with what he had said. "No! We leave immediately! Every minute lets the enemy slip farther away! I will not allow them to escape!" cried Rahim vigorously.

Qorbani was taken aback by the VEVAK agent's forcefulness, but wisely gave the only acceptable response, "Very well, Major. My boat is this way."

They walked quickly through the office space of the harbor administrative building and exited by a side door. Qorbani turned away from the flaming pier and headed to the main berthing area just behind the building. Between two small coastal freighters was a very small boat. Its outboard engines were already idling; Rahim couldn't hear them, but he could see the exhaust. Two sailors stood at attention by the lines, ready to take them in at a moments notice. The lieutenant motioned for Rahim to board first, and then signaled the sailors to cast off as he jumped aboard.

As they pushed themselves away from the pier, Rahim stood stoically in the cockpit. If the boat blew up like the other two, so be it—*Insh'Allah.* When nothing happened, he offered a short prayer of thanks. Rahim was now convinced he was blessed, under Allah's divine protection. If the last explosion had been a mere ten seconds later, he would've been killed. Instead, he had been spared with only trivial injuries. Spared to fulfill his destiny, that of hastening the return of the Twelfth Imam.

The patrol boat slowly worked its way past the long arc of nested dhows, keeping as much distance between them and the fire as possible. Rahim ignored the occasional dull thump as the hull collided with something in the water. He'd have time to mourn the dead later. Right now, every fiber of his being was concentrated on finding and killing those accursed devils. They had managed to kill almost three dozen Iranians during the long chase; thirty-four martyrs had paid the ultimate price for defending the Islamic Republic. He vowed that their blood sacrifice would not be in vain. As for the two traitors, they would be severely punished both in this world and the next. Out of pure anger and spite, Rahim had already ordered the execution of both Akbari's and Naseri's mothers. A fitting punishment for the two women responsible for bring such heinous criminals into the world.

Qorbani deftly maneuvered his boat past the harbor's mouth, and once into the channel, he gunned the engines. The small boat leapt to life as it accelerated, its bow rising above the water. As he rounded the outer break-water, Qorbani spun the wheel over hard and the boat skidded onto its pursuit course—due south. Rahim glanced at the speedometer. They were traveling at forty-two knots.

A private poked his head into the cockpit, tapped the lieutenant on the shoulder, and gestured for him to pick up the radio. Qorbani nodded and reached over for the bridge handset. Rahim saw that he was talking to someone, but between the ringing in his ears and the din from the outboards, he couldn't hear what Qorbani was saying. After a minute, Qorbani placed the handset in its cradle and leaned over to Rahim.

"That was headquarters. Two other patrol boats are heading to assist us." He pointed toward the northwest. "There is a *Torough*-class boat over there. It's based on the Swedish Boghammar, so it's fast and well-armed. Over here, to the northeast, is one of the new ten-meter rigid inflatable boats. It is also well-armed and very fast. Its maximum speed is fifty-three knots."

Rahim was pleased with the Pasdaran lieutenant's report, but they still had to find the Americans. "Lieutenant, any reports on the Americans' position?"

"No, Major. All we know is that two patrols reported them heading in a southerly direction. The lone survivor from the ambushed patrol also said they were in a small speedboat fitted with a single outboard engine," Qorbani explained.

"How close do we have to be before we can see them on radar?" asked Rahim.

"With two small boats? I'm afraid the range will be quite short, perhaps five to seven nautical miles."

"That's all?" Rahim was surprised by how short the range was. He'd seen radar ranges out over twenty miles from a coastal station.

Qorbani nodded his head, affirming his assessment. "Yes, sir, radar range is based not only on target size, but also on how high up the radar is. Small boats don't have much height of eye." He slapped the roof of the cabin to emphasize his point. The navigation radar was mounted just on the other side. Then shrugging his shoulders he concluded with, "Physics, Major. Not much we can do about it."

The lieutenant's description of their sensor limitations troubled Rahim; the pursuit had to be better organized if they were to locate their prey. Surely three patrol boats should be sufficient to do the job.

"Can you make a calculation to estimate an optimal interception point? We need to coordinate the search better. I will not tolerate them escaping again!" shouted Rahim.

"Yes, sir, I can. But without any contact data, it will be a rough estimate," Qorbani responded cautiously.

"Just do it!" Rahim demanded.

Qorbani nodded and signaled his sergeant to take the wheel. Politely pushing the obsessed VEVAK agent to the side, the lieutenant reached under the counter and pulled out a large laminated sheet of paper with numerous circles, scales, and a nomograph at the bottom. Rahim watched with rapt curiosity as Qorbani placed points on various circles and then traced out several lines with a grease pencil. He measured distances with a pair of dividers and drew more lines across the nomograph. After five minutes working the Maneuvering Board, Qorbani made a small circle around a point where four lines intersected.

"All right, Major. Assuming that they headed due south, with a maximum speed of thirty to thirty-five knots, and with a fifteen-minute head start, this is my best estimate of where we should vector our boats." Qorbani tapped the circle with his finger.

To Rahim, the circles, lines, and dots looked like gibberish. Frowning, he asked, "Can you provide courses and speeds for the other boats?"

"Yes, sir. Here they are for the *Torough* and the ten-meter RIB. If I'm correct, we should pick them up in twenty to thirty minutes. If I'm wrong, one of the other boats should get them," replied Qorbani, trying to sound more confident than he felt.

Rahim looked at the paper again and saw that it would be almost an hour before they would be in range to attack. He had to move fast. "Send the information to the other boats," he commanded.

8 April 2013
0517 Local Time/0217 Zulu
Twelve Nautical Miles South of Iran

Ramey watched his GPS receiver display as the latitude number ran past 26° 17' 30" and kept on going. "Okay, people," he shouted, "we are now in international waters. We are officially out of Iran."

"Hooyah!" screamed Phillips.

Jerry was stirred from his dozing by Phillips's howl. He carefully stood up, stretched, and looked behind them. The sun wasn't up yet, but the twilight glowed on the horizon. The country of Iran was no longer in view.

"Congratulations, Matt. That was some display you put on as we left. Do you think you got all of the patrol boats in Bandar Lengeh?" asked Jerry.

Ramey shrugged. "Don't know, XO. But that isn't the question that's bothering me. What I really want to know is how close were the patrol boats that were at sea when we bolted? Harry and Philly did a fine job picking a good boat for us. She's doing thirty-five knots, that's damn respectable. But most of the Iranian boats do forty-five knots or better. If they were close enough, they'll catch us."

"And we're blind," Jerry add.

"Bingo."

"Did you try to contact *Michigan* yet?"

"A couple of minutes ago. Didn't get a response," answered Ramey.

"Strange. They must have had to dodge a surface contact. Do you mind if I try?"

"Knock yourself out, XO."

Jerry put on the headset and made sure his personal radio was set to the right frequency and the power level was cranked up a few ticks. Depressing the transmit button, he phoned home, "Starbase, this is Gray Fox, do you read, over?"

No response. He waited for a few seconds then tried again, "Starbase, this is Gray Fox, do you read, over?"

"Gray Fox, this is Starbase, good to hear from you guys. Over." Jerry waved for Ramey, and pointed at his headset. The platoon leader put on his headset and dialed in as well.

"Gray Fox"—Jerry recognized Guthrie's voice—"report status."

"Sir, we have just crossed into international waters. We are on course south, speed three five knots. No sign of pursuit but we have extremely limited detection capability. Is there a UAV up in our vicinity?" inquired Jerry.

"Affirmative, we are doing a quick search. Wait one."

"Standing by," Jerry replied. He then pointed toward the backpack with the laptops. Ramey grabbed it and dragged out a machine. He had it open and firing up when *Michigan* responded with bad news.

"Gray Fox, you have three inbound patrol craft." Frederickson was now speaking. "The first contact bears zero six seven, range eight nautical miles, speed four two knots. The second contact bears zero nine eight, range one six miles, speed four six knots. The third contact bears two five two, range one six decimal five miles, speed five three knots. How copy, over?"

While Jerry repeated the data, Ramey brought up the images. Lapointe, awakened by the chatter, rolled over to see the screen. Fazel also joined him; curious to see just how much trouble they were in. Ramey froze the frame on the first contact and took a good look at it.

"It's the patrol boat I saw pulling into Bandar Lengeh. Intel data says it's an Ashura II WPB. It's armed with a 7.62 machine gun and small arms. We could probably fight this guy off if we had to." Ramey moved on to the second contact. He paged through the freeze-frames until he found a good side view. Zooming in, he let out a sigh.

"The second boat is an Iranian-built Boghammar. It's armed with a 107-millimeter multiple-rocket launcher and a DShK 12.7-millimeter machine gun. I'm not worried about the rocket launchers, but that .50 caliber is a big problem." Ramey shook his head as he spoke.

Panning to the third contact, Ramey zoomed in. Immediately, his eyes opened wide and his face took on an exasperated look. Fazel and Lapointe both grimaced.

"What's the matter?" Jerry asked. Concern grew within him as soon as he saw the SEALs' expressions.

"The third patrol boat is one of those Fabio Buzzi thirty-three-foot RIB racing boats. It has the same armament as the Boghammar, only faster. We are completely outgunned here."

Ramey turned the screen so that Jerry could see it. The patrol boat was sleek, sexy, and deadly looking. "Starbase, please advise as to the best evasion course," asked Jerry.

"Gray Fox, you are currently on the best course. Inbound hostiles will intercept in approximately two zero minutes."

Jerry felt discouraged; the fortunes of war had flipped on them once again. The others, too, looked worried, which aggravated Jerry's fears.

"We can't outrun them, and we can't outfight them," Ramey said firmly. "We are going to need some help with these guys."

Jerry agreed. "Starbase, it is the opinion of the platoon leader that we do not have the ability to fight off the incoming hostile boats."

"Gray Fox, understand your assessment of the tactical situation. Help is on the way. ETA is approximately three zero minutes."

Jerry looked down toward Ramey. The lieutenant was shaking his head. "Not soon enough. These guys will be here in about twenty minutes."

"Starbase, be advised that we're going to need assistance sooner. Request Cormorant support."

"Gray Fox, we are already preparing to launch a Cormorant. Please stand by."

"Standing by," Jerry responded.

8 April 2013
0528 Local Time/0228 Zulu
Kilo-Class Submarine, *Yunes*, SS903

Mehr sat patiently in his chair in the central post, waiting. Hunting a submarine was a slow, exacting game, best played by chess aficionados. They had arrived at the coordinates of the missile strike seven hours earlier and immediately began an expanding box search. Just before entering the area, Mehr had recharged his batteries near the inbound shipping lanes, hoping that the noise from nearby merchant traffic would mask his own diesels. The captain had ordered a strict ultraquiet routine; nonessential equipment was either turned off or placed on its lowest setting. All off-duty personnel were confined to their bunks. No videos, no music, no talking. They had to be one with the sea. With a full can, and a reduced electrical load, *Yunes* moved silently through the shallow water, stalking their whale.

It was warm inside the boat. With many of the recirculating fans and air-conditioning secured, the temperature had risen to an uncomfortable, but tolerable, level. Mehr wiped the sweat from his brow. He was glad that it was still spring. This kind of maneuver would have been impossible during the summer months.

"Captain! Mechanical noise bearing red five zero," reported the sonar operator from his cubicle behind Mehr. Russian sonar systems display azimuth information based on relative, vice true bearings. Thus, all directions are measured with respect to the ship's bow from zero to 180 degrees. Bearings to port are red, while bearings to starboard are green.

"Any propulsion plant noise, Sergeant?"

"No, sir. It sounds like a large object is being moved."

"Deck officer, sound battle stations, but quietly," Mehr spoke softly as he walked to the sonar cubicle. The operator offered him a headset; donning it he heard a number of creaks and squeaks, followed by a loud sharp thud. Something had just locked into place. Allah be praised. They had found their prey; Mehr knew he needed to act quickly.

"Helmsman, left ten degrees rudder. Steady course three one zero."

"Coming left to new course three one zero, aye, sir," repeated the helmsman.

"Sonar, stand by to go active on main and mine-hunting arrays. Fire control, flood tubes one through four. Stand by for rapid salvo."

8 April 2013
0530 Local Time/0230 Zulu
Nineteen Nautical Miles South of Iran

"Gray Fox, Cormorant launch in three minutes. Please stand by to take con . . ." Guthrie stopped talking in midsentence. Jerry could hear the WLY-1 acoustic intercept receiver beeping away in the background. What he heard next sent chills up his spine.

"Conn, Sonar, Shark Teeth and Mouse Squeak transmissions bearing one three zero! Contact is close. *LAUNCH TRANSIENTS!*"

Jerry heard Guthrie spitting out orders, then abruptly signed off with, "I'm sorry, Jerry, you're on your own!"

23

WHALE HUNT

8 April 2013
0530 Local Time/0230 Zulu
USS *Michigan*, SSGN 727

"*TORPEDOES IN THE WATER!*" shouted Buckley over the intercom.

"Where, Woody?" yelled Guthrie. He didn't have time for the intercom and just shouted down the passageway.

"Conn, Sonar, first torpedo bears one two two. The second bears one three seven."

Guthrie motioned to Simmons, the battle stations OOD, to acknowledge the report. He glanced at the fire control display that Ensign Sandy Wagner had manned, and there was nothing there on their assailant. He *has to be in our baffles, behind us,* Guthrie thought. *This guy was dangerous.*

"Weps, launch an ADC Mark 4 countermeasure from the starboard launchers. Helm, right fifteen degrees rudder, steady course north, all ahead flank!" Guthrie's immediate concern was the two torpedoes, but he couldn't ignore the shooter. He knew they had to get him out of their baffles and into view so they could start tracking him, but they had to jam his sonar as well.

Guthrie looked over at the intercept receiver. The WLY-1 warned them about enemy sonar transmissions, and it had lit off the same time as Buckley's warning of incoming torpedoes. It showed two Russian-made sonars, the MGK-400 Rubikon and MG-519 Arfa. Those were fitted on Iran's Kilo-class subs. The countermeasure should have some effect.

The captain dodged as other members of the fire control party took their positions. Lieutenants (jg) Sean Porter and Daniel Hogan had set up the geoplot and were starting to plot the bearings to the torpedoes.

"Sean, Daniel, just plot raw bearings. We don't have time to fair them. I need to know if I have to turn, ASAP."

"Aye, aye, sir," replied Porter as he drew out a bearing line on the paper.

"Conn, Sonar, first torpedo bears one one seven, drawing slowly to the right. The second torpedo is in our baffles, but was last seen drawing left. Neither weapon is active," reported Buckley more calmly.

"Very well. Find that Kilo, Woody!" shouted Guthrie as he shuffled over to the geoplot. Lieutenant Erik Nelson showed the bearing spread on the two torpedoes. "Captain, this one on the left looks like it will miss us, but just barely. The one on the right will be a problem if we remain on our present course."

Guthrie nodded. The torpedoes had been placed exceptionally well. There was no way they could get out of the acquisition cones of both of them.

"Dmitry, deploy an ADC Mark 5 torpedo countermeasure and prepare the ATT launchers."

The weapons officer reached up, lifted a protective cover on the countermeasure panel, and punched the button. On the aft starboard side of *Michigan*, one of the external countermeasures tubes erupted, spewing out a long cylindrical canister. Once activated, the countermeasure transmitted a loud acoustic signal that a homing torpedo would hopefully find alluring.

"ADC away, and the antitorpedo system is online," reported Zelinski.

Before Guthrie could acknowledge the weapons officer's report, the WLY-1 acoustic intercept receiver screeched out another warning.

"Conn, Sonar, torpedoes have enabled!"

Kilo-Class Submarine, *Yunes*, SS903

"Captain!" shouted the sonar operator excitedly. "A sonar jammer has been deployed."

Mehr looked up at the MGK-400 sonar display and saw that it was now filled with numerous spikes in the direction of the *Ohio*-class submarine. "Calm yourself, Sergeant! We knew he would do this," he admonished the nervous operator. "I just launched a sonar jammer myself, so settle down."

"Captain," interrupted Lieutenant Kashani, the fire control officer, "the torpedoes are nearing their activation point."

"Very well," Mehr said. The enemy would know soon enough that he had done more than just harass them with a sonar lashing. It was time to change their position.

"Helmsman, left full rudder. Steady course two two zero, speed eight knots. First officer, stand by to deploy another MG-24 countermeasure." As he watched his crew carry out their orders, he marveled at how well the attack was proceeding. The shot was picture-perfect. At least one of the torpedoes he fired would acquire the target. Evasion would be difficult as the American was almost dead in the water. He was a sitting duck.

Steady yourself, Ebrahim, he said to himself. The battle isn't over yet, and the American has yet to take any overt action. This is only the beginning.

"Captain, torpedoes are active," reported the fire control officer. "Torpedo on the left is clear, no contacts. The torpedo on the right has acquired a target. . . . No, wait! It's being jammed!"

Mehr smiled. The torpedo from tube two had found his quarry. But more important, that torpedo was the one with the guidance wire. "Offset the torpedo's course one point to starboard," he ordered.

"Aye, sir. Change course one point to starboard," replied the fire control operator. He rotated the wire guidance selector switch to "Transmit," flipped the direction toggle to "Right," and punched the course change button twice, ordering the torpedo to turn right by eleven and a quarter degrees, one point of the compass. "Course change completed, sir."

"Very well, Lieutenant. If the torpedo's course starts to drift to the left, just reset it to the right. Once it is past the decoy, we'll turn it back to the left. Understand?"

"Yes, sir," responded Kashani.

USS *Michigan*, SSGN 727

"Torpedo number one has changed course to the right," Zelinski said nervously. "It looks like it's being steered past the countermeasure."

"Just my luck," complained Guthrie cynically. "I always evade in the direction of the torpedo that is wire-guided." It was a poor attempt at humor, but he had to keep his own fear in check. His crew had to see him as the Rock of Gibraltar, even when things looked really, really bad.

"Weps, launch a salvo of two ATTs at torpedo number one and pop off another ADC Mark 5," Guthrie ordered. He then glanced at the speed indicator; they were only making ten knots. If this didn't work, it would all be over in less than a minute.

Zelinski targeted the incoming weapon with two antitorpedo torpedoes and hit the launch button. Another set of external tubes in the submarine's after superstructure ejected their contents, and the minitorpedoes sped off down the bearing to their target. The ATTs were small compared to one of *Michigan*'s Mark 48s, only six-and-three-quarter inches in diameter and ten feet long. Designed to destroy attacking torpedoes, they were a new addition to *Michigan*'s defensive suite.

Development of the ATTs had been troublesome, vexed with numerous technical difficulties, and caused the program to suffer one delay after another. Test trials had shown that accurately tracking a torpedo in the water was considerably harder than tracking a missile in the air, even though the latter was many times faster. But despite the less-than-desired hit rates, everyone agreed they were better than nothing.

The three underwater missiles closed each other at a combined speed of eighty knots. In a little under twenty seconds, the first ATT streaked past the Iranian weapon—a clean miss. The second ATT, however, locked on, homed, and exploded within inches of the incoming torpedo, destroying it.

Kilo-Class Submarine, *Yunes*, SS903

The entire crew cheered when they heard the explosion. They had "harpooned their whale!" Everyone hugged each other and patted their captain on the back. He had to shout at the top of his lungs to be heard. "Be quiet! Man your posts!" he screamed angrily.

The men, chastised by their captain, returned to their duties but they still bubbled with excitement and joy. Lieutenant Commander Khadem looked at his skipper with confusion. He was just as perplexed by Mehr's behavior as everyone else in the central post. Leaning over, he whispered, "What's wrong, sir? Aren't you pleased? You nailed that American dog!"

Mehr simply shook his head, it just didn't feel right. "It was too easy, Navid. Far too easy."

"But everything worked just as you planned," the first officer protested. "You foresaw everything. Truly Allah has given you a great victory!"

"Perhaps," Mehr replied quietly. "If so, then it costs us nothing to indulge my caution. We will stay on this course for a little longer, then turn west and slow down. Once those jammers die off, we'll know for certain if we got him. In the meantime, we remain at battle stations."

USS *Michigan*, SSGN 727

The explosion caused *Michigan* to rock slightly, but it wasn't close enough to cause any damage. The control room had become absolutely silent while the ATTs raced toward the incoming TEST-71 torpedo. A collective sigh of relief was the only indication that people were breathing again. The acting executive officer, Lieutenant Commander Harper, was the first to break the stillness. "Operational test of the ATT completed satisfactorily, sir."

"Amen!" cried Zelinski.

Guthrie chuckled, but quickly composed himself. That was just round one. This fight wasn't over yet. Looking around, he could see everyone in the control room staring at him, waiting for him to tell them what he was going to do next. Clearing his throat, he announced the basic tenet of his battle plan.

"Attention in Control. My intention is to stay on this course for a few more minutes to clear datum. I will then slow and come about to the southwest and attempt to find the Kilo. Once we detect him, I will deploy a mobile decoy to draw him away and maneuver the boat into position to engage with a Mark 48 ADCAP torpedo. Carry on."

The captain's declaration to shoot back electrified everyone in the control room. No submarine had ever fired a Mark 48 in anger, and the very idea jumpstarted the fire control party to provide the best possible firing solution. With his battle plan articulated, Guthrie had time to just think. Immediately, he found his thoughts going back to Jerry and the SEALs. He'd abandoned them, left them alone to fight a far superior enemy. *Should*

I just try and get away and see if I can get off a Cormorant? he said to himself. How long would that take? *No! Stop it!* Guthrie pounded his fist on the countertop. He didn't have time for this kind of second-guessing. *I have to fight for my ship.*

Guthrie joined Simmons on the periscope stand; he needed to take a look at the sonar display. The Iranian Kilo was still out there. But before he could find them, he had to clear his own countermeasure. After waiting patiently for several minutes, Guthrie started acting on his battle strategy.

"Weps, make tubes one and two ready in all respects, with the exception of opening the outer doors."

"Make tubes one and two ready in all respects, with the exception of opening the outer doors, aye, sir," repeated the weapons officer eagerly.

"Alright, people, here we go," said Guthrie. "Helm, all ahead two-thirds."

"All ahead two-thirds, aye, sir. Maneuvering answers ahead two-thirds."

"Very well, helm. Left fifteen degrees rudder, steady on course two two five."

"My rudder is left fifteen, coming to course two two five."

Guthrie reached up to the intercom. "Sonar, Conn, we are coming left to clear the ADCs, keep a sharp ear to the south."

"Conn, Sonar, aye," Buckley replied.

Kilo-Class Submarine, *Yunes*, SS903

"Helmsman, left standard rudder. Steady on course two seven zero. Make turns for four knots," ordered Mehr.

"My rudder is left standard, coming to new course two seven zero. Speed is slowing to four knots," acknowledged the helmsman.

"Very well." Mehr rose and looked around the central post. He wanted to make sure everyone was listening to him.

"Attention in Central Post. We are separating from our jammers to enable us to search for the American. I am not yet convinced we got him, so stay focused on your duties. *If* he is still out there, and we do find him, we'll need to quickly make another attack. We no longer have the element of surprise, so stay alert!"

Khadem listened to Mehr's proclamation and noted the emphasis on not becoming complacent. While he was still skeptical, his captain was the

best in the Iranian Navy, and he didn't get that way by pandering to the senior officers with showy demonstrations. Mehr knew his boat, and his men.
If he had an itch between his shoulders, it was because something wasn't
quite right.

"Sir, tubes two and four have been reloaded. And another MG-24 jammer is in the countermeasure launcher," Khadem reported.

"Very good, First Officer." Mehr's eyes remained focused on the sonar
display.

Khadem hesitated, standing by his captain, struggling to find the rights
words with which to question him, to ask him to justify his actions.

"You're still convinced we got him, aren't you, Navid?" Mehr preempted
him.

"Yes, sir. Everything points to that," the embarrassed first officer replied.

"And you want to know why I don't agree?" There was a slight smile on
Mehr's face. Khadem nodded silently.

"I don't for a moment believe the Pasdaran's propaganda about Americans," the captain spoke sternly. "The Americans are more professional than
the Pasdaran could ever hope to be. And they don't normally promote fools
to be captains of their submarines. My intuition tells me that this captain is
not a fool, and he had a trick up his sleeve. No, I don't think we hit him. The
weapon may have detonated because of the countermeasure, but my gut tells
me he's still out there listening for us. If I'm wrong, we have nothing to lose
by remaining vigilant for another hour. If I'm right, it just might save our
lives."

USS *Michigan*, SSGN 727

It was a long three minutes. Guthrie paced around the periscope stand,
pausing only to look occasionally at the sonar display. Nothing. The ADC
Mark 4 sonar jammer he had deployed was exceptionally loud and affected
the BQQ-10 hull arrays just as much as their adversary's sensors. They had
to get clear so the fancy signal processing equipment could digitally screen
out the influences of their countermeasure.

"Conn, Sonar, new contact, bearing one three five. Designate new contact Sierra-five seven."

"Sonar, Conn, aye," replied Simmons. Guthrie was already on his way to the sonar shack.

"What do you have for me, Woody?" Guthrie asked eagerly, as he entered the darkened space where four sonar operators worked their magic.

Buckley pointed to the passive broadband display showing the input from the spherical array. "Here is the weak trace we just picked up off the sphere. There is nothing on the low frequency bow array—no narrowband tonals—but without a towed array we can't be confident of this. The initial cut on bearing rate suggests he's close, about two degrees per minute, drawing left. My chief here says it's a submerged contact, and I concur, sir."

Although Buckley couldn't see it, there was a big grin on Guthrie's face. "Well done, gentlemen, well done. We'll stay on this course for another minute or two, and get a good first leg. Then I'll turn us to the southeast. Don't lose 'em!"

"Aye, aye, sir!" exclaimed the occupants of the sonar space.

Guthrie walked quickly over to the geoplot and gestured for Harper to join him.

"What do you have so far, Erik?" the captain demanded.

"Sir, we have two decoys. One bears one three zero and the other one three seven. If you add in the bearing spread from the torpedoes, that puts the Kilo somewhere down here." Nelson pointed to a circle two thousand yards in diameter, five thousand yards to the southeast.

"Very nice, Erik. Well done. You, too, Sean and Daniel." Guthrie was pleased with what his junior officers had put together given the sparse data they had to work with; but they had missed an important clue. "However, I think we can improve upon this a little. Hand me the ruler, please, Daniel."

Guthrie took the ruler and marked lines between the bearing cuts for the two torpedoes, explaining as he drew. "If you assume these weapons were fired nearly simultaneously, then the respective ranges to them should be fairly close as well. By linking the corresponding bearings together, you get rough positions, which we can trace back to their point of origin."

The captain then aligned the ruler along the position dots and drew two more lines. Guthrie finished by drawing another line through the two bearings to the decoys. The three lines formed a small triangle within the much larger circle constructed by his JOs.

"Sweet," whispered Hogan.

"This last line is more of a swag," admitted Guthrie, "but it's not that sensitive as long as it's roughly in an east-west direction, the direction of his travel. That, gentlemen, is where the Kilo fired from. Now let's figure out where he's going."

Porter and Hogan plotted out the rest of the bearing information and merged it with their skipper's initial starting point. In less than a minute, they had worked out an initial solution of course two six three, speed six knots, range four thousand yards. For all the high-tech ASW hardware his boat carried, nothing conveyed more information to Kyle Guthrie than a good old-fashioned paper plot. He wrote down the initial solution on a fire control chit and handed it to Harper. "Have Sandy put this into her analyzer and start stacking the dots against it," he ordered.

"Yes, sir," replied the engineer. He took the information and read it to Ensign Wagner, who quickly entered the starting solution into the fire control console. She immediately began manipulating the passive sonar bearing information by adjusting the course, speed, and range knobs until the bearing dots formed a nice neat vertical stack. The initial solution was a good one, and the dots stacked up quickly. They had a good first leg. Harper gave the skipper a thumbs-up sign.

"Attention in Control," Guthrie announced. "I intend to come left, and execute a second leg for an Ekelund range. As we turn, we'll deploy a mobile decoy to distract the Kilo skipper's attention. After a good fire control solution has been generated, we'll launch a single Mark 48 ADCAP. Stay on your toes. This isn't over yet. Carry on."

"Skipper, won't turning to the left get us awfully close to the Kilo?" Simmons voice was edgy with apprehension.

"You're correct, Isaac, we'll be closing the target. But if he's where I think he is, his sonar will be staring straight at the ADC Mark 4 countermeasure that's still cranking out a ton of noise. It should not only mask our approach, but also our shot. To quote our XO, 'we'll be coming at him from out of the sun.'"

Simmons face fell when Guthrie mentioned the XO. "I sure hope the XO and the other guys are okay. We left them high and dry."

For a brief moment Guthrie took the comment personally, but quickly realized that his navigator was merely expressing the same feelings of concern that they all shared. "I hope so, too, Nav. But right now, we can't afford to think about it."

"Helm, left fifteen degrees rudder. Steady on course one three zero," commanded Guthrie.

"Captain, my helm is left fifteen, coming to course one three zero."

"Very well, helm. Weps, stand by to launch a mobile decoy, course two two five, speed eight knots."

Zelinski quickly punched the buttons on the countermeasure panel, double-checked the settings, and reported, "Standing by to launch mobile decoy, course and speed laid in."

"Launch countermeasure!" barked Guthrie.

"Countermeasure away, Captain."

Let's hope he falls for this, Guthrie thought. *If he doesn't, it'll get* real *interesting*, real *fast.* Looking around the control room, he saw his crew carrying out their duties calmly and with determination. Pride filled him as he watched the team that he and Jerry Mitchell had worked so hard to train functioning like a well-oiled machine, preparing for the moment when he would order them to shoot.

It just seemed so bizarre; he had gone through this procedure countless times during his career, but that was in the attack trainers or on a test range. This was real; he was going to launch a warshot torpedo at a hostile target that had already taken a shot at him. The Kilo skipper was about to get what he deserved; no more, no less.

"Open the outer door on tube one."

Kilo-Class Submarine, *Yunes*, SS903

There was an old joke posted on the squadron headquarters bulletin board from some Western defense journal that read, "ASW means Awfully Slow Warfare." Mehr couldn't agree more. It had been a little over ten minutes since their initial attack, and there still was no sign of the *Ohio*-class boat. Had they truly hit the Americans the first time? Or had her captain decided that discretion was the better part of valor?

All but one of the deployed countermeasures had ceased to function and sank to the bottom, clearing up the sonar picture immensely. This last one, deployed by the Americans, was still causing some problems. Were they hiding nearby, lying in wait? Mehr dismissed the idea, because to use a countermeasure effectively in that manner he'd have to know exactly where *Yunes* was. And that was most improbable.

The Iranian skipper stood up and stretched. He was starting to get drowsy in his chair and he needed to get his blood moving. It would be bad form to fall asleep in the middle of the hunt. He strolled around all of the watch stations, checking in on his men, who had to be just as tired as he was. After speaking with Lieutenant Kashani at the MVU-110 fire control console, Mehr wandered back to the sonar cubicle. He leaned up against the door to the closet-sized space and looked inside; the two operators seemed to be in a trance, both watching their displays and listening intently to the waters around them.

"Any luck?" inquired Mehr politely. Neither man answered. He was about to address them more formally when the sergeant vigorously waved his hand and said, "Ssh!"

Mehr froze in place. The last thing he wanted to do was disturb these men if they were on to something. For what seemed an eternity, but in reality was only about twenty seconds, he hovered over the two sonar operators. Finally, the sergeant looked at his captain and reported, "Faint contact moving away from the sonar jammer. Bearing green three four."

Mehr patted the sonar operator on the shoulder and said, "Pass the tracking data to fire control." Marching into central post, he immediately began spitting out commands.

"Fire control, begin tracking the new contact. Stand by for rapid salvo firing."

"Yes, sir," Kashani replied, as his fingers mover swiftly over the console.

"Sonar, stand by to go active on both main and mine-hunting arrays."

"Aye, Captain."

"First officer, deploy a MG-24 countermeasure on my command."

"Aye, Captain."

Mehr leaned over Kashani's shoulder and looked at the fire control's position display. The contact was just off his starboard bow; he was in an excellent position from which to execute another attack.

"Captain, the contact has no blade noise at all. The bearing rate is high, drawing left. Evaluate the contact as a submerged submarine," reported the sonar operator.

"Very well, Sonar." Mehr evaluated all the data; this had to be his prey, his whale. "Time to end this game," he muttered softly.

"Fire control, open bow caps on tubes one and three."

USS *Michigan*, SSGN 727

"Captain, we have a firing solution," declared Harper confidently, while extending his hand with a fire control chit in it.

Guthrie grabbed the piece of paper and looked at it closely. "Course two seven three, speed five knots, range two eight hundred yards. Boy howdy, he's close!"

"Yes, sir. And getting closer, I might add," observed Simmons.

Guthrie gave his navigator a sour look and handed the chit back to Harper. "Plug it in, Eng."

Harper gave the data to Zelinski, who read it off to the fire control technician. Soon the Mark 48 ADCAP torpedo in tube one would have all the data it needed to find and kill the Kilo.

"Conn, Sonar, transients from Sierra five seven. Sounds like he's opening torpedo tube outer doors," reported Buckley.

Guthrie's heart sank. Had they been detected? Before he could acknowledge the report, the WLY-1 receiver began chirping. The Kilo had gone active.

"Snapshot, tube . . ." shouted Guthrie, but he was interrupted by Buckley before he could finish his command.

"Conn, Sonar, Sierra five seven has gone active, but we are not in the main beam. Repeat we are not in the main beam. WLY-1 is picking up a side lobe."

"Belay my last," barked Guthrie. "We'll stick to our original plan. Get those weapon presets in pronto, Weps."

Kilo-Class Submarine, *Yunes*, SS903

"Contact, Captain, range to target thirty-two hundred meters." The sonar operator's tone was understandably excited. They were much closer to the target than the first shot.

"Rapid salvo fire, tubes one and three!" cried Mehr determinedly.

"Tubes one and three fired, sir!"

USS *Michigan*, SSGN 727

"Conn, Sonar, torpedoes in the water. Bearing one nine one. Torpedoes are drawing right rapidly. They're going away from us."

"Sonar, Conn, aye." Guthrie smiled. He'd taken the bait. The Iranian captain had fired on the mobile decoy. *Now it's my turn,* he thought.

"Firing point procedures, Sierra five seven, tube one," he said calmly.

"Solution ready," answered Harper.

"Ship ready," replied Simmons.

"Weapon ready," responded Zelinski.

"Shoot on generated bearings," ordered Guthrie.

Zelinski nodded to the fire control technician, who grabbed the firing handle and rotated it to the left. "Set . . . Stand by . . . Shoot!" called out the tech.

On the word "shoot" he rotated the handle all the way around to the right, completing the firing circuit. Down in the torpedo room, the firing valve on the starboard tube nest opened with a pop, allowing high-pressure air to run through the blades of a turbine. The turbine drove a titanium pump impeller that spun very rapidly, driving hundreds of gallons of seawater into the torpedo tube. The force of the seawater literally threw the 3,700-pound Mark 48 ADCAP torpedo out of the tube with the acceleration equal to three Gs. Once clear of the submarine, the Mark 48's Otto fuel engine kicked in and propelled the deadly weapon toward its target.

"Normal launch," announced the fire control tech. "Torpedo course one nine five, medium speed, four zero knots, run-to-enable one five hundred yards."

Nelson immediately had the plotting team place the torpedo's course and designated enable point on the geoplot. Guthrie hopped down from the periscope stand and looked at the tactical situation displayed on the paper plot. He liked what he saw.

"If we've done this right, he'll be completely surprised when the torpedo enables ninety degrees from where it's supposed to be," stated Guthrie.

The captain watched as Porter and Hogan drew out the bearing lines to the Mark 48. At forty knots, it would take just a little over a minute to reach the enable point.

Kilo-Class Submarine, *Yunes*, SS903

Mehr was puzzled as he looked at the tactical display on the fire control console. The target he fired at wasn't doing anything! No reaction whatsoever. He surely couldn't have missed the active sonar pings bouncing off his hull. What was that man doing? Suddenly, his blood went cold with realization. That wasn't a submarine they shot at. It was a decoy! He had to get out of here, now! Pivoting toward the helmsman, he was about to give his orders when an alarm went off. *"TORPEDO ALERT, GREEN ZERO NINE ZERO,"* screamed the sonar operator.

USS *Michigan*, SSGN 727

"Detect. Detect. Detect. Homing," the fire control technician sang out. "Own-ship's unit has acquired the target. Bearing to target one nine three, range nine double oh yards."

"Bull's-eye, Skipper," said Harper.

"We haven't won yet, Eng," remarked Guthrie. Then raising his voice, "Helm, all ahead standard. Weps, stand by countermeasure station."

Kilo-Class Submarine, *Yunes*, SS903

"Launch countermeasure," shouted Mehr. He didn't bother waiting for his first officer's response. Mehr had other things to do if they were going to survive. "Helmsman, hard left rudder, steady on course two three zero, all ahead flank! Fire control, steer torpedo number one ninety degrees to the right!"

"Sir?" stammered Kashani with confusion.

"He's on our starboard side, you dolt! Turn the torpedo!"

Kashani started inputting the turn commands, but the elderly Russian fire control system was slow and klutzy. He had to execute one turn, wait for the weapon to respond, and then do it again.

Mehr could feel the vibrations as the boat accelerated. But he knew that if the countermeasure failed, it wouldn't matter.

USS *Michigan*, SSGN 727

"Conn, Sonar, target zig, Sierra five seven. Contact is cavitating and has deployed a countermeasure." Buckley's voiced boomed from the intercom speaker.

"Sonar, Conn, aye," Guthrie replied. "Any indication the countermeasure is affecting our weapon?"

Zelinski looked at the torpedo control panel, and asked his technician before he responded, "No, sir. It doesn't look like own-ship's unit is being affected at all by the Kilo's countermeasure."

"Time to impact," requested Guthrie.

"At six five knots, impact in two zero seconds," answered the fire control tech.

"Conn, Sonar, one of the torpedoes is turning toward the right. Bearing two four nine."

"Sonar, Conn, aye. Keep an eye on it. I need to know if it keeps turning toward us," said Guthrie. Glancing at the plot, it wasn't a threat, yet.

Kilo-Class Submarine, *Yunes*, SS903

"Incoming torpedo still closing." The sonar operator was sobbing as he spoke. Mehr didn't respond. It no longer mattered. The countermeasure had failed to decoy the American's torpedo, and at its maximum speed it was three times faster than his submarine. The whale would swallow them after all. He closed his eyes tightly and prayed for Allah's mercy.

Five seconds later, the Mark 48 ADCAP's 650-pound high explosive warhead detonated right next to the Kilo's hull, crushing it like a sledgehammer hitting an empty soda can. The twisted and mangled hull plowed into the bottom of the Persian Gulf.

USS *Michigan*, SSGN 727

"Conn, Sonar, loud explosion bearing two one six!" Buckley announced gleefully.

The fire control party erupted into a loud cheer, while Guthrie placed his head on the plotting table. They'd done it.

"Sonar, Conn, aye," replied Simmons. "Do you hear anything else?"

"Conn, Sonar, propulsion noises for Sierra five seven have stopped. There are . . . there are breaking-up noises on the same bearing. The torpedo isn't turning anymore. It will pass well astern of us."

"Sonar, Conn aye," Simmons responded soberly.

"Is it legal to congratulate you now, Captain?" asked Harper.

"Later. Let's get our ass up to periscope depth and see if we still have an XO," replied Guthrie wearily.

24

BARRIER

8 April 2013
0440 Local Time/0140 Zulu
Over the Persian Gulf

General Yuri Tamir commanded Operation Halom, Israel's strike on Iran, but he wasn't in the lead aircraft, and he wouldn't be delivering any ordnance. He'd flown both the F-15 and the F-16, but he was also an electronics specialist and the Israel Air Force's most expert computer hacker.

Tamir rode to battle on board a plane named the "Shavit," a Gulfstream 550 business jet converted by Israel Aircraft Industries. One side of the plane's interior was lined with operator consoles. A narrow aisle separated them from racks of electronic equipment on the other side. Tamir's battle staff sat at the front of the cabin, working with a large video screen on the forward cabin bulkhead.

Externally, the white-painted Shavit looked like any other business jet, especially with the blue IAF insignia painted over, as long as one didn't get too close. A careful inspection would reveal a long "canoe" radome under the forward fuselage and smaller antennas sprouting from other places. The canoe radome did not house a radar dish. Instead, a bank of antennas inside swept the ether for hostile radar signals, radio, microwave transmissions, and computer data links.

The Israeli Air Force called the Shavit a "Special Mission Electronics Aircraft." It could listen for hostile radars and passively plot their location.

It could listen in to enemy communications and warn pilots of hostile air-craft movements. It could also collect data from other sources and build a comprehensive picture of the battle, which was very hard to do in a blacked-out fighter cockpit while also trying to fly the plane. That's why Tamir would run the battle from here.

But the Shavit's mission was also offensive. Once it was in range of enemy territory, it attacked not the radars or enemy SAMs, but the air defense net-work itself. Analyzing, transmitting, intruding, it used sophisticated hacking tools to gain access to an opponent's air defense network. Digitally dressed in the enemy's uniform, they could read their status boards and duty roster, then scramble orders and add some of their own.

The Shavit had help with its mission. Long before it had taken off, two Eitan long-endurance UAVs had launched from Palmachim Air Base. With straight wings wider than a 737's, and a single turboprop engine, the Eitan cruised at a stately 120 knots—glacially slow compared to most military aircraft. But it could fly for thirty-six hours at forty thousand feet, and its composite airframe was almost invisible to radar. Each Eitan carried a full set of antennas like the Shavit. This let the Shavit's operators instantly triangulate any signal, and hack into an enemy network from more than one location.

General Tamir had overseen the development of the Shavit's electron-ics, designed the tactics, and had used them to great effect, not just in exer-cises, but in battle. When Israel attacked the secret Syrian reactor in 2007 during Operation Orchard, then–Colonel Tamir had run the electronic in-trusion of the Syrian defenses. His tinkering with the Syrian air defense computer network had the same effect as a "Jedi mind trick," obscuring the Israeli strike, hiding it while in plain sight. The Syrians never got off a shot.

Tamir's aircraft had taken off from Nevatim Air Base in Israel an hour before the rest of the strike. Registered as a civilian private charter, the plane had crossed Saudi airspace, then turned right when it reached the coast. Slowing slightly, it was flying down the length of the Persian Gulf. In the forty-five minutes it had before the strike's arrival, it scouted the elec-tronic spectrum, preparing its attack.

Standing behind the operator's chair, Tamir had grinned with almost predatory joy. The console displayed the complete Iranian air defense pic-ture: the condition of its radars, the status of every fighter squadron. At the moment, the operator was simply gathering data and monitoring Iranian message traffic. It had proven easier to get in than they thought, and with the extra time, Tamir felt the temptation to get creative, but he fought it. "Let them sleep, Dvir." The young lieutenant nodded.

Tamir let his deputy, Colonel Epher Okun, run the battle "up front." The general preferred to move from console to console, watching operators work like gunners at their posts. He'd trained this team until they could think and work as a single entity, but this was the Big Show. No more simulators, and they would only get one chance.

The radar intercept station was next to the intrusion station. Its map of the region was overlaid with symbols for the different radars—friendly, hostile, and neutral. The Shavit's computers matched the signals with known sources and plotted their position.

"Any changes, Ari?" Tamir asked the young lieutenant.

"No changes to the Iranians, General, but the American E-2Ds are moving east and north. They may be picking up our strike. Calculated detection range for their radars is three hundred and fifty nautical miles."

Tamir nodded. "The timing works. Don't worry, those surveillance aircraft will keep their distance. They don't want to be too close when we pass by. They'll watch us as we attack, and they may learn a few things, but they won't get close."

The communications intercept station was next to the radar intercept console. Tamir turned to the operator, a senior captain, and asked, "Are you picking up any transmissions from those E-2s, Yoni?"

"No, sir. I can't see their data link back to the carrier. It's going via satellite, and it's encrypted as well. I've watched them rotate the fighters escorting the Hawkeyes, and all their UHF stuff is encrypted."

"And nothing new out of Bandar Abbas?" the general asked. The captain shook his head firmly. The headquarters for the Iranian Southern Air Defense Command was located there. If the incoming raid was detected, the Southern headquarters would start talking to many people, very fast. Tamir was prepared to do something about that, but not until it was necessary. Eventually the strike would be detected. One couldn't hide a hundred tactical aircraft forever.

Okun's voice came over his headset. "Yuri, feet wet in ten minutes." Tamir checked his watch. The strike was on schedule, to the minute. In ten minutes the lead plane would cross the Saudi coast and be over the Persian Gulf. That was also the Initial Point, or "IP," technically the start of their attack run, although they were still hundreds of miles from the target.

Tamir checked the intrusion display again. All quiet. He patted the lieutenant's shoulder. "It should be about thirty more minutes, Dvir. Then we'll have some fun. These are not the planes you're looking for."

And if they did their job right, the Iranians would never even know they'd been hacked.

8 April 2013
0445 Local Time/0145 Zulu
USS *Ronald Reagan* (CVN 76)

Commander Tom "Heretic" Dressler, squadron commander of VFA-147, the Argonauts, waited patiently in his Super Hornet for the deck crew to move into position and ready him for launch. He'd elected to be the last in his squadron to launch, both because it gave him a few more minutes in the air, and so he'd know if any of his guys had trouble getting off the deck. Besides, his tactical displays were already up. Even with his radar safely off, the data link from *Reagan* showed him exactly what was going on.

Nobody ever lit off their radar on the flight deck. The microwave energy it put out would cook someone where they stood before they could even feel what was happening and get out of the way. But more than that, *Reagan*'s air group was launching "quietly," with no radio or radar transmissions by any of the aircraft. They wouldn't energize their radars or break radio silence until Taz said to.

The squadrons were taking off in reverse order, the Black Knights of VFA-154 went first, then the Argonauts' sister squadron VFA-146 the Blue Diamonds, then it would be the Argonauts' turn. Theoretically, each catapult could launch a plane every two minutes, and *Reagan* had four, two at the bow and two at the waist. That meant one plane every thirty seconds, but it all depended on the plane handlers and the rest of the flight deck crew.

Flight deck operations on a carrier have been called a "ballet." Like ballet, it's a precise art, and the performers on *Reagan* practiced and rehearsed it daily. But imagine the precision of a ballet combined with the noise and danger of a stock car race, where the stock cars are carrying high explosives. To complicate matters further, it was pitch black and the wind was whipping down the length of the flight deck at over forty knots.

Ready to launch, each Hornet weighed twenty-five tons, and was parked inches apart from the next. Almost any collision between two planes would render one or both unable to fly. The plane handlers had to move each plane in the proper order to its assigned catapult, line up the nose gear so the launch bar on the strut was engaged by the catapult shoe, and not get sucked into an intake or fried by an exhaust in the process.

Reagan's flight deck crew was putting over fifty aircraft, a full deckload, into the air. Everyone would be flying in fifteen minutes.

A plane handler in a bright blue shirt ran over and stood in front of his aircraft, holding lighted wands so Heretic could see his arm signals. As much as it depended on the plane handlers, Dressler had to do his part, and follow their orders precisely.

Heretic released his brakes and gently increased power, taxiing past the other aircraft to the outboard port waist catapult. To the commander's eyes, with his nose pointed toward the portside edge of the flight deck, it looked like the handler was going to put him over the side, but at the right moment the petty officer ordered the squadron commander into a hard right turn, almost pivoting on the right wheel. The Hornet ended up aligned perfectly with the catapult. The handler inched him forward, and he felt the catapult shoe engage the launch bar on his nose gear.

He had time to watch the plane ahead of him in the launch order—the last of the Argonauts except for him—spool up his engines to full afterburner and launch. Heretic watched the catapult officer, reflexively bracing his helmet against the seat behind him. He felt the nose of the plane drop as the catapult put tension on. Then he hit full burner, waited for the displays to settle, saluted the catapult officer, and grasped the handhold with his right hand. The computer would handle takeoff.

Heretic hardly noticed the blackness around him as he climbed to join his squadron.

8 April 2013
0450 Local Time/0150 Zulu
Over Western Saudi Arabia

For Colonel David Zohar, it was all about fuel. Everything else had been argued over, rehearsed, modified, and polished until there was precious little left to manage except the fuel.

Zohar commanded 69 Squadron, "The Hammers," which flew the F-15I Ra'am, or "Thunder." The squadron's name was especially appropriate on this raid. Each plane carried a five-thousand-pound GBU-28 on the centerline, a monster weapon that could penetrate meters of rock and concrete. Each of his twenty-four aircraft carried one GBU-28, two smaller GBU-31s, two drop tanks, and air-to-air missiles for self-defense.

The formation had just finished in-flight refueling from KC-707 tankers, something that would have been impossible without Saudi permission. But thanks to their agreement, every plane would start their attack run with virtually full internal and external tanks. Even so, it might not be enough, if they had to use too much throttle, or had to deviate from the planned flight path, or suffered battle damage.

The tanker aircraft were hurrying back to base as quickly as their portly airframes allowed, where they would fill up again and take off to meet the returning planes. Recovery tankers have saved many pilots and planes, and the Israeli Air Force would go to great lengths to make sure everyone came home.

Reflexively, he scanned the horizon, then the sky above and below them. There was precious little to see from that altitude at that time of day. The lights of a few urban areas, especially farther west, glowed against the dark landscape below them, but there was nothing on the horizon and nothing above them.

His radar was off, his radio unused since he'd climbed in the cockpit. He didn't need the radar or radio to navigate. Modern nav systems and GPS laid rails for them in the sky.

And he wasn't blind. A Shavit electronics aircraft had taken off before them and surveyed the enemy defenses. A data link from the Shavit via satellite gave Zohar a complete tactical picture without having to send out a single electron. He could see the Iranian defenses, the American carrier strike group and its aircraft, surface traffic in the gulf, even Saudi fighters patrolling to the east if he wanted to expand his view.

Right now, he kept the displays centered on his route, studying the Iranians. In ten minutes he would begin to descend from thirty-five thousand feet down to five hundred feet, a carefully calculated downward slope designed to keep them below the horizon of the enemy's radars.

But he wanted to stay at high altitude as long as possible. The Ra'am's jet engines worked best in the thin air up high. At low altitude, they'd guzzle fuel at almost twice the rate, and the thick air also slowed them down. As long as they were undetected, he wanted to stay high.

Zohar's back-seater was working the problem, but wasn't helpful. "Colonel, I recommend we descend as planned. The hostile radars are performing as expected. If we push it now and are detected, they gain ten or even fifteen minutes' reaction time. We might have to fight our way to the target."

Which they had all discussed, and planned for. If the Shavit's efforts were detected, or some fluke of atmospherics increased detection ranges, the Iranians could be wide awake when the raid arrived. But what was the worst that could happen?

Every radar and SAM site along the raid's path was being targeted, just in case. With enough warning, the Iranians could get some fighters in the air, or at least more fighters than with no warning, but none of the Iranian planes were a match for the Israeli aircraft. In fact, Zohar had been forced to punish a few of his boys who were too overconfident. But there were two squadrons of F-161 escorts between the Iranian interceptors and the strike aircraft, and once the two squadrons of strikers had delivered their load, they were equally lethal in the air. The Iranians would have better luck trying to take a bite from a chainsaw.

Daniel was a junior captain, but was one of the best back-seaters in the squadron. And it was best not to take chances. "Understood, Dan. We will descend as planned."

"This is Yuri to all squadrons. The lion sleeps. You are cleared through the IP." General Tamir's message was a little redundant, since they planned to proceed unless ordered otherwise, but positive confirmation was worth the effort. The voice transmission was via satellite, and encrypted like the data link, so the chance of detection was nil.

Zohar looked at the American surveillance aircraft on his display. They had a perfect position to watch the approach. There was nothing they could do to stop the Americans, but nothing they needed to do about it, either.

Daniel's report came on schedule. "Five minutes to IP."

The colonel was watching the clock count down and reviewing the descent plan when the symbols started appearing on the display. His threat warning receiver was almost shouting at him, displaying multiple air intercept radars—more than he could count—ahead of them.

"Daniel, do you have this?"

8 April 2013
0455 Local Time/0155 Zulu
Over Western Saudi Arabia

General Tamir forced himself to step away from the console operator. Breathing down Ari's neck was not helpful, and he could see the screen fine from a few steps back. He just could not comprehend what he was seeing.

The raw sensor display was almost useless, covered with bearing lines from literally dozens of fighter radars, all appearing in the last ten seconds.

"They're all American—APG-73 and APG-79 radars, General." That meant Hornet and Super Hornet fighters from the U.S. carrier.

The shock filling the lieutenant's voice was not just from the sudden appearance of so many signals, but their position. The fighters lay in a band directly across the raid's path. Altitude was hard to determine based on passive signals, but Tamir would bet they were at the same altitude. That location could not be an accident.

Okun's voice pulled the general away from the console. "Yuri, someone's calling the raid on military distress." The international military distress frequency was standardized at 243 megahertz, and was a good way to talk to a military aircraft if you didn't know which frequencies he'd be using. Meeting his deputy's eyes, Tamir tapped his headset with one finger, and Okun switched him over.

"Israeli aircraft, this is United States Navy carrier air group commander. Turn around and return to base. If you continue to approach Iranian airspace, we will fire on you."

Tamir quickly hit the channel selector switch on his headset. "David, this is Yuri. Do not acknowledge. Do not respond to the American transmission. Confirm by voice."

Colonel Zohar responded, "I heard the transmission, Yuri. I will not respond." Zohar managed to sound like answering the Americans was the last thing he'd do. "Interrogative, over."

"Stand by." *Interrogative was right*, Tamir thought. What was the Americans' game here? Did they really want to stop the attack? Although he'd been briefed about Israel's disagreement with the U.S., he'd marked it up to caution and distance. They didn't feel it was their fight, but the U.S. had as much to gain as Israel did, although he . . .

"General!" It was Dvir, watching the Iranian air defenses. "The Kolchuga array near Bushehr is picking up the American radars. They're still trying to sort out the picture, but there's a lot of traffic between the operators and southern sector headquarters."

The Kolchuga was one of the few modern sensors in Iran's air defense network. Designed by the Russians, Iran had bought the system from Ukraine after the collapse of the Soviet Union. It used broadband ground-based receiving stations to detect and quickly triangulate the position of planes using radar. Kolchuga could actually detect planes much farther out than radar, because the signal from a radar antenna continued to be detectable long after it was too weak to send an echo back to the plane that transmitted it.

That cut it. With the Iranians' attention attracted to this part of the sky, the raid's chances of catching the Iranians by surprise had just dropped from excellent to nil.

Tamir grimaced. "Ari, watch for changes in their radar status. Yoni, sit on Southern Command headquarters. Tell me if they start talking . . ."

"Yuri, the American is still calling for them to turn around. Distance is down to one hundred miles." Colonel Okun sounded worried. Did he think the Americans would really shoot?

"I'm going to push them, Epher. They may be posturing. Being so openly against us may get them points with the Muslim world." *But we will remember how this tipped off the enemy*, Tamir thought.

Switching voice channels back to the raid leader, he said, "David, energize your radars and lock up the Americans." There's no point in being quiet now.

"General, I'm getting jamming signals." The intercept officer pointed to strobes on the screen. "It's affecting communications as well as the radars. We've lost the data link to the raid. The Americans are jamming that, too."

Tamir turned to the communications officer. "Get me a channel on military distress!"

8 April 2013
0503 Local Time/0203 Zulu
Over the Saudi Coast

Zohar didn't need the general's order to energize his radar. Without the data link, the raid was blind, and he couldn't afford that now.

The American was still talking on 243 megahertz. "Israeli raid commander, this is U.S. Navy carrier group commander. You must abort your attack. I am under direct orders from my president to open fire if you do not turn around. Please acknowledge."

"David, I'm having trouble getting a lock." Daniel's voice on the intercom cut though the American's voice. "The jamming knocks me off every time I try to track one of them. And detection range is way down as well."

"Stands to reason, Daniel. The Americans sold us these radars. We're lucky we can see anything at all. We'll be in range for heat-seekers soon." Zohar wondered how long they would continue to jam. Would the Americans stop if he could get the raid past them into Iran? Would they really shoot?

"Israeli commander, what's your fuel margin? Can you afford to fight us and still attack your primary? We won't let you divert to Iraq afterward. Any Israeli plane that lands there will be permanently impounded."

That was bad news. Zohar had told all four squadrons that in spite of the deal with the Saudis, if they were damaged, to head for a U.S. air base in Iraq first, either Baghdad or Tallil. Better chance of getting both the plane and pilot back than with the Saudis, he'd thought.

The descent to low altitude had been forgotten. There was no point, now. In less than fifteen minutes they'd be across the gulf and into Iranian airspace. Zohar tried to buy time. "Why are you doing this?"

"Greetings to the Israeli Air Force. The time for explanations is long past. I have my orders."

8 April 2013
0505 Local Time/0205 Zulu
Over the Persian Gulf

General Tamir listened to the dialogue but said nothing. Revealing his presence wouldn't help. "Dvir, what can you do about the American jamming?"

The lieutenant shook his head. "We're not set up to hack the U.S. network. Even if we were, we'd have to abandon our intrusion into the Iranian air defenses."

Tamir looked at the main display at the front of the cabin. Going around wasn't an option. The American fighters lay between the Iranian coast and the strikers. They'd just shift the barrier left or right, with the range closing all the time.

He was confident of their ability to fight their way to the target against an alerted enemy, but he had never imagined fighting the Americans first. One of his staff had been tasked with figuring the odds. It was not a simple task. "Give me what you've got, Lev."

The major shook his head. "It's the multiple shots at close range. Even with good countermeasures, you need to see the missile coming at you to use them properly. We could lose twenty aircraft, maybe more. They'd lose less, because of the jamming, but still fifteen at least."

The communications offer reported, "General, Tel Aviv is calling. It's Minister Lavon."

8 April 2013
0507 Local Time/0207 Zulu
Over the Persian Gulf

While Zohar had been talking, his back-seater had been working with the radar to find targets and set up Python shots. The Python was a good missile, bigger and longer-ranged than the American AIM-9X, and its seeker was just as smart. Normally, the first salvo in an air battle would be at long range with AMRAAMs, but American jamming had taken away that option. Instead, they'd start with Pythons. When they got closer, in the dogfight, they'd burn through the jamming and use the AMRAAMs in boresight mode.

Of course, the Americans would do the same thing with their AMRAAMs, and they weren't being jammed.

"Israeli commander, our radars won't give you any warning of when you're locked up, so I'll tell you you're locked up, and you'll just have to believe me."

"You're going to lose a lot of airplanes and pilots," Zohar said angrily.

The American's voice was calm, as if this were merely an exercise. "Your losses will be just as bad. Will your tactics work with a half-assed strike, an alerted enemy, and no fuel reserves? You will lose people to no purpose! Turn around."

"Our purpose is clear."

Daniel's voice cut in again. "One minute to Python range for the lead aircraft."

Zohar said, "If you shoot, the Iranians win."

"So they tell me," the American voice answered. "And if you shoot, you won't either. Now you have to decide the best way to cut your losses."

Frustrated, fuming, Zohar was about to give the order to engage when Tamir sent the abort order. "David, this is Yuri. Abort. I repeat, abort. Confirm by voice."

Resigned, defeated, and still in a state of shock, Zohar responded, "Yuri, this is David. Confirm abort order. Returning to base." The Iranians would still be there tomorrow.

25

BLESSINGS REMOVED

8 April 2013
0530 Local Time/0230 Zulu
Nineteen Nautical Miles South of Iran

Jerry stared into space, his mouth hanging open, struggling to wrap his tired brain around what he had just heard. Ramey, also listening in on the circuit, was dumbfounded. *Michigan* was abandoning them.

Lapointe and Fazel had seen the sudden change in their expressions. "What happened, Boss?" asked Lapointe.

"Guthrie's ditchin' us! He's not sending any help!" exclaimed Ramey, furious.

"What!?" Lapointe and Fazel blurted out simultaneously, astounded by their platoon leader's words.

"Shut up, Ramey!" Jerry bellowed. "He can't help us because he has problems of his own!"

"What do you mean, XO?" demanded Fazel.

"The last thing I heard before the Skipper signed off was the WLY-1 beeping in the background and a sonar operator warning of active sonars and launch transients." Jerry sat as he explained, forcing himself to calm down. "I think they were being attacked by an Iranian sub, one of their Kilos."

"But I thought only the IRGC operated in the gulf now," said Lapointe, confused.

"That's what I thought, too, Pointy, but only a Kilo has the sensors I heard being reported, and you wouldn't hear any launch transients from a surface ship or air-dropped weapon. And if it's a Kilo class, that means the Iranian Navy."

Jerry took a deep breath, looked at the three SEALs and continued, his voice laced with worry. "Captain Guthrie has a tough fight on his hands. Staying to launch a Cormorant would have made him a sitting duck. He has over a hundred and fifty people on board *Michigan* that he's responsible for, including most of your platoon. It's not like he wanted to leave us to fend for ourselves."

The four men sat in silence, their desperate situation weighing heavily upon them. They were outgunned, they couldn't run, and they couldn't hide. What else could they do? It was Ramey who finally broke the gloomy stillness. "All right, we need to start figuring out what we're going to do when those patrol boats get here."

"The only thing we can do is fight," observed Fazel. "We certainly can't outrun these guys."

"Agreed, but the trick is how do we fight off three boats at the same time, Doc?" questioned Ramey. "We don't have nearly enough firepower."

Jerry heard the words, "at the same time," and it suddenly dawned on him that Ramey was defaulting to a worst-case scenario. "Whoa, wait a minute, Matt. You're assuming they'll make a coordinated attack."

"Yeah, what about it? It's a reasonable assumption," responded Ramey defensively.

"No argument there, Matt. And it would be appropriate if we were talking about a highly trained, professional military unit, but we aren't, are we?" Jerry countered.

"I see where you're going, XO. You think it's more likely they'll attack piecemeal," Fazel concluded.

"Exactly! Think about it. The Pasdaran are aggressive, impatient, and right now, really pissed off. That means they'll be even more impulsive than usual. On top of that, these are small patrol boats we're talking about. They don't have tactical data links, just voice radio, and they're coming at us from three different directions. A coordinated attack may be a reasonable worst-case scenario, but I'd argue it's the *least likely* scenario in this case," Jerry explained.

"But they will eventually all get here," Ramey contended.

"Agreed, Matt. But if they come in one at a time, we at least have a chance to thin out the herd. Not a great one, mind you, but it's still a lot better than taking all three on at the same time. And, we can improve our odds a little by using our one advantage," remarked Jerry cryptically.

"Advantage? What advantage?" Phillips didn't see it.

But the others did. "We have eyes on the targets; we know where they are. But they're unsure of where we are," stated Ramey.

"Correct, and that allows us to choose when and whom we fight first," Jerry declared. Using his hands, he showed the relative positions of the pursuers to their boat. "The RIB is on our right. The Ashura and Boghammar are on our left. If we alter course to the right a bit, we force the engagement with the RIB and put the other two into more of a tail-chase situation. That gives us a little more time to take out the RIB, which is also the fastest of the three bad guys."

"XO, we can't sink a RIB, at least not with small arms. I've been on boats very similar to the Iranian models. Those things use closed cell foam in their hulls. They're almost impossible to sink," observed Lapointe.

"Who said anything about sinking them, Pointy?" Jerry replied with a smile. "Our target is one of the outboard engines. We take out an engine and he's out of the game."

"What you're suggesting makes a lot of sense, XO. But dealing with the DShK heavy machine gun will be crucial. Even on a small boat it has a serious range advantage over our best weapon," Ramey stated thoughtfully.

Jerry was relieved to see that Ramey had swiftly recovered from the initial shock of *Michigan*'s abrupt departure. They had all been flabbergasted, overwhelmed when they realized Guthrie couldn't send help. But the platoon leader had rebounded quickly and was dealing with their problems, not just agonizing over them.

"Yes, Matt. On paper a .50 caliber machine gun has, what? . . . about twice the range of Harry's sniper rifle?"

"More or less, usually more, it depends on the specific model. But when mounted on a small boat the effective range drops by about a third," Ramey replied.

"Well, this isn't your basic paper drill; we're at sea and that changes everything," said Jerry.

"How so?" asked Ramey.

"When I was at postgraduate school, I read a lot about the Navy's research into the Iranian small boat swarm-attack problem—lots of small boats mobbing one of our own ships, a destroyer or cruiser. The Navy's been putting .50 caliber machine guns and 25-millimeter cannons on our ships, because they concluded the larger five-inch and three-inch guns were too easily overwhelmed and didn't handle small boats that were in close. But even with these smaller, fast-firing weapons, accurate engagement ranges was well inside eight hundred yards, and those Iranian patrol boats are a lot smaller than a destroyer.

"We are both in fast-moving, bouncy boats, with unstabilized guns, aimed by a Mark 1 Mod 0 eyeball. And the IRGC trains to attack big lumbering targets, not nimble little speedboats. I'd be surprised if they could hit us at more than two hundred yards under these conditions. They'll have to get really, really close to score any hits. And at those ranges, I'll bet on your marksmanship over theirs any day of the week."

"Well, I'm glad to see we're good for something," Phillips quipped.

"Just drive, Phillips," chastised Ramey, then he said more seriously, "Okay then, here's the basic plan: XO, you take on the navigation issue and figure out the best course to close the RIB. My guys and I will do what we can to protect Dr. Naseri and prepare for the fight. Any questions?" There weren't any. "Then back on your heads, people."

The collective brainstorming session had buoyed their confidence; the situation wasn't completely hopeless once it was broken down. With renewed assurance that they had a fighting chance, the SEALs began preparing with gusto. While Jerry worked out the best course to take to close on the RIB, Ramey and Lapointe looked at ways to prevent the enemy from doing to them, what they planned to do to him—take out an engine. At the same time, Fazel concentrated on finding a way to give Shirin some protection from at least small-arms fire.

It took Jerry only a couple of minutes to do the math, and he ordered Phillips to change course twenty degrees toward the west. If his mental gymnastics were correct, things would get really interesting in about ten minutes.

8 April 2013
0540 Local Time/0240 Zulu
Twenty Nautical Miles South-Southwest of Bandar Lengeh

Rahim tapped his fingers on the coaming. It had been over thirty minutes since they'd left Bandar Lengeh and there was still nothing on the radar screen. Visibility had improved considerably as soon as the sun broke over the horizon, but the lookouts had spotted nothing. Agitated, impatient, and just a little green from the patrol boat's choppy motion, the VEVAK agent was in a foul mood. "Lieutenant! You said we should have detected them by now!"

"Yes, Major, I did. However, there were a number of assumptions behind that statement. If even one was incorrect, then the estimate would have been incorrect as well." Qorbani kept his tone respectful; this wasn't the first time he had to deal with someone that didn't understand the maritime patrol problem.

"Could they have gone more to the west?" demanded Rahim.

"Of course they could have, sir. But to escape Iran, they have to move away from our coast, not parallel it. Besides, such a course would send them directly toward one of our secondary bases on Kish Island. A westerly course would be foolish. Since these are not fools we are dealing with, a southerly escape course makes the most sense. There is nothing more we can do but continue on toward the intercept point and wait," Qorbani answered.

Rahim didn't like the lieutenant's answer, but his explanation was logical. Frowning, he peered through his binoculars, straining to catch some sign of his prey. *They have to be out here somewhere,* he thought. Allah would surely not abandon him at this crucial juncture.

Suddenly, Qorbani shook Rahim's shoulder. He turned to see the Pasdaran lieutenant on the radio. He repeated the contact report back for accuracy, as well as for Rahim's benefit. "Understand the ten-meter RIB has contact on a high-speed craft heading south-southwest. Visual contact expected in four minutes."

8 April 2013
0543 Local Time/0243 Zulu
Twenty-Five Nautical Miles South of Iran

Jerry leaned against the forward part of the control console and scanned the starboard side. "Nothing yet, Matt," he reported.

"Keep looking, XO. He's only about three miles away, broad on our starboard beam," shouted Ramey, as he watched the UAV video feed. "Yeah, they have us on radar. One of the sailors keeps pointing in our general direction."

Fazel had tucked Shirin as far forward in the small boat as he could. She wore one of the tactical vests and her head was sandwiched between two of the backpacks. It wasn't much protection. A direct hit from any of the larger Iranian weapons would likely go right through, but it would provide her some shielding from splinters if the boat's hull was hit.

At the opposite end of the boat, Ramey and Lapointe had wrapped two tactical vests around the head of the outboard engine and stacked the remaining packs along the back end. Again, the protection was minimal. A .50 caliber bullet would have no problem going through, but smaller rounds might be stopped. Ramey also set up firing positions for Fazel and himself, the goal being to limit their exposure while hopefully reducing the effects of the boat's movement on their own shots.

Lapointe tried to assume a prone position, but the bouncing hull kept slamming into the knee on his wounded leg. And try as he might, the pain made even limited aiming impossible. Both he and Jerry would provide supporting fire from behind the console. Phillips volunteered to stay on as the driver. He and Ramey went over a basic evasive steering plan that would complicate the Iranians' ability to hit them, but not limit their field of fire. Being the most exposed, Phillips wore the last vest. After a short discussion, it was decided that Jerry would be the backup driver in case Phillips was wounded and incapable of steering the boat.

"Tallyho!" shouted Jerry. "Contact just abaft the starboard beam!" He made repeated motions with his arm, pointing in the general direction of the Iranian patrol boat.

Ramey raised his scope and swiftly confirmed the sighting. "Got it, XO! Okay, everyone, take your positions."

Shirin was shaking with fear. Never had she felt so exposed, so isolated. She let go of Fazel's hand with great reluctance, and only after he repeatedly said he had to take his place aft. As he left he motioned for her to get down and stay down. Without Yousef's reassuring presence, she felt utterly alone huddled up in the bow.

* * *

While the corpsman scooted passed Jerry to his defensive position, Lapointe loaded a high-explosive dual-purpose 40mm grenade into the launcher mounted on his SCAR. He only had eight grenades and he planned to use them sparingly.

During the planning, Ramey had instructed Lapointe to wait until the patrol boat steadied itself, an indicator that they were probably going to shoot, and then fire a grenade at their bow. Jerry was uncertain of what Ramey hoped to achieve with this tactic and asked Lapointe, "Pointy, how can you possibly expect to hit a small, high-speed craft with such a low-velocity weapon?"

Lapointe at first looked at Jerry incredulously, then snickered. "Who said anything about hitting them, XO? That would be the golden BB of all time! The boss figures that the Iranians will turn wide enough to avoid the grenade, giving him or Doc a clear shot at an outboard."

"Oh, yeah. Disregard the silly question," Jerry replied, feeling more than a little embarrassed. Lapointe laughed.

Although the RIB had been spotted at a range of nearly five thousand yards, this was far beyond the range of any weapon on either side. For seven agonizing minutes, Jerry and the SEALs could only watch as the Iranian patrol boat slowly closed on them. Through his sight, Jerry could see the long, slender wedge bouncing on the waves, throwing water out to either side. He knew they'd have to slow down considerably if they expected to hit anything. With the hull undulating up and down as the Pasdaran boat skipped along, he could see the machine gun barrel wandering all over the place. Sometimes it wasn't even visible as the boat's hull pitched upward.

Lapointe had taken over monitoring the UAV feed from Ramey. Both he and Fazel were now in a prone firing position, their weapons resting on the boat's transom and held firmly against their shoulders. "Shot warning!" Lapointe sang out. "The gunner has just pulled back on the cocking handle."

"Steady on course, Philly," Ramey shouted. "Don't turn until Pointy tells you to." The junior enlisted gave him a thumbs-up sign, acknowledging the order.

Jerry leaned over and looked at the UAV feed. The unmanned aircraft was bore-sighted on the RIB, keeping a steady eye on the pilot and gunner. It felt bizarre to be watching in real time as someone took shots at you, sort of like looking at a video game in reverse.

"Shot! Right slow!" yelled Lapointe. He could see a flare of infrared energy around the muzzle as the weapon fired. Phillips altered course slightly to starboard. The splashes from the rounds landed well to port.

"He fired too soon," criticized Ramey, then he said to his men, "Hold your fire. He needs to get a lot closer."

The Iranian crew didn't seem to realize this as another three wild volleys were fired before they stopped and concentrated on closing the range. Within another couple of minutes, the range had shortened to less than five hundred yards. This was the point when Phillips would begin using more radical turns to chase the splashes of the previous burst, to throw off the Iranian gunner's aim.

"Shot! Left hard," Lapointe called out again. Phillips banked the boat hard left. The splashes were to the right; immediately he shifted his rudder, and headed in their direction. The RIB was starting to get really close.

"Now, Pointy!" Ramey commanded. Lapointe raised his weapon, placed his sights ahead of the RIB's bow and pulled the trigger. A dull pop and a little smoke was the only sign the grenade launcher had been fired. Seconds later a small white plume of water marked the explosion. As anticipated, the Iranian turned hard right and Ramey and Fazel took a couple of aimed shots. Both missed.

"He's got to get closer, Boss," Fazel observed. Ramey nodded his agreement.

The RIB crew recovered quickly from their rude surprise and brought their racing boat back on to a pursuit course. The two boats weaved back and forth, the range dropping with each turn. During their maneuvers, Lapointe fired off another three grenades, each shot a little closer to the Iranian boat than the one before. Each time they swerved hard, with Ramey and Fazel taking aimed shots. Suddenly, Fazel saw something fly off one of the outboards. "I got a hit!" he yelled.

Jerry and the three SEALs all watched for some indication that the RIB's speed had been reduced, but it seemed unaffected as it continued to close. Another burst of .50 caliber fire came perilously close to the boat's stern—off by a mere foot. Water from the splashes sprayed on Ramey.

Phillips instantly zigged to the right, but the Iranian gunner had finally caught on to the American's strategy and immediately let loose another volley. Several rounds hit the gunwale between Jerry and the corpsman, tearing away chunks of the hull as they passed through.

"Son of a bitch!" yelped Fazel, as the bullets zipped over his head. Unfazed, he took several more shots. He scored some hits, but they were on the hull and thus totally ineffective. The RIB was only a couple of hundred yards away.

Lapointe shifted his body as best he could to put more weight on his good leg. This allowed him to lean a little to the left and brace himself up against the control console. He lined up his sights, well in front of the RIB, and placed his finger on the trigger. He then patiently waited for Phillips to finish executing a weave turn, checked his aim point, and fired.

The grenade hit the water several yards in front of the boat and exploded directly under the RIB's hull. The plume from the blast lifted the bow higher into the air, causing the racing boat to plane at an unsafe angle. The aerodynamic forces on the hull at such high speed pulled the bow even higher, and in the wink of an eye, the RIB went airborne, rotating end over end as it flew through the air. Pieces of the boat were ripped away and thrown skyward as it hit the surface, cartwheeling to a stop.

Jerry's jaw dropped as he watched the RIB sail into the air. Dumbfounded, he looked at Lapointe; and he wasn't alone. Ramey, Fazel, and Phillips were equally astounded. No one was quite ready to believe what they had just seen. Lapointe, too, was awestruck. Everyone repeatedly looked back and forth between Lapointe's grenade launcher and the capsized Pasdaran RIB.

It was Jerry who broke the silence as he patted Lapointe on the back. "Bravo Zulu, Pointy! That was one hell of a golden BB!"

"Awesome shot, Nate!" congratulated Fazel.

Ramey just shook his head, a big grin on his face. "No one back at the SEAL team will *ever* believe this," he lamented.

Lapointe acknowledged the accolades from the XO and his teammates with a simple, "Thanks." Then looking toward Jerry he added with a wink, "That was a bit sloppy, but I'll take it."

Jerry and the others laughed, relieved that the most dangerous threat had been eliminated. But it wasn't the only threat they faced, a fact Ramey reminded them of when he pointed toward a new contact on the port quarter. "Enough celebrating, everyone, the second boat is inbound and the third isn't far behind."

Rahim and Qorbani were both watching through binoculars as the ten-meter RIB appeared to be closing in for the kill. The VEVAK agent was silently urging the RIB's crew on, encouraging them to quickly finish the threat to his and Moradi's plan. Moments later, they stared in horror as the Pasdaran boat flew into the air and tumbled back down on to the sea. It didn't take a genius to realize that the chances of surviving such a violent crash were nil. Anger filled Rahim. The Americans had once again outmaneuvered him. It was incomprehensible how they always somehow found a way to snatch victory from his grasp. He swore that the long chase would end here and now.

"Lieutenant! I want you to fire on that boat at the earliest opportunity!" he ranted.

"Yes, Major," responded Qorbani, shaken, but angry now as well. "We will be in range in a few minutes."

Ramey and Lapointe watched the UAV feed as the Ashura patrol boat slowly closed the distance between them. They either missed the destruction of the RIB, which was very unlikely as they were well within visual range, or they were pressing on despite the dramatic loss of one of their more powerful patrol boats. Although the Boghammar was faster, it would take several minutes more before it would appear on the scene. For the moment, the odds were more even.

"Everybody back to their positions," shouted Ramey. "Ammo check."

Fazel had gone forward to check on Shirin. Physically she was unharmed; no bullets had come near her. Psychologically, it was a different story. Without Yousef, she had no one from which to draw strength and she was clearly running on empty. The corpsman stayed as long as he could, reassuring her that their situation would soon improve. She had to hang in there for just a little bit longer.

"Sorry for the delay, Boss," he said. "Dr. Naseri is more or less okay. She hasn't been hit, but if this doesn't give her post-traumatic stress disorder, I'll be surprised."

"How are you set for ammo, Doc?" Ramey asked patiently.

"I'm good, sir. I have three full mags plus a partial in my weapon," replied Fazel, still looking toward the bow into Shirin's terrified eyes.

"Doc." Ramey grabbed him by the shoulder and gave it a good shake. "I need you here. Focus on the fight, okay?"

"Yes, sir," said Fazel, as he turned away and prepared for another battle.

A quick check of the rest of the team showed they had sufficient rifle ammunition, which included Jerry who only managed to get off a few shots. However, they were down to only three grenades for Lapointe's launcher. Repositioned and ready, they waited silently for the next patrol boat to get in range.

The rate of their closure was maddeningly slow, and Rahim thought he would lose his mind as they clawed their way closer to their prey, one meter at a time. Qorbani explained that with only a seven-knot speed advantage, it would take them nearly eight minutes before they would be in effective range for their forward machine gun.

"Major, the *Torough*-class patrol boat is just coming into visual range." Qorbani pointed off toward his left. "They will join us in the fight in approximately six minutes."

"Are we in range yet?" growled Rahim.

"Just barely, sir."

"Then what are you waiting for? Fire!"

"Shot warning!" Lapointe yelled. Phillips began his evasive maneuvering, while Ramey and Fazel tried to get a good setup to return fire. The first rounds from the Ashura's 7.62mm machine gun were wide right. The gunner really didn't try to correct for his fall of shot, but just punched out one short burst after another. None came near.

"You imbecile! What are you shooting at?!" a furious Rahim screamed. Pointing at the gunner he added, "Relieve that moron before I shoot him!"

Greatly embarrassed, Qorbani sent his sergeant out to take the gunner's position. "Aim for the engine, Sergeant!" he instructed. Spinning the wheel, the lieutenant lined the boat up for another pass, a closer one.

"Here they come!" warned Lapointe. "They're making a straight dash in."

"Stand by!" Ramey ordered.

"Shot! Left hard." Lapointe shouted. Phillips pulled a hard left turn causing the Ashura to pass quickly to their right. The machine gun bursts missed again, but they were much closer this time.

"Open fire! You, too, Pointy!" Ramey, Fazel, and Jerry started firing at the exposed machine gunner with their SCARs, while Lapointe placed one of his last grenades just to the right of the patrol boat. The explosion showered the enclosed bridge with water. The Ashura immediately peeled away.

"What are you doing?" seethed Rahim. "Close the enemy!"

"Major, they have a grenade launcher! I am taking evasive action!"

Rahim would hear nothing of it. His face red with rage, he unholstered his pistol and pointed it directly at the Pasdaran lieutenant. "Close the enemy now, Lieutenant Qorbani, or I will shoot you where you stand!"

Tight-lipped, Qorbani spun the wheel and pointed his bow back toward the small speedboat. He was sure the VEVAK agent would order him to ram if they didn't start getting some hits.

"He's starting another pass," observed Fazel. "And he's coming straight in."

"Evasive maneuvering, Philly," Ramey instructed. "Open fire!"

Lapointe fired another grenade. It also exploded near the patrol boat, but this time it roared right on through the plume. Phillips jinked left and then put the helm over into a hard right turn. The Ashura failed to follow in time, but for a split second the Pasdaran gunner had a clear shot at their outboard.

He didn't waste the opportunity, and let loose with a long burst. He missed the outboard, but not Ramey and Lapointe. The platoon leader was hit twice in his left arm, while Lapointe took a second hit to his injured leg. Both men cried out in pain. Fazel also took advantage of the momentarily stable target and let go with several two-round bursts. The corpsman watched with satisfaction as the gunner on the Ashura patrol boat collapsed and several of the windows on the bridge shattered.

With rapt fascination, Rahim watched as the gunner clearly hit one of the men in the back of the boat—one less American devil to worry about now. He had only a second to gloat before three windows on the bridge exploded inward. A bullet whizzed by his head, so close he could feel the air as the projectile passed. He laughed aloud and bellowed toward the fleeing Americans, "I am blessed! You cannot win! Allah has judged you!"

Qorbani shattered Rahim's reveling when he shouted, "Replacement gunner!" Looking down, Rahim saw the sergeant slumped over at his station.

"Sir," yelled a corporal. "The *Torough* patrol boat is setting up to make an attack run."

"It will be over soon," mumbled Rahim.

Fazel watched as the Ashura backed off, probably to replace the gunner he had hit. Taking advantage of the temporary respite, he turned toward Ramey. The lieutenant's arm had been badly hit. The bone was obviously broken. The corpsman quickly put on a tourniquet, cinching it tightly. There was no way Ramey could hold a weapon.

"Philly!" cried Fazel. "The Boss is down. I need your gun in the fight. Have the XO take over."

Jerry jumped up and grabbed the wheel. "I have it!"

Phillips rolled out of the seat and picked up his weapon. He pushed Ramey to the side as gently as he could and took up his firing position. Lapointe waved Fazel off. The round had gone through his foot, and while incredibly painful, it was not life-threatening.

Fazel, being the next senior SEAL team member, assumed tactical control. Taking a quick look around, he saw the third patrol boat closing in from off the port quarter. They were being boxed in. "XO, patrol boat to port!"

Jerry nodded vigorously and drove the boat as well as he could away from both Iranian pursuers.

"Harry! The Ashura is making another run!" screamed Phillips. Grabbing Lapointe's weapon, Fazel loaded the last grenade and fired it at the rapidly approaching boat. It missed, exploding to port, but the blast caused the patrol boat to swing to starboard.

The relief gunner fired a long burst just as the grenade exploded, whipping the machine gun across the Ashura's bow, the bullets spreading out in a long arc.

The Plexiglas windscreen in front of Jerry shattered, startling him. A fraction of a second later, he felt a searing pain in his left shoulder. His left hand went limp, and the boat lurched to starboard as he tried to compensate. He couldn't recall if he screamed or not.

"XO! What the hell?" Fazel shouted angrily. Looking back he could see the bloodstain growing around Jerry's shoulder. He couldn't do anything about it now. "Can you still steer the boat?" he asked.

"I'll manage, Doc," Jerry yelled back. He looked behind him. They had a patrol boat on each quarter, closing fast. With three shooters down, and no grenades, things looked bleak. He wanted to think of Emily, but his mind wouldn't let him. *Focus on the fight*, Jerry thought. *Even if it's the last thing you do.*

Rahim was elated; another American had been hit. And with the *Torough* patrol boat now attacking from the other side, victory was assured. The chase would be over. Dahghan would be avenged. The traitors would die.

A loud *SHWISH* distracted him. He could see a faint smoke trail as it streaked toward the *Torough* patrol boat. Suddenly, it disappeared in a violent explosion. The boat was gone, disintegrated. All that remained was a burning pool of fuel on the ocean's surface.

"Helicopter gunship!" screamed a panicky Qorbani. He spun the wheel over, taking evasive action.

Rahim stood motionless. "No," he said softly.

A flash from the dark spot on the horizon testified to the launch of another missile. Rahim couldn't make out what Qorbani was shrieking. What was happening couldn't possibly be real.

"No," he repeated, only louder this time. "I am *blessed*," he repeated with conviction. The impacting Hellfire missile ended the debate.

Jerry blinked, not quite sure of what to think. The two Iranian patrol boats simply vanished in twin balls of smoke and flames. He felt woozy, tired. He could hear Fazel talking on his radio. Something about wounded team members. He saw Phillips near him. The young petty officer was grabbing the wheel.

"I've got it, XO," he said.

Slowly, Jerry released the wheel and then fell back into Fazel's arms. The corpsman lowered him carefully onto the blood-covered deck and started administering first aid.

He saw Phillips talking on his radio to the MH-60R helicopter that was hovering near them. Turning the shot-up speedboat westward, they headed toward the *Arleigh Burke* destroyer that was closing on their position at flank speed.

8 April 2013
0630 Local Time/0330 Zulu
Uranium Enrichment Facility, Natanz, Iran

General Moradi hung up the phone in total disbelief. Rahim was dead. The three patrol boats he was leading had been wiped out by the Americans. The traitors and all their information were safely in American hands. Soon the world would know of the farce that was the Iranian nuclear program. There would be no denying that they had lied, repeatedly. Their inability to successfully produce a weapon after years and years of effort, even with consistent covert foreign assistance, would make them a laughingstock. The damage to Iran's global image was unfathomable.

Worse, the Israeli strike had been intercepted by American carrier aircraft and forced to turn back. The Americans had done the unthinkable; they openly challenged the Israelis and defended Iran. Everything he'd planned, all the careful preparations he had put into play, would now be known as the lies that they were.

He was sure VEVAK would be out for revenge. They had lost two of their most senior agents. Someone would have to be held responsible. There would be a reckoning.

EPILOGUE

22 April 2013
1400 Local Time/1900 Zulu
Washington, D.C.

They had decided to do everything on the same day. A lot of people had to travel from other places, and it simplified the security arrangements. Jerry still marveled at the logistics. WTOP, the local Washington news station, had actually issued traffic alerts for the Arlington area.

Jerry thought the weather and the season had helped. The skies were clear, with temperatures in the mid-60s. A lot of trees were flowering, and the drive down the parkway was beautiful, but it was really the publicity that had drawn folks to say good-bye to someone they'd never met.

It was almost five miles from the National Cathedral to Arlington Cemetery, but Massachusetts Avenue and Rock Creek Parkway had been lined with people, some in uniform, but mostly civilians. Jerry saw families, too, the kids waving little American flags. Emily tried to estimate how many there were. His sister Clarice from Minnesota took pictures of the home-made signs they held.

The police escort peeled off after they crossed the Memorial Bridge and entered Arlington proper. From that point on, the Arlington staff would handle the traffic and the crowds. The press was already down by the gravesite, and the onlookers, there by accident or intention, were kept well back.

By the time it was Jerry's turn to get out of the car, Higgs's casket was already loaded on the caisson, the American flag neatly draped over the top, with the blue field over his left shoulder. The six caparisoned horses stood immobile as mahogany statues. The military chaplain, the escort, the band, and the rest were taking their places.

Jerry helped Emily and Clarice out of the car first, then Ellen Guthrie, with the skipper emerging last. He had to be careful of his left arm, still healing from the gunshot wound. One car in front of them, Nate Lapointe, now in a full leg cast and with crutches, managed a near-graceful exit with help from Phillips. Neat and well-groomed in their dress blues, Jerry had to work to remember these were the same grimy, camouflaged men he'd seen in the speedboat, or trudging across a dark landscape.

One car behind, he saw Harry, or Special Warfare Operator Second Class Heydar Fazel, get out and lend his arm to Shirin. She'd had a lot of help finding maternity clothes suitable for a funeral. Her hijab beautifully framed her face, while also being solemn.

The last few cars were still unloading when the band started. They led the cortege, playing the "Navy Hymn," then Higgs's college fight song, and the "Missouri Waltz," for his home state. Judy, the kids, and the rest of Higgs's family were right behind the caisson, along with the senior officers and dignitaries. Lieutenant Matt Ramey, his arm also in a cast, was her official escort. He'd known both Vern and Judy long before they were married, and was a close friend. She'd lean on him when the time came.

Barrineau, Carlson, and the rest of Charlie Platoon followed close behind, then *Michigan*'s wardroom and the members of the crew that had been able to attend. Out of a crew of just over 150, more than half had made the trip from Washington State. Following them were the rest of the SEALs from SEAL Team Three that were not deployed, plus representatives from every other SEAL Team in the Naval Special Warfare community.

It was a lot, but not compared to the service. The National Cathedral had been filled past its thirty-five-hundred-person capacity, and Judy had allowed it, for the sake of giving Vern a proper sendoff. It was clear official Washington and the public wanted to honor Lieutenant Vernon Higgs, and she was grateful. But the graveside service was for "family."

It wasn't a long walk, although it was long enough to give Jerry time to remember. This wasn't his first trip to Arlington. He'd visited it before as a tourist, of course, but then he'd helped say good-bye to Dennis Rountree, a crewman on *Seawolf* who'd died in their collision with *Severodvinsk*. Since

then, he'd felt differently about the place. He'd make time after the ceremony to go and say hello to his shipmate.

The band, in perfect step, marched to its assigned position and the rest
followed. While the casket was moved from the caisson to the stand, guides
escorted Judy and the others to their chairs. There was some jockeying
among the brass as they found their seats.

The Swedish ambassador had a place of honor, in front, close to the family. After the public release of the files from Shirin's flash drive, the Iranians
had been so desperate for any good press that they'd almost begged the
Swedes to take custody of Higgs's remains. His body was returned home in
just over a week, while the words "Iranian nuclear program" had become
the new catchphrase for any undertaking that was fantastically expensive,
destined for failure, or both.

The top American official present at the funeral was the secretary of defense. Although some had suggested President Myles attend, his presence
would attach too much significance to the circumstances of Higgs's loss.
While the SEAL's death and return had been very public, and was obviously
linked to the release of the Iranian files in some way, most of the events connecting the two were still Top Secret, and would hopefully remain that way.

Instead, President Myles had shown his appreciation that morning,
before the service. The award ceremony had been held at the Pentagon so
the presence of so many military service members would not draw attention. Charlie Platoon and *Michigan*'s blue crew, along with their entire
chain of command from the president on down, watched as Jerry and
Ramey received Navy Crosses for their extraordinary gallantry and service
to the United States at great personal risk. Lapointe, Fazel, and Phillips each
received the Silver Star for their efforts, as did Guthrie for his overall han-
dling of the crisis and his successful engagement against unspecified "enemy
forces." Frederickson got the Meritorious Service Medal for his efforts in
directing the critical reachback support that ultimately resulted in the successful conclusion of a mission of "significant importance to the United
States." And of course, Jerry, Ramey, and Lapointe received their Purple
Hearts. *Michigan*'s blue crew was awarded the Presidential Unit Citation.

Family members quietly clapped with each presentation. Shirin had
teared up watching Fazel get his award. Emily and Clarice had hugged each
other, but then Emily had just buried her face in a hanky and cried, relief
mixing with pride.

Judy Higgs had stood in line with Jerry and the SEALs, the kids standing quietly on either side of their mom. Myles posthumously awarded Higgs the Navy and Marine Corps Medal, along with his Purple Heart. After reading the citations and handing her the medals, he leaned close to her. They whispered softly to each other for several moments, then the president straightened and stepped back. Later, Judy refused to tell anyone what they had talked about.

At the reception afterward, Jerry had found Patterson and Hardy. "The medals look good on you, Jerry," congratulated Hardy.

"Too bad I'll never be able to tell anyone what they're for," Jerry joked. Unfortunately, it was true. The president had read a glowing but somewhat generic citation to the assembled group before giving the awards. The actual citation was classified. Anyone who looked in Jerry's service record or those of any of the others would find a form instructing them to call a special office in the Navy Personnel Command, assuming they had the clearance.

"I'm sorry we couldn't do more to help you, Jerry," Joanna lamented.

"You were busy trying to stop a war," Jerry said. "You're lucky the Israelis only PNGed you. What will happen if they find out using *Reagan*'s fighters was your idea?"

"Oh, they know," Hardy said, "and the problem is that I really liked Tel Aviv. I was hoping we could go back some time and play tourist."

Joanna reassured him. "Israel and the U.S. need one another. We'll sort it out. Give them time to see that we saved their rears, and elect a new government." Putting a hand on Hardy's arm, she turned to Jerry and said with considerable pride, "The president was very impressed with his diplomatic skills."

"Which meant I know which end of the two-by-four to use," Hardy joked. "I doubt if Andy Lloyd will want me in the State Department."

"But I think you're going to be offered a seat on the Foreign Relations Committee," she countered.

They'd decided it wouldn't be appropriate to come to the funeral, so Jerry had been grateful for the chance to see them.

At the gravesite, Jerry ended up sitting right behind Secretary of Defense Springfield, with Emily behind the chief of naval operations and Captain Guthrie behind the commander of the Special Operations Command.

It was almost instinctive for junior officers to be nervous in the presence of such senior officials, to defer to those who bore such great responsibility, but Jerry saw their presence as an acknowledgement by the chain of command of Higgs's service and sacrifice. To Jerry, the real dignitaries were the rows of warriors filling the seats around him.

The service was very short—some prayers, a Bible reading, and a hymn sung by a vocalist from the Navy choir. The escort fired three volleys, which seemed surprisingly loud to Jerry, given what he'd experienced, and a bugler played "Taps" without missing a note. Then the six sailors acting as pall-bearers pulled the flag taut and began giving it the thirteen folds, while a lone bagpiper, a retired Navy SEAL, played a solemn "Amazing Grace." The honor guard finished their work with a neat blue and white triangle. Not a hint of red was visible.

The escort passed the folded flag to the commander of Seal Team Three, who knelt in front of Judy Higgs and handed her the folded triangle, the straight edge facing her. He started to speak, "On behalf of a grateful nation . . ." and the SEALs sitting around Jerry began to stand and form a line to one side of the casket. Jerry stood as well, and spotted Lapointe, who nodded to him and made space for him to stand.

The SEAL at the front of the line waited until the commander had finished and took his place at the head of the line. Then Lieutenant Ramey gently let go of Judy's hand, stood, and walked over to join them. The SEAL commander helped Ramey, Higgs's closest friend, but hampered by his cast, remove the gold SEAL Trident from his uniform blouse and position it on top of the casket. With two sharp raps, Ramey pounded it straight and square into the wood surface. Stepping back, he rendered a final salute to his friend, his comrade in arms. As Ramey returned to his seat, each SEAL came up in turn, added his own trident pin, and rendered honors.

As he stood with Lapointe, Jerry watched petty officers and commissioned officers, from third class to captain, remove their tridents and pound them into the casket.

As they approached the front of the line, Jerry whispered, "Good thing it's not a metal casket."

"We'd manage," Lapointe said firmly.

Jerry took another step forward and saw Judy, holding Ramey's hand. Her face looked drained, weary. She'd sacrificed much, but she wouldn't be left behind. There'd be a long line of supporters to help her through the difficult days ahead; SEALs take care of their own.

Lapointe was the last SEAL in line. He slapped his trident into the wood, saluted, and hobbled away smartly. Now it was Jerry's turn. Jerry removed his gold dolphins and carefully placed them in line with the other insignia, and gave them two sharp raps. The pins bit deeply into the lid. By now, two rows of gold tridents ran the length of the coffin, and he was adding to a third.

It was more than just saying good-bye. Even in death, they wouldn't leave their comrade. He would never be alone.

GLOSSARY

1MC—General announcing circuit, shipwide public address system

ADC—Acoustic Device, Countermeasure

ADCAP—Advanced Capability

ASAP—As soon as possible

ASDS—Advanced SEAL Delivery System

ASW—Antisubmarine Warfare

ATT—Antitorpedo Torpedo

Bisht—A loose cloak worn on special occasions

BMC—Battle Management Center

BMP—A Russian armored personnel carrier. In Russian it stands for "Boyevaya Mashina Pekhoty" and is translated into English as "Infantry Combat Vehicle."

CAG—Carrier Air Group

CAP—Combat Air Patrol

CENTCOM—Central Command

CIA—Central Intelligence Agency

CJCS—Chairman of the Joint Chiefs of Staff

CNN—Cable News Network

CNO—Chief of Naval Operations

CO—Commanding Officer

COB—Chief of the Boat

CPA—Closest Point of Approach

CRRC—Combat Rubber Raiding Craft, phonetically spoken as SIRK

CSG—Carrier Strike Group

CT—Cryptologic Technician

CVN—Nuclear Powered Aircraft Carrier

DShK—A Russian 12.7mm machine gun. In Russian it stands for "Degtyaryova-Shpagina Krupnokaliberny" and is translated into English as "Degtyaryov-Shpagin Large-Calibre."

GBU—Guided Bomb Unit

GPS—Global Positioning System

Growler—Electronic warfare variant of the F/A-18F Super Hornet

Hadiths—Written reports of statements or actions of Muhammad, or of his tacit approval of something said or done in his presence

Halal—A term designating any object or an action as permissible according to Islamic law

Hijab—A term used to describe both the traditional head covering worn by Muslim women and modest Muslim styles of dress in general

HUMINT—Human Intelligence

IAEA—International Atomic Energy Agency

IAF—Israeli Air Force

IED—Improvised Explosive Device

IR-40—Iranian 40 megawatt (thermal) heavy water reactor

IRGC—Islamic Revolutionary Guards Corps, aka Pasdaran

JO—Junior Officer

Ka-bar—U.S. military fighting/utility knife

Klick—Slang for kilometer

KL—Iranian copy of the Russian AK-47 assault rifle

KPH—Kilometers per hour

MBITR—Multiband Inter/Intra Team Radio

MEK—People's Mujahedeen Organization of Iran. In Farsi, it stands for "Mujahedeen-e-Khalq."

MG-24—A Russian submarine deployed acoustic countermeasure. The Russian designation means "drifting compact device active sonar interference."

MG-519 Arfa—Mine-hunting/collision avoidance sonar on Russian submarines

MGK-400 Rubikon—Sonar suite on Russian Project 877 Kilo-class submarines

NAVSEA—Naval Sea Systems Command

NAVSPECWARCOM—Naval Special Warfare Command

NGA—National Geospatial Agency

NIC—National Intelligence Counsel

NIE—National Intelligence Estimate

NIO—National Intelligence Officer

NOFORN—Not Releasable to Foreign Nationals

NSA—National Security Agency

OIC—Officer in Charge

ONI—Office of Naval Intelligence

OOD—Officer of the Deck

PKM—Russian 7.62mm light machine gun. In Russian, it stands for "Pulemyot Kalashnikova Modernizirovanny" and is translated into English as "Kalashnikov's Machinegun Modernized."

PNG—Persona Non Grata

POTUS—President of the United States

Pu-239—Plutonium 239

RIB—Rigid Inflatable Boat

Rivet Joint—RC-135 signals intelligence aircraft

RPG—Rocket Propelled Grenade (slang). In Russian, it stands for "Ruchnoy Protivotankovy Granatomyot" and is translated into English as "handheld antitank grenade-launcher."

S8G—Submarine, 8th generation reactor, produced by General Electric. Reactor plant fitted in *Ohio*-class ballistic missile and cruise missile submarines.

SAM—Surface-to-Air Missile

SATCOM—Satellite Communications

SAVAK—National Intelligence and Security Organization. In Farsi, it stands for "Sāzemān-e Ettela'āt va Amniyat-e Keshvar."

SCAR—Special Operations Forces Combat Assault Rifle

SDV—Swimmer Delivery Vehicle

SEAL—Sea, Air, Land, U.S. Navy Special Forces

SECDEF—Secretary of Defense

Sierra—A U.S. Navy designation indicating that a contact was detected and being tracked by a sonar system.

SIGINT—Signals Intelligence

SM-3—Standard Missile 3, U.S. Navy ballistic missile defense system

SOCOM—Special Operations Command

SOF—Special Operations Forces

SSBN—Nuclear Powered Ballistic Missile Submarine

SSGN—Nuclear Powered Cruise Missile Submarine

Thobe—Arabic for garment. Generally a long tunic worn by men.

TWCC—Tomahawk Weapons Control Center

UAV—Unmanned Air Vehicle

U-235—Uranium 235

U-238—Uranium 238

VEVAK—Ministry of Intelligence and National Security. In Farsi, "Vezarat-e Ettela'at va Amniyat-e Keshvar."

VFA—Naval Strike Fighter Squadron

VIP—Very Important Person

VTC—Video Teleconference

WINPAC—Weapons Intelligence, Nonproliferation and Arms Control Center in CIA

WMD—Weapons of Mass Destruction

XO—Executive Officer

Zodiac—aka Z-bird, type of combat rubber raiding craft

Zula—Military designation that indicates a time is in reference to Greenwich Mean Time (GMT) or Universal Time.